Deep South Gold

Jo Stewart Wray

Writers' Branding
(877) 608-6550
www.writersbranding.com
media@writersbranding.com

Table of Contents

Chapter 1 1
Chapter 2 19
Chapter 3 36
Chapter 4 53
Chapter 5 58
Chapter 6 63
Chapter 7 67
Chapter 8 70
Chapter 9 81
Chapter 10 82
Chapter 11 86
Chapter 12 88
Chapter 13 91
Chapter 14 93
Chapter 15 95
Chapter 16 97
Chapter 17 103
Chapter 18 108
Chapter 19 111
Chapter 20 114
Chapter 21 122
Chapter 22 124
Chapter 23 135
Chapter 24 137
Chapter 25 143
Chapter 26 153
Chapter 27 159
Chapter 28 169
Chapter 29 173
Chapter 30 189
Chapter 31 192
Chapter 32 197
Chapter 33 200

Chapter 34 207
Chapter 35 211
Chapter 36 216
Chapter 37 224
Chapter 38 227
Chapter 39 231
Chapter 40 235
Chapter 41 240
Chapter 42 245
Chapter 43 249
Chapter 44 254
Chapter 45 257
Chapter 46 258
Chapter 47 263
Chapter 48 266
Chapter 49 268
Chapter 50 279
Chapter 51 285
Chapter 52 297
Chapter 53 299
Chapter 54 304
Chapter 55 306
Chapter 56 311
Chapter 57 314
Chapter 58 316
Chapter 59 320
Chapter 60 325
Chapter 61 327
Chapter 62 334
Chapter 63 336
Chapter 64 344
Chapter 65 346
Chapter 66 349
Chapter 67 351

Acknowledgements

I would like to thank the following people for their help and support while I was working on this novel: Carol Costilow for her work as editor, and Richard Wray for his support and belief in my talent. This story is rated R (Restricted for Mature Readers.)

No part of this publication may be reproduced, stored in a retrieval system or transmitted in any way by any means electronic, mechanical, photocopy, recording, or otherwise without the prior permission of the author except as provided by USA copyright law.

Scripture quotations are taken from *The Holy Bible, New King James Version* 1982.

This novel is a work of fiction. Names, descriptions, entities, and incidents included in the story are products of the author's imagination. Any resemblance to actual persons, events, and entities are entirely coincidental.

Others books by Jo Stewart Wray:
The Cheapskate's Guide to Home Decorating: How to Make, Find, or Buy Inexpensive but Stylish Décor'

Dedication: This book is dedicated to all the people who are my readers.

Chapter 1

It was as cold as a well digger's behind, a saying Granny used to say often. Chill bumps danced on Jane's arms and down her back. Catherine Jane Lynch followed the busty, spinster house mother Miss Ward, an old maid of thirty years old, as she carried her antique, half-empty, suitcase up two flights of wooden stairs to the dormitory room in Bacon Hall. *People said that Miss Ward practiced voodoo, that she had worked in a brothel in New Orleans, and that she arrived to the United States from Paris by way of that port city. Some even said she had worked for Marie Laveau.* People said other things about Miss Ward, things that made Jane blush. Jane didn't think she was French, but Miss Ward was fluent in French, Mrs. Laveau's native language, and she wore the latest fashion designs from Paris which were a touch too fancy to work as a house mother at The Central Mississippi Institute for Girls in French Camp, Mississippi. Miss Ward's attire was sometimes the talk of the dormitory, especially when a large, new package wrapped in brown paper arrived at the French Camp Post Office for her. Sometimes the packages contained sexy lingerie. The girls wondered how she afforded them, and they wonder who she wore them for since she didn't have an obvious boyfriend.

Jane didn't have many clothes. Sewing had come second in her life to simply surviving. Today she wore a simple black, ankle-length wool skirt and a black jacket with button-up cotton, a long-sleeved blouse with pearl buttons down the front along tiny pin tucks. Granny had made the blouse. The worn, black leather suitcase had belonged to Jane's aunt Mable before she had inherited it. Jane figured it had been Granny's before Aunt Mable's, so it really was an antique of about seventy-five years. It reminded Jane of a doctor's bag because the leather was worn and cracked, but it was larger. It was plenty large to hold her merger belongings, including her homemade cotton underwear.

December in Mississippi was sometimes freezing cold, and on occasion, snowy. This December was no different than those before it. To make up for her lack of warm clothing, Jane often layered several summer items underneath her skirt so that no one was the wiser. It made her look plumper too, even with the corset on.

Bacon Hall was one of three girl's dormitories on the campus of The Central Mississippi Institute for Girls in French Camp, Mississippi. French Camp was located on the Natchez Trace in Choctaw County. The school had opened in 1885. Homeless and wayward girls and female Native Americans went to CMI for Girls. *Which of those categories fits* me? Jane often wondered.

French Camp was a small town with only a saw mill, livery stable, general store, post office, church, and a few saloons. In addition to the girl's school, there was also a school for boys. Both schools shared a cafeteria called the food hall and the campus. They had teachers from everywhere. Most were from French Camp originally and had come back home. Others made their way here by way of New Orleans, such as that dark and attractive, Professor Huerta. Jane and the other girls fantasized and dreamed about him. Jane was relieved that only a few students were around because it was two days into Christmas vacation, and she should have been at home with her parents near Kilmichael. But Jane's parents were not there.

Jane shared the history of Kilmichael. Well, only that Kilmichael, Mississippi, had been renamed in 1845 when the name was proposed in a town meeting by Duncan McKinley after a town in his native Ireland. *Kill* meant church. She knew a few more facts about the people there, but she kept the secret for the sake of some of her relatives. Later these secrets would make her a fortune.

Her stepfather had been arrested for murder back in August, and then her mother had died last November. Jane and her baby brother Tommy lived with Granny in Kilmichael. So it really hadn't been a normal Christmas with strings of popcorn on thread strung on a real cedar tree that they had gone into the woods to cut and handmade ornaments that looked like brightly colored quilt squares. She missed the popcorn with golden honey drizzled over it and the other Christmas goodies like Granny's fruit cake and rum cake. *Nothing had been normal after her mother married Tom Lynch. He wasn't normal.* Jane thought.

Most of the other dormitory students were at home with their families. Well, those who had families. Victoria Watson and Sylvia Vanlandingham shared the room with Jane. It was very stark. There were no Christmas decorations. Thick layers of dingy, pale gray and tiny pink flowered wallpaper covered the boards of the wooden walls. Some of the wallpaper was peeling in large places. The floor was old, aged pine boards that had been torn out of another building. Jane despised the dull, brown color of the floor and how it showed every speck of dirt and trash. There were no rugs to soften footsteps and protect your feet from the cold. Jane wore black, woolen stockings with all her dresses. She also wore two summer petticoats to help stay warm.

It was Victoria's father, Deputy Watson, that her step father Tom Lynch had murdered, and yet she and Jane were still best friends. Mainly because Jane couldn't control her step father, and Victoria knew it. Victoria's father had been the deputy sheriff in Sheriff Marks's office.

"What's that smell?" the Miss Ward asked as she and Jane entered the room. She wrinkled her nose is disgust. "It smells like pine oil—like in a hospital." *For a woman who does voodoo rituals, smells shouldn't bother you.* Jane thought. Of course, Miss Ward's clothes couldn't be laundered in anything as strong as pine oil. For the most part, they couldn't even get wet.

"My roommates must have been cleaning. Rules and regulations, you know. We try to keep it as neat as a pin. I would hate to get reprimanded or sick during Christmas vacation. Wouldn't you, Miss Ward? You know, we might miss a celebration or something," Jane said sarcastically. She waved her hands back and forth in the air. She wondered if Miss Ward had heard about her father's arrest and her mother's death. Jane was certain that she must have heard. News like that traveled fast.

Everybody had been talking about the murder. One neighbor passed the news on to the next over the nearest fence or sent letters by the mailman. Jane thought.

Jane surveyed the room for evidence of tobacco or cigarette papers. None were visible. She really liked the smell of tobacco whenever her grandfather smoked his pipe. He used a cherry tobacco on special occasions. It was Jane's favorite. His pipe smoke had a wonderful cherry fragrance. She could smell it when all the older folks in the family sat out on the porch at night when the weather was warm enough, but smoking wasn't for her. She just liked the deep, rich smell. *That's what some people said about coffee, but Jane didn't care for coffee either.* On regular days, Grandfather smoked Prince Albert cigarettes. He had rolled so many cigarettes that his nails and the skin on his fingers had been stained by the tobacco.

Jane knew that her roommates had been rolling and smoking cigarettes and had sprayed the dorm room with a lye soap solution or pine oil and perfume to mask the odor. They had asked her to steal some of her grandfather's tobacco for them to roll and smoke. They usually kept a bottle filled with some strong smelling, homemade lye solution for this fumigating purpose. At first, they had sprayed the room with perfume from an atomizer until it was empty. Then Victoria had taken the perfume atomizer and filled it with the lye solution.

Looking around Jane saw that her bunk had been stripped of its rough, cotton sheets Granny had made her of flour sacks and a quilt. *I wonder where they are.* Jane thought. Her ticking-covered feather mattress was lying on the top of the wire box springs. The feather mattress was flat as a pancake.

My mother would have a hissy fit that no one had fluffed that feather bed since many fowl had lost their lives to make it. Jane thought. *A feather bed is fun to sleep on and heck to make up.*

Jane heard her mother's voice in her mind. Her mother liked the mattress fluffed to about 8 inches high. The other two bunks were made, so Victoria and Sylvia were on campus somewhere. No one slept in the top bunk above Jane. This suited Jane. She liked her privacy. She liked to read her Bible. Actually, it was her mother's Bible. Jane liked the notes that her Mama had written in the margins. Somehow it made her feel closer to her deceased mother. Mama had filled the front of it with the birth, marriage, and death records of the family. Recently, Jane had added her mother's death date. She hadn't added anything about Tom Lewis Lynch, her stepfather. She liked it better that way.

Miss Ward looked at her with soft brown eyes through horn-rimmed spectacles. Although she was years older than Jane, she still wasn't married at thirty years old. She worked at the school to support herself because she had no husband to make a living for her, a fact that Jane didn't understand because she was attractive enough. Miss Ward moved toward the door, and Jane could tell that she was ready to leave. She acted like someone was waiting for her. "I'll check with you later to see if you need anything. I'm sorry about your father and your mother's passing," she said and stiffly hugged Jane. She took a step toward the door and stepped through its opening closing the door behind her.

"Stepfather," Jane corrected her to the closed door. She wondered if Miss Ward was meeting a man.

Tom Lewis Lynch, Jane's step-father, had lived with Jane, Mama, and Jane's little brother Tommy in a small community near Kilmicahel. Kilmichael was in Montgomery county seventy miles northeast of Jackson, Mississippi. In 1885, Tom Lynch had been in the Mississippi State Insane Asylum in Jackson, Mississippi. He had received bleeding and purging therapy while there, but he escaped, and typical of his diagnosis of lunacy with hallucinatory experiences and nervousness, he had been prescribed some very strong medicines. He didn't take any of them or they didn't work. *Jane didn't know which.* And neither did the bleeding and purging therapy. Nothing worked; although some days, he had seemed fine. Some days he could fool you. Some days nothing seemed to be bothering him.

Jane had overheard her mother talk about all the insane things Tom Lewis had done after he lost his mind. According to Mama, one time Tom had chopped down an oak tree near their house because he thought God had directed him to do it. For the life of her, Jane couldn't figure out why her mama had married him. She had heard Mama tell her sister Mable that he had been good-looking, romantic, and sweet until his mind left. Now, folks around where he lived considered him crazy although he was one of the hardest working men in the county and the strongest. Mama had thought she could change him or help him. She at least tried to get him to take the medicine the doctors had prescribed to calm him. Mama had prayed for him every night when she prayed for the others in the family, but it seemed to Jane that he got special prayers. *Lawd, he needed them.* Jane thought. Now, Jane believed in God, but she didn't think that God ever told people to cut down oak trees or other mundane work tasks.

Over the years, Tom's sickness had gotten progressively worse. Once he thought monsters from the sky were after him, so he dived into a pond and hid under the water in a beaver hole in the bank. Apparently, there was air to breathe in the beavers' hole because he stayed under the water all afternoon. Everyone, who was looking for him, thought he had drowned. Mama had got Sheriff Marks and some neighbors to drag the pond with a fish net that was supposed to be used to catch minnows. Except for a few catfish and a couple of turtles and some crawfish, the nets had come up empty. Then hours later, Tom Lewis emerged from the muddy pond.

Jane remembered the way he had looked as he walked up the hill and into the back yard all covered with mud from being in the beaver dam. He was dripping wet. His sparse gray hair was matted with mud, and no amount of agitating his dirty clothes with the wooden paddle and lard-based lye soap in the black wash pot on laundry day was going to get all the mud stains out. Everyone talked about how he was a crazy man until Jane got tired of hearing it. They would say, "How's Tom Lewis?" and "If y'all need any help, we'll come out there and we will help y'all." They didn't really mean it. They were just being nosey and condescending, so whenever they asked Jane that question, she replied, "Fine. He's just fine."

One thing was for sure, Tom Lewis was obsessed with religion as were others with his sickness. He began going into houses and preaching to the occupants and also interrupting church services. He wanted to save the sinners and heathens there. He could quote whole chapters of the Bible by heart. He even thought that God communicated with him through lightening. Tom Lewis blamed everything he did on God or God's instructions and the Bible. Tom Lewis said that his shoulder and arms throbbed whenever he was in the presence of a sinner. *His arm and shoulder must throb all time because there were sinners everywhere.* Jane figured.

Jane remembered a time when Tom Lewis thought he had lice crawling all over his body. To get rid of the lice, he shaved off all the hair on his head and his body with a straight razor, stuffed tobacco up his nose, painted his body with black walnut stain, and sprinkled sulfur on his food to keep the bugs out of his urine. He ingested so much sulfur that he passed blood and had dysuria. *Grandfather on my mother's side cured his dog of mange that way. That must have been where Tom Lewis got the idea.* Jane thought.

That day after the murder, Tom's arrest had sent her mother into a deep depression and within a month, she had passed away; so Jane had returned to school in French Camp. Her baby brother Tommy was left with Granny. Since Jane was still a young girl, there was nothing to do in Kilmichael except go to church or school, but Jane could go to church in French Camp. Kilmichael was a little larger than French Camp, but Granny was so strict that she hardly let her out of the house. There were some blacks who lived on their property who were really nice, but Granny didn't let her associate with their children. In many ways, Jane was very naïve. Jane loved her baby brother, but she didn't like staying at Granny's house, and she missed her mother terribly. For some reason, her mother was buried in the French Camp cemetery, so to talk to her; Jane needed to be in French Camp. She also didn't like thinking about the day Tom Lewis had shot and killed Victoria's father.

Jane had witnessed Tom Lewis murdering Deputy Sheriff Jimmy Watson in cold blood the day that he and Sheriff Marks had ridden out to their house to pick Tom up on a warrant.

It had been a hot, steamy day in the summer. August. People had reported to Sheriff Marks all the strange things that Tom Lewis had been doing. The people in Montgomery and Choctaw counties were afraid of him. Tom Lewis thought that he was a prophet of God. He thought that the town's name *Kilmichael* meant Kill Micah, so he walked the dirt streets wearing a hand-painted sign saying: Repent the Eastern Gate of God has Been Seen. God is going to destroy 90% if you don't repent or hell. Pray-the keys + Holy Bible. The sheriff had been before Judge Bond and a warrant had been issued. Somehow Tom Lewis found out about the warrant, so he was waiting with a loaded gun when the sheriff and his deputy arrived. He acted paranoid that everyone was out to get him. When he was in the insane asylum, he even thought the doctor's fed him glass. That was after one of the severe medical treatments.

Jane lay on her bed and buried her face in the pillow ticking. *Several times she had awakened from a deep sleep, and the cotton gown she slept in was wringing wet because she had been dreaming about one or the other of her male professors.* She tried not to think about Tom Lewis Lynch. *I wish someone would take my side. No one has hugged me since my mother's funeral. Granny Folly is so very stern and because Tom Lewis's in jail, he isn't there for me either. I miss him when he is "at himself." Although Tom Lewis probably isn't too fond of me now since I testified about seeing him shoot Deputy Jimmy Watson. I had to tell the truth.* She thought as she got up and changed her nightgown.

She didn't want to think. She didn't want to think about Mama. She especially didn't want to think about baby Tommy. Her feather pillow had absorbed the smell of her roommates' tobacco, but it was the cheap Prince Albert. She fell asleep on the top of the flat, feather mattress in her daytime dress and didn't wake when her roommates came in.

At 6:30 the next morning, Jane awakened with a tickling on her nose. She wiggled her nose. It tickled again. She raised her right hand to scratch her nose and rubbed something that felt sticky over her face. Shaving soap. She smelled the soapy fragrance and thought of Tom Lewis shaving in the morning. He held the shaving mug with the round soap in the bottom of it and swished the damp, boar bristle brush around and around working up a soapy lather. She had lived with him since she was eleven, and sometimes he had been like a real father to her.

This morning she opened her eyes to see four eyes staring back at her. Victoria and Sylvia laughed at her. She felt the sting of the shaving soap on her nose and cheeks. Their laughter irritated her.

"Dang, you two." Instead of laughing with them as she usually did when they played practical jokes, she jumped up, grabbed her grooming basket, and ran down the hall toward the water closet where they bathed.

Turning the corner in the hallway, she ran squarely into Professor Huerta. He smiled when he saw her, and without thinking she smiled back. His salt and pepper hair and dark brown eyes looked right with his dark complexion. He was a handsome man of Creole decent, and Jane had dreamed about him often. Jane liked his accent best. She loved to hear him talk. He was from New Orleans and talked with a Cajun or Creole accent. She liked the deep southern richness of his voice. She didn't exactly know why. He told everyone that Marie Laveau II was his wife, but few at the school believed it because Laveau was said to be a horrible woman. She was supposed to be a voodoo priestess or witch from New Orleans. Mostly, the young girls didn't want him to be married.

Tears were making rivers down her shaving lather covered cheeks like rain running down a window pane. She longed for someone to comfort her and Professor Huerta must have sensed it.

"What is wrong, Miss Jane? What is all over your face?" He asked while gripping her chin in his hands.

Surprised to see him in the girl's dormitory since members of the male sex weren't allowed upstairs, she asked, "What are you doing here? I mean, upstairs in the girl's dorm?" *I shouldn't have asked that question.* Jane thought as soon as she had said it. She had been taught to respect her elders. She knew that girls often sneaked boyfriends into the dormitory through the windows. She had watched some of them having sex without them being aware that they were being watched, but she had never sneaked anyone into her room. She didn't even have a boyfriend, and she had never had sex. She was still a virgin.

For the last few months, Tom Lewis's trial and baby brother Tommy required most of her free time, so Jane hadn't had time for a boyfriend. *I'll probably turn out like Miss Ward, an old maid at thirty years old.* Jane thought. Since she had witnessed Tom Lewis shooting the deputy, Jane had to testify at the trial, and boyfriends didn't seem important at the time. She had been required to tell the truth about what she saw and she had, causing Tom Lewis to be incarcerated.

"Get that off your face, Miss Jane. That lye will burn your pretty skin. I will see you in the food hall in fifteen minutes and no less for breakfast, "Professor Huerta demanded in his smooth Cajun voice. He smiled at her with beautiful, white teeth. She wondered what kissing him would be like.

He hadn't answered her question about why he was in the girl's dormitory. I wonder how old he is and if he ever smiles at other girls like he smiled at me. He looks to be about forty-something years old, but his hair is already turning white or salt and pepper as her granny called it. Jane thought as she opened the door to the wash closet.

The walls of the tiny wash closet were covered with the same gray wallpaper as the dorm room, and the shades were drawn behind dingy lace curtains so no one could watch while the girls bathed. Tables with tiny mirrors held large ceramic basins and pitchers of water. Over to one side there was a large galvanized metal tub that you could use if you wanted to fill it with hot water for a full bath. Today Jane poured tepid water from the pitcher into the blue and white ceramic basin. A black girl named Oma had to be summoned if you needed more water. It was her job to service the girl's water closet. Jane removed her clothing down to her pantaloons that really looked like bloomers and her corset. *Today she would take a spit bath as Granny called it.* Jane thought. She took a cotton cloth and soaked it in the water in the basin. Then she washed her face to remove the shaving soap. The cleansing felt good to her but the strong lye of the soap still left a tingle on her skin, so she finished bathing the rest of her body with the cotton wash cloth and didn't add more soap. She was tingling in more places than the skin on her face. Jane took her time redressing. She wore the same long, wool dress that she had slept in. She took her damp hands and smoothed out some of the wrinkles.

She looked at herself in the full length mirror. She admired her fullness of her breasts beneath the thick wool. She wondered if Professor Huerta had noticed.

She left the wash room and walked down the hallway and down the stairs to the lobby. The food hall was across the campus from Bacon Hall. Early mornings were usually busy at the school, but this was Christmas vacation. Few people moved about. When she entered the usually bustling cafeteria, she noticed that the noise changed to silence. *Am I becoming as paranoid as Tom Lewis?* She walked to the counter where a whole row of large, black ladies stood dishing out the food that they had cooked. Jane picked up her breakfast plate of scrambled eggs, hot biscuits with honey and walked to where Professor Huerta was sitting. There were two male students sitting with him. One of the boys was from Kilmichael. His name was Ruben Andrew Jackson Stewart. Ruben and his family had moved into the area from

Alabama. Jane had seen them at church. The other boy whispered something to Ruben about her sending Tom Lewis to prison. She only heard parts of it, but she figured that was the reason for the silence and stares.

Professor Huerta motioned for her to sit down at his table as he rose and pulled the chair out for her. They had finished eating, so he told them that they needed to go. "You boys need to mind your manners. Whispering. You are being rude, and it seems that you are finished eating, so please remove yourselves from the food hall." His thick, deep voice was demanding and authoritative. His face was blood red even under his dark complexion. "But before you go, apologize to this young lady."

Ruben sheepishly apologized. "We are sorry if we offended you, Jane," Ruben said, and he and the other boy rose from the table and walked away. *Ruben must be the one with manners. He wasn't even whispering.* She thought.

Jane heard the other boy say in a hushed tone as they left, "Your highness."

Jane didn't think that he meant the apology, especially since it had been forced. She was more embarrassed by the fact that Professor Huerta had made them apologize than she had been by their whispering. She could feel her facing glowing red as she sat down to eat at Professor Huerta's table. She had thought that coming back to school would help her escape the town's gossip, but Kilmichael was only seventeen miles south of French Camp, and Tom Lewis had been the talk of the town there for a while now. She just wanted her mother to still be alive and for them to be able to play with Tommy. She felt the tears gathering in the corners of her eyes. She wanted to do things with her family and Tom Lewis like they had done when she was younger and before Tom Lewis got sick and lost his mind.

She needed something to take her mind off her home situation.

"Jane, we are having a picnic and dance in the grove tonight. Would you and your roommates like to come?" Professor Huerta asked. "You do dance; don't you? I'll pick y'all up in my buggy in front of the food hall after supper. My friend plays the fiddle."

"I'll ask them." Jane said. She didn't really intend to mention it to them. She was angry at them for the trick they had played on her this morning. She poured some of the thick honey on her biscuit, but instead of sopping it like she would have done if she were at home; she ate it with her fork.

"Good. See y'all at seven?" he said. He rose to leave the table. He strode out of the room like an important man. The tails of his long, black coat flapped against his strong, muscular legs.

"I'll be there," she replied. She felt excited to be going to a party. Now the glow on her cheeks wasn't from the lye soap. After she finished her breakfast, she went back to her dorm room, and for the rest of the day she thought about going to the party. Although she could not get rid of a knot that was forming in her stomach, she took special care with her appearance.

She asked Oma for hot water and filled the galvanized tub half way to the top. She shampooed her hair first, rinsed with fresh water, and then bathed, caressing her long arms, her firm breasts, her legs, and finally her hands moved between her legs. She hummed her favorite song to disguise the moans that her caressing caused. She caressed until the water's temperature cooled, and her temperature rose. She stood and wrapped herself in a large, dry towel. She puttered back to her room. Lazily she hung around her dorm room, making her bed with granny's sheets and quilt that she found in the closet. Then she hung her clothes in her cubby. Finally she read until the time passed. At five o'clock, she began to get dressed for the party although it was still two hours before Professor Huerta was to pick her up in his fancy, black buggy.

Finally, it was time for her to go to the food hall to eat supper. They had cooked fried chicken, mashed potatoes, butter beans, and hot corn pone. Jane always added local honey to her plate whether she had biscuits or corn pone. She got her plate and a tall glass of sweet tea. This was one of her favorite meals. She carried her plate to a table for two with a red checked cloth where she could see the front door in case Professor Huerta came inside. She didn't want him to have to look for her.

She watched the front door, but he didn't come through it. At five minutes until seven, Jane went outside and stood on the wooden steps of the food hall. Three other girls were waiting on the steps with Jane. Some of the girls lived in the dormitory with Jane, but she didn't know their names. *I wonder who they are waiting for.* She thought and then she saw a single horse and buggy coming down the dirt street from the livery. It was Professor Huerta. He crawled down from the buggy, and Jane noticed that he wore tall, black boots like Englishmen wore to fox hunt and that his entire outfit was black. His silver white strands of hair stood out in contrast against the black hairs. He had on black pants and a black shirt with a black leather vest. *Jane thought he looked very handsome.* "Load up in the buggy," he instructed the girls. This wasn't what Jane had anticipated. She had fantasized about this being like a date.

Have I lost my mind? Mama wouldn't approve of this. Jane thought.

"Come on, Honey Chile," one of the girls called. She and the other two settled into the back buggy seat. "You can sit beside us. We'll slide over."

Jane grabbed the front of her long skirt and climbed into the back beside these other girls. All four of them barely fit across the buggy seat. The front seat was for the driver, Professor Huerta.

The buggy was black with leather seats. It had a top cover with fringe around the edges. It was much more elegant than the old wooden wagons that her family used for transportation. *It must have come from New Orleans too.* She thought. Huerta climbed back into the front seat and lightly tapped the horse with the reins. He drove down a narrow trail toward the area of the campus called the grove. Some said many freed slaves had escaped to the north through it. Black berry bushes and small sweet gum saplings grew on each size of the trail to the grove. The farther away from town they went, the thicker the undergrowth got. The roughness of this area of the campus and the stories of stow-a-way slaves kept many people from entering the grove, but Jane had heard that it was a popular meeting place for lovers. *Who is Professor Huerta's lover? Or does he have one?* She wondered. *Maybe it is Miss Ward.*

Bouncing around in the back of the buggy was an empty, wooden, whiskey barrel; it was the kind moonshine was often stored in and left to age. *I wonder if he makes or drinks moonshine.* A blond-haired girl that Jane had seen in the dorm lobby and also waiting outside the water closet in line for her turn to go inside crawled into the back of the buggy and sat on the old barrel like it was a horse. She pulled her long skirts up around her knees and straddled it instead of riding side-saddle. "Rid 'um cowboy," the girl said, laughing. She bounced in the air when the buggy wheel hit a large rock. She threw her head back and swung her long hair around like she was bucking on a real horse.

Professor Huerta glanced back at the girls and laughed loudly in his deep, Creole voice. *Many girls at the school commented about his deep voice and his Southern charm.* Jane reflected. She hoped none of these other girls were his girlfriend.

Jane hoped that this party would be fun, but the knot in her stomach wouldn't go away. The girl on the barrel seemed like she would be a fun person to be around, but Jane made up her mind that she was walking back to the dorm whenever he stopped the buggy in the grove or sooner if he would stop. "Stop this buggy, please. I don't really want to go to the party. I've changed my mind," Jane said loudly.

Professor Huerta acted like he didn't hear her.

Jane reached up and tugged on Professor Huerta's sleeve to get him to stop. "We will be there in a few minutes, Jane. Be patient."

Just as he had said, they reached the grove quickly. The ground was wet and mushy, and the opening in the grove was empty except for one person who was standing near an old barbeque pit. Jane couldn't tell if it was a man or woman. Huerta stopped the buggy next to the pit. The girls crawled out of the buggy, getting mud on their skirt tails. "Lawdy! I'm getting mud on my new clothes," the red haired girl said.

The other person in the grove was Miss Ward. Jane was very surprised to see her. Miss Ward wore the same black outfit the Professor Huerta had on except he had on tall boots and Jane couldn't tell if she did or not because of her long skirt.

The other girls agreed to leave. *Jane decided that these girls always agreed with each other because they were friends.* All of the friends began to talk at once.

Jane looked at Miss Ward who seemed to be waiting for them. *Somehow her presence didn't make Jane feel better.* Miss Ward was building a fire in the barbeque pit. Jane had never noticed these two people, Huerta and Miss Ward, being friendly at the school. *That's why he was in the girl's dormitory, but I heard that he was married.* She thought.

Since it was so cold and damp, Jane and the girls huddled around the fire in the pit enjoying its warmth. Jane could see the other girls' faces in the glow of the firelight. The fire's glow made the whole scene look eerie, and a knot in Jane's stomach grew. She knew that she should have given more thought to coming out here to this party. It felt strange. It didn't seem to be a party at all, but she had been so lonely without her mother and Tom Lewis. Her mother often warned her that if something didn't feel right, it probably wasn't. She knew that she shouldn't be here.

"Pretty good looking ones," Jane heard Huerta tell Miss Ward. "They look young enough; don't they? The blood of a young girl is purer and is a better sacrifice when we do the Lucifer spell. Marie Laveau taught me this spell."

"We need to get out of here," Jane whispered to one of the girls. "I heard that Miss Ward does voodoo. He's whispering to her about Lucifer spells and Marie Laveau, the famous voodoo priestess. "

"I heard that too," the leader in the other group said. "That scares me." Then she turned to the others. "Let's go back," she told her friends and started back down the trail toward the campus.

The other girls followed along down the trail that led back to Bacon Hall and the food hall. They walked in the grass near the ruts that had been made by the buggy. Jane followed them.

She was the last in the pack headed back to campus.

Huerta ran up behind Jane and picked her up. "Do not scream or you die," he whispered into her ear. He had a knife next to the front of her neck.

She didn't scream. She was afraid to. The tone of his voice reminded her of Tom Lewis's when he was having a very bad day. She had seen firsthand how strong a crazy man could be.

"I really need to go back to the school," she said, meekly. "It's too cold for me to stay out here. I need to go back with them."

"Oh, no. You are staying here with us. We'll have a good time. You'll see. We'll just talk for a while and then we will go back to the campus."

"Why are y'all dressed all in black?" she asked. She was terrified, but she knew if she became too frightened that she would lose. She had to stay in control.

Huerta set her down and whirled around to show her his outfit. "You like my outfit?" He glared at her with dark brown eyes that danced with the reflection from the fire making him look sinister.

Once he wasn't holding her, she tried to run. She knew that she needed to get out of here. She tripped on a large pile of bones and a group of rocks shaped like a pentagram.

Huerta grabbed her again. "Oh, Lucifer, help us. Give us power," Huerta chanted louder and louder in her ear. "Lucifer, help us. Give us power." Miss Ward joined in his chanting, but she danced too. She was twirling a large white scarf.

A Voodoo queen. Was she trying to be Marie Laveau? Jane wondered.

Jane began reciting The Lord's Prayer. "The Lord is my shepherd. I shall not want. The Lord is my shepherd. I shall not want. The Lord is my shepherd. I shall not want."

"Shut up," Huerta screamed in his smooth, south Louisiana drawl. He held Jane tighter and moved his hands over her breasts. Then he tried to tie her arms behind her back with a different white scarf than the one Miss Ward was twirling.

Jane jerked her arms free and fought back with all the strength she had. She kicked at his shins and clawed at his face, trying to poke out his dark eyes. Miss Ward still twirled and danced, not noticing the fight. Jane couldn't understand exactly what he was saying. She reached into the fire and grabbed a stick that was only burning on one end. She began brandishing the blazing end toward Professor Huerta. The flame touched Huerta's black coat, and it began to burn. The black fabric turned reddish orange and then black again. The flame singed his hair. The smell of burned hair mixed with his musky perfume was horrible.

"Help me," he screamed to Miss Ward who was still dancing. Suddenly, she stopped and took off her coat and began to slap it against the flames of his burning coat, putting out the fire.

This was Jane's chance to get away. She turned to run, but before she left, she sprawled face first in the mud. She could taste the mud mixed with her tears. Grass and pine straw stuck to her clothes and her skin. "I'm going to get out of here alive," she whispered to herself. She stood up, grabbed her skirt up around her waist, and ran for her life toward the campus. The heels of her boots dug into the soft mud. Oddly, no one was following her. She stumbled on the trail as she ran on toward the campus and got covered with mud again. She was more than halfway there, but she could still hear Professor Huerta's screams for help. She still smelled the smoke.

A horse and rider appeared suddenly on the trail, but he couldn't stop the horse in time to keep from hitting Jane. She felt her body fly under the horse's front legs. The left side of her head banged against a rock. She screamed in pain. The gritty sand on the rock ground into the side of her face skinning a large patch and also scrubbed into her left shoulder. She screamed again from the pain.

Oddly, the rider didn't stop, but rode away as if he hadn't even seen her. Blood oozed from her left ear. Her head throbbed with more pain than Jane had ever felt before. She saw a tunnel and a white light at the end of it. Her mother was reaching out to her.

Chapter 2

In Jane's injured state, she began hallucinating about the day Tom Lewis shaved all his hair off his body. Mama told her that he had shut himself in the water closet, swirled the shaving brush around in the shaving mug and spread the foamy lye soap over small areas of his body a little at a time, and with a straight razor, he began to remove his body hair. Jane figured that the whole process took a lot of effort because his chest and back looked like a bear. He was so hairy.

Mama had been in the water closet with him. "Please don't do this, Tom Lewis," Jane heard her mother begging. "Take your medicine. It will probably get rid of those bugs."

"Those lice won't get me," he said, coming out of the water closet. There were streams of blood running down his head from the nicks in his scalp he had made. His chest was bare.

Then he came into the kitchen and took the bag of sulfur out of the cabinet. He fixed himself a large bowl of beans from the black iron pot on the wood stove and sprinkled two heaping teaspoons of sulfur over them. *How can he eat that?* Jane wondered.

Jane watched as he ate the entire bowl of beans before he took the rifle down from over the fireplace and went outside to sit on the porch. He looked so strange with his bald head and bare chest, but his sitting with that rifle really unnerved her. *What or who was he waiting for?* Jane had wondered.

Then she felt someone taking off her clothes. She felt hot breath on her face and felt something gorge into her between her legs. The pain was almost as bad as the pain from hitting her head. Then she felt momentary pleasure and passed out again.

It was about five o'clock in the evening when they heard two riders coming down the dirt lane on horseback toward their house. The clop, clop of the hooves sounded like an introduction.

Before the riders rounded the bend in the road in her dreamy state, Tom Lewis picked up the rifle that he had propped against a post on the front porch. He carried it toward the barn and went inside, closing the barn door behind him. The two riders rode up to the front of the house, dismounted, and tied their horses to the rail. They weren't coming for a friendly visit, and Tom Lewis knew it.

"Tom Lewis Lynch," Sheriff Marks yelled. "We came to get you. We have a warrant signed by Judge Bond. You must go with us."

"I am not going," he yelled back from the inside of the barn. He had the rifle sticking out through a crack in the wood boards of the barn's wall. "Get off my property, you heathens. God told me that you were coming. He said not to go with you. He said y'all were all heathens."

By this time, Mama was out on the front porch. "Y'all get back in the house," Tom Lewis yelled at my mother and me. Immediately, she turned and went back inside. I rose from the rocking chair and hurried inside, too.

I watched out my bedroom window. Tom Lewis fired his rifle hitting Deputy Watson. Deputy Jimmy Watson fell dead where he stood. Quickly, Sheriff Marks swung back onto his horse and rode back the way he had come. *He didn't even check on his deputy.* Jane had thought.

They would need more men to take Tom Lewis in, especially in his crazed state. Jane thought.

Then Jane dreamed that Professor Huerta showed up and dragged her back to the grove. He stretched her over that whiskey barrel and began hurting her, but the feeling wasn't totally of pain. When he finished, he dragged her back to where the horse had run over her.

***

When Jane awakened, she shivered from the cold dampness and her bones felt stiff. She hurt all over her body, especially between her legs. Her black dress and boots were covered with mud. The sun peeked over the trees to the East. She tried to stand, but couldn't. She crawled on her hands and knees into the bushes beside the trail. She crawled farther to a sweet gum sapling and tried once again to stand by holding to its leafless limbs, but they were too limber. She fell back to the ground, getting mud in her eyes again.

She lay on the ground. She felt vibrations in the ground from some other horses and riders. She crawled through the mud toward the vibrations, wiping the mud from her eyes she crawled in the direction of the campus. She needed help. She made it to the edge of the campus. The earth was cold and damp from the morning's frost. She crawled next to a large oak tree so she wouldn't get run over again.

The rider of one of the horses stopped suddenly, "There she is. Go get some help." She said to the other. "There's been an accident. I think she's dead."

Oh, no. Not Miss Ward. Jane thought. *I don't wanna be near her.*

"No, I'm not dead," Jane tried to say but was choking on something draining down her throat. It tasted salty like blood tastes when you cut your finger and stick it into your mouth. She vaguely focused on Miss Ward's face.

"What happened to her?" Miss Ward asked.

Jane was confused more than ever. "Why am I lying out in the woods? Why am I in such pain? What happened to me?"

She passed out.

Jane wanted to wake up. She wanted this to be a bad dream and for the pain to go away. Someone standing in a bright, white light was calling her name. Was it her mother? No, it couldn't be her mother. Mama was dead.

She heard Miss Ward yell, "Someone help her. She's choking. Turn her over."

"Help me!" Jane moaned. She couldn't breathe. She gasped. Someone rolled her onto her side.

"No, don't move her," Jane heard someone else yell.

"Finally, a teacher. Where is Doctor Hill?" Jane heard Miss Ward ask. "Your name is Professor Huerta? Isn't it? Well, do something, Professor. Please do something." Jane heard her pleading with Professor Huerta. Jane tried to focus on his face as he leaned over to take a better look. He smelled of smoke and exotic musky perfume. He had been the one hurting her and giving her pleasure at the same time.

"Move back, people," Jane heard the deputy sheriff tell the crowd that had gathered around her. "Let Dr. Hill through."

Jane felt someone touching her. It was Dr Hill, but she still smelled smoke and perfume. She tried to remember where she had smelled smoke recently. Dr. Hill checked her. She felt him probing and cleaning the cuts on her head. She needed to vomit the thick, salty substance that was draining down her throat. It tasted like blood. She felt someone lift her up and carry her back toward the town.

The trip took an eternity. She thought. Then they headed toward the doctor's quarters. She heard Miss Ward insist on following along.

Once they reached the doctor's quarters, someone laid her on a soft bed.

"Help her," she heard Miss Ward demand. The man, who smelled of smoke and perfume, Huerta, was not there. Jane was glad.

"Ma'am, I can only sew up her cuts and bandage her head. First, I have to finish cleaning the wounds. Why was she out in those woods anyway? She was found in a wooded area of the campus out near an area we call the Grove." Jane heard Dr. Hill reply. "No young lady should be out there. It isn't safe."

Jane knew everything that was happening around her, but she could not communicate with them. Her voice was weak, barely above a whisper. She tried to talk to Dr. Hill, but he wouldn't listen, or he couldn't understand her. Finally, he finished checking her and sewing up her cuts and gashes. The caregivers removed her muddy clothing and shoes and bathed her. They redressed her in a clean, white, cotton gown.

Jane heard Dr. Hill tell Miss Ward, "We don't have to send her to a hospital. Besides, I don't think she would survive a wagon trip. She may have been molested. If I had to bet, I would say that she has."

"Get Granny Folly," Jane tried to tell the doctor. "I don't want to be here with Miss Ward."

Jane was confused by what she had heard the doctor say. She couldn't remember exactly what had happened to her or why she was lying in the trail or anything else that had happened for the last two days.

"Let me know everything she says," Miss Ward instructed the women as she left.

"We will," one of them replied as the door closed.

"Hmmp, who does she think she is? Giving us orders?" she replied after Miss Ward had left the room. Immediately, Jane felt safer.

The group of women moved into the room and fawned over her. Miss Ward was not one of them. Somehow Jane trusted them.

When she awoke, different women surrounded her than the ones she had seen in the doctor's office earlier. Still none of them was Miss Ward. Jane felt thankful. One of them gently washed Jane's hair and gave her more of a spit bath. "You have a slight concussion. Doctor Hill sewed you up. He said it was okay for me to wash your hair. Your scalp is intact. The small bones in your ear may have been broken, since some of the blood drained instead of clotting in your brain. You are one lucky girl. If the bones in your ear hadn't broken, you might have died. Your doctor's name is Dr. Hill. You are fortunate that he was on campus instead of out delivering babies or sewing up bullet holes."

After the bath ended, Victoria and Sylvia entered Dr. Hill's office room. "How are you doing?" Sylvia leaned over the bed and kissed Jane a small, affectionate peck on the forehead. "You really smell clean even if this place smells like a hospital. What do you remember?"

"Nothing," Jane said, shaking her head from side to side. But she knew that she was lying. She remembered the feel of Professor Huerta inside her.

Jane couldn't talk to her friends, but she understood everything that they said. Jane squeezed Victoria's hand. She wanted them to know that she understood everything that they said. She remembered leaving Granny's house and that is was Christmas vacation. The rest terrified her. Tears rolled down her cheeks and her head hurt so severely that she thought she would die.

"You, girls, aren't allowed to stay very long. She is getting upset, and she doesn't need to be upset," one of the women said. "She needs her rest, so y'all need to go now."

Victoria leaned close to Jane and whispered in her ear, "I love you, Jane. Hurry and get well. I'll take care of you after you get back to the dorm room. You don't have to worry. I'm going now to get some bandages and to clean our dorm room."

Jane could hear the emotion in Victoria's voice. *Jane knew the room wasn't really dirty.* More tears welled in Jane's eyes because she knew that Victoria cared for her deeply despite all that had happened to her father.

"You can tell me what happened to you out there later," Victoria said.

Jane shook her head again. She knew that something bad had happened to her, but she didn't want to talk about it. More tears rolled down her face.

"Y'all really must be going," one of the women said.

As Victoria and Sylvia were leaving, Miss Ward entered the room again. She wore another very beautiful dress that must have come from Paris. The caregivers wore their own handmade dresses and large white aprons. The comparison was exaggerated.

Jane reached out her hand to hold on to one of the women taking care of her. Jane looked at her with a pleading look that said, "Don't leave me."

The caregiver seemed to understand, so she stood between Jane and Miss Ward.

"I'm Miss Ward," she told the women. "Jane is one of the students at the girl's school; I'm her house mother. I've just sent a rider to contact her grandmother in Kilmichael. Dr. Hill told me that Jane is in a very serious condition, and although he couldn't tell me very much, he did seem like a smart doctor. She has a mild concussion, but it isn't as serious as it could be. He said that the bleeding was good, because it kept her from having a more serious condition. The bleeding relieved the pressure." Finally, she stopped talking and looked directly at Jane. "Oh, I'm sorry, honey. I didn't know that you were awake. That's great. I've been talking about you. I'm glad to see that you are conscious. What do you remember? Do you remember anything?"

More tears gushed from Jane's eyes, but she couldn't wipe her face because of her bandages. Jane watched as one of the women ushered Miss Ward out of Dr. Hill's office by taking her elbow and walking toward the door. "You need to go. We'll take care of her. She needs rest."

Then the other caregiver turned to Jane to explain about the blankets and pillows. We will furnish those if your family stays in the lobby past 10 P.M."

Whenever Miss Ward left, Jane noticed the smoky smell again. It was a strong, smell of burned hair and perfume. Jane knew that she had smelled that sickening smell before. She felt like she would vomit.

Eventually, the smoky smell cleared. And Jane fell asleep with one of the women sitting in a straight back chair beside the bed.

At five o'clock the next morning, Jane was awakened by that same sickening smell of burned hair and perfume. She opened her eyes and saw a man standing at the foot of her bed. She looked around the room for the woman who had spent the night in her room. She wasn't there. Vaguely, she made out a man's form. At first she thought that she was dreaming. She looked around the room for other of her caregivers, but none of them were there either. When she looked toward the end of her bed again, Jane saw the man slip into the closet and close the door almost shut.

Jane watched the closet door. Although he had the door cracked about an inch, the man remained inside. Suddenly, Victoria entered the room. She took Jane's hand in hers and slowly stroked it. Jane felt Victoria's warm hands, but with him inside the closet, she wasn't comforted. "Jane, how are you this morning? You are my very best friend. You've got to get well. I need you. "Jane looked toward the closet. *Was she imagining that the smell of burned hair and perfume and that she had seen a man in the closet?* She wondered.

Two caregivers entered her room. One of the caregivers opened the curtains. The morning sun shone through the window panes. It hurt Jane's eyes, and her head hurt so badly that she thought that she would not be able to stand it. Dr. Hill entered the room right behind them.

"She's in pain," one caregiver said to Dr. Hill. "Can't you give her something?"

"No, I can't; besides, she won't remember anything about the pain whenever she gets well. She probably won't remember anything about her accident or about that entire day either."

Dr. Hill checked Jane's bandages and her heart. "Do you know where you are?"

He seemed like a patient man.

"Yes," Jane looked around the room and nodded her head. *That man was still in the closet.* She thought. "The doctor's office." Her speech was garbled.

"What day is this?"

"Wednesday," Jane answered. "I smell burned hair and perfume." Jane answered, but he didn't understand what she was saying.

"Time will tell how well you progress, young lady. As of right now, you're doing great. Actually, I can't believe it. You are a very lucky girl. The blood that had collected on your brain from your injury drained through your ear to the outside. All your vital signs are good, and you have no other health problems as far as I can tell. We will have to keep some ointment and bandages on the scrapes on your face. You may actually never fully remember the accident. Do you have any questions?"

"No." Jane shook her head. "Pain," she said. "Tired." Then she pointed toward the closet. "Check closet."

"I'm moving you to a more private room. As a matter of fact, we're moving you right now. These ladies will roll this bed into the other room."

Jane relaxed. *The man in the closet wasn't moving with her.* She hoped.

***

Her private room was across from the doctor's main office. The caregivers moved with her. At ten o' clock, Granny rushed into Jane's room. She had come by wagon from Kilmichael. "Hi, honey. What happened to you?" Granny asked in a breathless tone.

"I can't remember. Well, not exactly, Granny, but since I've been injured, Professor Huerta and Miss Ward have been watching me from the closet. Well, Miss Ward comes into the room." Granny didn't seem to understand her words.

"Victoria told me that you had been a little confused lately, but that's understandable," Granny said. "What were you doing out there anyway? By the way, Tommy has started sleeping in a bed by himself." *She's still flighty.* Jane thought.

"Why I was there is one of the things that I don't remember. I don't remember anything that happened the day of the accident. How is Tommy? I miss him so much. He's not down here with you is he?" Jane asked. *Granny seemed to understand the word* <u>*Tommy*</u>. Jane noticed.

"Yes, she told me; and no, I didn't bring Tommy with me today. "

"You aren't planning to stay here with me are you? If you are, who is going to take care of Tommy?" Jane asked.

"I have to lssset Victoria stay here with you, Honey. She'll take better care of you than I could. I'm going back to Kilmichael after my visit. You know that I'm not a good nurse. Lawd, I have such a weak stomach that I couldn't clean up a mess if you made one. I make a lousy nurse. Your papa has to clean up his own messes. And speaking of Papa and Tommy, I've got to get on back home to see 'bout them. Papa is in a bad way with his heart problem."

"I'll be okay. Don't you worry about me. You have enough to worry about already. Please take good care of all of y'all. Anyway, Victoria was going to ask them to post a guard outside my door."

"Guard? Oh?" Granny raised her eyebrows and looked toward the door. "I didn't see one."

"Give Tommy and Papa a kiss for me."

Granny stayed about an hour more before she left to go back to Kilmichael. Jane wanted her to get back home before dark, but Victoria stayed the night in the room with Jane. The next morning everything went smoothly. Jane had improved. She was able to talk clearly although her voice was hoarse.

At noon, Victoria went to the cafeteria to get something to eat. A sheriff's deputy stood outside Jane's room while Victoria was gone. The caregiver had left, and Jane slept with her head under a pillow to block out the light from the windows.

Jane woke and peered out from under the pillow. She asked that the curtains remain closed because the bright light hurt her eyes, and most of the time she kept her head under the feather pillow. She squinted in the darkness. Again she saw a shape enter her room that looked like a man. He stood at the foot of her bed. *How could he have slipped past the guards?* Jane wondered. She knew that Victoria had instructed the guard not to let anyone into the room.

Jane felt someone touch her pillow, so she lay perfectly still. She felt that any minute she would vomit from the smell of smoke, perfume, and from terror. She felt the pillow being pushed down on her face; the door burst open and one of the caregiver's opened the curtains. "What in heaven's name are you doing in here? How did you get past the guard? You must leave, sir. Get away from Jane's bed." She walked to the door to get the guard.

"He isn't here," she said. "I'll be talking to Sheriff Marks about this. Sir, you must leave this room immediately. You ain't 'possed to be in here."

Although the bright light hurt Jane's eyes, she removed the pillow from her face long enough to took directly at the man. Professor Huerta. Jane felt intense pain in her stomach and her head still throbbed. She was so frightened that she was nauseated again. She leaned over the edge of the bed and vomited close to Huerta's feet. Some of it splashed on his clothes and tall, black boots.

Huerta turned and hurried from the room. He bumped into Victoria as she entered the room, knocking her to the side. Jane screamed a loud, shrill scream, and Victoria screamed, "Professor Huerta, what are you doing in here?"

Both of the girls' loud screaming brought more caregivers into the room. The guard, who was supposed to be outside, didn't come into the room. "Get the Sheriff and have him stop that man who was just here. He's been trying to kill me," Jane yelled.

One of the women left the room to get the Sheriff. Another said, "I'll be back when I find out why that man was allowed to come in here. But don't you worry none, I won't be more than ten feet from the door of this room. I promise you that this will not happen again. Summon me if you need me."

Jane and Victoria waited for word that Professor Huerta had been picked up and questioned by the Sheriff. After about thirty minutes, another guard was posted outside the room. When the woman came back she said, "Would you believe it? No one at the Sheriff's office had been scheduled to guard this room until just now when I asked. Someone had things mixed up."

"Sheriff Marks is coming to question Jane. Tell him about this Professor Huerta being in here," she said. *Jane thought that she was the woman in charge.*

After that, Victoria stayed with Jane the next day and night while she was still at the doctor's office room. One of the caregiver's had rolled a cot into the room for Victoria. Jane felt comfortable being with Victoria. Whenever Victoria needed to go to the outhouse, she made certain that one of the women caregivers stayed in the room with Jane until she returned.

Jane hoped that eventually she and Victoria would figure out what had happened to her. At the present time, she couldn't remember enough of what had happened to her to get Professor Huerta arrested, but she kept trying. Trying to remember something that was horrible affected her mental attitude and mood. She didn't know whom to trust, but she trusted Victoria.

"Victoria, all I remember is that Miss Ward was there in the Grove, and I fought Professor Huerta off with a burning stick from the fire. She helped him, not me. I'm certain he raped me.

"In public, they act like they don't even know each other," Victoria said. "Did you hear that she is a voodoo queen? I heard that she does all kinds of voodoo spells. Did she know that he raped you? Why don't we play a trick on her? My grandmother used to talk about voodoo spells whenever she didn't think I was listening with a black woman from Louisiana who was a tenant on our farm. They had some voodoo spells for good and some for evil."

"What do you have in mind?" Jane asked.

"Oh, I don't know. What about some talc in her shoes and a note that it is hot foot powder and a curse?"

Soon after lunch, two sheriff's deputies entered the room. Their names were Sykes and Callory. They showed her their badges to Jane and Victoria and introduced themselves. Vaguely, Jane remembered them standing in the courtroom during Tom Lewis's trial.

"Tell us your story and then Sykes will question the doctor and his caregivers."

Jane explained to Deputy Callory that she had no idea why Professor Huerta had come into her room, but that she thought he and Miss Ward had been out in the Grove that night.

"Doing what?"

"All I remember is that she was dancing in the firelight. I remember fighting Professor Huerta off me with a burning stick from the fire."

"Why would Professor Huerta attack you? Weren't y'all close? I mean people saw y'all eating breakfast together that morning in the food hall." Deputy Callory wore horn-rimmed glasses and had to peer over them to look at her.

"When? I don't remember ever eating breakfast with him. Who told you that?" Jane asked.

"Someone saw the two of you together in the food hall the morning before your accident," he replied. "What do you think happened to you? Were you with him between the time that you were seen eating breakfast with him and your accident?

"I don't remember eating with him," Jane cried. Tears rolled down her cheeks. "I don't remember anything, but no, nothing was going on as you have hinted about." She felt humiliated. *How dare he suggest such a thing.* She wondered.

"Please, Miss Lynch, don't get upset. I'm going to talk to Dr. Hill now and anyone else who might know what happened. Don't cry. I'm going to leave now, but I'll be in touch with you; I can tell you that at the present time we don't have enough to arrest Professor Huerta or Miss Ward for doing anything wrong. She is the person who found you on the side of the trail. It isn't illegal to visit someone in the doctor's office room and especially since you two were friendly."

"She told you that they weren't friendly as you call it," Victoria said. "What about the officer who was supposed to be outside that door? He was out there when Professor Huerta came in here. In other words, he let Huerta come in here. Why?" Victoria asked. "You mean to tell me that your office is doing nothing?" Victoria said. *She knows all the deputies by name.* Jane thought.

"Well, Miss Watson, as far as I know, we didn't have an officer scheduled to guard her door. We didn't send one until today. The sheriff's office was not contacted. "

Jane didn't want to continue this conversation.

"But what about the fact that he attacked her? And they were contacted. I contacted them myself." Victoria said. *Jane noticed that Victoria's face had gotten blood red.*

"I don't have an answer for you, but I plan to question everyone remotely involved. I promise that I'll do whatever I can to help y'all, but it doesn't look good," Deputy Callory said. He gave a long sigh.

Later that day, Jane was dismissed by Dr. Hill to go back to the dormitory, and Victoria went with her.

When they entered the room, a WELCOME HOME sign was hung across the end of the room. Sylvia had painted it with mint green room paint on an old flour sack sheet.

"Thanks, Sylvia." Jane said, "I just want to sleep." One of them had made up her bed and straightened the room. They had brought back the quilt that Granny, Mama, and Jane had quilted. The sign and the quilt comforted her.

"Sylvia is going to stay here with you, Jane," Victoria said. "I've got to go put some hot foot powder in Miss Ward's shoes." She giggled as she left the room.

"What is she talking about, Jane?" Sylvia asked. "Hot foot powder? What is that?"

"Victoria thinks that Miss Ward was trying to do a voodoo hex on me out in the grove. I really don't understand why, but Victoria is playing a trick on her."

"I knew that everyone called her a voodoo queen. I heard the Professor Huerta was married to Marie Laveau, but I don't believe it, Jane, I'm sorry we played a joke on you that morning of your accident. Victoria and I put shaving soap in your hand and tickled your face. You got it all over you and rushed to the water closet to clean up," Sylvia said.

"Oh, I remember that. That's when I ran into Professor Huerta in the hall," Jane replied. " I wondered why he was in the girl's dormitory. I remember asking him. But he didn't answer." Jane sat down on the bottom bunk on her quilt.

"I bet he was visiting Miss Ward, if you know what I mean," Sylvia said. Jane didn't feel surprised by Sylvia's statement. *Sylvia always spoke frankly and said whatever was on her mind.* Jane thought.

"He asked me to eat breakfast with him." Jane remembered and told Sylvia.

"Didn't you think that was unusual? I personally don't really like him, and I didn't think he was a good teacher. Besides, I heard that he's going back to New Orleans."

"I remember he was dressed all in black, and he was chanting and dancing around the fire in that party out in the grove west of the campus."

"Party? You went to a party with Professor Huerta?" Sylvia asked.

"Oh my, oh my, now, I remember. Oh, God. It was so horrible. He asked me to come to a party. But it wasn't a real party. I rode there with three other girls. Professor Huerta picked us up in his fancy, black buggy that he brought here from New Orleans. Both he and Miss Ward were dressed all in black."

"Who were the other girls?" Sylvia asked.

"They go to school here. I don't know their names."

"Miss Ward was there and Professor Huerta had a whiskey barrel. Do you think he was going to rape one of us?" Jane asked.

"Maybe he did."

Jane cried softly and turned her head to the wall. Memories came flooding back to her. "They were dancing. I fought him off with a burning stick. I caught his coat on fire. I got away while he put out the fire. And then I remember severe pain."

"What was Professor Huerta doing?"

"He was chanting, 'Master, help us,' like a Lucifer spell. I think he was doing voodoo."

"Jane, you know from his accent that he is part Creole. Well, I've heard the other teachers talk about him. Maybe he does voodoo, too, like Miss Ward. They are both from New Orleans. She's French."

"Oh, my, Sylvia. Do you think he was trying to use me for a voodoo ritual? What do you know about voodoo? Listen, Sylvia, what if there are more voodoo kings and queens here at the Institute? He may have used other students in his rituals like he tried to do to us. Do you think he will try to get me here in the dorm room? I may need to go back to Granny's for the rest of the Christmas holidays. 'Recon he knows where we live? I mean in Kilmichael?"

"Oh, come on, Jane. You don't really think that they practice voodoo at the Central Mississippi Institute for Girls way up here in French Camp. That's for New Orleans. We are a long way from New Orleans and a far cry from the way they act. Compared to New Orleans, we a just boring." *Sylvia was trying to make a joke.* "I don't know much about voodoo, but if you feel up to it, we could go to the library later to research it. Maybe you could compare what happens in the books to what happened to you. It's just a wild guess, but we have got to start somewhere," Sylvia said. She waited for Jane's answer.

"Ok. I do feel better than I've felt in the last few days, and I think that I'll continue to feel better if I find out what happened to me," Jane said. "And what else to expect. I know that Professor Huerta was trying to harm me, but I don't know why. Maybe he thinks that I remember more than I do and that I'll tell someone. I just remember that he was there. That's all."

"Tell me about the whiskey barrel," Sylvia asked. "Was there some moonshine in it? Did he try to get y'all drunk?"

"I really don't know much about why the barrel was in the back of the buggy, but one of the girls with us was riding it like a horse. I'm going to rest now. We'll talk later." Jane said and lay on the quilt and drifted off to sleep. She tossed and turned. She dreamed that Professor Huerta was chasing her with a composition that she had written in one hand and a knife in the other. "No, leave me alone. Stay away from me, heathens," she screamed out.

Victoria shook her. "Wake up, Jane."

Jane smacked Victoria hard across the face, leaving a handprint on her cheek.

"Quit, don't hit me again. It's me, Victoria. Wake up, Jane. You're having a nightmare," Victoria said, shaking Jane lightly.

Groggy and disoriented, Jane leaned up on her elbow and asked, "What? Oh, I dreamed that Professor Huerta was chasing me." Jane noticed the whelp on Victoria's face. "Did I do that? Oh, Victoria, I'm really sorry." Then she lay back on her feather pillow and tried to clear the fog from her brain. Remembering Professor Huerta and Miss Ward made her queasy. "We must go to the library to research voodoo."

"I'll get us a body guard," Victoria said.

Chapter 3

As they walked down the street toward the library, Jane noticed Professor Huerta leaning on the rail in front of a saloon across the street across from the dormitory. The Deputy Sheriff walked along with them. Seeing him, Jane tried to be calm, but her heart began beating so loudly that she could hear it. "Perhaps we had better wait until another time to go," she told her friends.

"Are you feeling sick?" Victoria asked.

Apparently, they hadn't seen Professor Huerta. Jane thought.

The professor gazed at them with his dark, muscadine brown eyes. Jane remembered some intense pain and the sickening smell of smoke and perfume, and terror gripped her heart again. She felt queasy. Then she remembered the whisky barrel. Her heart felt like it would burst through her chest. Her body shook and her heart pounded. *At any moment, my heart is going to burst out of my chest.* She thought. Adrenalin rushed though her. "I've got to find a way to get rid of him."

"I know, Jane, but you must promise me to be careful, "Victoria said.

It doesn't look like this deputy as a guard is going to be able to keep him away from me. I've got to find enough evidence to get him arrested and put away for a long time.

Jane watched out of the corner of her eye. When they reached the library steps, Jane didn't see Huerta anywhere, so they walked up the library steps. The deputy stayed outside on the steps. The library was about three stories high. It had been built to be used by the town's people and the students.

Jane walked straight to the card catalog, a five foot high cabinet with tiny drawers that had brass knobs and label holders on the ends. They walked to the left of the circulation desk and looked in the Vs drawer. An old, gray-haired lady stood behind the circulation desk. "There are several books listed, but they are located upstairs in the oldest part of the library in the stacks. Mrs. Sanford is in charge of the stacks." Jane picked up three scraps of white paper and wrote a call number on each. Holding the slips of paper in her hand, Jane slowly climbed the metal stairs behind Mrs. Sanford and the stacks.

"Hey, you must be feeling a lot better. I surely hope so. You are moving around pretty well," Victoria said.

"I just want to get this done and get back to the dorm," Jane lied. She felt more adrenalin rush through her, giving her energy.

"No one followed us. Did they?" Victoria asked. "Why don't we get Mrs. Sanford, the librarian to go get them for us?" The frail librarian stood on the first landing. Jane stopped for a minute. *If they needed help, this frail little lady would not be it.* She thought.

"Shush, young ladies. This is a library," Mrs. Sanford said, putting her finger to her nose.

Jane's adrenalin pumped more. "I've got to find the answer for a way to end whatever Huerta is trying to do to me. My heart can't stand much more of this." Then she turned to the librarian, "Please help us find these three books."

Mrs. Sanford looked at the call numbers on the slips of white paper and turned up her nose and grunted, but she seemed pleased that the books in the stacks were being used. She seemed displeased about the subject.

Jane and Victoria followed Mrs. Sanford to the dusty, smelly stacks. There were books there that hadn't been touched in years. Jane had heard a little about voodoo, but she really had never been involved in it although some of her friends had dabbled in it. *Wonder how Victoria's trick worked with the talc?* Jane thought.

Finally, they reached the stacks and walked through a doorway to a small room in the back. The call numbers on the books that she wanted were shelved three shelves down from the door. They were grouped together according to the system. Jane pulled all three from the shelf, sat down on the floor, and ran her finger down each book's spine. She stuck a piece of paper in the book that began the section on voodoo when she found the page. On page 312 in the second book, she found "voodoo spells." She added a piece of paper there for a bookmark too. A Lucifer spell was listed. She marked it.

Death was printed in italics under a picture of a spell going on near a table. *The blood of a young girl gives more power.* Jane thought.

"Oh, my, Huerta is actually trying to kill me—not because I saw them performing the spell, but because of the power he'll obtain if he does. She shivered. "Why me? What am I going to do? To outsmart him, I must get him before he gets me. The picture of the spell going on stuck in her mind.

Can I do it? She wondered.

Mrs. Sanford had exited, so it was just the three of them. She heard the vibrations of someone coming up the metal stairs. *The footsteps sounded too heavy for a frail woman.* She thought.

Jane slid across the floor and under a table behind a metal cabinet that held the library's vertical files. Victoria followed. Sylvia had stayed down stairs near the circulation desk. *Maybe that's Sylvia coming up here.* She thought. She and Victoria left the books that they were looking at on the floor where they had laid them.

The door squeaked as it opened. From their hiding place under the table, she saw a black pair of boots. She smelled the smoky and perfume smell again. Terror seized her. She froze in place, but she couldn't silence the beating of her heart. *He will hear my heartbeat.*

She thought. Her feet would not move, and she couldn't think about what to do. The confidence she had that she could get Huerta left. Anxiety took its place.

She watched Huerta walk to the place where they had left the three books open. He reached to pick one up. She heard him roughly drop it on the table above her. *I hope he can't hear my heart pounding.* She thought.

"Voodoo," she heard him say. "She's got to be in here somewhere." He was talking to himself.

Jane and Victoria stayed completely still under the table. Jane held her breath to help slow down her heart beat.

"Maybe she's hiding on the other end of the stacks," Huerta said. "Or gone to the other room."

Jane watched the boots move away from the table she was hiding under. She saw him walk toward the other end of the stacks. She signaled to Victoria that they were leaving. Her heart pounding, she crawled from under the table toward the door. Without looking back, she opened the door, and she and Victoria crawled out into the hallway. Jane stood as Victoria stood. The door still had two inches to close. It squeaked and banged shut. "Run," Jane yelled.

Jane didn't wait for Victoria. She hurried back down the stairs as fast as her injured body would let her. She held to the rails as she ran. "Don't run in the library," Mrs. Sanford said as they pushed past her. Huerta was too close behind them to even care about library rules.

On the north side of the library was a creek with a bank absolutely covered with privet hedge, an evergreen bush that took over banks and other areas if it wasn't trimmed back and controlled. The creek divided the town. North French Camp was where the blue-blooded, old money, southerners lived. The privet hedge grew on the southern side further dividing it.

Jane had played in that creek as a child. Jane knew that hidden under that hedge was an opening to a cave with markings of Choctaw Indians on its walls.

Jane and Victoria ran out the front door of the library and past the Deputy.

Professor Huerta was a few steps behind them. They split up and Victoria turned to run south. Jane hurried to the edge of the creek and waded into the shallow water. The water was freezing cold, but she was more frightened of Huerta than she was of the creek. She had been in it before, and she didn't think he would follow her.

"Dang," Huerta said as he missed a step and tumbled to the bottom of the library steps. The Deputy was behind him.

Jane watched over her shoulder as he tumbled down the steps. With this chance to hide, she slipped under the water and opening her eyes under the water, she saw the opening to the Indian cave and made her way inside it. She hid within twenty feet of Professor Huerta, but she knew that he couldn't see her because of the water and the privet hedge. The other side of the cave was wide open and sunlight filled the opening. She peered through the privet at Professor Huerta. The cold water or her terror made her shiver, so she made her way to the sunny opening in the opposite direction. Before she reached the opening, she heard a shot from a handgun.

Revulsion overcame her. She hated Professor Huerta. "I must get away from him," she said aloud.

Jane's teeth chattered, and her head ached. She felt sick. She had to get out of this cave, so she stuck her head out of the opening. Victoria saw her and began to laugh. "Jane, get out of there. Professor Huerta is gone. After he tripped on the steps, he got up and hobbled away. Deputy Callory shot toward him, but I don't think he hit him. Come on. We need to get you back to the dormitory. I should have remembered that you knew about that Indian cave. Remember when we used to play in there when we were children?"

Deputy Callory came to the edge of the creek, "Come on out of the water, Miss Lynch. As soon as you get cleaned up and warm, we need to have a talk."

"Where did Professor Huerta go?" Jane asked.

"Deputy Callory shot at him, and he ran," Victoria replied. "Maybe he's gone. Maybe he will give up." Jane knew that she was trying to sound optimistic. "When we get to the dorm, we'll talk about what we found."

They walked back to the dormitory. Deputy Callory followed them.

"I know that he's going to follow us. That's why I asked Deputy Callory to accompany us," Victoria said. "He was a close friend of my father."

"Victoria, I just figured out how to get rid of Professor Huerta. I know what to do. I'm so relieved. After we talk to the deputy, I'll explain my plan to you." A flood of relief swept over Jane. It was as soothing as the fear of him killing her had been gripping at the core of her.

They reached the dormitory, and Deputy Callory strode into the lobby behind them. He sat in a large, red Victorian Queen Anne couch and they went upstairs, "I'm going to get cleaned up. You talk to him, but don't mention the voodoo to him," Jane said.

Jane went inside their room and removed her wet skirt, blouse, and underwear. She dressed quickly in an old robe. She walked down the hall to the water closet and asked Oma for some hot water. Then she sneaked back to the top of the stairs to listen to Deputy Callory and Victoria's conversation. At the present time, Jane didn't trust this deputy either. She listened while Oma filled the tub inside the water closet. She heard Deputy Callory say that he had not seen anyone suspicious in and around the girl's dormitory. Hearing him talk made Jane feel queasy; so she went into the water closet, added bubbles to the tub, dropped the robe, stepped into the hot water, and lay back to relax. She tried to remember the details of what had happened to her, but she couldn't remember anything that had happened after she had seen Miss Ward in the grove. The warmth of the water or the wetness from the creek made her bandages fall off, but her wounds were healing. After a while, she shampooed her hair and soaked in the tub until Victoria came to the door to check on her. Jane began to feel better.

"Are you going to come down stairs talk to Deputy Callory? I brought you a clean dress to wear."

"Yes, but why is he in a hurry? I thought he was watching the dorm for us. Won't he be staying the night?"

"Yes, I guess so, if you want him to. I just thought that you might hurry since he was kind enough to rescue us today."

"Oh, I thought that was his job," Jane replied, clearly agitated. She grabbed a towel and climbed out of the tub.

She redressed her wounds with clean bandages, dressed in the clean brown dress and sweater that Victoria had brought her, wrapped her long, dark hair in a large, white towel and went into the lobby. She sat down on a Victorian couch to talk to Deputy Callory. "I'm sorry that I took so long, but I was under the impression that you were staying the night to guard us and that I could talk to you later; besides, I felt very tired and sick and had to dress my wounds with new bandages since those got wet."

"Well, Miss Lynch, I am staying if you want me to, but I thought that I might be able to help you get a restraint against that man because he is stalking you," he said leaning back in the large, red couch.

"What good will a piece of paper do? How will that keep him from trying to kill me? I'd rather have a real person guard us," Jane said. She didn't trust Deputy Callory even if he did shoot at Professor Huerta. He hadn't hit him.

"I know that, Ma'am, but we can't provide a guard all the time. We don't have enough officers as it is. Now, tell me what happened. Why were you with him?"

"He invited me to a party. "

"You went to a party with him alone."

"Listen, if you are one of those men who think a woman gets what she deserves from the way she dresses or the way she acts, you might as well leave here now. No, I wasn't going to a party with only him. We were not alone. There were several other girls with us in his buggy. Besides, I trusted Professor Huerta. He was my teacher and, I guess, my friend." Jane said. She choked back her tears.

"I'm sorry, Miss Lynch, I didn't mean to upset you. I can see how you could have gotten yourself in this situation. You know, being lonely since your mother had just died and all."

"Leave my mother out of this," Jane said, rising from her chair. "I didn't cause what he did to happen. You talk to him, Victoria. I'm tired and I'm going to bed," Jane said. She abruptly left the room, but stopped at the top of the stairs to listen.

She heard Victoria talking to Deputy Callory after she left. "She's been through so much lately. She gets upset easily, but we would appreciate it if you would arrange for someone to guard the dorm tonight. I have a feeling that Professor Huerta is coming back."

"I'll do better than that. I'll guard it myself. I'm sorry that I made her so upset. I didn't mean to," he said.

After hearing him, Jane wished that she hadn't been so abrupt.

As soon as he went outside, Jane got out of her bed and went into the kitchen. She and Victoria made some ham sandwiches for dinner. While they were eating, Jane said, "The book that I found says a voodoo sacrifice often ends in death. That's supposed to be the supreme sacrifice, a Lucifer spell. Somehow I've got to get rid of Huerta, or he will use me as a sacrifice. I think he is deeper into voodoo than we thought. Now, I've got a plan, but I'm not certain that it will work. If I could get the sheriff to arrest him for attempted murder and get him convicted, I would be rid of him."

"You aren't planning to stay here is French Camp. Are you?" Victoria asked. "I thought you were going back to Kilmichael."

"Yes, that's exactly what I'm going to do until next semester starts. I'm hoping by the time the doctor releases me, the sheriff will have arrested Professor Huerta. If not, I'll have to help them catch him doing something else wrong. I've got to do some more thinking and planning. Someone else must be aware of what he did to me, and I'll be willing to bet that I am not the first student that he's done this to. Actually, he probably isn't the only staff member who's involved. Did you know that Miss Ward is his girlfriend? She may be able to help us catch him. I'll think about this tomorrow. I'm tired now and I'm going to sleep."

"How do you know about Miss Ward?"

"I used to walk at night on campus with some other girls, and I've seen them. They sneak out with each other at night."

By seven o'clock that night, they had both gone to bed. They locked themselves in their rooms. Miss Ward still wasn't in the dorm. Jane felt relieved.

The afternoon's events had taken their toll on Jane. Since she was exhausted, sleep came quickly to her, but it was fretful. The wind outside began to blow. Jane got up to open a window to get some fresh air. One of those rain storms with pink lightening was popping in the west over the Big Black swamp. *Grandmother Folly says that rain usually follows water. I wonder where Miss Ward is.* Jane opened the window. Then she looked at the clock on the mantle. *Ten o'clock.*

She looked out the window again. She saw someone coming toward the dormitory, carrying something large. She pushed the curtain back to get a better view. A black form was making its way to the porch. Jane saw the person when the lightning flashed. Jane watched the form. The form carried a container of something. He walked toward the dormitory. She rushed to Victoria's bedroom to wake her.

"Wake up, Victoria." She shook her. "Huerta's here." Jane put her finger to her lips. Then she motioned for Victoria to follow her. Neither of them put on their shoes. When they reached the hallway, Jane said, "We need to get out of here. Out the back way." Jane peeked through the hall window and saw Huerta dousing kerosene along the front porch of Bacon Hall. Then he walked off the end of the porch into the darkness.

Jane and Victoria watched through the window. "He's going to burn down the dormitory. Jane panicked. "Where is that deputy sheriff? We've got to get out of here." They tiptoed down the stairs and toward the back of the dorm. They both yelled, "Fire," as loud as they could and ran outside. Once outside they ran across the yard and hid behind the outhouse. They weren't a moment too soon.

Jane heard a loud boom, like the sound of hundreds of guns being fired at once. Next, the dormitory was engulfed in flames. Some of the girl students and Oma crawled out their windows. Some wore their gowns and were barefooted like Jane and Victoria. Jane counted, counting herself and Victoria ten people got out. Jane did not see Miss Ward in the crowd.

Immediately, the entire town was in the street. The number of houses on this street hadn't changed in years and neither had the way they looked. All were made of wood and were in danger of burning too, if a spark or ember floated or blew their way. There was less than thirty feet between the houses and the backyards were small. Most had a small vegetable garden in the back. "Was anyone inside the dormitory?" a neighbor asked.

"I think most all the girls went home for Christmas," another neighbor answered. "I saw some crawl out the windows. Ten got out." Jane had never seen this woman before. She dressed is a nightgown similar to one that Granny wore and she had a scarf tied around her head to protect her hair.

"What about the dorm mother, Miss Ward?" Someone asked.

"She wasn't there," Victoria answered. "We didn't get anything out of the dormitory. We should have at least gotten some of our clothes and favorite possessions before we left."

"And our shoes," Jane replied, looking at her bare feet. *I'm just glad we got out safely. Clothes and shoes are replaceable.*

"We were trying to save ourselves. At least we did that. Everything else can be replaced, I guess, except things my father gave me," Victoria cried. Jane hadn't seen her cry often. It broke her heart, so she hugged Victoria tightly to her.

A long line of men formed between the well near the livery and the dormitory. Some got water from the troughs on the sides of the street where the horses drank. Jane and Victoria stood with their neighbors helplessly watching the men passing buckets of water to each other. The last one threw the water on the flaming dormitory. They tried to put the fire out, but it was too late. The dormitory was a total disaster.

Finally, Miss Ward arrived from somewhere across the street, "Oh, my Gosh. Are you two all right? I certainly hope so. What happened? Were you able to save anything? Our dormitory is ruined," she sobbed, hysterically. *She is genuinely upset about her things.* Jane thought.

"She apparently didn't know that Huerta was going to burn the dormitory," Jane whispered to Victoria. "Where is Professor Huerta? He set this on fire. We can charge him with this crime. We need to talk to Sheriff Marks."

"Where is the deputy? Wasn't he here?" Miss Ward asked.

How did she know that? Jane wondered. *How did she know that we had a deputy guarding us? And how do we know that she didn't move her things before he started the fire?*

"We saw a man pouring kerosene on the porch before we ran out the back door. The deputy was supposed to be out here somewhere," Victoria said. "It was Professor Huerta."

"All our belongings. And oh, no. My clothes from Paris." Miss Ward turned to the girls. She acted like she hadn't heard the Professor's name. "I'm extremely glad that you two are all right. I knew that I should put some of my clothes in another location. Something told me that something else bad was going to happen." She looked at the two girls. "You poor darlings don't have your shoes on. You were barely able to get out before the dormitory blew up; weren't you? You poor darlings." She didn't look either girl straight in the eyes. She tried to hug Victoria. Jane moved out of her reach.

"She puts on a good show. " Jane whispered to Victoria. "She is such a phony. We can go to my grandmother's house tonight. I'm certain that she will be glad for us to stay with her." Jane tried to put her arm around Victoria to console her.

"Okay. Where is the deputy?" Jane asked. "I'd like to find out what he saw tonight. He can take us to Granny's. How did Miss Ward know about the deputy?" She walked across the grass to find him. Many of their neighbors watched as the fire was finally contained. Jane asked them if they had seen anything, but no one had.

Finally they found the deputy. He said that he had walked to the saloon to get a drink of water. He hadn't seen anything either. Later after the fire was almost out, he went to the livery stable. He borrowed a buggy and drove them the seventeen miles to Granny's house in Kilmichael.

***

The boards were cold to Jane's feet as she walked up on Grandmother's porch. The house was painted white and had gray trim. It had two large porches that ran across the front and back. At the back of her house was Mr. Petey's barbeque shack. Jane felt numb from shock and cold. She knocked on the glass pane in the front door.

"Who is it?" Granny asked, opening the door about two inches. Recognizing Jane she said, "Child, come on in this house. It's freezing out. Where is your coat? Where are y'all's shoes? You'll catch yo' death. What y'all doing out dressed like that in this weather?"

Granny smelled of her homemade cold remedy that she put near her chest before she went to bed. For the remedy she mixed kerosene and honey and poured it on a folded cotton bandage. This she pinned to the inside of her nightgown. She was dressed in her long, red flannel gown and a blue-flowered house coat. They were not really a matching set like the rest of Granny's house, but comfort was her strong suit not beauty.

"Oh, Granny, it's terrible. Our girl's dormitory of The Central Mississippi Institute burned," Jane said, barely audible through her sobs. "The dormitory just burned. We stood and watched it." She didn't tell her about the man with the can of kerosene that she thought was Huerta.

"Y'all can stay here. I'll make up ya'll a bed." She lightly hugged Jane as she invited them inside which was unusual for Granny who wasn't a hugger. "My house is small, but you are welcome to stay here with us, Victoria. I've already gotten Tommy to sleep. He is so sweet.

He always asks for Jane before he goes to sleep. He'll be surprised to see y'all in the morning."

The deputy left for French Camp to return the horse and buggy he had borrowed to bring them here. The trip had taken them two hours to get the Kilmichael, so Jane figured it would take him two to get back. At least, he wore a coat.

Jane and Victoria sat down on the couch while Granny made them some beds and added some of her hand stitched quilts to keep them warm. Jane loved looking at them and remembering the different dresses or shirts family members had worn from looking at the quilt pieces.

"We talked to the deputy on the way here, Granny. He was supposed to be guarding the dorm, but he said that he went to get a drink of water. We'll talk about it tomorrow. I guess that we had better get some sleep. Tomorrow we will have to go back to the school to salvage anything that wasn't ruined in the fire." They lay on the beds at Granny's and within a couple of minutes Victoria was snoring.

Jane was having trouble going to sleep. *I wish I could sneak into the bed with Tommy and sleep with him.* Jane thought. She got up to go to the bathroom and peeked into Tommy's room to check on him. He was sound asleep. She stood looking down at him in the soft glow of the lantern. Then she leaned over his bed and kissed him on the cheek waking him slightly. He made a soft grunting sound and turned over to go back to sleep.

Jane walked back into the main room. The fireplace was on the outside wall and two rocking chairs sat on each side of it. A cuckoo clock sat in the middle of the mantle. It was one of Granny's favorite possessions that had come from France. She heard Victoria still snoring. She went into the kitchen and took Granny's sweater from the hanger beside the door. She borrowed Pop's shoes that were sitting beside the back door. *I need some air. I think I'll sit on the back porch for a while. I always could think better out there since it's so peaceful.*

The smell of smoke from the fireplace drifted through the damp night air to where she sat on the porch. She hated the smell of smoke now, and she used to love it. Two horrible memories were connected with the smell of smoke. The pink lightening was over. Jane looked across the road toward Mr. Petey, a black man's joint where some people were cooking barbecue ribs on the grill. They usually smoked them all night to give them a sweet, smoky taste. The ribs smelled so good. The owner came outside to check the progress of the ribs. His name was Petey. Petey waved to Jane. Jane waved back to him. Then he walked out into the road and made his way to where she sat on the porch. "Hey, Miss Jane. I hated to hear about yo' school, and about all the bad things that been happening to you. Your mother…she was a fine lady…I used to work for her some when you was a baby. And I heard about what that man did to you at that school. I got a daughter up there. Oma works in the water closet. She came home tonight because the dormitory burned and told me all about it. She just barely got out. She said y'all did too.

"Oh, yes, I know Oma. She stayed in the dormitory where I did."

"She done told me that some strange things are happening at that place, but I thought that she was stretching the truth. That Miss Ward. She can't stand my Oma."

"I'm sorry, Mr. Petey. Now, since the dormitory burned, Oma doesn't have a job."

"It's all right, Miss Jane. I know you been having enough problems of your own there. If I cans do anything for y'all, let me know. It's been a while since we talked. Seeing you rambling around in the neighborhood used to be a common occurrence. I used to see you walking about at night when you was visiting your granny. You couldn't been more that thirteen or fourteen years old. Things so' was a lot different back then. You know, Kilmichael is a very small town and everybody knows everybody, but it's not the same anymore. It's more dangerous. I thought things would have been better after the war, but I can't say that they are. At least, I can go and come as I please, but making money is hard."

Jane heard a buggy come slowly down the road that ran perpendicular to the barbeque joint. It looked like the buggy that

Professor Huerta drove. They both noticed it. Jane got up from her seat and moved into the shadows. The moisture dripped slowly from the eve of the tin roof of Granny's house.

"Mr. Petey, please sit down on Granny's steps like you are by yourself. I don't want that man in that buggy to see me. I'll bet you that he had something to do with the fire at the school."

"Sho' nuff, Miss Jane. Can you sees who he is?"

She waited until the buggy went around the corner; then she moved back next to him.

"Let me axe you a question, Miss Jane. Oma said some man chased you out of the library today. Is that him?" Petey asked.

"Yes, that's him," Jane replied. It was refreshing to find someone who believed her without being condescending or asking her a bunch of embarrassing questions.

"Honey, I promise you that he won't bother you no more around here if I gets my way," Petey reassured her. "I ain't gonna tell the law neither. They not too good at helping black folks anyway. We've got a way of taking care of our own problems. Just you never mind. Leave it to old Petey. You spend your energy on getting well and getting yo' schooling. Yo' mama was so proud of you."

"What do you know about voodoo, Mr. Petey?"

"I knows a little bit. Why you ask?"

"That man Professor Huerta, the one harassing me, he's into voodoo. I heard that his wife is Marie Laveau from New Orleans."

"I'll see what I can find out. I gotta go check on the barbeque," he said. With that, Petey waved good-bye to Jane and went back to check on his barbeque.

Jane was getting cold and she was afraid that Huerta would come back, so she went back inside Granny's house. She hung Granny's sweater back on the hook and left Pop's shoes where she had gotten them.

Victoria crawled out of the bed and said, "Jane, what on earth are you doing outside at this time of night? I awoke because I'm hungry. Do you mind if I get some milk?"

"Of course not, go ahead. Make yourself at home."

Victoria began to sob hysterically. "What am I going to do? I don't have anywhere to live and all my things are ruined."

"Well, the first thing tomorrow, we need to talk to Sheriff Marks. The person who set fire to our school needs to be arrested. We can tell him that we saw him. Perhaps they can find some incriminating evidence or maybe someone else saw him. I've got an idea. Let's get the sheriff to find out where Huerta was at that time of night. Victoria, I've been thinking."

"Victoria, what do you know about voodoo? I was talking to Mr. Petey out on Granny's porch tonight when Huerta rode by in his buggy. I'm going to ask Mr. Petey some more questions about it."

"You saw Huerta here last night? You were outside on the porch with Mr. Petey?" Victoria asked. "Have you lost your mind? What were y'all talking about?"

"Voodoo."

"Why are you asking about voodoo? That's just spells. Professor Huerta is a real threat," Victoria said. "We've got to get some sleep. We'll talk tomorrow."

Jane heard the flap on the mailbox clank as the lid was slammed shut. She got up and looked out the window in time to see Huerta ride away in his buggy. She slipped out the door and got the envelope from the box with her name printed in large red letters on the front. They reminded her of the *Scarlet Letter*. It was sealed. She recognized Professor Huerta's handwriting from her grammar class. Jane slid her fingernail under the flap of the envelope. A piece of folded paper was inside. The letter read: If you tell anyone, your friend Victoria, and your grandparents die. Don't forget that you have a little brother and also a step-father in jail.

Jane rushed back inside the house, and with shaking hands, she took a long fire poker that Granny used from the set that rested near the fireplace. She stuck the end of the letter into the fireplace to catch it on fire. Then she shoved it deep into the cinders and coals.

After most of the stationery burned, she poked the rest under the coals and waited for it to burn too.

She had to get Huerta without putting anyone else in danger. She couldn't go to sleep. She had to come up with a plan.

Chapter 4

Her plans had three parts. First, she would go back to The Central Mississippi Institute for Girls, stay in a different dormitory, and not lose her scholarships. She knew that they could double up to make room for more girls in one dorm. Second, she would get some other evidence of Professor Huerta's involvement in voodoo and use it against him. Third, she would do what Granny always said and, "Give him enough rope and he would hang himself." *In her mind, she could see Huerta swinging from a noose.* With his setting fire to their dormitory, he was close to hanging himself now.

Jane didn't tell Victoria her plans and she didn't tell her about the warning Professor Huerta had put in the mailbox.

Jane and Victoria went back to the Institute the following Sunday afternoon. This suited Jane. It was part one of her plan. She would not lose her scholarship. The administrators had assigned them to another dormitory. Sylvia moved back in the house with her mother. They were moved into a girl named Rachel's room with her.

As soon as they were settled in Rachel's room, Victoria went to find her boyfriend. Jane liked Rachel immediately. Rachel had long dark hair and beautiful brown eyes. She was about Jane's size, and to listen to her talk, she was rich. Her family lived in Vicksburg, Mississippi.

"Want to smoke a cigarette?" Rachel asked Jane after Victoria left.

"No, I don't smoke, but Victoria does."

Rachel lit the cigarette and filled the dormitory room with blue smoke. "You look so slim. How do you look like that?"

"I work in my Granny's garden. We live on a farm outside Kilmichael. Do you know where that is?"

"No, not really. My! I don't like working in a garden. My mama used to try to make me work in the garden with the Negroes."

The two of them talked a long time. They talked about their families, boys, and the school. Jane showed Rachel the pine oil trick in a perfume atomizer.

The next morning at breakfast Jane sat with Rachel in the food hall. Rachel had loaned Jane a beautiful dress and matching shoes to wear. The dress looked like it came from Paris. It wasn't handmade like those she had worn that Granny had made. It was a mauve color with beige lace and pin tucks. The length was perfect for her. The waist was fitted and had a row of lace around it.

Not many students had gotten up early enough to eat breakfast because it was still Christmas vacation. There was a slow rain falling. So they stayed inside the food hall to wait for the rain to stop. She watched Professor Huerta slowly saunter up to their table. Jane had spotted him the minute that he walked into the cafeteria and put his umbrella beside the door, but she had tried to act as if his presence didn't matter to her. She was determined to show him that she wasn't afraid of him. She didn't look directly at him. Her heart beat loudly against her chest. She tried to silence it. It was so loud that she thought everyone in the food hall could hear it. She reached deep within herself for strength because she hated him. She turned to face him.

At her table, he turned his face toward her and away from Rachel. He mouthed, "If you tell anyone anything, they are DEAD and so are you." Then he walked back to his own table and sat down to eat his breakfast of soggy, scrambled eggs and toast. Jane noticed that a jar of honey sat on each table today instead of jelly.

Rachel looked at Jane and raised an inquisitive eyebrow. "What?"

Jane ignored her question. She watched him calmly eating his breakfast. *I hope he chokes. Burning the dormitory was a mean thing to do, but using her as a voodoo sacrifice was sick.* Jane thought.

"What was that all about?" Rachel asked, her brown eyes dancing. Both were looking straight at Huerta when he motioned with a quick movement of his hands and eyes for Rachel to come to his table.

Rachel moved to get out of her chair.

"Don't go over there," Jane said as she placed a hand on Rachel's arm to stop her.

"Why? He's my grammar teacher. I have to." She got up and walked to the table where Professor Huerta sat.

Jane watched. Rachel smiled and looked like she was saying *yes.* She nodded her head. Rachel quickly returned to the table to tell Jane all about it. She had two pieces of paper in her hand. "Professor Huerta gave us tickets to the musical comedy tonight in the show tent." Rachel said holding up the tickets.

Jane was terrified. "No, I don't want to go. No, we are not going." *I wonder what I've gotten my roommates into.* Jane thought. "I saw him setting fire to our dormitory."

"Speak for yourself. I'm delighted," Rachel said. "Are you certain that he is the one you saw? He wouldn't do a thing like that." She carefully tucked the tickets into a pocket on her dress.

"We can't do that. He'll…" Jane did not finish her statement.

"But it is for your birthday. I wasn't supposed to tell you. It was supposed to be a surprise," Rachel said.

"Who said that it's for my birthday?" Jane asked.

"Professor Huerta did. Aren't you in his grammar class? Does he always give presents to his students?" Rachel looked at her with a questioning look.

Suddenly it occurred to Jane. In ten days, she would be twenty years old. She remembered Huerta asking for the youngest one in the group. She remembered what the book about voodoo had said. Perhaps she would be too old on her twentieth birthday for him to be interested in her. She felt his stares burning through her. *Who would he prey on after she turned twenty? She had ten days to get him before he got her. Well, now nine more.* She thought.

Huerta was watching for her reaction. She was terrified beyond words, but she held her emotions in check. She had to appear strong even with that large knot forming in her stomach. She would not let him know how frightened she was. Professor Huerta motioned for Jane to come over to his table just as he had motioned for Rachel.

On wobbly legs, she stood and walked toward him. Her knees felt rubbery, but instead of walking to his table, she walked out of the food hall into the pouring rain. *If she was going to go through with her plan, it was time to start part two, but voodoo terrified her. From what she had read, she had to have a talisman with protection properties to avert Huerta's evil.* She thought.

Huerta had followed her the last time that she left the school to go to Granny's. She had put her family in danger from him. She tried to shake her terror, but she needed some evidence to put him away forever. The burning of the dorm would be hard to prove. Even Rachel didn't believe her. She was going to that tent Chautauqua, but she wasn't going to let him know ahead of time.

The knot in her stomach would not go away. Her stomach always hurt when she was frightened. On the day of the concert, she wrote Victoria a note: *Rachel and I are gone to the musical comedy in the show tent. Wish you had been here to go with us. We'll tell you all about it when we come back. Don't worry. I've got everything under control. Just keep doing what you are doing. Tell your boyfriend 'Hi,' for me.*

Finally, it was 6 p.m. Jane and Rachel walked inside a large show tent with side flaps that reached to the ground. It was set up in a large flat area near the edge of town. It had ropes and stakes holding the large faded red tent in place. Long lines of people had formed to buy their tickets. They were loud and cheerful. Traveling entertainers rarely stopped in French Camp. Jane and Rachel were able to bypass the long ticket lines because Huerta had given Rachel the tickets. Again, Jane's legs felt wobbly. They had to walk all the way to the front of the stage for their seats in the rows of folding chairs. Most girls Jane's age would have killed for backstage passes to any show. They had them, but Jane felt cold chills run down her back. The hair on the back of her neck stood on end. Clearly, Jane was afraid of Huerta, but she was more determined than ever to win over his brand of evil. He was nowhere to be seen when they got there.

The smell of food from the vendors outside the tent made her feel queasy as she and Rachel found their seats. *I wonder where the outhouse is.* Jane thought.

Then Huerta showed up arm in arm with one of the black comedians in the show. She was a woman dressed as a male character. He looked very excited, intoxicated, and his facial expressions were animated. Jane heard him call her Tela. Tela was Negro with very dark eyes and velvety, honey colored skin. She was well built with tight muscle tone and long limbs.

Jane shuddered at the sight of him and this young woman. She surveyed the crowd for a familiar face. She saw a few that she knew. Plan one, coming back to school had worked. Plan two had to be a success too, so she fought the urge to flee. She needed physical evidence to use against him.

Miss Ward strode through the door on the side of the show tent near the front of the stage. From the look on her face, she did not like the way Professor Huerta was holding on to the young, honey-colored actress, Tela. Miss Ward walked up to him and although Jane couldn't hear what was said, it appeared that she and Huerta got into a heated argument. Miss Ward's arms and hands began flying and a physical confrontation followed. Huerta knocked Miss Ward into a seat near the front of the stage.

Then he turned and walked up the steps to the stage, across it, and behind the curtain, leaving her half-sprawled on the dirt floor. Tela followed him.

Chapter 5

Jane wanted to see what Huerta was doing behind the curtain, so she excused herself as if to go to the outhouse. As queasy as her stomach felt, she thought she might need to find the outhouse first. So she made a detour. The red show tent was packed. There were people sitting in the folding, wooden chairs and some had even brought chairs from somewhere else. *Perhaps the saloon.* Jane thought. The master of ceremonies came to the center of the stage and the show began. Jane looked at Rachel who was engrossed.

He introduced the main characters, who wore grotesque costumes and face paint. Jane couldn't tell which were male and which were female.

The music began and the show started. Jane hadn't noticed much about what was happening on stage, but several male actors came on stage and began a funny dialogue. Everyone laughed. She sneaked down the outside of the tent and found the outhouse before she made her way behind the stage. The line at the outhouse was as long as the ticket line had been, so she didn't stop. She walked into the edge of the wooded area behind the show and threw up. Then she walked toward the back of the show tent. Jane felt the vibrations of the loud music pulsing through her body. A drum and a trumpet played jazz. She heard the contagious laughter of the packed audience.

Her adrenalin increased and her heart beat loudly. She made her way around the stakes holding the back of the red tent in place and peeked inside. Huerta stood there with that young actress, Tela. The two were dancing and chanting something. *Tela is another voodoo queen.* Jane thought. Huerta and Tela shared a pipe. The tobacco smelled like cherry. *It reminded Jane of her Grandfather's pipe.*

Jane moved closer inside the opening to be able to hear what they were saying. "Come to the cemetery tonight. As a matter of fact, I'll teach you a new spell that communicates with the dead. It is the Lucifer spell." Huerta laughed loudly, smiled at Tela, and flicked a match onto the floor. Suddenly, the match caught the dead, dry grass on fire. The fire moved at rapid speed to the tent curtains; and Jane watched as the dry, brittle curtains of the stage caught on fire. The curtains burned toward the ceiling and the stage. Jane couldn't move from where she stood. Then the dry, unpainted wood of the stage caught fire. It all happened so fast that Jane stood there watching with horror. Her legs felt heavy. She couldn't move.

At first, the audience acted like this was part of the show. Then someone screamed, "Fire!" Jane snapped out of her shock. People in the audience scrambled to leave and tried to exit through the side entry and the front doors. They knocked chairs over and a few people fell to the ground trying to escape the smoke and flames that quickly filled the tent. The fire ruined her plan to catch Huerta doing something backstage. *Where was Rachel?* Jane wondered.

Jane could handle her queasy stomach no more. Although she had already thrown up, she could hold back no longer. The excitement of the burning tent wasn't helping. Bitter bile rose in her throat. The smell of the show food got the best of her. She puked all over the front of her dress. In her bent over stance, someone running from the tent bumped her, and she fell to the ground. She crawled to the side of the dirt lane to keep from getting trampled by the fleeing crowd. Disgusted, she took some dry grass from the ground and wiped most of the vomit off her dress. When she looked up, she saw

Huerta standing over her, and he was holding Rachel by the upper arm. His leer terrified her, but Rachel was oblivious.

Rachel didn't even look in the least bit frightened. "Professor Huerta rescued me." She babbled. "How did you get out of the tent? Who rescued you?" Rachel asked. She seemed pleased to have Huerta holding her arm.

Jane shuddered and didn't answer. She wanted to run at the sight of Huerta, but she didn't want to leave Rachel. Being that close to him made her remember some of what he had done to her and part of the voodoo ritual. She began to shake.

"Come with me. It isn't safe with this stampeding crowd." He grabbed Jane's upper arm. "My, you are shaking," he said to Jane.

"Where are you taking us?" Rachel asked as Tela joined them.

"I can't go. I'm sick." Jane said and she vomited again.

"Oh, my dear, what is wrong with you?" He let her go.

Composing herself, Jane ran in the opposite direction of the cemetery. She slipped into the shadows and turned to see if Huerta was chasing her. He was not.

Huerta, Rachel , and Tela walked in the direction of the cemetery beside the church near the end of town. Less than one hundred people had been buried there, but Jane hadn't known any of them except her mother. Jane slipped through the shadows, following them. *It is sacrilege to desecrate a grave.* She thought.

"Why are we going to a cemetery?" Jane heard Rachel ask. "I'm afraid to go out there at night. Cemeteries give me goose bumps because I'm afraid of ghosts."

"You'll see," he said, teasingly. "I'll protect you from the ghosts. See I have a lantern here to light the way."

Tela laughed. Her dark eyes danced in the glow from the burning tent, but she didn't seem at all concerned that it was burning and her job would be over.

"Are ghosts afraid of the dark?" Huerta asked and joined in Tela's laughter. It sounded eerie for them to be laughing so loudly about a cemetery.

Jane knew what exactly to do. She ran across the street to the current girl's dormitory and found Miss Ward rearranging her sparse belongings in her room. Jane told her, "Huerta has carried that actress Tela to the cemetery." She didn't mention Rachel.

"That bastard," Miss Ward said. Her jealousy showed from the expression on her face. "He will be sorry."

"Do you know Tela?" Jane asked.

Miss Ward acted as if she already knew Tela, but Jane saw the hot, fiery sparks in Miss Ward's green eyes as she jumped up out of her straight-backed chair, grabbed a red globe lantern off the white tablecloth-covered table, and marched out the door and down the old wooden steps. Then she marched toward the cemetery down the center of the street. Giving her a few minutes to get a head start, Jane watched Miss Ward's lantern go almost out of sight. Then she followed, making her way down the middle of the street now. *I need a lantern too.* She thought. Although the glow of light from the windows helped, it ran out after she passed the last store. She had followed the light from Miss Ward's lantern to know where to go after she was away from the town and from the glow of the burning tent.

As Miss Ward got to the cemetery, she turned off her lantern. Jane slipped into the depths of the hedges making its fence around the cemetery to be able to hear and see what was happening. Miss Ward had joined Huerta, Rachel, and Tela at the head of Jane's mother's grave. They all seemed to be getting along.

It had been about a week since Jane had put flowers on her mother's grave, and since it was December and the weather was so cold, they wilted quickly. That is where they were standing. *Why are they standing there?* Jane wondered.

She saw the four of them standing near a tall, granite gravestone statue of an angel. *My mother's grave is next to that angel. Rumors about the angel's eyes following you wherever you were in the cemetery came to mind.* Jane sneaked closer to the angel.

Huerta had his and Miss Ward's lanterns sitting on the rectangular bottom of the granite angel's base. He passed around a bottle of whiskey to all of them including Rachel, and then he poured some on Jane's mother's grave. *The fact that Miss Ward was there with Tela and Rachel didn't seem to be a problem.* Jane thought.

Huerta pulled several items from the pockets of his coat. He chanted over them as he placed them on Mrs. Lynch's grave. Jane saw some white things that looked like chicken bones, a fruit jar of clear liquid, and a six-inch long black thing like a turkey beard, some coins, and some paper. *I wish I had made my talisman already. I don't think Rachel or Miss Ward is going to be helpful to prove Huerta's involvement in voodoo. He's trying to get to me by voodoo through my dead mother.* Jane thought.

Jane watched Rachel slowly backing away from the other three. She wobbled as she walked, looking intoxicated. "No, I need you to stay," Jane whispered to herself. "I need you to testify that he's into voodoo." None of the others noticed that Rachel had left. Soon Rachel made it to the darkness of a cornfield next to the cemetery. Jane watched her disappear into the darkness.

Jane crawled to the end of the graves from where she hid. Then she crawled behind a large gravestone. "We can finish the spell tonight. Then Jane Lynch will be under my control." Jane heard Huerta tell the two women. Jane crawled back toward the hedges. Then she stood and ran as fast as she could back to the town. She stumbled and staggered in the roughness of the dirt road as she slipped past the livery and one of the saloons. Finally, she made it to the dormitory.

Chapter 6

Jane slipped back into the dormitory through the back door in the kitchen. She wriggled the hook latch just so and the locked door opened. It was a trick she had used at Granny's house. She ran up the stairs to her new bedroom. Since she was still frightened, she pushed Victoria's bunk bed in front of the door and crawled into the bottom bunk and covered her head. Rachel slept on her bed and was snoring. She was in an alcohol induced sleep.

I wonder how she got back to the dorm. She must have been as drunk as Cooter Brown. Jane thought.

Jane fell asleep immediately.

The next morning Jane and Rachel woke with the clang of the morning bell, signaling time for them to get up. The black cast iron bell had an iron ball to clang against its sides. It resided on top of a wooden cedar pole outside the front of the school building where they went to classes. Jane looked around and rubbed the sleep from her eyes. Victoria hadn't come home to their dorm room last night.

"Why do you have Victoria's bed in front of the door?" Rachel asked, rousing from her sleep by the sound of the bell. She looked at the black streaks that Jane was making by sliding the bed back across the brown tile floor.

"The disinfected smell of this room is too strong this early in the morning." Jane felt sick to her stomach and her head ached. "I was scared of Professor Huerta and Miss Ward." Rachel seemed to be in agreement this morning.

"Look, Jane, I know they are into voodoo. My head still feels about twice its regular size."

"Alcohol seems to be part of their rituals," Jane said.

Then Jane was silent. She knew that more was involved than Rachel ever imagined, but she didn't really trust Rachel. When she had lived with her grandmother, Granny had warned her of the evils of dabbling in voodoo. She had called it a satanic practice. One of the old, black women who lived on their place had tried to teach Jane about voodoo, but Granny had a hissy fit and forbid her to mention it to Jane again and especially forbid her to teach Jane how to do any of the spells.

This morning Jane's throat tightened every time she thought of what Huerta had done to her, although she still couldn't remember all of it. She thought about the smell of smoke and exotic perfume, and it made the bile rise in her throat. She choked it back. When her throat tightened, her voice became high pitched and emotion filled.

In her emotion-filled, high-pitched sound Jane said, "Did you know that was my mother's grave they were doing the voodoo over? We need to watch Professor Huerta and Miss Ward. I think that Tela woman will leave with the entertainers. If they leave, that is? They may be out of business since their tent burned. I am frightened of all of them. Aren't you?"

"Well, after last night, I am. Were you at the cemetery? I had a feeling that you were watching from the shadows."

"Yes, I was hiding in the hedges. I saw what they were doing to my mother's grave. I saw you crawl off into the cornfield."

"I didn't want to go to the cemetery anyway. It's too creepy out there for me," Rachel said.

Abruptly, Professor Huerta and Miss Ward entered the dorm room. *Miss Ward must have shown him which room we were staying in now.* Jane thought. *And he doesn't mind breaking the rules by coming into the girl's dormitory.*

"We were just going to breakfast," Jane lied, hoping Rachel would take the hint.

Jane felt Huerta's stare burning into her. His cold, dark eyes never left her face.

"We came here to tell you ladies about the show and the fire and about the party we had afterward," Huerta said. "Since you missed it. What happened to you?" He directed the question to Jane.

"Well, I couldn't stay out past my bedtime, so I came back to the dorm," Jane lied. *You don't need to know that I saw you in the cemetery.* She thought.

"We'll catch you later." Huerta assured Jane with his double meaning. He hadn't lifted his cold stare one time since he had come into the room.

Rachel looked from Jane to Professor Huerta and then to Miss Ward. "Hey, what's going on?" *The tension in the room was impossible to miss.* All four stood looking at each other. The bell for the beginning of breakfast clanked.

The two turned and abruptly left the room.

Before going to breakfast, Jane looked for Victoria, but could not find her. When she went to the food hall, Miss Ward and Huerta sat across the room in another stall from Rachel and Jane. They were unaware that Jane could hear their conversation.

"The secret and mystery of the ritual will be what captures that girl. Physical force will not be necessary. We will use plan A—using the addictive powers of sex and voodoo first or plan B –force. She can be wooed and intrigued. Let's plan a harmless party for her birthday. We can give her a real present. I'll suggest a ritual at midnight on her mother's grave since she skipped out on us last night." He drank his morning coffee and poured local honey on his biscuit. He gobbled it down quickly.

"Do you really need it to be Jane?" Miss Ward asked. Couldn't that girl Tela do just as well?"

"Yes, Drucilla. I really need it to be Jane. We'll get Rachel to bring her. She seemed enamored," he said.

Jane looked toward Rachel. It didn't seem like she had heard a word that they had said. Jane saw them get up and walk across the food hall. They noticed her and came toward her and Rachel. "We're having a birthday party after hours today. You two are coming." It wasn't an invitation. It was an order.

Then Huerta turned and walked out the door. Miss Ward followed.

"I've got to find Victoria," Jane told Rachel. She needed a chance to go to the sheriff's office.

Jane hurried across town to the Sheriff's office. She burst through the door. "I need to talk to Sheriff's Marks," she said, trying to calm her hysteria.

"Sheriff Marks, I need for you to go with me to the cemetery. Professor Huerta and Miss Ward have been doing a voodoo ritual on my mother's grave. Also, I saw Huerta pouring kerosene on the dormitory porch last night, and then he set it on fire." Jane's voice was high-pitched and sounded nervous like she felt.

"Calm down, young lady. Tell me that again," Marks said.

"I saw Professor Huerta and Miss Ward doing a voodoo ritual on my mother's grave last night," Jane said. Her heart raced, and she panted and gasped to catch her breath.

"What were you doing in the cemetery last night? There was a huge fire in the show tent. I thought that I had seen you there, but no matter, I was coming to find you anyway. I've been informed that your step-father has broken out of prison and is headed this way."

Jane collapsed to the floor in a pile of dress and long, brown hair. The pins had slipped out of her hair, letting it fall to the floor.

Chapter 7

When Jane awoke the next morning, the sun streamed in through her dormitory window. She didn't remember walking back to her dorm room. She tried to turn over in the bed, but she hurt from head to toe. She pulled the sheet up over her head and drifted back to sleep. Dreams of Tom Lewis Lynch, her step-father being angry with her filled her with fear.

Someone was shaking her. Gently. Was it in her dream or was it real? She was afraid to open her eyes, but there were other times that she had been dreaming and waking up had been a relief. *Would Tom Lewis be there when she opened her eyes?* Jane wondered.

Reaching deep into herself for the last bit of strength she could find, she opened one eye slightly and looked through her lashes. Victoria was trying to wake her. Was this the same person that she had been dreaming about? The soreness of her muscles and bones let her know that it was real.

Jane let out an unintelligible sound and sat up in the bed. "He's out," she told Victoria.

"Who?" Victoria asked.

"Tom Lewis."

"Oh, my God. How?" Victoria asked. "We've got to get out of here. He'll know exactly where to find you."

Someone pounded on the door, but neither of the girls went to open it. "Who's there?"

"It's me, Rachel." Victoria opened the door, and Rachel tumbled into the room frightening Jane even more with her urgency.

Jane dashed to the water closet down the hall. "I want to be left alone for a while. I need to think." She yelled as she ran down the hall. She asked Oma, the attendant, for enough hot water to take a bath. Once the tub was filled, she added a few drops of lavender and soaked in it a while, letting the water trickle down her back with the bath sponge. A few of her wisps of hair worked loose and got wet from the sponge, making them curl more. She reached for a bottle of honey and poured a little in the palm of her hand. It was her favorite beauty ritual, so she dabbed some on her face and relaxed in the hot water. The hot bath cleared her mind. She had to think of another plan to get the evidence on Huerta that she needed. As much as she wanted to go somewhere to hide, she needed to finish out her time at The Institute so she would graduate.

I need to go back to talk to Sheriff Marks.

Victoria came to the water closet. "Jane, you have a visitor. Sheriff Marks is waiting to talk to you in the lobby downstairs."

Jane took her time rinsing the honey from her face and drying her body and getting dressed. Then she slowly walked down the dormitory stairs. The honey and the warm water made he have a pinkish glow.

Sheriff Marks was looking out the window when she walked up behind him. "Good morning, Sheriff," she said.

"Good morning, Miss Lynch. I went out to the cemetery this morning after you collapsed in my office to check on your mother's grave. I saw nothing except some footprints. Are you feeling better?"

"Yes, thanks," Jane replied. "Did you see any evidence of the voodoo ritual I told you about?"

"Well, no, not really, but I did see a lot of shoe or boot tracks out there as if lots of people had been standing near her grave. That didn't worry me as much as the fact that there was one extremely large shoe print. It could have been Tom Lewis Lynch's shoe print, and it probably was. Most of the men around here have small feet, but I remember that he had size thirteen shoes."

"Oh, my goodness. So you think he's here in French Camp?" Jane asked.

"There is a good possibility. I think this is the first place he will come to. It is familiar to him, but everyone doesn't know him here like they do in Kilmichael, and he still has sinners and heathens to save." Sheriff Marks had a smirk on his face that Jane didn't like. "How are you feeling? You worried me when you passed out."

"I'm okay. Thanks for asking. I'll let you know if I see him," Jane assured the sheriff.

"I'm posting a guard on this dormitory just in case he shows up," he said.

Chapter 8

After about a week, Jane hadn't seen anything of Tom Lewis Lynch. She didn't think that Sheriff Marks had either since he hadn't contacted her. *He's gotten as far away from here as possible.* Jane figured.

Every day or late evening Jane went to the cemetery to check her mother's grave. She liked watching the sunset in the distance from that vantage point. She checked for new footprints in the dirt near her mother's grave. She checked for some large size thirteen tracks. She checked for strange objects on the grave. She wanted to make certain that Professor Huerta and Miss Ward hadn't been out there again doing their voodoo.

Jane hadn't been able to come up with a talisman yet, but she had given it some thought. *She thought about dolls, handkerchiefs, and jewelry, but she couldn't settle on any one thing.* So as of the moment, she had nothing.

Huerta had left French Camp in his fancy, black buggy, but no one knew how long he would be gone, and school started back around the second week in January. Everyone figured he went back to New Orleans to see his family. A trip to New Orleans would be dangerous. Secretly, Jane hoped that he wouldn't make it back. She knew that lots of serious problems could befall someone traveling from New Orleans to French Camp. She had heard tales of robbers and others kinds of thieves along the trail. Part of it was quickly getting the name Natchez Trace. She also figured that he had gone back there to see his wife, Marie Laveau, and that was the reason he hadn't taken another woman with him. *Jane wasn't certain whether that visit to New Orleans was good or bad.*

Miss Ward had stayed at the Institute instead of going to New Orleans with Huerta although Jane didn't figure that she had been invited. She was receiving packages of new clothes from Paris almost daily to replace what had been ruined in the dormitory fire. She wore them around the school as if French Camp and the Institute was part of a fancy school in Paris.

Often she opened the packages of the fine lace blouses and dark velvet dresses in front of the girls. *She really is cruel. Her clothing choices fit the finery of some areas of New Orleans not the ruggedness of French Camp.* She thought.

Jane still borrowed clothes from Rachel, and Granny had brought some from some people in the churches of Kilmichael. Jane had bought a new pair of boots. Victoria received a large box of clothes anonymously, so as far as Jane was concerned, they were doing alright. They wouldn't have dressed like Miss Ward if they could have.

The comedy show actors and actresses left town after about a week. They had repaired the scorched tent and charred stage as best they could. Their covered wagon parade to the north was refreshing, and Jane wanted the best for them. *A part of her wanted to join them, to be free as a gypsy of the problems here at the Institute and in her life.* No one could tell Jane where Tela was. She was not with the comedy show actors and actresses. *Perhaps she went to New Orleans with Huerta. Perhaps she would stay there.* Jane thought.

Late one afternoon, Jane walked to the cemetery next to the old, white church to check on her mother's grave. As she walked through the gate toward the church, Jane thought she saw a figure standing near the church sign at the foot of the steps. It looked like a man walking toward Mama Lynch's grave. Since the church was old and white, any figure next to it showed up. Someone had erected a flag pole, and the Confederate flag flew there although the Civil War had long been over, and the slaves were freed. Jane saw that the flag was blowing in the wind, but there was no wind. She spit on her finger and held it in the air to see the direction of the breeze. There was no breeze.

A ghost had been reported being seen in that cemetery and around that church. Since a Civil War battle and an Indian massacre had happened in Choctaw county area, Jane didn't doubt that the area was haunted. Jane wasn't certain that she believed in ghosts, so that report didn't stop her from going to the cemetery to check on her mama's grave. Mama came first. So far, she hadn't seen a ghost. Mostly, she liked to talk out problems to her mother. Hearing them aloud lessened there severity.

As she reached the front of the church, the flag fell down and hung next to the flag pole, and the figure disappeared. *How curious.* Jane thought as she followed the path she always followed through the cemetery to her mother's grave next to the large angel gravestone.

As she got to her mama's grave, she felt a strong gust of wind. The sun dropped behind the trees, making eerie shadows dance around. At this time of afternoon, the wind usually dropped too. She looked toward the flag. Again it danced at the top of the flag pole. She looked back at the ground to see if she saw any evidence of footprints or a voodoo ritual such as bones or turkey beards. She saw large foot prints on her mother's grave.

Suddenly, something or someone grabbed her and dragged her toward the back of the large angel gravestone. Or was it in it? She felt a large hand over her mouth, so she wasn't able to scream a sound that could be heard by anyone. She screamed into the palm of the hand that covered her mouth. A gargled, muffed sound was all that could be heard which wasn't nearly enough to be heard back at the town.

Tom Lewis or Huerta? Jane wondered.

A dark space large enough to stand up in opened at the base of the gravestone. The large man dragged Jane inside the opening. Then the opening closed. *Something smelled familiar.* Jane thought. She had expected this to be Huerta. He wasn't Huerta. Huerta smelled of exotic perfume with a musky scent.

Jane realized that she was inside a tunnel and that she was standing, and the person who had dragged her deep inside the tunnel was Tom Lewis Lynch. He let go of her, and he lighted a torch on the side of the tunnel and held a lantern near his face so Jane could see him. She didn't scream because she didn't know how Tom Lewis would react, or her scream had no sound because it was stuck in her throat. She wasn't sure which. Her heart lurched. Terror gripped it.

"Hello, Jane," he said. "It's been a long time. I've seen you out here every day since I got back. You check on your mother's grave; don't you? I really appreciate you taking care of her grave."

He sounded rather sane to Jane. "Yes, I come out here often. Professor Huerta and Miss Ward had been doing voodoo out here, and I have to check on my mama. It is dangerous for you to be here. Someone might see you."

Tom Lewis laughed his strange laugh.

"I mean they are looking for you." She told him.

"Mr. Petey told me what happened to you. He is in here somewhere. I trust Mr. Petey," Tom Lewis said. He didn't address the fact that he had escaped from jail.

"Mr. Petey?"

"Yes. Don't you trust him? He said you did," Tom Lewis said.

"I do," Jane replied, but at this point, she didn't know whom to trust. He didn't mention the trial or prison. "Where are we? What is this place?"

"This is a secret tunnel that the Confederate Army used during the Civil War. They hid from the Yankees and often the Yankees thought that this cemetery and church were haunted. Mr. Petey brought me here when I went to get him to help me hide out. He told me about it. He said that few people knew about the tunnels under the church—only a few elderly folks and some black folks. He said it had been used as a stop on the Underground Railroad. That's how the black folks knew about it. The church is for white people, and as far as I know, they, blacks and whites, still don't go to church together. Some Choctaw Indians knew about it too. He said, during the war, the Rebels could be out here one minute, and then disappear into thin air when the Yankees showed up."

"Where is Mr. Petey?" Jane asked, wishing for a friendly and sane face.

"He went to get me some food. I'm hiding you from that Professor Huerta until Mr. Petey and I get even with him for what he did to you. I can't be seen around here or Sheriff Marks will take me back to prison."

Jane was afraid to talk about the subject of prison, so she said nothing.

"I think Professor Huerta went back to New Orleans," she said. "I heard that he did."

"He will be back soon. Then we will take care of him. He's a heathen. He will suffer the wrath of God." Tom Lewis sat there whittling a triangular object. Jane didn't know what it was and she didn't ask. Seeing him with a pocket knife was enough to scare her into silence. She noticed that he had several of the same shaped objects in his coat pocket.

Jane's question as to Tom Lewis's total sanity or insanity was answered. This frightened her too since she was his prisoner. *If he got rid of Huerta, and if he didn't blame her for sending him to prison, she might be alright.* She thought.

"Mr. Tom, it's me," Mr. Petey said. He had entered the tunnel from the opposite end of where they were. "I brought you some corn bread and sweet milk. Mr. Petey walked into the light of Tom Lewis's lantern. He carried a red cloth sack that looked like a flour sack or a chicken feed sack.

He untied the flour sack and spread it as a picnic on a large boulder that lay inside the tunnel. "Well, Miss Jane it sho' is nice to sees you again. I told Mr. Tom about that Professor harassing you. Then he turned to Tom Lewis, "I think I saw his fancy, black buggy in the livery stable this evening. He's back from wherever he's been, and he brought that girl Tela back with him."

Jane's heart sank. *The voodoo is back here.* She thought.

Tom Lewis took the information in without comment.

"Jane, have some milk and bread," Tom Lewis said. He reached out and offered it to her with his large hands. Jane noticed that they were no longer callused and rough. They had softened while he was in prison. He had been one of the hardest working men she had ever seen. And one of the strongest. When he sat with his legs crossed, she noticed a hole worn in the sole of his shoes. *From pacing in the cell?* Jane thought.

"Thanks. You eat it," Jane told him. "I'm certain that you are hungrier than I am. I ate just before I walked to the cemetery."

Quickly, Tom Lewis crumbled the cornbread into the milk and spooned it out of the jar like cereal. *Jane thought about the salty and sweet taste of it.* Once he was finished eating most of it with the spoon, he turned up the Mason jar and drank the rest. Then he wrapped the dirty fruit jar and spoon the same way Mr. Petey had brought them to him.

"Mr. Petey will carry you on into the secret room under the church, Jane. Get comfortable there. You need to stay here in this secret place until I get Huerta," Tom Lewis said.

"The folks in town will miss me. They'll be looking for me," Jane said. She knew that Victoria and Rachel would, but she didn't mention Victoria to Tom Lewis. She said nothing to remind him that she had had a part in sending him to prison.

"If Professor Huerta is back, they'll think he did something to you again." Tom Lewis laughed in that insane way that frightened Jane. *She thought about the many times that he had frightened her.*

"They won't be looking here," Mr. Petey said. "Come, Jane, let's go to that secret room."

Jane was glad to go with Mr. Petey even if it was deeper into the tunnel. She needed a chance to talk to him. Once they were out of Tom Lewis's ear shot, Jane whispered, "Is he still insane? He scares me when he's not "at himself.""

"Oh, off and on, Miss Jane. Off and on," Mr. Petey replied. "But you are safer with him than you are out there with Huerta. I think the Professor plans to kill you, and apparently that Sheriff and his office can't do much with him. You know Tom Lewis loves you. He can't help his insanity. He does try sometimes. I've seen Mr. Tom control his insane reactions for days. We know Huerta burned y'all's dormitory, but did he get arrested? No. That Sheriff had rather lock up folks like your stepfather."

"You are not afraid of Tom Lewis?" Jane asked.

"Oh, off and on, Miss Jane. Off and on. I told you he can't help it. You know."

"What is he doing now?"

"He's watching for Professor Huerta to show up out in that cemetery and he's whittling. He said that he'd show up sooner or later. He said you would too and you did."

"What's he gonna do to him?" Jane asked.

"I really can't say. It's hard to tell what Mr. Tom's gonna do at any given time."

"Will you stay here too? I'm not as frightened when you are here." She looked at Mr. Petey with a pleading expression.

Mr. Petey seemed to be considering her request as they made their way deeper into the tunnel. Finally he said, "I'll see if he'll let me take you to my house behind Granny's. I bet he won't 'tho 'cause that is the first place Huerta would look for you. Remember that night he burned y'all's dormitory? We'll be to that secret room in a minute."

"Yes. I remember," Jane said, looking down at Rachel's borrowed clothes. They reached the secret room and entered it. It was a 12ft. X 12ft. chamber with stone walls. Somehow the stones reminded Jane of the ice house in town where they stored ice to keep it frozen for use later. Over to one side was a large wooden door with an iron cross piece, locking it from the inside. A pallet made from a folded old quilt lay on one side of the floor. A pile of wood shavings was next to the pallet. She supposed it was Tom Lewis's pallet or bed. *She wondered how long he had been here. He had been escaped from jail for a few days and no one had seen him.* In one corner was a blue granite, chamber pot. There was evidence of someone living inside this room.

"How did you get inside here?" Jane asked. "Isn't there a way to get outside besides that door?"

"No, Miss Jane," Mr. Petey replied. "If it is, I don't know about it, and you probably can't raise that wood beam by yo'self."

"How can I stay here? What will I eat and where will I sleep? And more private matters?" Jane asked. Tears slowly flowed down her face.

Tom Lewis entered the secret room behind them. "Don't cry, Jane. I'm gonna take care of you. Mr. Petey will bring us food and water. He said that Professor Huerta was back in French Camp. It's just a matter of time before he comes back to yo' mama's grave to have another voodoo ritual. Just be patient. Make yourself comfortable. Mr. Petey and I take turns watching for him. God's gonna deliver him to me. His voodoo is an abomination."

Jane dropped onto the pallet where Tom Lewis slept. It smelled of him. She covered her face with her hands and cried herself to sleep. His smell was familiar, but disturbing.

When she awoke, neither of the men was in the secret room with her. She sat up and surveyed the room as best she could in the soft glow of the flambeaux. There were only two ways out of this room that she could see--one led back to the cemetery. She hadn't noticed how to open that end of the tunnel in the base of the angel, so she took the lighted lantern off the wall and eased through the tunnel toward the cemetery. She remembered the flag flapping in the wind. *That flag must flap more when the tunnel is open, so there must be another opening inside the tunnel.* She thought. Suddenly, she felt a strong breeze flowing through the tunnel. *She wondered if Sheriff Marks knows about this tunnel and this secret room. A secret like this would be hard to keep quiet in a small town like French Camp.* Jane concluded.

Eventually, she saw Tom Lewis and Mr. Petey sitting near the opening at the end of the tunnel. She felt only a slight breeze now. *They must have the base of the angel mostly closed.* Jane thought;

Tom Lewis turned toward her and motioned with his finger for her to not make a sound. Then she heard voices. People were in the cemetery. It was a large group. Jane had no idea how long she had slept. She just knew that she had been very tired recently. She didn't know if it was night or morning.

"There is a funeral going on," Tom Lewis whispered. "I think old, Miss Turnipseed died if I heard correctly. You know her. She lived in Kilmichael on Stone Street for a while. She'll be going straight to hell. In fact, I bet her soul was knocking on Satan's door within five minutes after she died. I know judging people is a sin. Since it is ten o'clock in the morning, they can't see our lanterns. As soon as her funeral's over, Mr. Petey is going to get us some food. He's also checking on Professor Huerta's where-a-bouts. I'll bet you anything that he is back from New Orleans."

Jane heard someone praying and others wailing. Every once in a while she heard Miss Turnipseed's name said. Then she heard more praying. *Jane wondered how a woman who never married could have such a large group of mourners. She probable had money.* Jane thought.

Soon the mourners filed past the angel statue going back to the church to eat their noon meal as was a custom in the area. Usually the ladies in the church of the deceased's burial location fixed covered dishes to feed the family and anyone else who came to the funeral that wanted to eat since the funeral lasted until dinner time. They usually cooked fried chicken, mashed potatoes, creamed corn, fried pies, cakes, biscuits and local honey or molasses, corn bread, and ham. On days when a funeral wasn't happening, it was called "dinner on the ground." Today's feast would be eaten inside the church because of the weather. It would be delicious. *Thinking about this food made Jane's stomach rumble.*

"As soon as they finish putting the dirt over her casket and all is quiet, we'll open this wide enough to get more air, and Mr. Petey will go out," Tom Lewis said.

She wondered how they got air last night while we were locked inside.

Jane felt the vibrations as mourners walked over the tunnel going back toward the church. "I wish I could eat with them. I'm famished," she whispered. *She didn't look forward to being alone with Tom Lewis, and she was so hungry that she thought she would pass out.* So Mr. Petey's excursion to get food was a welcome happening. She held her stomach to control the rumblings.

"I'll get us some food, I promise, Miss Jane," Mr. Petey assured her. He smiled at her holding her belly. He gathered up the flour sack and the Mason jar that he had brought the milk and bread in.

Jane sat quietly and listened to the movements above them. Her stomach growled and rumbled. She heard what sounded like shovels rubbing against rocks as the dirt and gravel was thrown on to the top of Miss Turnipseed's casket. This part of a funeral was the saddest to her. *She thought about her mother's funeral.* Tears rolled down her face. She wiped them away with the back of her hand. She wanted to hide the tears from Tom Lewis.

Tom Lewis looked at her. "I miss her too," he said. "She was the only woman who ever loved me."

Usually, he showed no emotion. Perhaps he was more "at himself" today. Jane thought.

Jane choked back a wail. *I am so emotional recently. I wonder what is wrong with me. Perhaps it's because I miss Mama so much.*

Finally, all the funeral noises in the cemetery were gone, so Mr. Petey slipped through the opening and disappeared.

Tom Lewis and Jane sat in the dimness of the lantern in silence. He whittled on a piece of wood that he kept in his pocket.. Jane had no idea what to say and there was nothing to do except wait. *She didn't think it mattered anyway because Tom Lewis didn't usually carry on a conversation. He was usually listening to the voices in his own head. Sometimes he answered these voices. He was exceptionally scary whenever he did that.*

They sat there for what seemed like hours—listening, watching, and waiting-- until they heard noises coming toward the cemetery.

Sheriff Marks. Jane recognized Sheriff Marks's voice.

"She's not out here tonight," he said. "And with all the tracks out here near her mother's grave from that Turnipseed woman's funeral this morning, there's no way to know if she's been here or not. Her friends at the Institute said that they haven't seen her since yesterday when she said that she was coming here to check on her mother's grave."

Jane wanted to scream out to let Sheriff Marks know where she was when she heard another familiar voice. *Professor Huerta. Professor Huerta was with Sheriff Marks.* Jane thought.

"Oh, no," Jane whispered. "Tom Lewis, Sheriff Marks has Huerta with him. I can hear his Creole voice."

No wonder I can't get anything done about Professor Huerta. They are friends. Jane thought.

She reached out to touch Tom Lewis's sleeve. He turned to her with his finger to his lips in shushing gesture.

Finally, Sheriff Marks and Huerta left the cemetery together, leaving Jane with only Tom Lewis to help her. She had never felt so alone in her life. Terror gripped her. She felt as if she couldn't breathe. Her lungs wouldn't take in air. She was afraid to exhale. *What if Mr. Petey didn't make it back? What if she was left here in this tunnel with Tom Lewis? How would she get out of this tunnel and secret room? How would she get away from Tom Lewis?* She wondered. There had to be another way out of here.

Chapter 9

Jane and Tom Lewis again sat in silence waiting for Mr. Petey. Finally, he came back.

He brought three full meals of fried chicken, local honey, mashed potatoes, peas, cornbread, and sweet tea. *Jane wondered if he had gone to the inside "dinner on the ground" with the mourners, but Mr. Petey was a black man. Mourners hardly mixed in the Southern churches, so she knew that he hadn't.* Jane smelled the food as soon as he walked into the tunnel with the large flour sacks with the tops tied. He handed her a red one and the other he handed to Tom Lewis. Finally, he opened his green printed one. The sweet tea was in sealed, blue Mason jars. Jane hungrily drank hers. She was so thirsty. The two men did the same.

"Professor Huerta is back," Mr. Petey told Tom Lewis. "His fancy buggy is in the livery stable."

"I know. He was out here earlier with Sheriff Marks," Tom Lewis said. "I've got a feeling that he'll be back out here tonight to do more of his heathenish voodoo. We'll get him then."

"The Sheriff was with him?"

"Yep."

Chapter 10

After eating the wonderful southern cooking that Mr. Petey had brought, the men leaned against the stone walls of the secret room and slept a while. In the dim light, Jane searched the walls for any irregularity in the walls or for any indication that there was another opening. She watched the direction of the flames—the way they blew when the cemetery end of the tunnel was closed as it was now. Finally, she found it.

At the side of the door that went into the church was a different looking section of stone. The stone in that section of the wall was a slightly darker beige shade than the rest of the wall. Jane said nothing to the men about her finding. She didn't know where that part of the tunnel led, but the way the air currents flowed, she knew it led out somewhere outside.

The minutes clicked by. They slowly turned into hours until it was finally dark outside. Mr. Petey and Tom Lewis moved back to the cemetery end of the tunnel to wait for Professor Huerta and his voodoo queens, Tela and Miss Ward. *She figured that they would be with him.* Jane waited in the secret room, using the excuse of needing some privacy. As soon as the two men were out of sight, she moved to the darker section of the wall where she had noticed the change in the stone. She touched the wall and moved her hands over it to feel any indention or change in it. She knocked on it lightly, trying not to make enough noise for Tom Lewis to hear because sounds echoed in the tunnel and secret room. Suddenly, the wall moved. A small crack turned into a larger one. Not knowing what to do next, she pushed it back shut into place. She stepped back to view the wall. It looked no different than it had looked earlier. *I'm not ready to enter that part of the tunnel.* She thought.

She picked up the lantern, and opened it slightly to get a faint beam of light, and made her way toward the end of the tunnel where the two men sat. She knew that it would be close to midnight before Huerta and his voodoo queens came back to the cemetery. Although she didn't know exactly what time it was, she knew it wasn't that late yet. She felt that they had the opening wide on their end of the tunnel because she felt the cool, strong breeze. There was a faint scent on the breeze from the funeral flowers.

She opened the lantern covering and watched the flame in her lantern as she made her way to the cemetery end of the tunnel. *Perhaps there are other tunnel openings down on this end of the tunnel.* She thought. She rubbed her hand along the tunnel wall as she went.

Finally, she felt another change in the tunnel wall. Holding the lantern up to it, she noticed the same darker brown colorings in the wall. *She wondered where these tunnels led and what was inside them.*

"They won't be out here until around midnight," Jane whispered, as she extinguished her lantern.

"How do you know that, Miss Jane?" Mr. Petey asked. "You been to one? I mean, you been to a voodoo ritual?"

For a minute Jane was silent. Then she nodded. "Yes." She didn't want to tell them about it.

"It is around ten o'clock. We need to be quiet," Tom Lewis whispered. "Jane, you might want to go back to the secret room. You might not want to see this. It could get rough out here."

"What will you do with the women he brings with him?" Jane asked.

"They are heathens too, Jane. Jezebels," Tom Lewis said. "Just sinners and heathens." Tom Lewis scratched his head.

"Maybe so," Jane said. She didn't know what to do. "Could Mr. Petey take me to his house while you get even with Huerta? I don't want to be in the way."

"Maybe so. Mr. Petey, what do you think?" Tom Lewis looked at Mr. Petey. "What do you think, Petey? I don't want Jane to get hurt."

Mr. Petey paced back and forth in the tunnel. "I'll take her out the other end of the tunnel while you wait here, Mr. Tom. If Huerta comes here tonight, he won't see us. It would be better that he not see Jane. Mr. Tom, you gon' be ok by yo'self?"

"Yep. Take her to safety," Tom Lewis said.

"Come on, Jane. Huerta definitely doesn't need to know that you are with us here. The moon is shining, so we won't need a lantern." He took Jane's hand and led her toward the secret room.

He took her by the shoulder and ushered her back into the secret room. "You can get cleaned up and get a change of clothing at my house. It is a long trip. Are you up to it? I'm not sure how we will get there tonight. If Mr. Tom gets Huerta and 'em women, you don't need to be here. I think you will be safe at my house, but I don't want your granny or anyone else to know you are there. I want you to be safe. Huerta might hear that you are there and come after you there in Kilmichael instead coming out here."

"Won't Oma and Mis' Shug be at home?" Jane asked.

"They may, but they won't tell nobody if I ask 'em not to," Mr. Petey said. They had reached the secret room, and Mr. Petey removed the metal bar from the door lock and opened the door into the old church. Jane was so excited to get out of the secret room and tunnel that she forgot about telling him about the other tunnels.

When Mr. Petey opened the door to the church, Jane heard a familiar voice and the footsteps of several people leaving by way of the front door. Jane's heart lurched. She was so frightened. "That's him. I recognize his voice," she whispered and grabbed Mr. Petey's shirt. "What do we need to do now?"

"While I have you free," he replied, "I'll taking you on to my house. Whether Mr. Tom captures Huerta or not is on him now. Be very quite. They're going out not coming in."

Jane was relieved to be getting free of that secret room. She stayed as near to Mr. Petey as possible. They waited ten minutes inside the sanctuary of the church to exit the front door. Then Mr. Petey and Jane exited as quietly as possible. They closed the door behind them. A full moon shone, lighting their way. They slipped in the shadows toward town to the livery to steal or borrow a horse.

Chapter 11

Tom Lewis waited in the opening of the secret tunnel. His gut feelings told him that Huerta would be out here tonight. He noticed the yellow brightness of the moon's glow. The full moon assured him that something unusual was going to happen tonight. Finally, he heard noises coming into the cemetery from the direction of the church. At least one of the voices belonged to a woman.

He watched as Huerta, Miss Ward, and Tela came nearer and huddled over Mrs. Lynch's grave. The moon shone brightly in the cemetery. His anger was about to boil over. Still Tom Lewis waited on his chance. *Heathens.* He thought. He watched Huerta throw something white like stones or bones onto her grave. It looked like some chicken or animal bones. Then he poured a clear liquid from a Mason jar on the dirt. The three of them joined hands and chanted something looking up at the sky.

Idiots. Heathens. Sinners. He thought. But still he waited.

Finally, he slipped out of his hiding place and around behind them. Suddenly, in a mad frenzy like the crazy man's reputation he had, he grabbed Huerta and Miss Ward both by their upper arms and with the strength of a demon dragged them inside the opening of the angel gravestone. Tela ran back toward the church. He let go of the two and closed the opening behind them. They were locked inside the tunnel. She couldn't have gotten them if she had wanted to with the angel's base closed. They were in total darkness. Huerta screamed, "Who are you? What are you doing? Let us go." Miss Ward cried hysterically.

"No chance of that," Tom Lewis said. "This is for Jane Lynch." Huerta and Miss Ward huddled together in the darkness of the tunnel. He left them inside the tunnel on the stone floor where they huddled together, frightened of this crazy man. Tom Lewis rushed to the other end of the tunnel and through the secret room, extinguishing all the flambeaux as he went. He left them in total darkness. Then he slipped through the secret door into the church. Since the door locked from the inside, he took several of the rectangular pieces of wood that he had whittled and jammed under the door, so they couldn't get it open from inside the tunnel.

He walked out the front of the church into the moonlight. It was so bright that it hurt his eyes. *What do I do with these heathens?* He wondered.

Chapter 12

Jane and Mr. Petey slipped into the livery stable. It smelled of horses, manure, and hay. They took Huerta's horse and bridle, but they didn't take his saddle or a horse blanket. "He's not gonna miss this horse for a while," Mr. Petey said. "Maybe never."

Jane laughed, nervously, grasping her neck lightly. *Horse thieves were hung in these parts, so what about murderers? Folks like Tom Lewis were the only ones who could do something and live to see another day even if it was in jail.* Jane thought.

"When we get to my house in Kilmichael, we'll let the horse go. We won't keep him. That way, he ain't stolen; just borrowed or got loose." *It was as if Mr. Petey was reading her mind. A black horse thief would be hung sooner than a white girl, but a horse thief was hung. It was a simple fact. Jane thought about the horror stories she had heard about a hanging tree between Bethsaida Church and Poplar Creek where horse thieves were hung.*

Jane rode behind Mr. Petey, and they rode bareback since they hadn't stolen a saddle. The horse's backbone cut into Jane's legs.

The moonlight made it easier for them to guide the horse down the shadowy, seventeen mile trail toward Kilmichael. They would be riding near the hanging tree on their way. *Jane wondered if the area near the hanging tree was haunted.* Neither of them talked and they saw no one over the few hours it took to get to Mr. Petey's house. Jane was so tired that a few times she fell asleep and almost fell off the horse. One time when she wobbled to the side, an owl flew out of a tree past them and frightened the horse, making it side step. He snorted and Jane screamed. She tightened her grasp on Mr. Petey's waist and tried hard to stay awake.

Finally, they reached Mr. Petey's house. Jane felt achy and sore from riding so far without a saddle. She looked forward to a long hot bath and to sleeping in a regular, soft feather bed tonight instead of the stone floor of the secret room.

Finally, they reached Mr. Petey's house where he lived with his wife Shug and his daughter Oma. It was a white, shotgun house that had been inhabited by many blacks before them. They went to the back and slipped off the horse. Mr. Petey took the bridle off the horse and gave him a sharp slap on the back. It ran across the yard into the woods. They slipped into the house through the kitchen. Shug was sitting near the big fireplace, and she had started a fire in the fireplace.

Looking at the clock on the mantel and thinking of the lateness of the hour, Jane said, "I wonder if Tom Lewis finished his party yet."

"I wonder too." Mr. Petey said. Neither of them spoke Huerta's name aloud.

"I knew you would be home tonight," Shug told Mr. Petey. "Part of my seeing sense. Miss Jane, I made up a bed for you already."

In these parts, Mis' Shug was known for her ability to tell the future and for delivering babies. People went to her whenever they had problems. Young pregnant girls often went to her for help because they couldn't pay a doctor.

Jane didn't want to get into a clean bed without at least a spit bath, so Mr. Petey brought her a basin of warm water and some of Oma's nightclothes to change into. She had just finished her bath and gotten dressed when there was a banging on the front door. The loud banging woke the others in the house.

"Jane?" Oma said. She sounded like she was still dreaming. She turned over in her bed to look at Jane bathing in her bedroom. "How did you get here? Daddy, who's that beating on the front door?"

Mr. Petey removed his rifle from the rack above the mantle and opened the door. It was Tom Lewis Lynch. "I just wanted Jane to know that the heathens are captured. He and that woman are inside the tunnel. I'm gonna leave them there. But I've got to disappear again, so Sheriff Marks and the other lawmen don't find me. That was a great hiding place. I don't know where I'm gonna go now."

"I'll tell Miss Jane in the morning," Mr. Petey said. Jane, Oma, and Shug stood listening in the next room. Jane let out a huge sigh of relief. Then as quickly as he came, Tom Lewis disappeared into the night.

"Thank you, Mr. Petey. We will talk about what to do next in the morning. There are several important decisions to make. I don't know whether I should show back up at the Institute now, but I've got to finish school. Do we leave those two in that tunnel to die? He didn't say that they were dead, so I'm betting they are alive and that he just locked them inside the secret room. I'm just so tired. Did you know that there are other tunnels connected to the main one?"

"How you know that, Miss Jane?" Mr. Petey asked. He looked surprised.

"From the flambeaux and the breeze." Jane rubbed her eyes and yawned. "We will talk about it later. I've gotta go to sleep."

Shug and Oma showed Jane the bed in Oma's room where she could sleep. She crawled into the soft, fluffy, feather bed and pulled the flour sack sheets and quilts around her neck. This bed reminded her of granny's. She fell asleep about the time her head hit the pillow.

Jane dreamed of her mother and a dark baby with dark eyes and dark hair.

<h1 style="text-align:center">Chapter 13</h1>

"That girl's with child, if you ask me," Shug said to Mr. Petey early the next morning. She rubbed her stomach gesturing pregnancy. Jane stood in the bedroom at the entrance of the kitchen. Shocked and dismayed to hear Shug's diagnosis. Shug was the local midwife for the black women and some of the whites, but most of the whites used Dr. Hill to deliver their babies. Mr. Petey and Shug lived in a shotgun house. It was easy to hear what was said from one room to the next. The house had a long hallway that ran from the front door to the back of the house with one room opening into the next. It was said that you could shoot a shot gun all the way through the house from the front door to the back without hitting the wall.

"How you know that?" Mr. Petey asked. His voice sounded horrified.

"I can tell by looking," she said. "She glows, her breasts are fuller than the last time I saw her, and she is really tired."

"She should be tired, Shug. She's been in the secret room with Tom Lewis and me. Not exactly a place to rest."

"What are you gonna do? It will show up soon enough. You know they will kick her out of that Institute. They will make her go somewhere away from here to have her baby," Shug said. "Lots of girls in her condition from Mississippi have to go to Alabama."

"First, we are gonna talk to her about it. Or let me says. You gonna talk to her about it," Mr. Petey said. "Lawdy, what a mess. Poor girl. Who is *they* anyway?" He put his head in his hands.

"*They* is Granny. She would be so embarrassed that she'd ship her off to another state. Granny don't want no 'outside children.'"

Whenever he looked up, Jane stood in the room looking at the two of them.

Chapter 14

Jane burst into tears. She felt like the weight of the world sat on her shoulders. A baby. A baby by Huerta, and in Tom Lewis's definition, a heathen, and she didn't even remember. Try as she might, she couldn't remember what had happened to her. Horrors upon horrors gripped her. Her stomach lurched. *What was she going to do with a baby? She couldn't even take care of herself or her baby brother.* Fat tears rolled down her cheeks. She licked the salty taste of them. Pain gripped the pit of her stomach. She knew nothing about having a baby. She did know how to care for a baby. She had learned that from taking care of Tommy.

"Come here, sweetie," Shug said. She gave Jane a big hug. "You heard; didn't you? Let me wipe yo' tears. Everything will be okay. I'll help you."

"What am I gonna do? Granny will ship me off somewhere. She will give my baby away. It is a disgrace to have a baby in the South and not be married." She looked with pleading eyes at Shug and Mr. Petey. "Tom Lewis left Huerta in the secret tunnel. He may be able to get out. Today is my birthday. I'm twenty years old. I'm probably too old now for his voodoo ritual, but I can't let him know there is a baby. Mr. Petey, how will we know if he gets out of the tunnel or not? Your house is the first place he'll come if he does."

"You are right, Jane. I seriously doubt that he will get out, but if he does, we will be ready. Where do you think Tom Lewis went? I bet he'll wait a few days for them to get really hungry and then he'll go back there to see. He'll let me know."

Jane's face turned blood red. "We can't let Tom Lewis know that I'm pregnant. For that matter, we can't let anyone know. This is my last semester of school. School is over in four months. I'm going to finish." Then she turned to Shug. "Can you help me hide the fact that I'm having a baby for at least four more months? You can take care of me; can't you? Oh, Miss Shug. Nobody else can know."

"You need to hide out here until we find out about Huerta and Miss Ward. After a couple of days, I'll go check on them myself," Mr. Petey said. "Huerta needs to learn his lesson."

Chapter 15

Jane went back to the feather bed and crawled back under the covers, burying herself deeply. She cried herself to sleep and slept all the rest of that day. She felt so tired. The feather mattress and the soft quilts felt so good. The December wind howled and a light snow had begun to fall. She didn't know if her tiredness was from the events of the last few days or from being pregnant. She always wanted to have children, but this isn't the way she had envisioned it. She wanted to find a husband and get married first. She felt that hiding out for a week was the best thing to do. Then she would be beyond her twentieth birthday.

That afternoon she watched out the window of Mr. Petey's house for any sign of Granny, Tommy, Tom Lewis, or, of course, Huerta. Once she saw Tommy playing in Granny's back yard. *She wondered where Tom Lewis was. She wondered if her baby would look like Tommy or her or God forbid, Huerta.*

On the third day, there was a sharp rapping on Mr. Petey's front door. He went to open it.

"Have you seen Tom Lewis Lynch?" Sheriff Marks asked. "Someone said he was seen at the house next door." Jane and Oma crawled under the beds to hid in the adjoining bed room. Jane hoped that he wouldn't decide to search the house. "Also, did you know that

Jane Lynch is also missing? My guess is that he took her off somewhere to get revenge against her for helping send him to prison."

Jane felt relief flood over her. She rested her head on the cold wooden floor. *He wasn't gonna search the house.*

"Miss Ward and Huerta are missing from the school. Have you seen them?" He fired questions at Mr. Petey without giving him a chance to answer.

Mr. Petey stood silently while Sheriff Marks fired questions at him. "Tom Lewis, Jane, Huerta, and Miss Ward? Hmmm? Well, I ain't seen narry one of 'em. But I'll let you know if I sees any of them," Mr. Petey lied.

I hope he believes Mr. Petey, Jane thought.

"If I get Tom Lewis this time, I'm gonna see that he hangs. I ain't got time to chase him all over the country. He's crazy as a loon. I pity that girl if he's got her."

"If I sees any of them, I'll let you know." Mr. Petey said again.

Chapter 16

The stone floor of the secret tunnel felt cold to Huerta's hands, but oddly it didn't feel damp. *He wondered if he was buried alive. Or was going to be.* He rubbed his palms along the walls against the cold stones feeling his way toward the end where he and Miss Ward had been dragged inside. *He thought it was an opening in one of the large gravestones. He remembered a large, granite angel standing next to the Lynch woman's grave, but he couldn't remember whose name was on it. If we were put in this entrance, so we should be able to get out this way.* He felt the granite door of the inside of the statue. He ran his hands across the smoothness of the granite up toward to top of the opening, noticing that he could stand up. So he did.

"Huerta, where are you?" Miss Ward asked. Her voice sounded weak and scared. "That is you that I hear moving around. Isn't it? Is this a cave? I can feel the floor and one wall."

"I'm looking for a way out of here. No, this is a tunnel. You stay still where you are, and I'll come get you whenever I find how to open this thing from the inside."

"Where did that crazy man go?" she asked. "Farther on into this cave?" She sounded very scared to be left in that tunnel.

"He left in the other direction. This is a tunnel; not a cave. At least, this part of it is a tunnel. The walls are too smooth to be a cave although they are made of stone. Do you have any matches in your pocket?" Huerta asked.

"No. I don't carry matches. He put out all the lanterns. Didn't he?"

Huerta didn't answer. He continued to rub his hands along the granite, trying to find a way to open it. Finally, he found a loose stone and struck it against the other granite of the door, making a spark. "If we can find something to burn, we can catch it on fire with this. You got anything?"

"Like what? Paper? I have this paper that we were going to use in our voodoo ritual."

"Let me have it," Huerta demanded. He took the paper and struck the granite rock against the hardness of the granite door to the tunnel. He made another spark, but he couldn't strike the rock and hold the paper at the same time, so he said, "Miss Ward, would you please hold this while I make a spark? We've got to have some light to see how to get this door open."

Miss Ward struggled to her feet and rubbed her hands along the walls of the tunnel, moving toward him. "It's black as pitch in here. Is this a vault, like in the cemeteries in New Orleans?"

"Move toward the sound of my voice," he said. "I don't think this is a vault. I think this is an Underground Railroad hiding place or a Confederate tunnel. I've heard my students talk about a Confederate tunnel of that sort being somewhere around here, but none of them actually knew exactly where it was. He didn't tell her what they said was hidden inside."

Finally, she inched toward him until he felt her hand touch his. "Here take hold of my hand," he said, grasping it.

"Okay, hold this paper. I'll strike the stone on this granite," he said.

He struck the stone two or three more times until a spark landed on the paper, igniting it. It blazed. Huerta held it in his hand and surveyed the granite door and then the tunnel. He saw that the opening was tall enough for a grown man to stand in. The floor was stone as were the walls and ceiling. *Someone had gone to a lot of trouble building this tunnel,* Huerta thought. The opposite end from where they stood led into a vast blackness.

He blew the flame out.

"Why did you do that?" she asked. "I hate to be in total darkness in here since I don't know what's in here. It is like being buried alive in here. And it may be filled with spiders, snakes, or bats."

"Those are only monsters in childhood fantasies. Don't be afraid. We are going to inch along the wall toward the opposite end, toward the south. We are going the same way that crazy man went. This piece of paper won't burn very long. We must find a lantern or something to have light. Then we will strike the granite again and light the lantern."

"What are the walls made of?" she asked. "You may have to bring the lantern back here. I'm frightened."

"Okay, then you wait here for me. I'll inch my way down the other direction. I assume that the tunnel is straight and runs north to south."

"Okay, but I don't like this." Miss Ward said.

Huerta took the piece of paper with him as he inched his way toward the south end of the tunnel. Slowly and carefully, he rubbed his hands along the wall in the darkness. Stone by stone he rubbed moving southward on the wall until he had gone about twenty feet. Suddenly, he felt a change in the smoothness of the stone wall. Then he felt an air draft around the edge of one section of the stones. He ran his fingers over the stones following along with the draft. It was slight, but distinct. He wished for the light of the lantern to be able to see. Slowly, he moved farther south along the wall.

He bumped his head on something and that something moved. Metal clanked against stone. He reached up to see what it was. He rubbed his hands over it. It felt like a lantern. He grasped it and lifted it from its hanger. Then he cradled it next to his stomach and moved back toward the north end of the tunnel where Miss Ward waited.

"Huerta, is that you?" she asked.

"Yes, I found a lantern. You have to help me light it. We'll light that paper again to light the lantern."

He stumbled into her, moved over her, stepping on her toes, and felt along the wall until he felt the granite again. He set the lantern on the floor between his feet. "Come here. Hold this paper again."

She followed him to the granite door. "Here, hold it like this," he said. He rolled the paper into a long strip like a homemade cigarette and handed it to her to hold one end.

She grasped the end of the paper. He struck the granite rock against the granite door again making a few sparks.

Finally, one of the sparks hit the rolled end of the paper, caught fire, and blazed. He stooped to pick up the lantern from between his legs and opened the globe on it. He held the paper next to the cotton wick in the lantern and the wick ignited. Slowly, he closed the globe and adjusted the wick. At first there was a faint light.

"And then there was light," Miss Ward said. "Now, if you can just find a way out of here, I'm ready to leave."

"There probably isn't much kerosene in this lantern. We will have to hurry to find a way out of here or find another lantern. I couldn't figure out how to open this door from this side, so let's move toward the other end. I think that crazy man who kidnapped us went out down that way," he said. "We can too. I think that was Jane Lynch's stepfather, Tom Lewis Lynch. He won't be hanging around down there because Sheriff Marks is looking for him to take him back to prison."

Carrying the lantern, he led the way back down the tunnel where he had come. Miss Ward followed. He stopped where he had found the draft around the stones and again ran his hands over the stones.

"What are you doing?" she asked. "Is that the way out?"

"Maybe," he said. Opening the globe on the lantern, he again examined the stone, but this time with more light. The flame flickered near the areas where he had found the drafts. He knocked on each stone. He knocked on the stones of the tunnel wall. There was a distinctly different sound. Then he knocked on each stone within the drafty area. Suddenly, one of the stones opened. He held the lantern up high to look inside. The light shone into the opening. Within he saw another tunnel. He reached his hand inside the opening. There was something cold and made of iron on one side of the opening. It was a lever. He reached inside and pulled on the lever. The heavy, stone door opened. He peered deep inside the opening. There was another tunnel. He held the lantern to look inside, searching for a way to exit. This tunnel was filled with spider webs, telling him that no one had been in this tunnel in a long time. Bats hung from the ceiling. The light from his lantern disturbed them, and two of them, awakened by the light from his lantern, flew toward the light into the tunnel where he and Miss Ward stood. She screamed and fell to the floor covering her head. Huerta shined the rays of light deeper into the opening. Something shiny reflected in the light. There were stacks of it stacked on the floor. It looked like shiny bars of gold and over to one side were large sacks of something lying on the floor. It didn't look as if these stacks or sacks had been disturbed for many, many years.

Gold bars. This is the Confederate treasure the students had told tales about. Huerta thought. *How could he be this lucky?*

"We don't want to go that way," he told her. "That is a cave. And it is full of bats, spiders, or snakes. I heard you say you are afraid of those. To tell you the truth, I am too. They will bite you." He closed the stone doorway and replaced the stone that opened to the iron door handle.

"Well, let's go on south the way that crazy man went," she said.

"Let's do. One end or the other and we will get out of here," Huerta tried to control the excitement in his voice. He tried to slow his breathing and calm his rapid heartbeat. Miss Ward hadn't realized that the bats had to exit through an opening on the other end of the cave from where they lived. There would be an opening in there that led to the outside, but it might not be large enough for a person to crawl through.

Huerta held the lantern, and they made their way south toward the secret room. In about twenty more feet, the tunnel opened up into the secret room. The opening to the church stood wide open.

"If we get out of here, do not tell anyone that we were held prisoner in this tunnel. Promise me," he said, holding her so tightly by the arm that it would have a bruise. "No one must know!"

"I promise," she said. "I just want to get as far away from here as possible, and I won't breathe a word." The relief was apparent in her voice.

Huerta believed her. He and Miss Ward hurried through the secret room into the church. She didn't even stop to talk about why he wanted to keep this a secret. He watched her as she ran out the front door of the church and back up the street toward the Institute.

I've got to make certain that she doesn't talk. He thought. *I just don't think that she will. I can't believe my luck. Marie is going to be ecstatic.*

He found another lantern inside the church, lighted it, and went back inside the secret room. He stopped once inside and put the bar across the door, sealing the opening into the church from the inside of the tunnel. He didn't want anyone else wandering into this tunnel. He hurried back to the end of the tunnel in the cemetery. He had to figure out how to open that opening from the inside and from the outside. The opening in the base of the angel stood wide open. *Tom Lewis Lynch had come back to let them out.* Huerta thought. *He could be waiting for them in the cemetery.*

Huerta slowly exited that end. Once outside, Huerta looked for Tom Lewis Lynch, but he wasn't in sight. He sat down on a gravestone to think and to figure out how to open the tunnel from outside. He looked toward the town and saw Miss Ward hurrying up the street. *There was Confederate gold or some other kind of gold inside this tunnel and from the looks of the cobwebs and bats, he was the only one who knew where it was.* He thought.

Chapter 17

Jane waited with Shug and Oma for Mr. Petey to come back from the cemetery. Finally, he entered the back door of the shotgun house.

"They escaped," he said. "Neither Huerta or Miss Ward are inside there. I went through the entire tunnel and someone had locked the door to the church from the inside. They must have exited through the cemetery."

At first Jane was relieved. *Being a horse thief was bad enough, but accessory to murder? Then she thought about how she was going to survive until school was out and stay alive and hide the pregnancy.*

"I've got to go back to the school. School won't be out for four more months. I can't let Huerta keep me from graduating. Mis' Shug, I'm really gonna need your help. I can't let anyone know about the baby."

"Honey, yo' secret is safe with us. It ain't gonna be good for you to be under so much stress. That baby might come out looking like a haint if you don't relax. I packed you some of Oma's clothes. They are bigger than the ones you been wearing. That baby's gonna need some room. And I packed y'all some food. A woman with child has gotta eat often and rest lots."

Mr. Petey brought the wagon around to the back of the shotgun house, and Jane climbed in beside him. They rode in Mr. Petey's wagon back to the Institute. She kept a lookout for Huerta's horse, but didn't see it anywhere. The long ride was rough, but it gave her a chance to think and sort through her feelings. As soon as she reached the Institute, Victoria ran out the front door of their dormitory to give her some news. "Miss Ward and Tela left French Camp early this morning for New Orleans. She quit. We don't have a dorm mother. Huerta is back, but he has no helpers with his voodoo rituals. Miss Ward gave no reason for quitting her job. She just packed her fancy clothes and left. Tela left with her. They make strange bed fellows as my granny used to say."

"Great," Jane said. At least two of her problems had left the country. She told Mr. Petey good bye and climbed down from his wagon. "Victoria, help me get these clothes to our room. I'll tell you where I've been."

Jane spent the afternoon telling Victoria about Tom Lewis and the secret tunnel and room. She also told her about his kidnapping Miss Ward and Huerta. "He must have gone back to let them out of that tunnel if they came back here to the Institute," she said.

"You have to take me to that tunnel," Victoria demanded, the excitement in her voice was evident. "Let's go tonight. Maybe that is the secret tunnel that the Confederates used. I know that you have heard the story."

"No, not tonight with Huerta free and knowing about it, I'm afraid he would lock us inside. Besides, I don't know how to get the base of the angel open, and the other end can be locked on the outside or the inside. That's how Huerta got locked inside. Tom Lewis whittled these triangular wedges and shoved them under the door, so they couldn't get the door open from the inside, but he could get out. Otherwise, you lock it from the inside with a wooden beam. He must have sneaked back out there and open the cemetery end to make certain that they could get out. We will go sometimes when Huerta is out of town, and yes, I have heard that story. I do want to check that tunnel out, but I can't chance getting locked inside."

"You said that Mr. Petey was there. We'll get him to go with us," Victoria said. *Victoria won't rest until she has seen that tunnel and secret room for herself.* Jane thought.

"Well, that tunnel isn't going anywhere. It's been there for ages, so we can go anytime that Huerta isn't around. It has been there for a long, long time." Jane turned her bed back and lay down. "I've got to get some sleep, Victoria. I'm very tired."

"Okay. I'll go get us some food from the food hall. I'll sneak some out for you. You take a nap while I'm gone. Put that dresser in front of the door, so Huerta can't come in here. At least Miss Ward is gone, and we don't have to worry about her bothering us. I'll knock three times, so you will know it's me." Victoria grabbed a large purse and headed out the door. Jane moved the dresser in front of the door, and then removed her dress that Oma had given her and lay down for a rest.

She dreamed of the secret room and Professor Huerta. Her sleep was fitful and not restful at all. She tossed and turned. She awoke in a fit and a puddle of sweat.

When the three knocks came on the door, she was changing into clean pantaloons and changing the bed sheets. She had discarded the corset after Mis' Shug said she was pregnant. "Just a minute. I'll be right there." *She wondered how she was going to keep her pregnancy hidden from Victoria. It would make changing clothes in front of her impossible.* She thought.

Jane rolled and slid the dresser from the front of the dorm room door and opened it. Victoria stood there holding the stuffed purse and a Mason jar of sweet tea. *The Mason jar reminded Jane of eating in the secret room.*

She took the jar from Victoria and removing the lid, drank half of it before she looked at the food that Victoria spread out on the bed. She had brought biscuits and honey, ham, and baked sweet potatoes. Jane devoured all the supper that Victoria had brought because she was ravenous.

Jane and Victoria went to the water closet to do their nightly rituals before bed. Jane applied the local honey to her face and neck. She had to pin her hair back so it wouldn't get honey in it. She then washed it off with a clean cloth leaving a slight residue or it to nourish her skin overnight. Victoria didn't see the need, so she skipped the honey ritual.

Finally, they put on their nightgowns and left. Then they got back in their dorm room and lay down for the night. Victoria started asking questions.

"How long is that tunnel?" Victoria asked.

"I think it is about forty-five feet."

"Where is the entrance in the cemetery?" Victoria asked.

"It is in the base of that angel gravestone statue next to my mother's grave," Jane said.

"How do you open the statue?" Victoria asked.

"I already told you that I don't know," Jane said.

"Well, I bet that I could figure it out," Victoria said. "I'm not sure that I can sleep tonight. I'm wondering how that thing could open. And the tunnel ends inside that old white church? I went to Miss Turnipseed's funeral. Were you inside that tunnel then?"

"Yes, but Tom Lewis was kinda holding me hostage. So I had to be quiet. I could hear y'all, but I couldn't say anything," Jane said.

"You know, I bet that tunnel and that cave where you hid from Huerta at the library in that creek are connected," Victoria said, gazing off into the distance.

"Probably are," Jane answered. She had already thought about that. Her eyelids felt so heavy since she had eaten all that food. She lay down on her bed and fell asleep while Victoria kept talking and asking questions.

Early the next morning on January 10, the sun peeked into the room and Jane woke with a start. Today was the first day of their last semester of school. Jane wanted so badly to tell Victoria about her pregnancy, but a secret like that was hard to keep quiet, especially in a small community like French Camp. Since she wasn't married and didn't remember being raped by her teacher, keeping it a secret was more important than ever. Jane dressed hurriedly and then woke Victoria. "Time to get up. We've just got one more semester to go. Up and at 'em."

Chapter 18

Three Months Later

Three months into the second semester was spring break time, and until that time Jane had managed to keep Victoria out of that secret tunnel because she didn't know how to open it, and Tom Lewis had not been captured yet. Mr. Petey hadn't been back to the Institute and although she had been to the cemetery to check on Mrs. Lynch's grave, neither of the girls could figure out how to open the base of that granite angel. Huerta left French Camp for the week for a trip to New Orleans supposedly to see his wife, so they would have their chance while he was gone. It was just what Victoria had waited for. *Secretly, Jane hoped he didn't bring Miss Ward and Tela back with him if that was where they went.*

Once Jane saw the back of his buggy going around the bend in the road, she hurried to the cemetery. Victoria had gone to the library. *If anyone sees me out there, they would think she was checking on her mother's grave.* She thought.

She was running her hands along the base of the granite angel when at about that minute, the base of the angel opened and Tom Lewis appeared, coming from the inside. "What are you doing out here?' He asked.

So this is where Tom Lewis has been hiding, and Huerta must not have told Sheriff Marks about being inside the tunnel. I wonder why? I wonder what Huerta found while in there. I wonder if he found what's inside that other tunnel. Victoria and I have to see if he got the gold. Jane thought.

"I want to know how to open this angel," Jane boldly asked Tom Lewis.

He looked at Jane with his crooked smile and stuck his hand in his pockets, the smile that always frightened her, the smile that he had whenever he wasn't "at himself" and said, "Young lady, I'll show you but you can't tell a soul, and you don't let anyone know where I'm hiding out. Tonight I've got to go to Kilmichael to preach to the heathens and see Mr. Petey."

"I promise that I won't tell," Jane told him, trying to control the excitement in her voice. Finally, everything was working out so they could see about that gold. "Give my best to Shug and Oma."

"Look here." He closed the base and then knocked on a special area of the granite angel and the base reopened. "Let me close it again and you try knocking here."

Jane made a fist and knocked on the same area of the granite angel and the base opened. Then he reclosed it. "Thanks. I just came out to check on mama's grave. And it seems alright, so I've got to go back to the school. You be careful on your trip to Kilmichael." Jane made her way back to the front of the church and back up the street.

She could not get back to the library to find Victoria fast enough. When she reached the steps of the library, she was totally out of breath.

She sat down on the steps to rest and to wait on Victoria to exit. Suddenly, the doors of the library opened and Victoria came rushing out.

"I know," Jane said, excitedly. "I went to the cemetery to check on mama's grave, and Tom Lewis was there. He's been staying in that tunnel. That's why Sheriff Marks hasn't found him. He told me how to get into that tunnel by opening the base of that angel." She took a deep breath and continued. "And Huerta left for New Orleans for the week. But, he hasn't been back to that tunnel since he got out, and he didn't tell Sheriff Marks about being locked inside there. I think he found that extra tunnel that I found. I think something like gold or other Confederate treasure is inside there. "

Chapter 19

"I know how to get inside the tunnel, Victoria," Jane said, rubbing her neck and trying to hide her excitement. "That Confederate tunnel in the cemetery. I know how to get inside. It starts in the angel statue near my mother's grave and ends in the church. While I was checking it out, Tom Lewis appeared out there. He showed me how to open the end by knocking on a certain place at the base of the angel gravestone. I want to go back out there tonight. I've got to check for the secret room or tunnel that I just know is there. Remember, I told you about the flames flickering. Are you afraid to go in there with me?"

"I thought you were afraid of Tom Lewis," Victoria said. "Well, I would be. If he doesn't lock us inside, I'm not afraid of much. Well, let me say that I actually am afraid of him. I think you are too or you should be. He isn't aware of what he's gonna do next, so how can you be?"

"I am kinda afraid," Jane replied. "But I don't think he'll be out there. He went to Mr. Petey's house tonight and then to preach in Kilmichael probably at the Baptist church. They are having revival. You know, he's gotta save the heathens."

Victoria laughed and shuffled an armful of books. She reshuffled the load from one arm to the other. The hard spines of the books were making red streaks on her arms. "Let me take these to the dorm. It's about dark, so we will get lanterns and take a look inside that tunnel. If Tom Lewis isn't there, I won't be afraid. What if he's there and I'm with you? How do you think he'll react? I know he's crazy, Jane. He needs to be back in prison. You know it too."

"Yes, I know," Jane said. Thinking about Tom Lewis made her sad. She never knew what to say about him to Victoria or anyone else for that matter, so she changed the subject. "I don't want to light the lanterns until we get there. Somebody might see us with the light going to the cemetery at night. As far as I know, Huerta is still gone, but he could return at any time. Maybe you should check the livery for his buggy."

"Well, I've got another idea. Let's sneak into Huerta's living quarters and search through it. I overheard two librarians talking at the library, and they said he wouldn't be back until tomorrow or the next day, but if he is going to New Orleans, he will be gone longer than that. There's no telling what we might find in his room," Victoria replied.

Huerta's living quarters were in the boy's area of the campus, so they would have to sneak in a window or through the kitchen or something. Jane thought.

Jane followed Victoria back to their room, and she threw her armful of books on the bed. She was researching the history of the Confederates in the area, hoping to find out more about the use of secret tunnels by the South, and she had a book about Marie Laveau I, who was supposed to be Huerta's mother-in-law. Somehow all the women in the Laveau family had Marie in their names. Victoria had told Jane that she wanted to find a map of the tunnels if there was one. So far, she had only an inkling of their war strategies, but none that she knew involved tunnels. She also had checked out some books about voodoo. Seeing these, Jane really hoped that Victoria didn't get sucked in by the voodoo rituals and beliefs. She knew it was very powerful and kind of like devil worshiping as far as getting a person hooked.

"Let me sneak into Huerta's room to search it, and you go on to the cemetery," Victoria said. "It will be easier for just one of us to sneak in there. Just give me about thirty minutes. Where do you think he'd hide his voodoo stuff? In his mattress? Or under his bed."

"I don't really know, "Jane said. "How will you know his voodoo stuff when you see it?"

Victoria shrugged.

"I'll gather a couple of lanterns, but I'm going on to the cemetery before it gets dark. Do you think that you can get there without a lantern?"

"Let me see? Sure. The moon is supposed to be big tonight like it was last night. I think I can make it," Victoria replied. The excitement in her voice was evident.

They separated, Victoria going toward Huerta's living quarters, and Jane went to the livery to borrow some lanterns and make certain the Huerta was gone. Victoria left the dorm and instead she sneaked to Sheriff Mark's office. It was in the same direction as the boy's section of the campus, so Jane didn't notice exactly where Victoria was going.

Jane looked inside the livery. The stable attendant, Mr. Charlie, was there, but he was lying on a pile of loose hay and snoring loudly. He sported a long, gray scraggly beard like Santa Clause that badly needed trimming. His beard was full of stray pieces of hay. He wore thick pants and a blue, plaid, flannel shirt and a ragged, old, gray wool coat. He never roused from his hay bed, and he kept snoring, so she took a couple of lanterns and some matches. Then she eased back out of the livery stable door and down the street to the cemetery.

Once she reached it, she sat at the base of the angel gravestone and waited for Victoria.

Chapter 20

Victoria's footsteps made clicking sounds as she strode into Sheriff Mark's office and announced to him that Tom Lewis Lynch was currently headed to Kilmichael to preach to save the heathens. He was sitting in a straight back chair and leaning back with his feet propped up on the antique, wooden desk. "I really want him to be put back in jail where he belongs for killing my father," she said. "He's the one who is a heathen. I don't know which church, but Kilmichael isn't that large. I think probably the Baptist. You can figure it out. Don't ask me how I know where he is going, and don't tell anyone how you knew where he was."

"I'll ride over there tonight and pick him up," Sheriff Marks assured her, taking his feet off the desk.

"Just be careful," she said. "He's crazy as a Betsy bug."

"That's putting it mildly," Sheriff Marks said, taking off his hat and rubbing his hand through his sparse, gray hair.

Satisfied that he would capture Tom Lewis if he really wanted to, Victoria turned and abruptly walked out of his office. She tip toed down the wooden board sidewalk and around to the back of the dormitory where Huerta resided. Then she looked to see if anyone had followed her or was in the alley where the window was. Since no one was in sight, she raised a window from the outside to sneak inside. Luckily, the window wasn't locked, and it opened into his living quarters. Pushing the curtains aside, she climbed inside. Victoria knew it was his quarters immediately because there was a picture on the mantel of Huerta and his family from New Orleans. A beautiful woman stood in the photo beside him. The inside of his room looked the same as the inside of theirs. One side of the room was lined with classic books and literature texts. *Professor Huerta is very well read.* She thought.

She surveyed the room, looking for anything that would prove his interest in voodoo. Nothing was out and visible, so she started rummaging through drawers. In the bottom drawer of one of his chests, she found a book of voodoo rituals, some voodoo paraphernalia like pictures with the eyes cut out, wild turkey beards, bones, powders of some kind, and dolls. The room smelled of his exotic perfumes.

The deeper she looked in the drawer the more she found. Whenever she looked at the picture with the eyes cut out, she realized that it was a hand drawn picture of Jane. Seeing this gave her the creeps, but she gathered all the things that she found and wrapped them in her long skirt and climbed back out the window that she had entered, pulling it back down.

Carefully, so that no one saw her, she sneaked back to the girl's part of town and reentered the girl's dormitory and hurried to their room. Now, they had proof that Huerta was up to his eyeballs in voodoo. Victoria wondered what Sheriff Marks would say about this. She figured that she needed to find another way to use this information instead of telling the sheriff because she had entered Huerta's room illegally.

I'm going back before he comes home from wherever he's been and take his picture out of that frame and jab his eyes out. She thought. *Just like he did Jane's.*

Once she had hidden Huerta's voodoo paraphernalia in a wooden box under her bed, she walked down the stairs and out the door. It had only been twenty minutes since she and Jane split up. Victoria definitely didn't want Jane to know that she had told Sheriff Marks where Tom Lewis Lynch was going. Jane was her very best friend in the whole world. Victoria knew that Jane was afraid of Tom Lewis too, especially when he wasn't "at himself." Darkness had descended on the town, making shadows on one side of the street. So Victoria wouldn't have any trouble hiding as she made her way down the street. She really did need a lantern, but she didn't want anyone to see her carrying it. So she carefully walked down the center of the street. Victoria knew that soon her eyes would adjust to the darkness. Also, telling Sheriff Marks where Tom Lewis would be got him out of town which was another good thing for Jane and her, so he wouldn't be out near the cemetery tonight. Excitement about looking in that Confederate tunnel flooded through her.

Inching her way along, Victoria made it to the cemetery. She was so excited that it felt to her like it took an hour to get there. Jane met her at the cemetery's entrance. "Hey, I think we can light the lantern with a match if we wrap out skirts kinda around it, no one will be able to see it," Jane said. She struck the match and lighted the lantern, and they huddled around it and held their skirts together in the back until they reached the angel gravestone. Then they turned the flame down very low and set it behind the statue so that no one from town could see it. Jane knocked on the base of the angel in the area Tom Lewis had shown her and it opened. They rushed inside, taking the lanterns with them. Jane pulled the opening in the angel almost closed and stuck a stick in it to keep it from closing completely.

She turned the globe on one of the lanterns to open it and brighten it. She lighted the other one.

"Whew, this is something," Victoria said. "So this is where the Confederates hid from the Yankees, and the slaves hid out as part of the Underground Railroad. I'm so impressed by the effort it took to build this tunnel and the history it has seen.

"We have to find the extra tunnel that runs off to the side. I think I remember approximately where it is. I feel certain that Confederate treasure will be inside it," Jane said, excitement sounded in the tone of her voice. She told Victoria to carry the lantern, and she felt along the walls of the tunnel until she found a section of stone that felt different. Victoria walked in front of her and held the lanterns so that Jane could see what she was doing. Finally, Jane found it. "Here it is. This is the section that I thought was another tunnel to one side. Let's see."

Victoria raised one of the lanterns, and they both examined the section of the wall. "See, Victoria, the wall is smoother here and watch how the flame flickers whenever you hold the lantern near this seam. I can feel a slight breeze. We've got to find how to open this section. Since the base of the angel opens from knocking, let's try knocking. I guess we had better do this systematically, stone by stone. We will need to remember how we opened it."

"Please let me," Victoria said. Her excitement was evident.. She began to knock on the stones one-at-a-time. Finally, one of the stones had a small opening. "Shine the light inside here. You know, there will be spider webs inside if no one has been in this part of the tunnel for a long time. This reminds me of reading Edgar A. Poe's *Tell Tale Heart* and *The Black Cat.*

"It will be more like years," Jane replied. She looked inside the opening and felt in the crevice. "There is an iron piece hanging down from the top. I'm gonna pull or push this iron handle." First, she pulled the iron lever and the entire wall moved. "Wonderful, Victoria. We got in." They pulled the section of rocks back to look inside the opening.

"Jane, look at all the cobwebs and bats. Let's be very careful not to disturb the bats. They bite." They shone the lantern inside the aperture. "Oh, my God. Do you see those shiny bricks of gold? I'm going inside to get some of them. Quick. Where can we hide this gold if we can get it outside?"

"Well, Victoria, I've been thinking about that. I've got about three ideas," Jane said. "The first is inside that grave box that is cracked in this cemetery. I think there is a Confederate soldier buried in that grave box. His name is Benjamin McCrary. We could remove the cracked corner and place the gold inside. The second idea is inside a hollow tree, but the best one I can think of is near Tom Lewis's house. The third idea is in the hearth of the fireplace at Mr. Petey's house in Kilmichael. What do you think about these ideas?"

"Jane, look over there. Wonder what is inside those brown burlap sacks?" Victoria rushed over to open the bags. Her rushed movement roused the bats. What seemed like hundreds of them flew toward the light of the lanterns. Jane dropped her lantern on the floor and covered her head and neck. The lantern globe cracked and the light went out. The bats made a squeaky high pitched sound and then most of them flew back to their roost. One bat landed on Jane's neck.

Jane screamed.

The bat bit her, so instinctively she knocked it off hard against the stone floor, killing it. "Oh, my. Victoria that thing bit me. We need to get out of here, and we need another lantern."

"Where is that one?" Victoria asked. "I bet I can light it again." They both felt around on the stone floor until Victoria found it. Victoria struck another match and held it close to the wick. There was enough kerosene in the wet wick to light it again. "Watch the glass," Victoria said. "It's scattered over the stone floor. Be careful. Let's get this gold out of here and get you to a doctor. Look inside the sacks." Victoria opened the string that held the top together. "Just as I figured. Gold coins. Remember reading about the Confederates borrowing gold from France to finance the war, but it got misplaced or stolen. Maybe this is some of it, and the men responsible are dead."

"Grab one of those sacks and I'll grab the other one. We'll drag them outside the door into the tunnel, and then I'll come back in here to get the gold bars one-at-a-time while you light that other lantern. Just remember to move slowly so we don't rouse the bats. Since we've got to get you to the doctor, we'll hide them tonight in that broken McCrary grave box. Is it close to the angel statue entrance?" Victoria asked. "If it is very far, we both need to pull the sacks over there together. These gold coins are heavy."

118

"Yes," Jane answered. "It's right on the other side of Mama's grave." *What am I gonna do about the rabies vaccine? I'm pregnant,"* she wondered. *I wonder what that vaccine will do to my unborn baby.*

Slowly and carefully Jane finally got the other lantern lighted. Victoria slowly removed the gold from the tunnel a little at a time without disturbing any more bats, and Jane resealed the opening. Then they dragged the gold sacks out of the opening in the angel statue toward McCrary's grave box with the broken corner. The grave belonged to a man who had died during the Civil War named Benjamin Forrest McCrary. As far as Jane knew, she couldn't think of anyone whose name was McCrary, so she didn't figure anyone would notice that they had removed the corner and placed the gold inside and replaced the corner. Carefully, Jane removed the broken corner from the thick top of the grave box, and they both grabbed the sack of gold coins that they had dragged to the grave, lifted it, and placed it inside. Then they went back for the second sack and then finally the gold bricks. One by one they placed the gold bricks inside the grave box with the two sacks of gold coins. They closed the opening inside the tunnel. Then Jane got a pine limb and swished it on the ground to disguise their footprints. They reclosed the angel's base that led to the tunnel, and then they made their way back up the dirt street to The Institute and Dr. Hill's office. Jane's adrenalin was pumping.

They reached Dr. Hill's office as he was about to leave for the evening. "I've been bitten by a bat," Jane told him. *I don't know what I'm gonna tell him about being pregnant.*

"Come in here and sit on this chair. Let me see where the bat bit you," Dr. Hill said. His blond hair was tousled, but Jane thought that he looked good with it that way. She admired his blue eyes and muscular body too. Victoria followed Jane into the examining room. "There is a vaccine that I can give you to prevent rabies that was recently developed by Louis Pasteur. It isn't recommended for children and pregnant women. What happened to the bat?"

"I killed it. I think," she replied. Suddenly Jane burst out crying.

"Don't cry, honey. You can take the shot. You aren't a child or pregnant," Dr. Hill said.

Sobbing and sniffing, Jane wipes her runny nose. "Mis' Shug, the local midwife in Kilmichael, says that I'm pregnant." Jane sobbed.

"Does your boyfriend know?" Dr. Hill asked. He seemed to already know the answer to his question.

"I don't have one," Jane replies, still sniffing. "If I'm pregnant, it is Professor Huerta's. He raped me. I think. I don't remember. I was knocked out."

"I figured he had something else in mind besides voodoo," Victoria said. Jane could tell that she was about to blow up to talk.

"I'm gonna give you the vaccine even if you are pregnant because if you come down with rabies you will die. The vaccine may not hurt the baby," Dr. Hill said. "I figured that you had been abused the last time you were here with that head injury whenever the horse ran over you. Well, I suspected it. Now, I have to report the suspected rape to Sheriff Marks, but no one has to know that you may be pregnant. Where were you when you were bitten by the bat?"

"Will you keep it a secret. The pregnancy I mean. I graduate in six weeks," Jane said.

"We were near her mother's grave in the cemetery when the bat attached," Victoria lied, answering the question for Jane.

"Okay. There will probably be more people getting bitten, but Jane is the first around these parts that I know of." Dr. Hill left the room to mix up the rabies vaccine.

At first, while Dr. Hill was gone, Victoria didn't mention Jane's pregnancy, but told Jane about the voodoo items that she found in Huerta's living quarters. Jane busted out crying again.

"I don't want to be pregnant," Jane said. "I want children, eventually, but not like this."

"Don't worry, honey. We are rich women now," Victoria said. "You can handle it."

"We've got to find another place to hide the gold. I've thought about a hollow log or tree, the fireplace hearths at Tom Lewis's, Granny's, or Mr. Petey's houses. What ideas do you have?"Jane asked.

"Let's bury it in the ground somewhere," Victoria said. "It'll need to have a permanent marker like a tombstone or perhaps under an old church. Another idea I had was to hide it in the bricks of a hearth like you mentioned, but the owners of the house would have to be informed and that could be disastrous. One thing is for certain, we don't need to leave it all in one place." She had tried to change the subject away from Jane's pregnancy, and Jane knew it.

"Okay. Let's divide it in half, and you hide yours, and I'll hide mine," Jane said.

"Sounds good," Victoria replied. She didn't ask more about the pregnancy."

"Time will tell if I am pregnant or not," Jane said. There was no way she could forget about it. "God, I hope not," Jane blurted out.

"We'll not to worry about that until you graduate, so they can't kick you out of school. We won't tell a soul," Victoria said. "Especially, Huerta. He doesn't need to know."

"Oh, my goodness. I hadn't thought about him being a problem. What more can he do to me?" Jane asked.

Chapter 21

Tom Lewis waited until the Baptist church in Kilmichael was in full swing during night time revival, and he could hear that the closing prayer was over. Then he burst through the side door near the pulpit, wearing the placard that he had made about the Eastern gate. "Heathens, repent of your sins. God hates sinners, *"God said in Ezekiel 44: 1-3 Then he brought me back to the outer fate of the sanctuary, which faces east; and it was shut."* Tom Lewis had their attention. *"And he said to me, 'this gate shall remain shut; it shall not be opened, and no one shall enter by it; for the LORD, the God of Israel, has entered by it; therefore it shall remain shut. Only the prince (meaning Jesus) may sit in it to eat bread before the LORD; he shall enter by way of the vestibule of the gate, and shall go out by the same way."* He was reciting. He didn't have a Bible in his hand.

*"The Golden Gate" was located on the eastern wall of Jerusalem; it was one of eleven gates into the city. It was sealed in the 16th century by the Turks. Jesus came down from the Mount of Olives and entered the temple, "*Tom Lewis said.

He was half-way through his sermon when Sheriff Marks burst into the Baptist Church through the front door. "Tom Lewis Lynch, you are under arrest. You are a fugitive from the correctional facility for the murder of Deputy Watson."

A cry went up from the congregation. "He's insane," one woman said loudly. Then she fainted in the pew and fell onto the floor. Her fellow pew church members grouped around her. Strangely, some men in the congregation moved quickly out into the aisle between the two rows of church pews that ran up to the side walls, blocking Sheriff Marks's path or perhaps trying to help the woman who had fainted.

"Get out of my way. You are interfering with an officer of the law," the sheriff screamed. "I could arrest all of you."

They moved out of his way, so they wouldn't be arrested as Tom Lewis removed his placard about the Eastern Gate and sprinted out the side door of the church. He had left his blue bicycle resting in the shadows against the steps of the church. He hopped on the bicycle that he had ridden to the church and pedaled away into the darkness. Luckily for Tom Lewis, Marks hadn't brought any deputies with him because of what had happened to Deputy Watson.

Marks ran to the side door and saw Tom Lewis disappear into the night. Tom Lewis was yelling, "The Eastern Gate, the Eastern Gate…the Eastern Gate. Just call me Nellie Bly."

Chapter 22

When Huerta reached New Orleans around seven o'clock in the morning. He felt bone tired. After traveling constantly for three and a half days with only the change of horses twice, he drove his buggy down the clickity-clack old bricks of Dauphine Street in the Faubourg Marigny (New Orleans) directly to Marie Laveau II's well-known establishment. Huerta felt excitement as he had never felt it before. Part of his excitement was due to seeing his wife, and the other was the gold. He couldn't wait to tell Marie about finding the Confederate gold. He eased up the stairs to her living quarters. Frightening Marie was never a good idea. He felt his news would make her take him back after their separation if for no other reason than the gold. He missed her. She was such a beautiful woman who never seemed to age. If he could get this Confederate gold back to New Orleans, she wouldn't ever have to worry about money ever again, because if it was enough to finance part of a Civil War it would be enough to finance her operations and to live richly for the rest of their lives. She could stop her liquor import business, her brothel business, her voodoo business, and even her on-the-side hairdressing business of doing the hair of wealthy, white folks. She wouldn't have to con the wealthy, white folks of New Orleans out of money any more.

Huerta knocked three times on her door. He used the same knock he always used and she would know it was him. She came to the door wearing a flowing, white, long gown. She had a white scarf tied around her hair, and her dark brown eyes were made up to look even more exotic than they naturally were. The white made her honey colored skin glisten. Marie was the daughter of the famous Marie Laveau I who was partially Creole, Haitian, and multiracial. "Marie," he said after she opened the door and grabbed her to kiss her.

She pulled away from him. "You look excited. Tell me. What?" Marie said in her melodic, Creole voice. Her perception and intuition both always kicked in, and she was seldom wrong. She didn't often let her emotions cloud her judgments.

"I've got great news. I've found some Confederate gold. Lots and lots of it. All we have to do is to go get it out of the tunnel where they had hidden it," Huerta said. His voice was higher pitched than usual.

"You lie," she said, looking at him as if he was trying some tactic of reconciliation on her.

"No, I swear," Huerta tried to convince her. "Why not come back to The Institute in French Camp, Mississippi, with me and see for yourself. You could come on the pretense of holding a voodoo rite. Maybe in the Big Black River. I'll take you inside the tunnel where the gold is hidden. At the least, you would have a little, fun trip up the trail that folks are beginning to call the Natchez Trace, perhaps make some money in the River, and I'll give you half of the gold. We are gonna need to bring it to New Orleans and perhaps take it out of the country to get the value out of it," Huerta said. He stood inside her apartment holding his hat in his hand in a humble gesture. "What do you say? Can you leave New Orleans for a short few days or maybe a week?" He had thought she would be more excited, but holding her emotions in check was a strong point of her personality. She also made decisions quickly.

"Give me a few hours. Say until nine o'clock this morning and I'll travel with you, but if you are tricking me and I don't feel that you are, I'll put a voodoo spell on you. You won't have a talisman for this one. At first, I didn't believe you, but your excitement is too real." Then she looked at her reflection in the large mirror in the living room. "I'm fifty-eight years old. Traveling that far will exhaust me, so I've got to mix some potions and make some arrangements with my people who work for me." She turned and walked into her kitchen. She had been cooking breakfast of grits, sausage, and eggs with homemade biscuits with local honey. Huerta followed her, still holding his hat in his hands. Smelling the food made his stomach growl and his mouth salivate.

Quickly, Marie went to work on her anti-fatigue potions, packed her travel bags with her clothes, toiletries, potion making bag including local honey that was the base of many of her potions and beauty remedies, and other voodoo paraphernalia; and within the hour she and Huerta headed out the door to find her employees and give them their instructions for her absence. Huerta had no doubt that they would follow her orders because they were terrified that if they didn't, she would put a voodoo spell on them. His spells never worked as well as hers, but he had tried to keep voodoo alive and in the family. Marie Laveau II was called a voodoo queen or a Voodoo priestess as she mother Marie Laveau I had been. Some called her a *witch* just like they had called her mother.

Huerta drove his buggy for her as they rode over the brick streets to her liquor warehouse. New Orleans, being a port city, was an excellent place to carry on an import business. Today he was her bodyguard. They stopped outside the warehouse long enough for her to go inside to give her instructions to the employees who were mostly Haitian immigrants who had immigrated to New Orleans. These people believed in her Voodoo. He waited outside in the buggy. Marie always had a bodyguard in New Orleans. Most of the people in New Orleans knew who she was and respected her or were frightened by her, but she had enemies who had threatened her three children. These enemies were jealous of her wealth or were some wealthy, white person whom she had blackmailed. To insure her children's safety, they were shipped to the Dominican Republic after someone had threatened to burn them alive, so she was jealous of anyone who was able to raise their own children in peace. Huerta had gone with them until they were old enough to take care of themselves.

When she returned to Huerta's buggy, he drove her to the brothel that she owned. Although he wanted to go inside with her to see some of his old friends, her instructions to them were private, so he waited in the buggy. He knew that she often got the girls to find out information from the men who frequented the brothel just as Marie herself did from the servants who worked for the wealthy, white people whose hair she fixed. Running cons and blackmail were two ways that Marie got money, but Huerta knew that if they could get this Confederate gold, she wouldn't have to do some of the things she was doing now.

***

At the end of the second hour, they were headed back to The Institute and French Camp, Mississippi, on the rugged trail from New Orleans to Jackson and then on the Natchez Trace trail. The trip was long and hard on him because he had just ridden down it to New Orleans, so part of the time he let Marie drive the buggy while it was still daylight. She could take care of things almost as well as a man. The trail was somewhat smooth because so many people used it to come back from Natchez, but it was still dangerous because robbers often preyed on the exhausted travelers.

The trail began somewhere in Tennessee and ended near New Orleans. Since travel on the Mississippi River was easier going south, people often floated boats, rafts, or barges south. Then they sold their goods, walked or rode horses back north. Therefore, it was well known that they had money on their walk back north, so robbers often preyed on these people. Luckily, Huerta had never been bothered by these robbers. It could be because he carried a sawed-off shotgun in his lap. And the visibility of this gun scared them off.

They didn't stop to camp at night, but they did stop to change horses a couple of times in places that Huerta frequented like Natchez, Mississippi, Jackson, Mississippi, and Kosciusko, Mississippi.

By the second afternoon, they reached The Central Mississippi Institute, and Huerta broke the rules by moving Marie Laveau II into his living quarters. At this point, he didn't care because he considered himself to be a rich man. Or he had counted his chickens before they hatched. Once he went into the room that was his living quarters, he sensed that someone else had been in there. Although his intuition wasn't as strong as Marie's, he could sense some things. Strangely, nothing seemed to be missing until he looked in the drawer where he kept his voodoo items. "Jane Lynch," he said.

"Who?" Marie asked. "Are you calling me by your girlfriend's name?"

"This student that I tried to use in a ritual," he replied. "She's been rummaging through my things."

"What do mean? You tried?" Marie asked. "Why has she been in your bedroom?" Marie asked. The jealousy in her voice was evident.

"Oh, it's not what you think," Huerta said. "I mean she broke in here while I was in New Orleans with you."

"Why would she care?" Marie said, sounding even more jealous. "What was she trying to find? Proof that you are a married man?"

Her statement about him being married surprised and delighted him. "Get some rest. Jane Lynch isn't important in the least. Her stepfather is the one who helped me find the Confederate gold. He kidnapped me and locked me inside that tunnel. That's where I found the gold.

We came back here to get Confederate gold. Let's sleep so we can be rested enough to get it. I'm exhausted. I haven't slept in days. You can sleep on the bed. I'll sleep on the floor," he said. When we get rested, we will go get the gold and then plan your ritual at the Big Black River. Then we will go back to New Orleans as rich people." *He knew that as soon as he laid his head to rest he would fall asleep.*

"When we get ready to go to the tunnel, I'll give you one of the potions that I mixed up. You will have plenty of energy then. Why did he kidnap you? Were you sleeping with his stepdaughter?" Marie said with an angry twinkle in her eye.

"Nope, he's insane." He answered her with the simplest answer he could think of that was the truth. She could always tell when he was lying.

"We will drink the potion in the morning. It works every time," Marie said, dismissing the other topic for now.

Huerta hoped that she would forget about Jane Lynch.

The next morning before daylight Marie and Huerta awoke from the sound of a rooster crowing. The man at the livery stable raised chickens. Huerta was glad to be awakened this early.

Marie handed him one of her potions, and she drank the other one. "It's time to go get the gold. Where are we going to hide it until we go back to New Orleans. We can't hide it in here. You already said someone rummaged through your things," Marie said.

"I've already thought about this problem and I've a solution. There is this hollow section in the bottom of my buggy. Since we will be traveling back to New Orleans in it, let's hide it in there," Huerta said. He wanted to keep Jane Lynch out of the conversation. He wanted to keep Marie's mind on the gold not on the sex. Money and power were her driving forces, and she had done well with both in New Orleans. *She was making a name for herself the same as her mother had and one day she would be as famous as her mother.* Huerta thought.

"Will we go to the cemetery is the buggy? Gold is very heavy. How much is there? One bag?" Marie asked.

"No. I saw a stack of gold bricks and at least two, brown burlap bags of gold or another treasure. I didn't go inside the tunnel and count it. The tunnel is filled with bats," he told her. "Wrap a heavy scarf around your neck so they can't bite you, and I'll do the same."

"Huerta, I have a better way to keep bats away. I'll mix up a potion for that. It has a lot of garlic in it. It is the same I use to keep vampires away. They are the same. Bats and vampires," Marie said. "Can I mix it in here? It has a very strong smell."

"Go ahead. We aren't gonna stay here long anyway," he said. "If they kick me out, it will be a blessing since we will go back to New Orleans as rich people."

Quickly, Marie mixed the potion to ward off the bats. She slipped the glass bottle with the cork top into the pocket of her skirt. "I'm ready," she said.

They slipped out the door of Huerta's living quarters and down the street to the livery stable. Huerta harnessed a fresh, rested horse to his buggy and left some paper money for the attendant, Charlie. He took two lanterns from those hanging on the wall in a group of seven. They opened the doors of the livery. Marie climbed into the buggy, and they rode toward the white church. Huerta noticed that the Confederate flag was hanging down next to the pole. To make things seem normal, he parked the buggy in front of the church and tied the horse to the rail so it couldn't leave.

"We enter through that large angel gravestone," he said, helping Marie from the buggy.

They walked through the rows of gravestones and markers until they came to the large angel. Then Huerta knocked on her base and it opened.

"Look at the flag," Marie said. "We must enter and close the base behind us," she said. "You can get us out of here if we close it?"

"Yes, light your lantern," he said, handing her a few matches. She lighted her lantern and dropped the rest of the matches into the same pocket with the potion to keep bats away.

"Put some of this potion near your neck," Marie said.

Huerta did as she instructed. He grimaced at the strong garlic smell. "No wonder they stay away. That potion smells horrible."

"It will wash off. A bat bite is deadly. Few people get over rabies," Marie said.

After lighting her lantern, Marie closely followed Huerta inside the tunnel. They reached the opening to the secret part of the tunnel that housed the Confederate gold. "I heard that the Confederates borrowed gold from France, but most of it never made it to the banks that were using it for collateral for loans. Some of it wound up in Georgia and one story was that it was divided up among the wealthy land owners and buried in their fields. Exactly how this gold got here must be buried with a dead Confederate soldier who stole it instead of taking it to Georgia."

"Let's just get it and get out of here," Marie said. "It's creepy in here."

Finally, Huerta found the section and knocked on the brick where he remembered the opening. He was amazed that she found anything creepy. He hadn't known her to be afraid of much. He knocked the second time. That stone opened to show the iron handle. He pulled it and Marie shone her lantern into the aperture. "I don't see anything except bats and perhaps some drag marks on the floor. Are you certain that no one else knew where this gold was?" Marie asked.

"Tom Lewis Lynch. He is the one who kidnapped me and locked me inside this tunnel. Let me look inside that aperture. Oh my, it is gone," his anger was overwhelming. He felt his new buckle. The blood colored his face and the veins in his head and neck became engorged with blood. He thought he would pass out.

"You lied to me, Huerta. There was no gold here. If this is your way to get me back?" Marie said. The fire in her eyes frightened him. This wasn't the first time he had been frightened by her.

"No, I swear. It was here. Come with me. We are going to Pete's house. He is Tom Lewis's friend and will know what happened to it," Huerta said in an embarrassed tone. "He'll tell us where the gold is or he will die."

"You are a fool, Huerta. Does Petey have a wife or a daughter? I can make them talk. We don't need to murder anyone and have the law looking for us. You mentioned that Jane Lynch's stepfather was Tom Lewis. If we can't find out about the gold from this man Petey, we are gonna kidnap her. That will draw Tom Lewis to us and if he is close to Petey, it will draw him too. Then we will find out what we want to know," Marie said.

"Yes. Petey has Oma and Shug, his daughter and wife. You are such a smart woman, Marie," Huerta said. "I am embarrassed,

Marie," he said. "Why don't we plan the voodoo rites in the Big Black River and have Jane Lynch there. That should bring both Petey and Tom Lewis."

"First, we are going to Petey's house. I'll get any information out of him that he has. I'll use Oma and his wife, Shug. Women often tell me things without meaning too. I can be very persuasive and hypnotic," Marie said.

"Let's go back to my living quarters and wash this garlic smelling bat potion off. As bad as we smell it will be hard to seriously harass anyone," Huerta said. "Thanks, Marie, for believing in me."

"I feel that you are telling me the truth, but if I find out that you have lied to me, you will be so very sorry," Marie assured Huerta.

Huerta tried to keep the worried look off his face, so he grinned widely at Marie. "Let's go." He carefully closed the tunnel opening where he had previously seen the gold, and they walked to the opening in the angel. He knocked on it until it opened and they exited. They left the cemetery and loaded up in the buggy.

A chicken snake lay across the dirt street and coiled at the sound of the horse's hooves. "Stop," Marie said. "Let me catch that snake. It will help us.'

Huerta stopped the horse as quickly as he could. It had seen the snake too and was skittish. Marie stepped down. She was chanting something that he had never heard her saying before. She walked over to the coiled chicken snake. "Stay like a stick. Stay like a stick. I need you, friend of Tombi. You were put on this earth to help me," Marie chanted. She reached down and picked up the snake. First, it looked like a stick and then it went limp at her touch. Then she stuck it into her pocket and climbed back into the buggy. "I'll wake it whenever we get to Petey's house." She told Huerta. "I'll use it on his wife and daughter, Shug and Oma. They will then do whatever I ask them to do."

"We'll stop off at The Institute," Huerta said. "Then we'll go on to Kilmichael to Petey's." For some reason Huerta didn't think Petey knew about the gold. His bet would be on Tom Lewis, the wild card." Since Marie had caught the snake, they would need to go on to Kilmichael today. He didn't want to stay in the room with that snake even if she had put it in a trance. She definitely had a way with snakes. She even had a pet one at home that she had named Tombi after an African god, but it stayed locked in a cage like terrarium. Still it didn't make Huerta comfortable.

When they got back to the dormitory, Sheriff Marks was waiting on him and he wasted no time telling him why he was there.. "Well, Huerta, you have been accused of raping Jane Lynch by Dr. Hill. I may have to place you under arrest. By the way, I just got back last night from Kilmichael at the Baptist church. Tom Lewis Lynch interrupted the revival service there, but they helped him get away. You know we are proud of our crazy folks in the South. He rode away on a bicycle no less. I guess the next thing I hear is that he's like Nellie Bly," he said. "Did you rape that young girl?"

"Of course not," Huerta said, hoping Marie believed him. "If she was raped, it was probably by that crazy stepfather she has."

"You are probably right. Could I get you to help me catch him? I thought we might tell him that you have kidnapped Jane. He would come running then," Sheriff Marks said.

Huerta couldn't believe his luck. Having Marie around made him lucky. *Thinking that he too wanted to catch up with Tom Lewis Lynch, Huerta thought that was an excellent idea, but he wasn't certain that he wanted Marie around Jane.*

"I think that is a wonderful idea, Sheriff. I'm planning to have a voodoo ritual rite in the Big Black River near Kilmichael this afternoon. Would you help us spread the word? Be certain that the congregations of all the churches know and post signs in the saloons. Tell people they can find out how to make requests, and have their wishes come true. That will bring them there. Say we do it at two o'clock," Marie said. "Oh, by the way, I'm Marie Laveau, Huerta's wife. I've been living in New Orleans, but have come up here for a visit."

Whenever she said her name, Sheriff Marks almost dropped his false teeth because his mouth flew open."It is nice to meet you, Mrs.

Laveau. I'm Sheriff Marks. Huerta and I are friends .Okay about the ritual, but how is that going to help me catch Tom Lewis Lynch?" Sheriff Marks asked, thinking that she was one of the most beautiful women he had ever seen.

"Jane Lynch will be part of the ceremony," Marie stated flatly. "You can tell them that," she said and watched Huerta's face for any sign of emotion. "They can learn how I can grant their wishes. Mention that too."

"I can't be a part of a kidnapping," he said.

"I'll do the kidnapping. You do the rescuing," Marie assured him.

"By the way, what is that smell?" he asked, politely.

"Bat potion. Marie mixed it up to keep the bats away," Huerta said.

"That's funny. Dr. Hill said that Jane Lynch had been bitten by a bat. Where are y'all finding all these bats? That's why she had gone to see the doctor," Sheriff Marks said.

Chapter 23

So far, Jane had not had any adverse effects from the bat bite or the rabies shot, and she had no idea whether Dr. Hill had reported the rape to Sheriff Marks. When she and Victoria went back to the livery to borrow the lanterns again, she overheard the blacksmith talking to someone about Huerta being back in French Camp and that he had brought his wife, the famous Marie Laveau, back with him. The blacksmith was putting up a flyer about her performing a famous Voodoo Rite in the Big Black River near Kilmichael today at two o'clock. "Says here," the blacksmith said. "Marie Laveau will show you that she can grant your wishes."

Jane left the lanterns and rushed back to their dormitory room. "Victoria, Victoria, he's back. Huerta. He brought Marie Laveau, his wife, with him. We can't move that gold today, tonight, or anytime soon. We can't move it with him in town. We will have to wait until he takes her back to New Orleans. And that's not all, the blacksmith was putting up a flyer about her doing a Voodoo Rite in the Big Black River near Kilmichael. It will be this evening at two o'clock."

"Calm down, Jane. Marie Laveau died in 1881," Victoria said. "I read it in this book right here."

"This is Marie II. She is the daughter of Marie Laveau I. She is a voodoo priestess too."

"Interesting," Victoria said. "I wanna go hear her or at least watch her from the bushes. She doesn't have to know that we are there. I heard that her mother had about twelve thousand spectators on the shores of Lake Pontchartrain to watch her perform her legendary rite on St. John's Eve."

"It scares me to death that she is here. Her voodoo really works. The blacksmith said that she will show you how she can grant your wishes." Jane had turned as pale as a ghost and her voice reflected her fright.

"Calm down," Victoria said. "If anyone should be afraid of her, it is Professor Huerta. She is supposed to be his wife. Didn't you say?"

"Why," Jane asked.

"Just forget I said anything about the gold. We really cannot move our gold while they are in town," Victoria said.

"I'm going to the cemetery to check on my mama's grave and our gold now. Then I'm gonna take a nap. I'm so, so sleepy."

"I'm gonna take these books back to the library. I don't want anyone to know that I checked out a book on Marie Laveau I with her daughter in town," Victoria said. "You be careful. I'll see you back here is a few minutes. Don't open that grave box. Someone might see you. Just look for tracks around it."

"Okay, Victoria. I'll see you in thirty minutes."

Chapter 24

Jane walked down the center of the street toward the cemetery. As she walked that direction, she thought that the Confederate flag was flapping in the wind. *Someone must have the tunnel open.*

She reached the entrance to the cemetery in front of the church. She walked between the markers and gravestone toward her mother's grave. As she reached the area two graves from her mother's grave stone, the flag fell to the pole. Jane surveyed the ground for tracks or evidence of voodoo. There were several large shoe prints near the angel gravestone and her mother's grave, but none were around McCrary's grave box where they had hidden the Confederate gold. Jane didn't walk any farther into the cemetery than her mother's grave. She didn't want to make fresh tracks near where they stashed the gold.

Then she decided to go inside the church to see if the door to the secret room was open or locked. She took her time going back down the trail between the gravestones, but whenever she got to the thick privet hedges near the church, someone jumped out from behind the hedge and put a black bag over her head. She smelled a faint garlic smell and the expensive musky fragrance that Huerta wore. He dragged her into the woods behind the church. She could smell the cedars there. Then he loaded her into his buggy.

"Leave the bag over her head," a woman's voice said. Jane figured it to be Marie Laveau. "Girl, you be still or I will put this snake on you. We need you for the Voodoo Rite that we are doing in the Big Black River. We need for your stepfather to come. But first, we need to stop at the man Petey's house. Can you help us with getting your stepfather to come to the Rite, or do I need to kill you to get him there?" Marie Laveau said. "Get down on the floor of this buggy. No one can see you with us, now."

It was too late. Victoria had seen everything that happened at the church and the cemetery, but she had felt powerless to help as if someone had put a spell on her. She had heard that they were taking Jane to the Voodoo Rite at the Big Black River near Kilmichael. Once they were out of sight, she ran all the way back up the shadowy edges of the street to get a horse from the livery. She figured that there was no use to go get Sheriff Marks to help her because she knew that he was Huerta's friend.

Finally, Huerta stopped the buggy at Mr. Petey's house. He dragged Jane out and across the wood planks of Mr. Petey's house. Marie followed closely behind them. Huerta rapped loudly on the front door and Shug opened it. Oma stood behind her.

"Just the people that I wanted to see," Marie said. "I'm Marie Laveau. We have Jane Lynch here. I'm having a Voodoo Rite in the Big Black River this evening. She will be part of it. We want Tom Lewis Lynch to be there or Jane dies."

Shug and Oma's eyes were as big as saucers. "I've heard of you," Shug said, "but I'm not afraid of you. Take that bag off her head. How do I know it's Jane?"

With that Marie removed the unconscious snake from her pocket. It began to wiggle. "You see this snake, Shug? You see it too, Oma? Aren't y'all afraid of snakes? It does my bidding. If you can't find Tom Lewis Lynch and get him to the Big Black River by two o'clock this evening, this snake and all its friends and relatives will visit y'all in your bed every night for the rest of your lives. This one isn't poisonous, but some of them will be, so your lives may be cut short. Watch as I turn him into a stick. Stay like a stick, stay like a stick, stay like a stick." The snake stretched out stick straight and then went limp. Marie put it back into her pocket. "Can you get Tom Lewis Lynch to the Big Black River?"

"Of course," Shug said in a trance-like voice. "He will be there." She seemed to have forgotten about helping Jane.

Huerta, Jane, and Marie Laveau turn and walk off the wooden porch of Mr. Petey's shotgun house. No one followed them. Although Jane tried to pull away from them, they forced her to climb back into Huerta's buggy, and again she put Jane back in the area on the bottom of the buggy where they were planning to put the gold.

"Let's go," Marie instructed Huerta. "We will need a boat and a hollow log or two. Actually, we will need three."

"Why do we need the logs?" Huerta asked.

"They will be put in the river for us to stand on."

"For people to believe me, I need to look like I'm standing on the water."

"There should be some on the bank that people had used to hand grabble with," Huerta said. "We will load them into a boat. I'm certain that there will be a boat there for our use, too."

He drove the buggy steadily toward Kilmichael. Jane had settled into the bottom of the buggy. Soon they stopped on the end of the wooden bridge that crossed the Big Black River. Just as Huerta had predicted, there were three hollow logs and a large boat under the bridge. He loaded the hollow logs inside and Jane and Marie got in the boat, too. As they pushed off from the bank, several cottonmouth snakes and water moccasins scurried away in the water.

Jane was truly frightened of these snakes, but they didn't seem to have an interest in climbing into the boat with them.

"Aren't you gonna put a spell on all these snakes?' Huerta asked.

"Not unless I have to," Marie replied. "Now, let's get our logs set up." She stood in the boat and surveyed the situation. "We need all three of the logs to be close together just under the edge of the water for us to stand on. Jane, can you swim?"

"Yes," Jane said. She had been too frightened to get away, but knowing that Tom Lewis would be at the Voodoo Rite gave her some peace of mind that he would help her.

"Roll one of these logs into the water here," Marie said. "This one is for me."

Huerta picked up the log and stood it in the muddy waters of the Big Black. "I can't swim," he said.

"The water isn't that deep right now. I'm certain that sometimes it gets deeper," Marie said.

Once he had that log where she wanted it, Marie instructed him to put his and Jane's logs side-by-side. He did this while they still sat in the boat. "We will take the boat upstream around the bend and come floating down whenever it's time. Then we will step out of the boat onto the logs as if we are standing on the water. People will be amazed and begin requesting favors and leaving donations."

"What about Tom Lewis?" Huerta asked.

"I'll instruct a snake to force him into the water to rescue Jane," Marie said. "Then I'll put him under a spell to divulge the location of the gold."

Whenever Jane heard that, she knew what they were looking for. They thought that Tom Lewis had stolen the gold, and he had no idea that there was any gold. Jane had to figure out what to do and a way to save Tom Lewis from Marie's snake spell.

"I hear people coming. It is time to move upstream. When the time is right and almost everyone is here, we will float down and step out onto the logs. After that, leave everything to me. After a while, Huerta, you will collect all the money from the people who want favors or wishes from me."

Hundreds of people started gathering on the wooden bridge and on both banks of the River. Finally it was time, so they floated down the river and first Marie stepped out onto her hidden log, then they floated a little farther and Jane stepped out on hers. Finally, Huerta stepped out onto his. Surveying the crowd, Jane saw that Victoria had come by horseback and stood on one end of the wooden bridge.

Tom Lewis, Mr. Petey, Shug, and Oma stood on the bank in front of them. Shug and Oma's eyes were still as large as saucers. There was a dark cloud forming in the west. Jane figured somewhere in the bushes that Sheriff Marks was hiding waiting on Tom Lewis to make a mistake.

"Welcome, friends and believers," Marie said. "I am the famous Marie Laveau from New Orleans. My mother was Marie Laveau I, the famous Voodoo priestess. Today you are about to witness something truly remarkable. Today I will show how the power of voodoo can change your lives."

"Let Jane go," Tom Lewis yelled. "You, heathen." He waded into the water toward them.

Marie took the snake from her pocket. "Be careful, sir. I control all the snakes," she chanted. The chicken snake coiled around her arm.

"I'm not afraid of a chicken snake," he yelled. "And I'm not afraid of you, heathen."

The crowd went totally silent. A whole group of snakes were swimming toward Tom Lewis. "Stay a stick, stay a stick, stay a stick," Marie chanted and the snakes began to float like sticks, floating on the water.

Tom Lewis kept coming toward them.

"Do something," Huerta said. "Marie, do something. He's insane. He's already killed one man."

"This girl, Jane is your girlfriend? Eh?" Marie asked him.

"No," Huerta answered. "You are the only woman for me, Marie. You are my wife."

"He raped me," Jane cried. Huerta fell off his log. "I'm having his 'outside child.'"

With this, Marie went crazy. Her own children had been shipped to the Dominican Republic. "Snakes attack. Snakes attack. Snakes attack," she screamed toward Huerta. The cottonmouths and water moccasins that had been floating as sticks turned back into snakes and floated toward Huerta. They attacked him with a vengeance, biting him over and over until it looked like he drowned. The dark clouds moved in and rain started to pour, sending people on the bank scurrying like rats, and the river began to rise. Jane jumped off her log and into the rising river with the snakes, but they didn't bother her. Tom Lewis had finally made it to her to help her to the bank. Sheriff Marks was nowhere to be seen. Jane climbed onto the horse with Victoria, and they rode swiftly toward The Central Mississippi Institute in French Camp, Mississippi.

Tom Lewis Lynch rode off on his bicycle like Nellie Bly.

Chapter 25

At Commencement Exercises at The Central Mississippi Institute for Girls in French Camp, Mississippi on May 25, 1884, Catherine Jane Lynch scanned the audience, looking for Marie Laveau's honey-colored face and the colorful scarf she tied around her hair. She looked for someone wearing a colorful head scarf and white linen. Jane didn't see her and sighed with relief. Maybe Marie was gone back to New Orleans; maybe Marie was done harassing her; maybe Marie had found some other interest; whatever the reason, if she had left, Jane was relieved. Marie Laveau frightened her in a way that she couldn't explain. Perhaps it was because Laveau was different, very different. Perhaps it was because Laveau was aggressive, very aggressive. Perhaps it was because Laveau knew things that she didn't. It definitely wasn't because of voodoo. *Marie's voodoo is fake.* Jane thought. *Her voodoo doesn't frighten me. My stepfather, Tom Lewis's, insanity frightens me more than her voodoo does.*

It was sticky hot as it often is in Mississippi in May in the auditorium. Brown, curly tendrils stuck to the sweat on Jane's neck; and the white, linen dress she wore stuck to her round, pregnant stomach. *If I had a colorful head wrap, I'd be dressed like Marie.* Sometimes when she sat very still, like she was now, the baby kicked and made the front of her dress jump up and down. Trying to conceal her expanding waistline had made selecting a dress to wear to her graduation ceremony very difficult, but Shug had helped her, and she looked presentable, if not pretty, and hopefully not pregnant. She hoped not pregnant.

Either no one had heard Jane tell Marie Laveau during that voodoo ritual in the muddy Big Black River at Kilmichael that Marie had forced her into participating in about Laveau's husband's "outside child" that she was carrying, or they had been too scared to admit to being at Laveau's voodoo ritual, even if they were only there out of curiosity. Often people who didn't believe got sucked in to Marie's ways. Anyway, no one had mentioned Jane's pregnancy to her face, so she was able to finish school and graduate, keeping her pregnancy a secret from most people and especially from Granny, who wouldn't have liked it at all.

Finally, the Commencement service ended. Everyone in Jane's class had received their diplomas to their relief, and school was over. Right before the audience stood to leave, right when Jane was so relieved she wanted to jump with joy, the school president, Cloyd Drane, invited everyone in the audience to join the graduating class at the reception dinner. There would be lots of the great, Southern delicacies: fried chicken, fried fish, hushpuppies, biscuit, corn bread, butter beans, stews, and other delicious foods. Jane had smelled the fried chicken before the graduation ceremonies started and felt like throwing up. Even at this late day in her pregnancy, the smell of greasy, fried food still made her feel nauseated.

Sharp pains and spasms began to radiate from her navel to her lower back. Jane hoped it was time for the baby to come. She hoped she was having contractions. She was tired of being pregnant, tired of feeling crowded, tired of hiding her bulging tummy, so the contractions were welcome. She was very tired of trying to hide the pregnancy. A few days ago, Shug had told her that her baby had "dropped" and would be born any day now. Shug was the local midwife in Kilmichael who had birthed numerous children--both black and white-- in the area. She was very good at birthing babies.

So Jane felt safe with her. Shug had become her friend and a mother figure to her after her mother's death. She trusted Shug with most things but not everything.

Victoria followed her to the banquet, reception room. On the banquet table, Jane saw a large, metal, white dishpan with a tiny red ring around the edge of golden fried catfish, a blue gray, granite dishpan of piping hot, fried chicken, several cast iron Dutch ovens of squirrel stew, large china bowls of butter beans, purple hull peas, potato salad, baskets of corn bread, hush puppies, a cast iron Dutch oven of sausage gravy made of gravy, flour, hunks of sausage and onion, baskets of handmade biscuits and quart Mason jars of local honey, jugs of sweet tea, and stacks of fried apple pies. It had taken many of the local ladies and men many hours to prepare this feast. *But today, Jane didn't think she could eat anything because she felt sick. What a shame.* She thought. *I hate missing all that good food.* Normally, the cafeteria's food was good, but this was a feast that didn't happen often in these parts except at church's "dinner on the ground" which was a saying for the times the church members shared a pot luck meal.

"Victoria, I bet you a plug nickel that there's some moonshine around here somewhere. Folks in these parts do one or more of three things: they raise corn to sell for making moonshine, they make moonshine, or they drink moonshine. Some do all three. And other folks make moonshine out of other things like strawberries, apples, and local honey. There are few exceptions," Jane said. She winked at Victoria.

"I'm gonna ask if anyone's got any. I'm old enough now to drink it I guess. You want some?" Then she hesitated, "Oh, I forgot. You can't," Victoria said. "We gotta make us some apple pie moonshine as soon as you can. I tasted some my daddy got. It was delicious. I can't wait until you aren't pregnant."

"Shush. Don't say that aloud." Jane replied, her voice full of pain. Another labor pain shot through her belly again. She hadn't felt pain like this before. It was different, strong, and happening about every 10 minutes. "Have you seen Shug around here anywhere? Find her for me. Please, Victoria. I really think that I need her." She tried not to let on that she was having contractions.

Victoria looked at her suspiciously. "You are fixin' to have that baby. Aren't you? Oh, Lawd. I gotta find Shug. I sure don't know what to do. Girl, you are scaring me to death," Victoria said.

Jane waddled to a straight-backed chair near the door to the cafeteria kitchen and sat down, holding her stomach. Within a few minutes, Victoria returned with Shug.

Shug took one look at Jane and said, "We've got to get her to her room. That baby's coming."

Then Jane's water broke and gushed down her leg.

"We don't have a room anymore. We had to move out yesterday before Commencement. The new students have already begun to move in," Jane said, the distress in her voice making it edgy and sharp.

"Well, where is a room where we can birth this baby?" Shug asked. "It's coming right here if y'all can't find a place."

"The water closet," Victoria answered. "It's private and there is a chaise lounge for her to lie on."

"Come on, Jane. We'll help you up the stairs to the water closet." Victoria supported Jane on one side, and Shug supported her on the other as they helped Jane up the stairs to the chaise in the water closet. Whenever they reached it, Jane lay down on the blue velvet, Victorian chaise lounge that sat outside the door in a kind of lobby, and Shug examined her to check the position of the baby.

"It is still breach. Get Oma or that other girl, Kizzy, up here. They are in the kitchen. Have 'em fill that big galvanized tub with warm water, but no soap. The baby needs to be turned or it's going to be born upside down, but before I put you in the tub, I'm gonna use moxa sticks to coax the baby into turning on its own," Shug said. "Sometimes these work by themselves. Sometimes not. Sometimes I have to use the tub filled with warm water, and that baby will turn around because he's floating in the water. Sometimes nothing works."

"What are moxa sticks?" Jane asked, thinking she had to smoke it. "I'm scared, Shug."

"They are dried, rolled mugwort plant that I rolled to form the sticks. They look like cigars. I grew the mugwort in my garden out behind Granny's house. Sometimes I sell the herb sticks to other midwives or even doctors," Shug said. "The heat from them will make a breach baby turn. Sometimes. Sometimes that baby's got a mind of his own. You don't smoke 'em. Don't worry."

Victoria helped Jane remove her white, linen dress and her high-topped, lace-up boots. She laid the dress over the top of a chest in the water closet to let it dry. Wrestling around with the pain caused the pins to fall out of her hair, and it lay on the chaise lounge like a shiny, brown halo.

Shug helped Jane slide her homemade, cotton slip up around her ribcage under her breasts. Then she lighted the moxa sticks like a cigar and held them near Jane's stomach, but still the baby didn't move or change into the birthing position. Shug pushed on the baby to force it to change position for a face-up birth. That didn't work either. The baby wouldn't turn.

Oma rushed into the room. "Mama, I've got the tub full of warm water. Is it time for Jane to get into it?"

"Victoria, snuff these moxa sticks out. They ain't gonna work," Shug said. "This baby is being stubborn. Maybe we can put Jane into the water and make him move because her belly will float in the water possibly makin' him move into the correct position for birthin'."

Jane rolled an embroidered handkerchief and put it in her mouth to bite down on to keep from screaming from the pain. Although she had graduated earlier in the day, she still didn't want anyone to know that she was having a baby. She felt ashamed and very unsure of both her and the baby's future. She had done little to prepare for the birth except to secretly make a few clothes, gather some cloth for diapers, and find a large basket for it to sleep in when it was first born. Shug had talked to her about nursing, but Jane didn't feel comfortable about anything pertaining to having a baby. It wasn't something she had planned. Having a baby was the result of her being abused.

Shug tried to help Jane remove the slip to get into the tub of warm water, but she was too modest and chose to keep it on. "Honey child, after you have a baby, you'll lose all yo' modesty. That'll be all gone," Shug said. "You won't even care anymore."

Jane carefully stepped over the metal edge into the tub of warm water. As she sat down, another pain shot through her. At any other time, the tub of warm water would have felt relaxing. Her baby was coming no matter what Shug did to turn it. She tried to relax and let the warm water get the baby to move into position. Still it didn't turn, but the pains kept coming.

Jane stayed in the water until it cooled as wave after wave of pain and contractions shot through her. She still kept the handkerchief in her mouth to keep from screaming, but it was soggy wet with saliva now. She needed to replace it with a dry one.

Shug tried to coax the baby into position, but still it refused. Finally, Shug took Jane's hand to help her stand and helped her step out of the tub. Shug wrapped Jane in a large, crisp, white and blue floral flour sack sheet that she took out of her large bag and helped Jane move back to the chaise. Shug had her prop her feet up next to her buttocks. Still the baby was breach, but it was coming. And it was coming fast.

"Push, Miss Jane," Shug instructed. "It's time. Push."

Jane pushed and Victoria bathed her face with a cool, wet cloth. She still had the wet, rolled cloth in her mouth to stifle her screams, so she gritted her teeth and held back the screams.

Finally, the baby presented itself in a face-down position. A caul or thin veil covered his head down to his shoulders. Carefully, Shug snipped the veil under his nostrils so he could breathe.

"It's a boy," Shug told Jane. "A special boy. Born with a caul. He'll have special powers." Shug carefully sliced through the caul membrane from his tiny head, being careful not to tear it loose from his tender skin in ways that would make scars on his face and neck. The caul was a thin sheath of skin covering his head. Shug was careful to keep this caul membrane. It would be worth a pretty penny. "Sailors like to carry these with 'em to sea. It's said that a sailor in possession of a caul can't drown." Shug said. "Yo' baby'll be able to tell the future," Shug proudly told Jane. "All I want for payment, Miss Jane, is this caul. I'll sell it to a seaman. That is unless you want it yo'self."

Jane shook her head *no*. This was all too much for her. She felt light-headed, like fainting, but she gritted her teeth. She willed herself not to faint. She had to be strong. She was responsible for another human being now, not just for herself.

Shug wrapped the baby in a clean, flour sack, pillow case. "I'm gonna get Mr. Petey, and we are gonna to take you to our house in Kilmichael until you get yo' strength back." Under her breath she added, "Hope that voodoo woman has left town. I hope she don't show up again."

Jane heard what Shug said and silently agreed with her. *Maybe Marie Laveau had gone back to New Orleans.* Jane thought.

After about an hour, Shug and Mr. Petey filled the back of the wagon with hay and covered it with handmade crazy quilts Shug and Granny had quilted, quilts that were made with abstract pieces of fabric in no particular pattern. Often these quilts were pieced by hand and hand-quilted by a group of neighborhood women who were careful to make tiny quilting stitches. Jane remembered looking at a quilt on Granny's bed and picking out different outfits that she, her mother, and Granny had worn. Jane had dressed in her linen dress again, so Mr. Petey picked her up from the blue velvet chaise and carried her to the wagon. Shug took the baby. On the way out of the dormitory, they ran into Kizzy who acted very interested in Jane's baby. Shug showed him off as if he were her own.

Jane and her baby boy snuggled together in the back of the wagon on the hay. Mr. Petey started the mule down the trail toward Kilmichael. Many wagons had traveled the rutted trail before them, so it was relatively smooth and dusty today. Since all the people had left the Commencement hall and surrounding area, no one saw them except the women cleaning up the kitchen and Kizzy.

When they rode close to the hanging tree near Bethsaida Church, Mr. Petey started telling stories of the "little people" who were supposed to live in a gully or a cave in this wooded area to pass the time until they reached Kilmichael. "I's got one of 'em little people' in a jug," he said, chuckling to himself. "It's a whiskey jug with a corn cob stuck in the top so that little fella can't get out. It's got a name on the side of the jug. The name is Zolly Coffer. Those folks are like rabbits."

"Naw, you don't. I let Zolly Coffer out," Shug replied, laughing hauntingly. "He's been keeping me company while you've been gone helping Tom Lewis."

Mr. Petey stopped the mule. "You did what?" You let Zolly out? That was a fool thing to do, Shug. I hear tell that they's set up a camp in the gully near that hangin' tree where yo' cousin was hanged. Now, their whole darn family's gonna be after me," Mr. Petey said. He laughed very loudly.

Jane couldn't tell if he was joking or not. She hoped he was.

"You's been in the moonshine again, Petey. I can smell it on yo' breath. You smell like apple pie and alcohol, but I tells you what, the next time you catch one of 'em little people, I'll let you keep it. I hear tell, they steal women and children, so let's get that mule moving again. I don't wanna be a little people's slave, and I betcha Miss Jane don't either," Shug said.

Jane covered her head with part of a crazy quilt. *Little people scared her, but they were the least of her worries. She had to worry about a voodoo woman and raising a baby without a home, job, or husband.* At least, Granny hadn't been able to ship her off to a home for unwed mothers in Alabama.

"Mr. Petey, that baby back there is a caul baby. I still got the caul that covered his little head," Shug said. She sounded so proud of herself as if she was the reason he was born with a caul. *To Shug, a caul baby was a prize possession worth more than gold.* Jane thought. When she looked at her tiny, little boy, she was inclined to agree with her. This baby was worth more than gold to her.

Jane uncovered her head to breathe in the fresh night air and to hear more of Shug's thoughts about him being a "caul baby." Jane hadn't ever heard of a "caul baby" before. *As she took a deep breath, she thought she smelled smoke and thought about what Mr. Petey had said about the little people. As far as I know, no one lives in this area.* Jane thought.

"Sho' nuff," Mr. Petey said. "They's kinda rare. Ain't they, Shug? I mean caul babies."

"Not as rare as these "little people" you speak about. I heard that they's angels; these caul babies," Shug said. "I was just trickin' you. I didn't let that 'un outta yo' whiskey jug, but I bet Zolly Coffer's good and drunk by now from licking on that jug. Turning to Mr. Petey, Shug continued, "Get us going again. I'm more afraid of ghosts around that hangin' tree than of "little people." One of my cousins got hanged out there by some old moonshiners who caught him stealing their liquor from their jugs. My old maw used to say that his ghost roamed these woods at night 'cause he wasn't finished living yet. Lawd, talking about all this has got my blood running cold. I got cold chills, and the hair is sticking up on the back of my neck. Angels, ghosts, little people, and a caul baby, we's hainted tonight. We sho' is. We 's hainted. Let's get this wagon back to rollin'."

"Shug, you forgot that the baby's daddy was a voodoo king. No wonder he's a caul baby." Mr. Petey said and started the wagon rolling again. "I tell you that's why he's a caul baby. His daddy. Sho' is. He's a special baby 'cause his daddy was a voodoo king."

Listening to them, Jane's exhaustion got the best of her, and both she and the baby fell asleep as Mr. Petey and Shug continued to talk about little people, ghosts, and caul babies.

She awoke as the wagon pulled up outside Mr. Petey and Shug's house in Kilmichael. It was around midnight and Jane was exhausted. Shug and Mr. Petey helped Jane down from the wagon and then helped her walk up on the porch. Jane loved the sound of frogs and birds chirping in the night. They made their way through the front room where Petey and Shug slept and into the bedroom that she had shared with Oma whenever she was hiding from Tom Lewis, her insane stepfather who had broken out of prison to help her get away from Marie Laveau's husband Huerta and then left the country on a bicycle. Shug's house was beginning to feel like home to Jane. She liked the crazy quilts that Shug had on the beds and the rag rugs on the floor. She liked the feel of hominess. Shug had gone to a lot of trouble to make this house homey, and it had a cozy, welcoming feel. Shug took the baby inside in the basket that she had gotten for him to sleep in. It was as large as a laundry basket with deep sides, the kind women took out to the clothesline to gather dry clothes. She laid him in the bed beside Jane and began to instruct her on how to nurse him as soon as Mr. Petey left, showing her how to tease him into taking her nipple into his tiny mouth. He already knew how to suck. It was instinctive.

As if reading her mind, Mr. Petey said from the other room, "I heard that Tom Lewis went out West on a bicycle."

Jane smiled. She wondered where Tom Lewis might be now and what he would think about her baby. She wondered what everyone else would think too. That is everyone but Granny, Jane already knew what she would say. She thought she'd name him Charles Lewis Lynch, like most people in the South he would have a double name. She would never tell anyone who the father of her "outside child" was, nor would she tell how he had been conceived because she didn't really remember any of the details of her abuse. Mr. Petey and Shug wouldn't tell either. Shug had to fill out the birth certificate and mail it in to the state capital, but no one else around here had would see it. Jane planned to ask Shug to leave the line for father's name blank if she could.

Chapter 26

Marie Laveau

Marie Laveau had not left French Camp as Shug and Jane had thought and wished, and she had an entire league of people who kept her informed about the happenings of her enemies and friends. She had counted the time and wasn't leaving until Jane had that baby. Jane, Mr. Petey, and Shug were in Laveau's enemy category. Laveau held some rituals and was staying with one of the women who often came to her meetings. One of these women was Kizzy, who worked at The Central Mississippi Institute for Girls. This was the same Kizzy who had seen Jane's baby right after it was born.

***

"Jane Lynch's baby's been born," Kizzy told Marie. "He's a caul baby. A special one."

"A caul baby boy," Marie Laveau said. The elation in her voice evident. She wanted that baby and she would get him. "Are they hiding out here in French Camp or did they go back to Kilmichael?"

"No, they ain't."

"If I know that midwife Shug, she took them to her house in Kilmichael. That's all the better. A caul baby boy. He will be a voodoo king one day. I'll teach him all I know, and then he can take over from me when I am too old and can't perform anymore. He'll know all about the voodoo gods. We'll keep it all in the family. He'll be able to make lots of money to take care of me when I'm old. He'll know Damballah. I'm going to Shug's house to instruct her on how to care for my little voodoo king until I come back after him."

***

Maire Laveau strode into the livery stable as if she owned the place and demanded a horse. She wore a long, flowing gown of white linen. It made her honey-colored skin glow in contrast. She wore her long hair in a bun with a colorful silk scarf tied around it. It was almost as if she was trying to hide her beautiful hair, but she didn't want to have more beautiful hair than her customers whose hair she fixed in New Orleans.

"Be careful, Miss Laveau. There's ghosts and "little people" in the woods 'tween French Camp and Kilmichael," Charlie, the livery stable man said, laughing loudly.

"Who said I'm going to Kilmichael," she asked, adjusting her head wrap in what seemed like an unconscious habit.

"You ain't the only one who knows things, Missy. I know you following that girl who had yo' man's "outside child." I heard 'em say it was a caul baby," Charlie replied. "I know you going to Kilmichael. That baby'll be better than you at telling the future and casting spells when he grows up. Bet you weren't a caul baby, Missy Laveau."

"Shut yo' mouth, old man, before I put a spell on you and make you bray like a mule and strut like a banty rooster instead of talk for the rest of your pitiful life," Marie said. She was angry. She glared at him with her dark eyes and fire seemed to shoot out of them. Her glare was used for intimidation.

"I know you are that voodoo woman, Marie Laveau from New Orleans. You need to go back where you came from, Honey. These folks round here ain't into Voodoo; they's Protestant. They are not like you. They don't believe in voodoo gods and snakes. I watched you that day in the Big Black River when you did that ritual pretending you walked on the water, but you don't scare me. I'm a Baptist and you ain't Jesus Christ. Y'all was just standing on logs in the water. You was not walking on water like you wanted us to think. Naw, you ain't Jesus. And 'em snakes, they are like dogs; they can smell fear. That Professor Huerta, he was scared of the water and the snakes. He couldn't swim. I done heard him say so before. The snakes knew his fear. Tom Lewis Lynch. He ain't afraid of nothing," Charlie said. "But you better watch out for him. He's crazy. I believe they call him insane. And his crazy has a long medical name. He killed that deputy sheriff. He don't care who you are. Voodoo woman or no voodoo woman. He won't care. You better be afraid of him. I repeat, he's crazy."

Marie stared at him and then climbed onto the horse. She adjusted her flowing dress, turned, and rode toward the dirt street. Then she turned again in the saddle and reaching into her bag, she removed a large black object and rolled a black ball of wax on the floor of the livery toward Charlie. It picked up pieces of hay and manure as it rolled his way.

His eyes got as big as saucers as the black ball of wax neared him. He was as afraid of it as if it were a snake. His terror showed.

Marie laughed hysterically at his terror.

"I'll get you back," Charlie yelled. "You ain't gonna get nothing on me. I ain't afraid of yo' voodoo. You's just an old witch. They probably named that place on the Natchez trail where the witches dance after you. I've seen those black spots where you and your witch friends danced, and the grass withered and died. It still ain't grown back. Everything you touch dies. You old witch."

I'll be back in a few days. Have me a horse and buggy ready. I'm heading back to New Orleans when I get back. She turned her horse toward Kilmichael.

She felt Charlie standing in the doorway of the livery watching as her horse went behind the trees out of sight. She felt his eyes on her. Her long, white skirt flowed in the wind behind her. She laughed hysterically which was part of her mystery.

Maire slowly rode down the trail toward Kilmichael. As she neared the area where the hanging tree was, a large, white owl flew toward her, screeching loudly and nearly knocking her off her horse. *I'm not frightened of owls.* She thought. Out of the corner of her eye, she saw movement about three to four feet above the ground in the growth of sweet gum bushes and black berry briars. She thought of the stories of the "little people," but hurried on down the trail, and to ward off evil spirits, she shrieked loudly herself.

***

Early that morning, Shug was singing in the kitchen of the shotgun house when Marie Laveau appeared in the open doorway.

"If you lived in New Orleans, woman," Marie told Shug, "you would learn to lock your doors. No matter, I can enter through the walls. I'm Marie Laveau." She said and laughed hysterically similar to the loud shriek she had made in the forest.

"I's know who you is," Shug said. "You a mixed-blood voodoo witch, but you's a fake. You trick folks outta they money. Like you did in the Big Black River." Shug's voice was quivering. "Charlie at the livery said that you one of 'em witches that killed that grass where y'all dance up toward the north on the trail. He says it won't grow back."

Jane heard this conversation, but stayed in the bedroom of Shug and Mr. Petey's shotgun house with Charlie. She didn't want to confront Marie Laveau although she knew that eventually she would have to. *If I stay out of sight, she might not know I'm here.* She thought. A shotgun house had one long hallway that ran through the entire length of the house. It was called a shotgun house because you could shoot a shotgun from the front to the back without hitting a wall. Jane had no desire to tangle with this voodoo woman, not today, not ever.

"Well, my dear, I hear you are an excellent midwife. Birthing a breach baby without harming it. Tell me about the birthin'. What is his name?" Marie said to Shug.

With that Shug smiled, Laveau seemed to be giving her a compliment. "His name is Charles, but she gon' call him Charlie. He was turned backwards and wouldn't turn into birthin position, but he's alright. As far as I can tell. He's perfect. Really. But the best thing, he's special," Shug said.

"A caul baby," Marie finished for her. "Very special indeed. Now, Shug, you take very good care of Charles. I'll come back after him when he's finished nursing his mama. He's gonna become the next voodoo king. He's the child of royalty. You treat him like royalty, or you'll be sorry. And tell Jane that she can't hide from me. I can always find her."

With that, Marie Laveau reached around her neck and threw a pouch on Shug's table. Shug recognized the pouch. It contained Oma's baby teeth. She had made it of red silk that was now faded to a slight pink from age. She put a drawstring on the top and a tassel on the bottom. She used it to keep a collection of Oma's baby teeth and a lock of her hair. It was something that Shug wore around her neck all the time.

"Where did you get that?" Shug demanded. "I's always wears that around my neck." She reached up to touch the place on her neck where the pouch usually hung. It wasn't there. It was lying on the table.

"Remember the snakes, Shug. Remember the snakes." Marie laughed loudly, turned, and left on the same horse that she had ridden there. Jane peeked out at her through the curtain at her flowing white gown hanging beside the horse until she rounded the corner out of sight.

After visiting Shug, Marie Laveau didn't think that she had ever been more excited. She thought about how she'd get that baby all the way back to New Orleans down the trail with robbers and bandits. Charles Laveau was his name or would be when she got him. Jane didn't know, but she had named him after Marie's father who was also named Charles Laveau. His name thrilled Marie as much as the fact that he was a caul baby. She smiled at the thought of having a caul baby to teach how to be a voodoo king.

I'll get him after he quits nursing, but I'll get him. Marie thought. *And I'll send Jane a husband to help me.*
She grinned inwardly at her cleverness.

Chapter 27

Catherine Jane Lynch

Jane alternated between living with Granny or Shug and Mr. Petey. After all, the houses were only a stone's throw away from each other. Shug and Mr. Petey's shotgun house was in Granny's backyard. And behind it was Mr. Petey's barbeque joint. Jane felt more at home at Shug and Mr. Petey's than she did at Granny's because Granny had some funny notions, like about how folks should act and what was proper and who to hang around.

Granny said, "Jane, it is a good thing that you graduated before they found out you were pregnant, or you would have been kicked out of that school on your rear. And, Honey, I'm so sorry but I can't let you live here with us all the time. What would people say? It's a disgrace to have an "outside child."

"But, Granny, it's not my fault. I didn't have a choice in the matter. I was forced. I didn't even know then. I still don't remember."

"Hmmmp. No, matter. You should not have been out there in those woods. You know better. If I'd known what you was doin' I'd 'a sent you to Alabama to live with my sister or to a home for unwed mothers. I still may send you to Alabama and get somebody to adopt that boy," Granny said. She clicked her teeth with her tongue in that way that annoyed Jane. "I'm embarrassed by you and that baby too."

"Oh, no, you won't. I'm old enough to make my own decisions." Jane stomped her foot on Granny's shiny wooden floor. "And, by the way, his name is Charles. You can't send me anywhere. Not anymore." Jane cried. "I'm grown." *Granny never had been a loving grandmother. She had always been more worried about what other people thought.* Jane thought. Granny hadn't taught her anything about sex, but Jane had found a long, descriptive letter about how women enjoyed sex, what to do, and how. She had been very surprised about the content of that letter. Granny had written the letter to Jane's mother many years ago, and Jane found it in her mother's trunk after her death. It described how a woman got aroused. It described how a woman's nipples became erect when stimulated and how her hidden button also got hard or erect when stimulated, too. Jane hadn't experienced these with a man, but she had alone. Thinking about that now, made her nipples erect and her button too.

"Lawd, if only your mother was still alive," Granny replied still clicking her teeth.

"Well, she isn't and we are, so Charlie and I'll go stay with Shug and Mr. Petey," Jane said. "At least, they love me and don't talk about sending us to some other state."

"I don't like that any either, living with darkies. You gotta get married if any man around here will want you and your "outside child." Granny really made Jane feel bad and very sad. It was clear to Jane that Granny would never love her baby as he needed to be loved. *Jane wondered how she treated her brother Tommy when she wasn't around.*

"At least, thanks for the baby clothes that you made him; otherwise, he didn't have many," Jane said, holding back the tears out of spite. Granny would not make her cry or even show a moment's weakness. "I appreciate them, and I've been sewing some for him, too. Shug has too. She loves me and him."

"Hmmm. You keep that baby under a mosquito net at night and late in the evening. Yellow fever is deadly and there ain't no cure," Granny said. "I ain't got time to take care of no sick baby."

Three Months Later

Jane walked from Shug's to church in Kilmichael, but she left Charlie at home with Shug. Actually, Jane had not thought of Marie Laveau's threat in weeks, and she hadn't seen her anywhere. Maybe she had left town and gone back to New Orleans. Somehow Jane felt safer now. Charlie was growing like a weed, and he was so cute that she could just eat him up and kiss him all over.

Jane sat on the back right pew in the very back of the Baptist Church in Kilmichael. Kilmichael Baptist was the largest church in Kilmichael. Reverend Mayfaire was still the preacher and the congregation had really grown while he was there. It was the same church that Tom Lewis Lynch, her stepfather, had gone in to preach and "save the heathens" as he called it. That was during their last revival and before he left on his bicycle trip out West. *I wonder where he is now.* Jane thought. *I could use his help. At least he always loved me and wasn't ashamed of me like Granny is.*

When Jane entered the church, she noticed a dark, handsome man standing at the front of the church leading the choir. He was so handsome that she couldn't take her eyes off him. Jane hadn't seen him before. The Pastor, Reverend Mayfaire, introduced him as the choir director. His name was Johnny Tingle from Picayune, Mississippi. She touched her hair to make sure the pins were holding all her brown curls in place.

Reverend Mayfaire's sermon gave Jane a warm feeling when he talked about God's gift to mankind and that through water and the Holy Spirit in Baptism, we are reborn. Then a baby named James McCrary was baptized. *Jane thought about Charlie and then she thought about the Confederate gold that she and Victoria had hidden in a Confederate soldier's grave box. His name was Benjamin McCrary. I've got to go check on that gold soon.* She thought. *But I doubt anyone has bothered that grave box.*

After the church service ended, Johnny Tingle, the new choir director, was surrounded by young women and the giggling sixteen-year-old Bennett twins who still wore their hair in ringlets. Jane felt compelled to walk to the front of the church. She felt the stares of some of the women and girls who were sitting in the front pews. *I guess it's something I've got to get used to. But I've done nothing wrong.* She thought. *Let them stare.*

Johnny seemed to be enjoying the female attention of the older women, but the giggling Bennett girls seemed to irritate him. When his eyes came to rest on Jane, he said, "What is your name, young lady?" she felt that he undressed her with his eyes, and she liked it.

"I'm Jane Lynch. I'm very pleased to make your acquaintance."

It was hard to miss the twinkle in his blue eyes whenever she heard her name. "Well, Miss Jane Lynch, will you accompany me to our 'dinner on the ground' picnic? I would really be flattered if you did." Then he leaned forward and hugged her and whispered in her ear, "I really would love to see your beautiful body naked."

"Oh, I couldn't eat dinner here. I didn't bring any food to share. It is a pot luck meal. It wouldn't be polite," Jane tried to excuse herself, but she was beyond excited by his request to see her naked. She couldn't take her eyes off his deep, blue eyes. She thought they looked like the color of the sky but softer and deeper if that was possible. The more she looked into his eyes the hotter she became. She wanted his mouth on her lips. She wanted his mouth on her nipples and his hands cupping her breasts. She wanted his lips on her neck. She wanted to see and feel his excitment. She wanted him.

"Hmmm, well, I did, so there is enough of my gumbo for the both of us." He looped his arm through Jane's and led her toward the picnic tables out back of the Baptist church under the large oak and pine trees. The other girls and young women stepped back and gazed at them. Jane saw jealousy in their eyes, and she enjoyed it. A couple of them whispered to each other but thankfully, Jane couldn't hear what they said. She would have to really learn not to care.

"Well, Miss Lynch," Johnny said. "Tell me about yourself. Are you from here? Kilmichael. I mean."

Shyly, Jane told him that she had graduated from The Central Mississippi Institute for Girls in French Camp, and that she had moved back to Kilmichael.

"You are holding something back." He acted like he knew more about her than she wanted him to know.

I guess I'll have to quit being so guarded. She thought and decided to open up and tell Mr. Tingle all about herself, except the part about the Confederate gold.

"I have a three-month-old son. His name is Charles Lynch," Jane said.

"So you are married?" Johnny asked. He had a disappointed look on his face. "You are a Mrs. Not a Miss."

"No, I've never been married," Jane began to cry softly. Big tears rolled down her cheeks. "But I do have a son."

Johnny reached up and wiped them away. Jane noticed one of the women of the church staring disapprovingly. Johnny seemed oblivious to the stares. *Jane thought that they could not hear what she and Johnny were saying.*

"Well, Jane, I build wooden toys for children. I'll make Charles a rocking horse. Don't cry. Everything is going to be fine. Your having a child intrigues me. I envy the man who was able to give you one."

Jane knew he was trying very hard to make her feel better. She didn't feel better yet.

"I must go. Thanks for the dinner," she said.

"No, Miss Lynch. You are not going to get away from me that easy. You must let me walk you home," Johnny said. "I want to meet your son. And your folks." He added as an afterthought.

"I live with my grandmother, and she wouldn't like for me to bring you home with me. Perhaps another time," Jane lied. She felt that she needed to get far away from Johnny Tingle. She didn't trust herself with her body so aroused.

"Perhaps," Johnny said. "I'll see you later at the church."

"Perhaps." Jane ran from the picnic area or dinner on the ground toward Granny's house.

Johnny watched her as she disappeared around the corner. Like Lott's wife, Jane turned once to look back once, but she didn't turn to a pillar of salt unless you counted the salty tears running down her face.

When Jane made it home to Shug's house, she rushed inside to see Charlie.

"What's wrong, Miss Jane? You look like you' seen a ghost," Shug said. She was stirring a bowl of cornmeal, an egg, and buttermilk to make corn bread. She had a cast iron corn bread muffin pan heating on the wood stove. Jane loved Shug's cooking.

"A man," Jane replied in a breathless voice. "The new choir director at the Kilmichael Baptist Church. He's building Charlie a rocking horse."

"Well, Miss Jane, you found yo'self a man?" Shug asked, pouring the corn bread batter into a hot muffin pan on top of the stove, being careful not to get any on to the sides.

"Oh, no, Shug. He's not a boy." Jane blushed when she said this. "I think I'm in love."

***

The next two Sundays, Jane was too shy to go back to the church, so on the second Sunday evening around three o'clock, there was a knock on Shug and Mr. Petey's front door.

Jane sat in the kitchen feeding Charles a bottle and was almost ready to burp him, but because of the layout of this shotgun house, she could hear everything that was said on the front porch.

A man's deep voice said, "Excuse me, Mame, but I'm looking for Jane Lynch. Is she home?"

"She sho' is. Would you like to come in?" Shug asked him.

"No, I'll just sit here on the front porch in the rocking chair admiring the blooms on the pear tree in the front yard if you don't mind. Would you tell Miss Jane that I'm here. That I've come calling."

"Would you like a glass of sweet tea?" Shug asked, politely.

"Yes, please," Johnny replied. Riding on that street is hot and dusty. We need a good rain."

Shug disappeared into the house to find Jane. She let the screen door close gently behind her instead of slamming.

"There's a gentleman caller for you on the front porch. He said that he'd take a glass of sweet tea," Shug whispered, picking up Charlie to finish his burping and feeding him.

Jane took her long, curly, brown hair and put it into a high ponytail and then pinned it down into a soft, loose bun. Then she pulled some of the curls loose around her face. She pinched her cheeks and bit her lips to make them pinker. All this was unnecessary because she was too excited to speak. Jane poured Johnny a glass of sweet tea and walked timidly onto the porch with it in her hand. The screen door banged shut behind her. He jumped with a start.

"Hello, Miss Lynch. I didn't think I was ever going to see you again," Johnny said."Why haven't you been coming to church?" He had his hat in his hands, but he reminded her of someone or something. Exactly, what she couldn't put her finger on. She looked at the way he was dressed. He wore a black suit, a white lace collar, and a tall pair of black riding boots, the kind that fox hunters in the pictures in her textbooks had worn. Then it hit her. He dressed like Professor Huerta had.

"Hello" Jane's voice was barely audible.

"I waited for you to come back to church. It looked like you weren't coming back to the church before I had to leave to go back to Picayune," Johnny said. He rested his back in the back of the chair.

"Oh, you are going back to Picayune?" Jane asked, looking at her hands and examining her fingernails, a habit she had whenever she was too shy to talk.

"Well, that all depends on you, Catherine Jane Lynch."

"Me? How did you learn my whole name? How does it depend on me?"Jane asked. She was totally puzzled.

"Miss Lynch, I'll be frank with you. I'm looking for a wife," Johnny said. A huge grin took over his face, the kind that makes your face sore the next day.

"Mr. Tingle, are you asking me to marry you? Why, I hardly even know you. We've only met once. Well, now twice." She turned a bright red color. She felt her cheeks burning, and she didn't know what to do or say.

"Will you marry me, Miss Catherine Jane Lynch? I would ask your parents for your hand, but I've been told that your mother is deceased, and your stepfather is unavailable." Johnny had a very sincere look on his face. He was being polite.

"This is too fast. How can I marry you? I don't even know you, and I have my baby, Charles," Jane said.

"We can get to know each other first, but if you say *no* I must return to Picayune. If you say *yes,* I'll stay here in Kilmichael until next Sunday. So as soon as possible, you will need to give me a definite answer." He finished his sweet tea and set the empty glass on the front rail that was used for tying horses and mules. With that Johnny rose and walked down Shug and Mr. Petey's steps and waited a few minutes. "Well, I guess I'll have to go back to Picayune without a wife." He hung his head and untied his horse from the rail as if he was ready to leave.

Jane looked at him and smiled. "*Yes,* I can't bear for you to leave the country and go back to Picayune. So the answer is *yes.*"

He ran back up the steps and picked her up off the wooden floor of the porch and swung her around, giving her a hug and then a long, hot kiss with his tongue exploring her mouth. She loved it and swept her off her feet. Her body melted against him, and she felt his erection full and hard against her.

"Thank you for the sweet tea. Miss Catherine Jane Lynch. It was delicious, but not as delicious as your kiss. When may I come calling again?" Then he leaned closer and whispered, "I can't wait to hold your naked body against my naked body."

"Next Saturday," Jane answered meekly. This was a situation that she had never experienced before, but she liked it.

"Okay, my dear Jane. See you at seven o'clock next Saturday." He bounded across the yard and swung onto his horse.

Jane sat gripping the arms of the rocking chair on the front porch and watched him ride down the street and out of sight around the corner. She didn't know what to do. She was very physically excited and in shock. She had never even had a real boyfriend.

"Well, he already knows about Charlie and where I live. How do I tell him about the Confederate gold or do I tell him anything?" She whispered aloud.

She went back inside and asked, "Shug, do you mind watching Charlie for a few days. I need to go to French Camp?"

***

On her trip to French Camp, Jane thought about what Mr. Petey had said about the little people living near the hanging tree, but she didn't believe in magic or little people or voodoo magic. Still she kept watching the sides of the trail in case these little people might be watching her. Only what had happened to her today seemed like magic or a wish come true or a prayer answered. It was a different kind of magic.

Once she reached the French Camp area, she went straight to the cemetery to check on her mother's grave and the grave box that housed the Confederate gold. It was about dusk when she reached it. She looked around to see if anyone else was there watching her. There had been no more voodoo activity near her mother's grave. Well, none that involved props that she could see. Jane looked up at the Confederate flag. It was lying next to the pole, so the tunnel that ran under the angel gravestone wasn't open, causing a draft, and she didn't see anyone else around.

She walked to the grave box. There were no tracks near it either. Since people swept or scraped the cemeteries in the South like they swept their yards, tracks were easy to spot in the dust. Jane moved the broken piece on the top of the grave box over to the side. She peeked inside. The gold was still there, so she replaced the broken corner piece and went to the woods to get a twig from a cedar tree to wipe out her tracks. *I wonder if Victoria wipes out her tracks whenever she comes too. She must.* Jane thought. *Or she hasn't been out here.*

Jane sat down to rest on the base of the angel statue that led into the tunnel where she and Victoria had found the Confederate gold. She needed to think. She had agreed to marry Johnny Tingle. *Now, she had to decide how to tell him about the gold or if she even wanted to tell him. Somewhere in the back of her mind, she felt that he already knew.*

Chapter 28

Late one evening the next week, Victoria knocked on Shug and Mr. Petey's door. Jane met her on the porch and Shug brought the two of them some sweet tea. Charlie was taking a nap.

"I'm going to take my half of the gold with me to Memphis, Jane. I've been checking on it very carefully. I've been very careful that no one ever saw me. It is still there, so tonight I'm going to load my half in my wagon and take it with me. Could you get Shug to watch Charlie, so you could go with me to get my part of the gold? I don't plan to get mine melted for a long while yet, but I may use some of the coins. What about you? I heard that you and Johnny Tingle are getting married. Have you told him about your part of the Confederate gold yet? Can you trust him?" Victoria asked, firing questions at her.

"Victoria, I'm really going to miss you. Trusting someone else like I trust you hasn't happened to me yet. So trusting Johnny is all I wonder about. I won't tell him that you have gold if I do tell him about mine. Maybe I'll tell him about part of mine, but not all of it. That way, I always have some insurance. I think that would be best. *To tell the truth, there's something about Johnny that worries me.* Jane thought. She stood and hugged Victoria. The fireflies twinkled in the front yard. "I guess I'll leave the other part of my gold here in the grave box until later. What do you think? Gosh, I really hate for you to move away from here."

"It's yours. Do what you want. Just don't talk about mine," Victoria said. "I know if we spend it too fast, someone will get suspicious."

"Let's go inside to ask Shug and Oma if they will watch Charlie while I help you pack. I'll ride my horse, so I can come back when you leave." Jane took Victoria's hand, and they went inside.

***

Jane saddled her horse and tied him to the back of Victoria's wagon. The two girls rode in the wagon back to French Camp. As they neared the hanging tree, Jane asked, "Have you heard the tale of the magical, little people? They are supposed to live in a gully near the hanging tree near Bethsaida Church. It's told that they come out at night and steal women and children to turn into slaves. It's an old Indian legend, but Mr. Petey believes it, and Shug does too." Suddenly, they heard a loud screeching sound. "Shug says that her cousins' ghost roams these woods near the hanging tree. Maybe that's him making that screeching sound. Or maybe it is bats."

Victoria pulled her sweater up around her neck. "Are you trying to scare me to death, Jane?" She answered. "You know I'm not afraid of magical, little people, ghosts, or even voodoo women like that Marie Laveau. I think they play on folks' fears and take advantage of them. On the other hand, I am afraid of bats." A large, white owl flew across the wagon trail. "That is what was making the screeching sound. I'm glad it wasn't bats."

"I'm really going to miss you, Victoria," Jane said. She laughed almost as loudly as the owl had screeched. "You mentioned Marie Laveau. She told Shug that she was going to take Charlie away from me, but I haven't heard anything from her since the Commencement Day. I'm not afraid of her either, but I know she hates me, and she wants my baby. She thinks he's going to be a voodoo king because he was a caul baby."

"Like I told you, Jane, I'm not afraid of her," Victoria said. "Or those other things either."

Finally, they pulled the wagon into French Camp, and Jane went to leave her horse at the livery with Mr. Charlie.

When Jane walked into the livery, Charlie was shoeing a horse, he said "Well, hello, young lady. I see that voodoo woman isn't got you yet," he said to Jane. He smiled a large toothless grin.

"Why is everyone talking about voodoo women?" Jane said in a soft whisper to herself. She wasn't amused. If there was anywhere else to leave a horse, she would have used it, but there wasn't another livery in French Camp. "I need to leave my horse here for a while, Mr. Charlie. I'll be back to get him when I finish helping Victoria pack. She's moving to Memphis."

"Memphis? They got the yellow fever up there. Y'all know that jungle fever. I think the darkies brought it over here. Folks is getting fever, headaches, backaches, and vomiting. My aunt did. She had all 'em things. Their pulses slow, their gums bleed, and they turn yellow. It don't last longer than three to six days. Then they die or not. Some get over it. They can't have it twice if they don't die. Sometimes they think they just got a cold with fever. Po' folks are dropping in both Memphis and New Orleans," Charlie said, rubbing his nose on his sleeve. "I'm staying outta both cities. It ain't come to French Camp yet. I hope it don't. I ain't got nobody at home to take care of me. No Missus' I mean."

I hope Marie Laveau gets it and doesn't survive. Jane thought.

"People think it is spread through the air. Not me. Folks been closing up their houses, wearing wool sweaters, and piling the blankets on the sick, feverish ones. Even with it so hot and humid. Can you imagine? Well, not me. I think it comes from mosquitoes. Actually, I think 'em mosquitoes bite them darkies from Africa and then bite someone of us and we gets it. I think storms blow 'em mosquitoes in. Lawd, I'm running on so, Miss Jane. Forgive me. How's that young un' of yours. I heard you named him after me." Charlie laughed a deep, belly laugh.

"Thank you, Mr. Charlie," Jane said. "He is named Charles. We call him Charlie. I didn't name him after you. Sorry."

Jane left the livery. First, she and Victoria stopped at Victoria's house and loaded her meager belongings into her wagon. They also loaded the wheel barrow.

Then after it got dark, they drove to the old, white church and cemetery called Berea. Victoria tied the mule to the hitching rail and pushed the wheel barrow to the grave box near the angel statue. Jane always checked the Confederate flag to see if it was flying. Tonight it lay still against the pole.

Chapter 29

Jane and Shug took in the waist of the white linen, graduation dress that Jane had worn to Commencement Exercises. Shug added lace, crochet, and pearl buttons, making the dress into a lovely, romantic, dress. It was to be Jane's wedding dress.

Johnny and Jane met at the Baptist Church in Kilmichael. Reverend Mayfaire married them. There were only two people in attendance, Shug and Charles, Jane's "outside child." Victoria had already left for Memphis, so she was absent.

Jane carried her floral bouquet of Queen Anne's lace and black-eyed Susans. Jane put a large arrangement of the same flowers and some ivy tendrils in the center table behind the pastor. There weren't any other decorations.

Johnny wore his same black suit and tall, shiny, black boots. He looked very handsome. He was very attentive to Jane in the two weeks since he had proposed to her. He'd even gathered some of the wild flowers and ivy for her to arrange for the wedding.

Immediately after the wedding, Jane gave Johnny a present. It was a gold bar. He unwrapped his present and was speechless for a few moments.

"A gold bar? Where did you get this, Jane? Did you rob a bank?" he teased her. "Will we be in trouble for having possession of this Confederate gold? Shouldn't we give it back to the government?"

"Which government? This is Confederate gold, not United States of America gold. How did you know it was Confederate anyway?"

"Well, I guess you have a point, Jane." Johnny couldn't hide his delight.

"I found it in a Confederate tunnel. I guess some soldier buried it and then died. Guess no one knew where it was but him." Jane didn't understand Johnny's delight. He seemed happier about the gold than about marrying her.

"We'll take it to New Orleans and get it melted and turned into gold coins; otherwise, it's no good to us," Johnny said.

"What are we going to do with the coins?" Jane asked. "Won't someone be suspicious? How did you know it was Confederate?"

"Lucky guess," he said brushing her question to the side. "Why, put them in the bank, my dear, or exchange gold coins for silver and live on it until we get work to do." Johnny walked to the back of the church with Jane. They got Shug and Charlie, who were already outside standing at the bottom of the steps waiting to throw rice on the married couple for good luck, into the buggy and rode back to Shug's house to get packed for their trip to Picayune and their new life together.

Once they reached Shug's house, they packed two bags for Jane and Charlie and the wooden rocking horse. They hid the gold brick still wrapped like a present in the secret compartment in the buggy. Within an hour, they started their trip to Picayune down the old Trace. The first part of the Trace was little more than an animal path and an Indian trail. There were trails that branched off to the sides.

They made their way slowly down the rutted trail until they came up behind another buggy and a wagon. The wagon was parked perpendicular to the trail so that the first buggy was trapped between them.

The buggy in the middle is getting robbed. Jane thought. She felt her heart beating hard against her chest. *Bandits.* They wore masks over their faces, but Jane saw that their skin was dark like that of Indians, but they spoke English.

She had heard tales of robbers attacking people who had floated south on the Mississippi River to sell their wares in New Orleans and were now making their way back up north. *She thought of Charlie and the gold. They had nothing else of value, and she didn't plan to give up either of them to these bandits.*

While the robbers took money and whiskey from the people in the buggy, Johnny jumped off the front seat and took the horse by the reins, he tried to turn the buggy around, but it didn't cooperate. He led the horse into a side trail to turn the buggy around, but one of the wheels fell into a hole. They were stuck. He frantically tried to move out of the hole, but the wooden wheel was stuck and wouldn't roll.

As soon as the robbers finished with the first buggy, they moved on to Johnny and Jane's buggy.

"Give me all your valuables," the man demanded.

"We don't have anything. Don't shoot us. We don't even have a gun." Johnny replied, still frantically trying to move the buggy.

We don't have a gun? Jane thought, horrified.

"Give us those bags," the robber demanded.

"We've only got a few clothes for the baby." Johnny said, trying to stall them.

"We've got babies," the robber replied. He grabbed the bags from the floor of the buggy, and one-by-one he emptied the clothes onto the ground.

"Leave us alone," Jane said. "That is just baby clothes."

"We'll take the baby," the bandit said. "We can sell him."

"No, he's sick," Johnny said. "We're taking him to a doctor in New Orleans if he lives that long. I think he's contagious."

Jane gasped in horror. She was superstitious about saying that someone was sick when they weren't, but she wasn't giving them Charlie unless they killed her. She tried to hold her breath to make her heart stop beating so hard. She could hear it and feel it in her temples.

"You know saying that a baby's sick if he ain't will put a spell on him. He'll get sick. Deathly," the robber said. "Let's go, Chico. We ain't doing no good here. Just wasting our time. I can't tell if he's lying or not." He and his partner hurried back to their wagon.

Then taking their mule by the bridle, they backed the wagon into a side trail and getting their mules back in the main trail, they left Johnny and Jane stuck and distraught but happy to be able to pick up their belongings, still have the baby and the gold.

Jane jumped out of the buggy and gathered their meager amount of handmade clothes that were scattered on the ground. She stuffed them back into their bags not caring whose clothes went into whose bags. "Let's find some wood or rocks to put under the buggy wheel to raise it out of the rut. Then we can try again to get it out," Jane said. *She wondered if she had more experience with wagons and horses than Johnny had.*

As they were putting tree limbs and rocks into the hole, a rider came from the south. He wore a uniform and was a post rider. He stopped to help them. "You young folks need to be careful in this wilderness. This isn't considered the safest or the best route for me either, but it shortens my trip carrying the mail. Y'all know there ain't no stagecoaches on this trail. Folks rather travel south down the river. I mean the Mississippi River." He pried the buggy wheel with a long tree limb while Johnny rolled the buggy backward until it was free of the hole and back on solid ground.

"This trail has had lots of names. The north part is called *The Chickasaw Trace*. Part of it is called *Path to the Choctaw Nation*. And it has been called *Path of Peace* even with its notorious criminal traffic. Ain't y'all heard? Some folks call it the Columbian Highway and the Nashville Road, depending on which way they were traveling--north or south. Maybe one day Washington will improve it for a safe route for travelers like y'all. They probably will because of the large amount of cotton being grown now and the United States' North winning the Civil War."

"Thanks for helping us," Jane told him. "I was scared to death." *She thought about their brick of Confederate gold.* "Those guys were trying to rob us, but we don't have anything. Just clothes and the baby."

"Young lady, you are very welcome," the post rider said. Then he went back to talking about the trace. "Y'all know that Meriwether Lewis died on this trail. Don't nobody know if it was suicide or murder, and "Old Hickory" got his nickname from walking with his army on this trail in 1813. His men considered him as tough as the hickory trees around them. Be careful y'all don't get bit by mosquitoes or horseflies. Yellow fever is bad in these parts. And to the south. Where are you folks headed?"

This man doesn't think we know anything. Jane thought. *And he never stops talking.*

Suddenly, Charlie began to whine and whimper. Jane touched his head to comfort him. He's burning up with fever. *She hoped it wasn't yellow fever like this post rider had just talked about. She wished Johnny hadn't told the bandits that he was sick because he would get sick. It never failed. Now, he had a fever.*

"If y'all ride on about ten mo' miles, there ought to be an inn, but watch out for the 'little people' between here and there," he said, mounting his horse. "When the first folks who settled here in the 1800s came to the falls, Indians told them that there was a race of little people who lived all about the region, but especially in caves, gullies, gorges, and behind falls. I hear tell they wiped out an entire party of Indians. So when you are in this area, keep yo' eyes peeled for movement you might see out the corner of yo' eyes." With that last statement, he rode his horse on down the trail.

"Whew," Johnny told Jane. "I appreciate his help, but he's a walking history lesson that could get old quick."

"How far did he say it was to an inn?" Jane asked.

"'bout ten miles. We should make it by midnight," Johnny said. "Did I hear you say that Charlie had fever?"

"Yes," Jane answered, taking him out of his basket to nurse. She was careful to keep her breasts covered so Johnny couldn't see them.

She kept her eyes peeled for any movements and her ears perked for any strange sounds. She and Johnny rode south in silence. She wanted to berate him for not having a gun, but she didn't

After they had ridden about ten miles, Charlie began to fret again. Jane gave him some water and put an herb poultice on him that Shug had made for her. It smelled of garlic and kerosene. In the clearing up ahead, Jane saw some smoke coming out of a chimney. She smelled food cooking. "Maybe that's the inn the post rider mentioned or the home of the "little people." Jane said, laughing, but inside she was truly frightened of "little people." She had been all her life.

"Well, I hope they want company for supper. I'm famished," Johnny said. "How is Charlie?"

"His fever is gone. Maybe he is just tired," Jane said. "It is probably too late for supper."

"Where are we?" Johnny asked. Perhaps a good night's sleep will make all of us feel better."

"Raymond Inn," Jane said. "It is what's written on the sign on the front of the inn." She was so glad to maybe get out of the wagon and able to stay in an actual bed tonight. "What are you going to do with the gold brick while we are inside sleeping?"

"I'm going to take it inside, too," he said as if guarding that gold was more important than anything else.

They had reached the front of the inn. Johnny went up on the wooden porch to inquire about them staying there. Wearily, he came back to the buggy. His shoulders were drooping. All their beds are full, but they said we could stay in the barn for free," he told Jane. "They invited us to eat breakfast with them at six o'clock. That is just about six hours. Can you find a way to get comfortable in the barn?"

"Let's see," Jane said. "At least, you won't have to move the gold out of the buggy. It'll be out here with us. I'm so tired, Johnny. I think I could go to sleep in the buggy sitting straight up," Jane said.

"Mr. Foote, the inn keeper, said that he would get us some quilts and a couple of cold biscuits and baked potatoes from Mrs. Foote. I'll make a bed down for us in the hay, and Charlie can sleep in the buggy for a while. Then I'll put him with you, and I'll sleep in the wagon. We don't want anyone going through the buggy again while we are asleep."

Jane was glad that Johnny was going to sleep with her. Charlie's fever had broken, so she was ready for the touch of Johnny's hands on her body.

Johnny spread a blanket over some hay while Jane put the sleeping Charlie to bed on a folded blanket in the bottom of the buggy. Then he pulled Jane down on the blanket with him. He kissed her, teasing her lips and mouth with his tongue until she melted her hot body against him. Slowly, he unbuttoned her dress and let it fall into a puddle on the makeshift bed. Johnny leaned back on the bed and admired Jane, "You are so beautiful, Jane. Please remove those bloomers and that uncomfortable corset, although I do like the way it holds up your beautiful breasts.

Jane leaned forward and let one of her breasts rest in Johnny's mouth. Her nipples were already erect.

He took her nipple into his mouth and flicked his tongue against it making it harder and sending electric currents down to her mound of hair between her legs and lower. Her mound tingled.

Jane's body was on fire. She was waiting. She wanted Johnny's body. She wanted him inside her.

She removed her bloomers and Johnny pulled her toward him and put his lips on her mound and licked. Tingles of electricity shot through her body. His tongue reached her sensitive spots. Juice slipped out of her and ran down her legs.

Johnny laid her on the blanket and entered her. He rubbed against her and moved deep into her. Again and again he thrust his hardness into her. She became wetter and wetter.

"Jane, you feel so wonderful. I'm so glad that we got married. Our life is going to be filled with these expressions of my love."

She wrapped her legs around his waist and pushed her body up to him against his thrusts, enjoying the way her body responded to him. He moved with her with his manhood again and again. Until both Johnny and Jane fell with an exploding passion that Jane knew she would crave for the rest of her life. Both fell to the bed and slept from passion and exhaustion of the trip.

Later that night, Johnny brought the sleeping Charlie to the hay bed and laid him beside Jane to sleep. He made himself comfortable on the floor of the buggy with the blanket that had been Charlie's bed.

***

At daylight, Mr. Foote rang the cast iron bell to call everyone to come for breakfast. Jane had been awake for a while nursing Charlie. She put him back into the basket that she carried him in and asked Johnny which way to the outhouse.

Johnny opened the barn door for her and pointed her in the direction of it between the barn and the house, but far enough away from the house to keep down the smell and flies. She left the baby full and asleep in the basket. He seemed content .Stretching her legs in the cool morning air was refreshing. The sun rose over the tops of the tall pine trees.

In the distance a rooster crowed. Jane remembered the roosters at Tom Lewis's house fondly. There were others from the Inn already stirring this morning, but so far Jane hadn't recognized any of them. She thought about trusting Johnny again. She realized that she had left him with the gold and Charlie, too. Trusting Johnny seemed to dominate her thoughts, so she hurried and went back into the barn because trust wasn't something she felt for him yet.

All was fine as far as she could tell when she got back to the barn. Charlie was still sound asleep, so she gathered the basket with him inside, and she and Johnny walked the few feet to the main house where the smell of fresh coffee, hot buttermilk biscuits, country ham, sausage, and sorghum molasses made her hungry. She remembered watching Tom Lewis help make sorghum molasses at French Camp. This food made her think of Shug and Mr. Petey's house at breakfast time. Both of them were excellent cooks. Then for some strange reason, she thought of Marie Laveau. She hoped that Laveau wasn't still in Kilmichael, but had gone back to New Orleans, so she wouldn't frighten Shug anymore.

"Good morning," Mr. Foote said. He showed them to the table. "We'll have to eat in shifts this morning, so there's no need to wait on the others. Make yourselves at home."

"Full house at the Inn last night?"

"Yes. I wish it was every night," Mr. Foote replied.

Jane and Johnny sat down with two other couples at the breakfast table. Soon two other folks came to sit with them too. Mrs. Foote brought each person's plate loaded with food. *Jane found it strange that she didn't ask what they wanted. It was "take it or leave it."* Jane and Johnny were famished since they hadn't eaten a real meal since noon yesterday, just the cold biscuits and baked potatoes Mr. Foote had given them. Food was something that Jane had forgotten to pack, but she knew how to forage in the forest for fresh food. She could find: mountain mint, wild garlic, lambs quarters, blackberry, poke salad, sassafras, may pop, evening primrose, bullhead lily, hardy orange, and persimmon. All these were not in season, but some were.

"Have any of y'all run up on some 'little people?'" One of the women at the breakfast table asked. *Jane noticed that she had an unkept, rough, nasty look. Jane decided that she would rather have slept in the barn on the hay than in a bed that someone like her had slept in. Jane thought of scabbies and lice, not to mention other bed bugs like pubic lice. She reminded Jane of the Southern saying "rode hard and put up wet." I don't ever want to look like that.*

Jane remembered the love she and Johnny had made last night and smiled. If she had her way, she would repeat that expression of love for the man she married many times.

"I've been living in the area that folks say the "little people" live in all my life. I've never seen them," Jane answered. "And I don't want to see them." She noticed that the conversation about "little people" had caught Johnny's interest, and he was listening intently.

"Well, I seen them," the man with this rough woman said. "They ugly little creatures and mean. Lawdy, they mean. They wiped out an entire party of Indians one time. This old Choctaw chief told me 'bout it. He did. They hide in nooks and crannies or caves. Why, if the Confederates had let them help, we'd have give 'em Yankees a whipping that they wouldn't never forgot. My ole daddy said he'd seen some of 'em living in a large hole in the earth. He said they shrieked like owls and made menacing movements with their arms and hands. He said that they always got what they wanted because they scared people to death."

Jane thought of the owl's shriek that she and Victoria heard on the way to French Camp. She thought of how frightened she and Victoria had been. "Have you ever heard them?" Jane asked.

"Naw, but my daddy don't lie," she said. "Well, unless he's 'liquored up' on moonshine." She laughed loudly as if being "liquored up" was a prize. "I was hoping I'd see some of 'em little people. They do magic. I hear tell."

"Well, I hope I don't see any of them," Johnny replied. "I ain't looking for them. Folks around here sure are superstitious."

"Well, son, where you from?" the man asked. He didn't sound amused.

"Picayune and New Orleans," Johnny answered. "Folks are superstitious there too, but not me."

Jane looked surprised. *New Orleans? That was the first time she had heard Johnny say that he was from New Orleans.* She thought. After he said that, her feeling of mistrust was stronger, and she had wished Marie Laveau had gone back to New Orleans. Well, it was a large city. Maybe she wouldn't run in to her, and the folks at the Inn said she was busy healing people of yellow fever.

They had finished their breakfast, so Jane carried Johnny and her dirty plates to the large, blue granite dishpan in the kitchen of the Inn. "We better get going before the "little people" get up." She winked at Johnny.

"Awe, honey, they roam at night. I guess they can see in the dark," the rough looking woman said. "I heard that they were like rabbits and constantly had sex with whoever was available."

Jane and Johnny loaded Charlie's basket into the buggy. Johnny checked for the gold brick in the secret compartment while Jane carried the pile of quilts that they had borrowed back into the Inn.

Then Johnny hitched the horse to the buggy. All seemed to be fine, so they crawled into the buggy and headed south. Once they had gotten about a mile down the trail, Jane said, "Mrs. Foote packed us some food for the trip. That was very nice of her."

"Yes, it was. They seemed like very nice folks."

"Johnny, you never told me that you were from New Orleans," Jane said. It was more a question because she wanted to know why he hadn't told her.

"Really? Well, I guess it never came up," Johnny told her. About that time Charlie woke for his feeding, so Jane dropped the conversation for now. *She didn't know if it would have made a difference to her if she'd known earlier, but Johnny's secretiveness was the reason she worried about trusting him.*

They rode on all day only meeting travelers walking or riding back up north. No one mentioned anything about seeing bandits or being robbed, so Jane felt better. They rode past different land marks that she had heard Mr. Petey talk about like Confederate cemeteries and other Confederate relics. When Johnny decided to stop that night, they were at Port Gibson Inn. "I want us to get a bed tonight. Sleeping in the buggy or on the hay and then riding all day long, will make old age come on fast. I need a place to wash up. I haven't seen a creek or water hole since we left Raymond. Well, nothing except that slough back a ways," Johnny said

"A good night's sleep would be grand, but until we do something with that gold, I don't think that's possible" Jane said. "You really seem worried about the gold."

"When we get to Picayune, I'm going to take that gold brick to the New Orleans Mint. They have security. I read in the *Times*

Picayune that they coin a large quantity of silver every year. Silver dollars. I heard they store them in the building instead of circulating them. Maybe we could make a trade of gold for silver coins. Then whenever we spent them, it wouldn't be so obvious. President Hayes appointed a Mississippi Senator as superintendent of that mint, Henry S. Foote. I wonder if he's related to those nice folks at Raymond Inn?"

"I read about that in the newspaper, too," Jane said. "I heard they didn't produce high quality coins. Can you trust them?"

"Well, I can make them afraid of me" Johnny said. "And we have to trust somebody because that gold brick has got to be melted. They won't mess with me."

"How?" Jane asked. "How can you make them afraid of you. You don't even carry a gun."

"Honey, never you mind. I won't do anything unless it is necessary."

If that was supposed to make me feel more secure. It did not. Jane thought.

Port Gibson Inn was the next inn on the trail that they had come to since leaving Raymond. Since they left before the others, Jane felt that they would be able to get a bed. The problem was as before, the gold, but worse than that was sleeping with Johnny. That was a problem that weighed on her. Since they had ridden all day in the wagon, Jane was famished and tired.

"If you will stop in the next swampy area, I'll gather some greens for us to eat. So when he stopped, Jane climbed down from the wagon and gathered corn salad, bittercress, and lamb's quarters. To this she added wild garlic. She washed the greens and mixed them together, seasoning them with wild garlic. They had salad.

"So you could survive in the woods and swamps without food," Johnny said. "I'm impressed."

They rode into Port Gibson before night fall. Jane noticed a cemetery on the right. Some of the graves had beautiful and colorful flowers growing on them and the others had weeds. Jane believed that those with weeds growing on them had been evil people. That is what Granny had always said. This cemetery was scrapped as clean as the one in French Camp where the Confederate gold was hidden except for the graves that had flowers or weeds, so Jane held her breath as they rode past. She didn't want to inhale the spirit of an evil woman who had been buried in black, had weeds on her grave, and had come back to haunt the cemetery.

Reaching Port Gibson just at supper time, Jane and Johnny placed Charlie in their room and took turns washing up. Jane surveyed the room while Johnny was bathing. Then she turned to view Johnny's body. He was muscular and toned. His stomach was rippled and tight as if he worked as hard as a farmer.

When he caught her looking at him, she turned her attention back to the room.

The walls were covered with tiny pink flowered, gray paper over tongue and groove board walls. Some of the paper was falling off the walls. The curtains were ancient lace, but Jane felt that one time they had been beautiful. The furniture in the room was homemade. There were two single beds. This delighted Jane, so for another night she didn't have to sleep in the same bed with Johnny. Johnny had put the gold brick in his leather bag with his extra clothing, so he moved it inside.

Well, I did give it to him as a present. She thought. She picked up Charlie to nurse him and again he felt feverish. He had gotten some teeth and nursing made her sore, but not so sore that Johnny's lips on her nipples wouldn't excite her. Perhaps his fever was caused by his teething. So she picked some cottonwood buds to make some cottonwood salve to rub on her sore nipples.

To alleviate Charlie's fever, she used one of Shug's herb and kerosene poultices on a folded cloth on his chest to help with the fever and clear any congestion. She pinned it to his diaper shirt. He had no other symptoms of yellow fever, and she had searched his little body for a mosquito bite. She thought about what Mr. Charlie at the livery had said. *Po' folks dying before they knew they even had the yellow fever.* She found no bites.

Shug's poultices seemed to help his fever. *Jane so wished that Johnny hadn't told those bandits that Charlie was sick. He'd come down with a fever soon after they left. She wasn't totally superstitious, but some things she never did or said, especially if her grandmother or mother hadn't done or said them either.*

Finally, Johnny returned from the bath, and she went to take hers. She had brought baking soda to add to the water to ward against yellow fever. It was a remedy she had heard that some people used. Instead of leaving Charlie with Johnny, she took him into the water closet with her. "I've got to bathe him." She told Johnny who didn't seem to mind. He didn't act too fond of Charlie anyway, or Jane didn't offer him to him to hold.

"He's got fever again, but I made another poultice, so I'm going to bathe him to reduce his fever, too." Jane took the basket containing the sleeping Charlie and walked down the hallway.

Quickly she bathed the baby and herself. She stood and put Charlie back into the basket. The bath made her feel more relaxed and fresher smelling, and Charlie's fever seemed to subside.

She never wanted people to think she was nasty like the unkept woman she had seen at the Inn, but clearly she had enjoyed the sex she'd had with Johnny. As she sat back in the tub of water, she rubbed her hands over her long legs, her firm breasts and her erect nipples, and let them come to rest between her legs. She remembered the electricity that Johnny's touch had caused in her body. It was so much more fulfilling than she could cause herself.

***

When she returned to their room, Johnny said the woman had said that supper was ready and that all present should eat together. *It* must be something *they all did.* Jane thought.

"I'm famished," Jane said. *I'm so much hungrier these days because I am nursing Charlie. My figure is snapping back quickly, so I feel just about like I did before I got pregnant by Huerta at that voodoo ritual.*

Jane shuddered at that thought. That was a horrible memory that she tried not to think about and large parts of what happened to her she still couldn't remember. Johnny had never asked her who Charlie's father was. *Somehow she felt that he already knew or didn't really care.* She didn't know which.

They seated themselves around the large wooden, pine table at Port Gibson Inn. Jane set Charlie's basket nearby so that she could see him. *The poultice had helped break his fever. The innkeeper brought each one of the guests their plates of food and a large glass of sweet tea. This innkeeper didn't ask what they wanted either. I guess it was "take it or leave it", too.* Jane thought.

They were served purple hull peas cooked with salt pork, game stew, and biscuits. Since Jane was starving, she didn't even ask what kind of stew it was. It contained meat, potatoes, onions, and tomatoes. What kind of meat she didn't really know. They had napkins made of well-worn pillow ticking. They were folded beside each person's plate. A stack of them rested in a basket in the center of the table. She and Johnny placed their napkins in their laps, but Jane noticed that none of the other guests even touched their napkins.

"They got an outbreak of yellow fever down south of here. It is really bad in New Orleans," one guest said. "Folks are dying by the hundreds. That woman Marie Laveau can cure it, so folks are flocking to her for help."

With the mention of Marie Laveau's name, Jane began to listen intently. That meant that Marie Laveau was back in New Orleans.

"Marie Laveau? That voodoo woman?" A woman asked. Jane noticed that this woman wore a single blue bead on a black cord around her neck. This was supposed to ward off witches according to superstition. "I heard that she was a witch. That Marie Laveau. I heard she had thousands of folks gathered at a Lake Ponchartrain at one of her voodoo rituals." The woman fingered the blue bead.

"I don't know much about voodoo," an elderly gentleman said. "But I heard that she also imports liquor and runs a brothel. She's a very well-known woman in New Orleans. Folks say she is very wealthy. She even goes to the prisons to visit with the prisoners, and she is a hairdresser for the rich, white folks. Some folks think she's a voodoo priestess, and I'd say with a gathering of thousands of folks, she's on her way."

"Did you say that she can cure yellow fever?" another man asked. "Well, in that case, why are so many folks dying from it?"

"What I said was that the folks she treats who have yellow fever usually live. They don't have it again. I heard she bathes them in an alkaline bath and gives them herbs and used poultices and gris gris."

"What are gris gris?" The first woman asked.

"Lawd, I thought that everybody knew what gris gris was. They are voodoo charms or spells. That's what makes her a witch," she added.

All this talk of Marie Laveau had ruined Jane's supper. "Please excuse me. The baby," She got up to leave the table on the pretense of changing Charlie's diaper.

"I never bothered a sleeping baby," the woman said. "Never did. If a baby's sleeping, he's doing fine if you ask me."

Chapter 30

Jane watched out the window as Johnny housed the horse in the barn at Port Gibson where, like before, it was fed and watered. There were three horses in the barn already, and the buggies were parked outside.

Then Johnny came into the room to go to bed. Jane had stayed in their room since supper. Charlie woke again to nurse and again Jane was glad that his fever has left. She changed him into a clean diaper and made him comfortable again in the basket that she used to transport him. She left him in this basket to sleep. The closeness of its sides seemed to make him feel comfortable. *Every time she used the basket, she thought of the story of Moses.* Then she reapplied the cottonwood salve to her breasts, and she hoped that Johnny wouldn't mind the salve because her nipples were tender. It was a remedy that seemed to help the soreness.

Jane slowly disrobed while Johnny watched. Her passion increased as Johnny's eyes caressed her body. Her salved nipples became erect, and she slipped under the covers with Johnny. She snuggled her hot body against him, and he rolled her over and kissed her running his tongue deeply into her mouth.

Then he moved to her breasts, and the salve didn't even slow him down. He nibbled, sucked and lightly bit them even with the salve on them. Jane forgot about the salve and thought about the feelings

Johnny was causing in her body. The more he fondled her breasts and nibbled on them; the more excited she became.

Finally, she moved on top of Johnny and guided him into her. He filled her completely. She moved on top of him and rubbed her mound on him while he thrust into her. She rubbed her firm breasts on his chest and let her nipples tease him. Suddenly she burst into a climatic explosion. Then Johnny did. They both fell asleep after being satisfied.

***

Early the next morning they again headed south in the buggy. This time she carried bread and biscuits that she had smuggled out of the kitchen. This innkeeper hadn't been as nice as Mrs. Foote, so smuggling was the best way to get some food for their trip.

"Where are we going to live when we get to Picayune?" Jane asked Johnny.

"First, we are going on to New Orleans to the New Orleans Mint. We have got to get this gold bar melted. Then we'll have some money to rent a place. Then we will look for somewhere to live."

Jane definitely didn't want to live in New Orleans. That was Marie Laveau's headquarters. *Of course, Marie Laveau's league of informers will tell her that we are there the moment we enter the city.* She thought.

Johnny drove their buggy through the city easily as if he knew exactly where he was going. Apparently, he didn't need a map. He drove up to the front door of the New Orleans Mint without even having to ask for directions. Although Jane hadn't seen it before it looked refurbished. There was a sign outside that read something about the Bland-Allison Act. Jane waited in the buggy with Charlie and the gold brick while Johnny went inside.

A group of black, freed slaves surrounded Jane and Charlie in the buggy. The chattered incessantly, but Jane couldn't make out what they were saying, so she just smiled and looked at them, trying to read their lips. Finally, she realized that they were talking about Charlie. They looked very excited.

Finally, Johnny came back to the buggy. He shooed the crowd of free, black slaves away from the buggy. But shooing them away didn't lessen their excitement.

Jane was glad Johnny asked them to disperse. She couldn't understand them. Their language was foreign to her, and they didn't act like they could understand her. It was as if they knew something that she didn't know. They didn't seem like they were trying to harm her. It was like she was magnetized.

"I don't see how those folks work inside there. I think there are about forty-something women working in that Mint. They sit along long, narrow tables and use scales to measure the precious metals. There is no air in there or open windows. I guess wind would change the scales because the windows and the doors are shut. Everything needs to be precise. Needless to say, it is hot as hell in there. I don't see why they don't die from heat exhaustion," Johnny said. He took the wrapped gold brick out of its hiding place.

"Are they going to melt our gold brick?" Jane asked.

"Yes, I got someone to say that it will get melted, so we are going to leave it with her today," Johnny said. "I already knew her, so I trust her. Her name is Matilda Mason. She used to go the Baptist church in Picayune where I directed the choir."

Jane didn't ask any of the details, but she did remember the name Matilda Mason. *I'm just glad I didn't tell him about all the gold at one time.* She thought.

Johnny took the gold brick, still wrapped like a present, inside; Jane waited in the buggy with Charlie. As soon as Johnny left her in the buggy by herself, the freed slaves congregated around her buggy again. They seemed to want a glimpse of her baby, Charlie.

"Baby special," one of them said in English. "Caul," another one said.

"How did you know?" Jane asked, very surprised.

"Ah, we felt it," she said. She placed her hand over her heart. "Special, all knowing baby."

Chapter 31

Johnny and Jane found a small house in New Orleans for rent. It was already sparsely furnished and still had bed linen and kitchen utensils. The previous owner had died of yellow fever. *The rent wouldn't be due until next week, so the gold should be melted by then.* She thought.

"Aren't you afraid that we'll contract yellow fever?" Jane asked.

"No," Johnny answered. "Not unless we are bitten by a mosquito. You heard what the folks at the Inn said and the post rider. They said you got it from a mosquito bite."

"Yes, and I also heard them say that only Marie Laveau was able to cure it. Well, I don't believe that she is better than the doctors and hospitals here. Do you?" Jane had settled Charlie inside his basket. She knew that he would soon be too big for this basket. Maybe they could get him a crib by then.

"She may be. Let's get this place cleaned up and livable. It looks like it hasn't been cleaned for years. There's an extra room for Charlie. Let's start with it," Johnny said. *Jane thought that he avoided the subject of Marie Laveau.*

Jane went into the bedroom that was to be Charlie's. It was sparsely furnished with only a small single bed and a rocking chair. Johnny brought the rocking horse and Charlie's bag in from the buggy and set it in that room. Jane found a straw broom and began cleaning the floor, making dust fogging. Perhaps it was a good omen. The former occupants had not taken the broom with them, but left it for her. Next, she got some damp cloths and dusted the bed frame and the rocking chair. She took an old rug that covered the floor in front of the side of the bed outside and beat it with a long stick. Dust boiled from the rug. Jane decided to leave it outside to air and sunshine. She moved it to the end of the clothes line and placed the feather mattress out in the warm sunshine too.

Then she dragged the mattress from the other double bed and put it out to sun too. She brought in fire wood and started the stove burning to heat water to clean.

Next, she started cleaning the kitchen. She found a large pot and some lye soap and set it to boil on the wood stove. Carefully, she took each of the dishes from the cabinet and dipped them in the boiling water and rinsed them in a gray granite dish pan of cooler water. Then she spread them out on a counter to dry.

"I'd better go get us some food," Johnny said. "I know where there's a market."

He didn't take the horse and buggy. He had tied the horse in the yard and then rolled the buggy inside the gate behind the tall, wooden fence.

Jane sat down to rest while Johnny wasn't there. *He really did know a lot about New Orleans.* She felt like her eyelids burned and her scalp tingled. *I wonder if he planned to come to New Orleans all the time or if my giving him that gold brick caused that? I don't feel like doing anything about it now. I feel feverish.* She thought.

It was almost supper time before Johnny came back with vegetables and fruit for supper. "I'm not feeling well," Johnny said. "I think I have fever. I'm going to go lie down to rest. I'll get hay for the horse and flour, meal, salt, and meat tomorrow."

***

By the time morning came, all three of them had yellow fever. Jane moved Charlie into her bed so that she could nurse him and change his diaper, although her fever had dried up most of her milk. She didn't feel strong enough to stand. She did hand some fruit and water to Johnny, so he wouldn't become dehydrated. She had never seen anyone as sick as Johnny was.

At dusk, a neighbor knocked on the door and asked to buy the horse. Jane was so sick that she didn't have the strength to say *no*. And she didn't have any money, so payment for the horse would get them food and rent and perhaps herbs and kerosene for poultices to help ward off the yellow fever. *I should have brought some of those gold coins, but I didn't think it would take a long time to get that gold brick melted.* Jane thought. *I didn't want to bring all the gold here. I saved some for later like my survival insurance.*

The same neighbor later came in to take care of them. Her name was Juicy. Jane felt that this woman was a spy for Marie Laveau and in her feverish state one night, Jane thought that Marie Laveau herself had been in the house instructing the woman on what to do. Jane dreamed that Marie was doing a voodoo ritual over Charlie:

Serpent, serpent- ole
Damballah Queen of the Voodons
You are a serpent,
Serpent, serpent-ole.

"Where is the gold?" Marie asked Jane, mopping her feverish brow with a cold, wet cloth.

"Leave my baby alone," Jane said.

"Charles is not just your baby, Catherine Jane Lynch. He also belonged to my husband. I heard you say so yourself; therefore, he is part mine. I will make a voodoo prince of him. He is already special. A caul baby. People are already drawn to him. Did you not see those freed slaves at the New Orleans Mint? You finish nursing him. He needs to be treated like royalty. He is royalty. His father, Huerta, was a king in Africa."

"Where is the gold?"Marie demanded.

Having high fever and feeling like she was dreaming, Jane answered, "Johnny left it at the New Orleans Mint to be melted with a woman named Matilda Mason. And Victoria took hers to Memphis."

"You mean that little friend of yours, Victoria, helped you?" Marie asked her. She sounded delighted to know that there was more available gold. "When did Johnny say that it would be ready?"

Was she dreaming?

"He didn't say," Jane replied or talked in her sleep. She watched as Marie Laveau took great care of Charlie, trying to get him to eat and drink. They had bathed him in baking soda solution every day. He seemed to be getting better, but they did not stop bathing him. Three times a day they fed him goat's milk with water because the fever had dried Jane's breast milk.

Jane suspected that they had added herbs to the goats' milk, too.

The woman filled a tub with water and sat it in the sun behind the wooden, board fence to warm. Then she poured in baking soda and added herbs to it. Jane was told to bathe Charlie in it and then to bathe herself. She did as she was instructed. Johnny was too sick to stand, so Jane dipped some of the warm water from the tub into a basin and carried it inside to bathe Johnny.

They were sick for five days. Each day the water was changed and each day Jane bathed herself, Charlie, and Johnny. The two of them seemed to be improving, but not Johnny. His fever was making him delirious. Each day a funeral wagon came down the street to pick up those who had died from yellow fever. They yelled, "Give us your dead for burying." It was an eerie sound that sent chills through Jane even through the fever. Finally on the sixth day, Jane and Charlie were better. Johnny had died in the night.

Not knowing what else to do, Jane let Johnny's body get picked up by the funeral wagon. They said that they would carry it to a large trench in the New Orleans cemetery and bury him with the other bodies they picked up that day. The marker would say that he died of yellow fever.

Jane realized that Johnny had tricked her into coming to New Orleans. He had even rented a house next to Marie Laveau's. None of what he had done had been an accident. He knew what he was doing.

Jane watched out the window as day after day a stream of people flocked to the house of Marie Laveau. They camped out in front of her house. When they saw Marie, they tried to get to her. They pushed and shoved and trampled on each other to get a glimpse of her. They acted like she was a famous person, and she was. She was getting more famous each day. When she entered a room, her presence and sexuality drew people to her. Jane hoped that they didn't see Laveau coming to and from her house. That hadn't been a dream.

She wanted privacy. *Then she thought of the freed slaves who had flocked around the buggy when she and Charlie were outside the New Orleans Mint waiting for Johnny. Would Charlie be like Marie? They said they knew he was a caul baby. Could that make him famous?*

The next evening Marie came to Jane's house carrying food and drinks of herb teas. Jane was so famished, and there was nothing in the house to eat. She brought all kinds of vegetables and a chicken. She brought spices, herbs, and medicines.

"Jane, I want to have Charles christened as a Catholic."

"You've been here all the time. You are the reason Charlie and I survived," Jane told her. "Why? Why did you save me?"

"I help people. Not harm them," Marie Laveau said. "Besides, I've got plans for you young lady. We live in the French Quarter, the best-known part of the city. Your loose morals will fit just fine in my brothel."

Chapter 32

"Brothel? I can't work in a brothel?" Jane cried. *Without the horse and buggy, the gold, and Johnny, Charlie and I are at the mercy of Marie Laveau.* She thought. I'm getting that gold, so then we can go back to Kilmichael. I'm not staying here. Jane didn't know how, but she would keep Charlie safe, but she wouldn't work in a brothel. *Well, if she did, she would sweep floors or something.*

"When you get well, you will work three days and four nights each week. Working in a brothel is hard work, so you will need to have your strength back. Keep doing the baking soda baths. Go outside each day in the sunshine to get some color into your cheeks. I will bring you some fancy clothes to wear especially some sexy lingerie. I've looked at yours. They are too shabby for that kind of work. You need to look attractive to my customers. You are at my mercy now. You will do whatever I tell you to do if you want to see Charles every day," Marie said.

Apparently, Marie didn't have plans for Jane to sweep the floors at the brothel.

"You mentioned Baptism of Charles. I do not mind that. I want him to be Baptist or Catholic," Jane said. *It will be better to appear to go along with her than to fight her until I can get me and Charlie away from here.* Jane thought. *She can never know that I am frightened by her and her voodoo followers.*

"His Baptism is this next Sunday. This is the day the Church celebrates the paschal Mystery. The Baptism should be done in the communal celebration in the presence of the faithful in the church and his relatives, friends, and neighbors who are all to take an active part in the ceremony. You be ready," Marie said. "You will present Charlie to the Church of St. Louis Cathedral for baptism."

"How can you be Catholic and a voodoo priestess at the same time?" Jane asked.

"Let me worry about that, Missy," Marie Laveau said.

***

The Sunday of the Baptism, Jane and Marie Laveau went to the St. Louis Cathedral. When they entered, the people were already singing hymns and the priest was dressed in an alb with a festive-colored stole accompanied the ministers at the entrance of the church where Jane and Marie Laveau were told to wait with Charlie.

They greeted all present and welcomed Charlie as a gift from God.

The celebrant asked, "What name do you give your child?"

"Charles Laveau," Marie answered before Jane could say anything. Jane didn't object to him being named Laveau.

"What do you ask of God's Church for Charles?" the celebrant asked.

"Baptism," Marie answered. "We ask that Charles Laveau be baptized." As usual, Marie was dressed in a flowing white linen dress and a colorful scarf around her head.

"Do you clearly understand what you are undertaking?" the celebrant asked.

"We do," Marie answered. A large smile spread across her face.

I don't. Jane thought. She didn't know what else to do, except remain silent. Marie Laveau frightened her to death, especially since she felt stranded in New Orleans.

"Charles Laveau, the Christian community welcomes you with great joy, in his name I claim you for Christ our Savior by the sign of his cross. I now trace the cross on your forehead, and invite your parent and godparent to do the same."

The celebrant drew a cross on Charles's forehead, in silence. Then he asked Jane and Marie Laveau to do the same.

They did.

Then he read Psalm 84: 7-9 aloud to everyone in the church: They go "from strength to strength; Each one appears before God in Zion. O Lord God of hosts, hear my prayer; Give ear, O God of Jacob! Se'lah "O God, behold out shield, And look upon the face of Your anointed. After this scriptural readings and prayers were said in unison. Others in the church read along in unison.

After the invocation, the celebrant said, "Almighty and ever-lasting God, you sent your only Son into the world to cast out the power of Satan, spirit of evil, to rescue man from the kingdom of darkness, and bring him into the splendor of your kingdom of light. We pray for this child: set him free and send him the spirit of the Holy Spirit."

Jane could stand this no longer. She didn't understand why Marie Laveau, if she believed in voodoo, wanted Charles to be baptized. Was she religious or Satanic? She fainted into a puddle on the floor of the church.

No one moved to help her. When she awoke, she saw a lighted candle in Marie Laveau's hand. Then the celebrant said the Lord's Prayer. He blessed them all.

Chapter 33

Marie Laveau drove the buggy to her brothel with Jane in tow. It was 9 o'clock in the morning. The brothel was an old, white two story house in the Red Light District of New Orleans. It looked like any other house on this street with a white picket fence and several single horses and horses and buggies tied to a hitching rail out front. There were shrubs and trees around. If it was like the houses Jane saw coming here, it had a courtyard in the back made of bricks and a black iron fence with a gate. Jane couldn't imagine anyone coming by a brothel at that time of day. "You will do everything you are asked to do by Madame Lucille, or you won't ever see your son, Charles, again."

Jane exited the buggy slowly. She wore the frilly, red frock that Marie had brought home for her to wear. She felt so ill at ease. Marie, a famous hair dresser of the rich white folks in New Orleans, had shown Jane how to pile her hair up on the top of her head with three large curls hanging down on the left side of her face. Marie had shown her how to gather her breasts up about the corset to blossom out of the top of the dress. Jane figured that she had gotten the dress from one of her wealthy, white patrons. Jane was more frightened than she had ever been, but she would not lose Charlie to this woman.

The two of them entered the brothel. It was mostly empty except for the woman who ran it, Madam Lucille, and the girls who worked here sitting in the parlor. Jane knew her job would be to entertain the men who frequented the place. *I'm not doing that.* She thought.

Marie had already told her. The lobby had white lace sheer curtains and red velvet curtains. The chairs the girls sat on were covered with red velvet. Over to one side was where liquor was served. *If I 've got to work here, I'll have to drink some of that liquor.*

Then Jane thought about Charlie, staying home with a nanny. Tears filled her eyes. *I was going to apply at the World's Fair Expo Building, the World's Industrial and Cotton Centennial Expo.* She thought. *If I've got to work and be away from Charlie, that is where I wanted to work. Not here. Not in a brothel.*

Jane didn't think that she would be able to do this, so in her pocket, Jane had brought some powdered mushrooms, the kind that caused death. A slight amount caused only sleep.

The woman, Madame Lucille, who was the boss at the brothel showed her where to sit. "You have to do what Madame Lucille tells you to do. You have to do what the customers pay for," Marie said. Marie handed her a list-type menu for the brothel. It contained a list of appetizers, parties, and specialty items. Jane had never experienced anything on the menu. "Get their money first. You can negotiate for a different price if you wish, but you are only here to make money. Remember that. Be sure that you are selling sex. Do not fall in love with any of them. You must bring me all the money you earn each week," Marie said. "You want Charlie do stay safe; don't you."

Jane looked at the girls and women sitting in the parlor waiting for customers to select them to go upstairs to one of the bedrooms. Some of them were younger than Jane, but some were in their forties. All were dressed in frilly, colorful dresses like Jane or their pantaloons and corsets or other sexy lingerie. They wore their hair up in the fashion that Marie had done to hers. Most were over-made-up with make-up. Jane was not.

The room was lavishly decorated with red velvet curtains and ornate features of carved wood. It was so fancy that Jane wondered why Marie Laveau lived as she did in the poor part of town. Two reasons came to her mind: the first was that Marie Laveau didn't want to appear richer than the poor people that she cheated out of their hard earned money when she preformed rituals for them, and the second was that she wasn't the sole owner of this brothel. *Probably, some rich white man in New Orleans owned most of it, and Marie brought in the women to work.* Jane thought. Jane hoped the latter was true because if it was she might be able to get his assistance to get out of New Orleans with Charlie.

Jane picked up a newspaper. The headline read: $ 1,777,000 of Louisiana Money Stolen by Edward A. Burke Fair Building Put on Hold. *That would have ended my dreams of working at the Expo for a while.*

One of the girls said, "Come with me. I'm Sadie." She grabbed Jane's hand and led her through the swinging doors to the back of the room on the first floor.

"Why are you here?" Jane asked the girl.

"Honey child, I've got four kids to feed. So the answer's simple. They would starve to death if I didn't work. My name's not really Sadie. It is Charlotte. What's yours?"

"I'm Jane Lynch," Jane said. "Why change your name?"

"I don't want my kids to hear that I work here," Sadie said.

"Marie Laveau is forcing me to work here. She wants my son. He's eight months old. I've got to get both of us out of New Orleans and away from her. Can you help me?"

"Not with Marie Laveau. She can put a voodoo spell on you," Sadie said. Her eyes got as big as saucers.

"Is there anyone here who's not afraid of her?"

"You ought'a be afraid of her, too. She's got you baby and all."

"Oh, I am, but I don't believe in her voodoo. Most of what she does is fake. She uses voodoo to make money."

"You need to meet Mr. Fares'. He can help you," Sadie said. "He comes in here almost daily. Well, almost. He'll pay you to sit and listen to him. He's a little sad because he'll talk to you like you are his dead wife. Her name was Delia. You just let him call you Delia. That's not all he wants. He wants to caress your naked body, especially your breasts. He's too old to perform, so he will want to have sex with you with his hand and lick and kiss you. Then he wants to sit and have you hold his hand for the rest of the evening. Whatever happens, don't tell him that he is crazy."

Delia Fares'. Jane thought. She looked over the menu of what customers could ask for and the prices that they would pay. Nowhere on the sheet was listening and hand holding. "How much does he pay for you to listen to him?"

"A few hundred a week," Sadie said. "Let's get you dressed or undressed. I bet Marie Laveau is waiting."

Sadie instructed Jane to remove her pantaloons. She loosened Jane's tight hair style. "Men who come in here don't like every hair in place no matter what Marie Laveau says." Jane didn't ask about the pantaloons.

"I feel totally naked," Jane replied. "Will Mr. Fares' come in today?"

"Probably. You just go out and sit with the rest of us until he gets here. Most of the girls avoid him or shun him because they say he's crazy, and they are scared of him. Well, he ain't crazy. Just lonely. I guess all the men who come in here are lonely," Sadie said, laughing. "They pay for someone to pay attention to them."

When Jane and Sadie went back into the parlor, Jane saw a sad, old man sitting on a red chaise. All the other girls had left the room. Sadie took Jane by the hand and introduced her to Mr. Fares'.

"Mr. Fares', this is Delia. She wants to spend some time with you upstairs," Sadie told Mr. Fares'.

"Upstairs?" He looked up and smiled at Jane with a wide grin. He stood and took Jane's hand. He led her up the red, carpeted stairs to a bedroom near the back side of the house. Jane timidly followed. Tears welled in her brown eyes.

He opened the door and instructed Jane to sit on the bed.

She remembered her lack of pantaloons.

"You are very beautiful today, Delia," he said. "But I see the tears. Honey, why are you so sad?" Mr. Fares' asked.

Jane burst out crying more loudly. "It's Marie Laveau. She is trying to take my baby boy, and she is forcing me to work here. Can you help me? Can you help me get out of New Orleans? I need to go back to Mississippi."

For a long time, Mr. Fares' sat on the bed beside Jane. He held her hand and patted the top of it. He looked longingly at her.

"I'm assuming that you don't have any money and that is why you are working here. What is it you need besides money? A horse and buggy perhaps?"

"Yes, Jane replied. "And someone to travel with us up the trail. That trail that they are calling the Natchez Trace is dangerous with Indians and bandits. If you can help me get back to Kilmichael, Mississippi, I can pay you back there. I have money there."

"I don't want your money."

"You can't leave dressed like this. You will stand out too much," Mr. Fares' said. "You are so beautiful that everyone will notice. I would to like to see you naked myself."

"I've got some clothing downstairs," Jane said quickly, but she didn't tell him it was pantaloons. "Maybe Sadie will bring it to me."

"I'll ask her," he said.

Mr. Fares' went out the door and back down the stairs to where Sadie sat in the parlor. He had left the door slightly ajar, but Jane couldn't even hear his soft footsteps on the stairs. He appeared to be a mild-mannered man.

Within a few seconds, both he and Sadie came back inside the bedroom door. Sadie carried Jane's pantaloons stuffed under her dress.

"These aren't the kind of clothing I had in mind," Mr. Fares' said. "I meant less fancy clothing."

"I cannot stay in here," Sadie said. "If Marie Laveau finds out that I helped you escape, she will put a hex on me." With that, she turned and left the room.

"Put your pantaloons on," Mr. Fares' said. He watched for a glimpse of her naked. "Climb out that bedroom window after dark tonight and then down the trellis that holds up the running rose bush. Until then, I'll stay in here with you. When you get outside, hide in the back of my buggy, and I'll take you to Marie Laveau's house tonight to get your baby. She will be dancing in the Square until midnight and having an orgy, like she usually does on Saturday nights. You can't miss it. She'll have a large bonfire. Who will be at her house taking care of your baby?" he asked. He walked over to the window and looked outside.

Jane pulled her pantaloons on under the cover of her long dress. "I don't know who she left at home with Charlie. Possibly, she carried him with her to the Square near St. Louis Cathedral. He is only eight months old.

"She won't have him at the Square unless she has someone there watching him." Mr. Fares' said.

"I'm loaning you a horse and buggy and my son to travel back up the trace to Kilmichael, Mississippi, with you. You can pay him when you get home, and he can return here with the buggy and payment. It is very obvious from your demeanor that you don't belong in a brothel. You are a very nice girl who is stranded in New Orleans."

"I do appreciate your taking the time to help me. Tell me about your Delia."

"First, let me tell you about my son who will be your traveling companion. He was a baseball player with the Gulf League, but he injured his ankle and can't play until it is healed. His name is James Fares'. When you get into the buggy tonight, he will be the driver. I'll instruct him to drive pass the Square near St. Louis Cathedral to make certain that Laveau is there and that your baby isn't," Mr. Fares' said. "You will need to disguise yourself, but he will help with that."

Jane was frightened, but grateful. She wanted to be back home in Kilmichael again. She missed her brother Tommy, Shug and Mr. Petey and even Granny.

"I will tie a red scarf on the horse's bridle, so you'll know my buggy and my son will help you. Remember his name is James."

***

Finally, the sun set and Mr. Fares' left the brothel. Jane waited an hour and then gathered her long skirt up around her waist and climbed out the window onto the rose trellis. As carefully as she could, she climbed down the trellis, trying to hold the long tail of the fancy red dress. When she was even with the top of the first floor, her dress got hung on a nail on the trellis. She slipped and her dress pulled over the top of her head, leaving her hanging in the air with her pantaloons shining.

Finally getting untangled from the trellis she looked toward the ground or the courtyard below, and saw a man waiting for her on the ground under the trellis. *I've been caught trying to escape.* She thought.

After a few seconds, the skirt tore and Jane dropped to the ground near his feet. She stood quickly and her skirt fell to her ankles. The man took her arm, and she heard only the swooshing of her skirt as they walked toward the buggy. "I'm James Fares'," he said as he helped her into the back of the buggy and covered her with a black blanket. "We don't want you to be recognized."

"I'm Jane Lynch." Jane watched him by peeking out from under the blanket as he limped to the front of the horse and untied the red scarf. He started the horse down the street. She was so glad that the man was James Fares' and not one of Marie Laveau's informants.

He stopped around the corner out of sight of the front of the brothel and said, "Miss Lynch, you may get up on the seat now, but wrap the blanket around yourself so you won't be noticed. We are driving to the Square near St. Louis Cathedral to see if Marie Laveau is still dancing. It is Mardi gras. Let me warn you. She may be doing more than dancing."

Chapter 34

During Mardi gras, it seemed that everyone in New Orleans changed their identities except Marie Laveau. She stayed the same. She dressed in the long, white linen tunics and skirts that flowed in the breeze and wrapped her hair in that colorful scarf. It was a profitable time for her. Many of her followers asked her for potions: love potions and hexes. During Mardi gras, white people rubbed paint on their skin to appear black, and black people dusted themselves with flour to appear white. Everyone seemed to want to experience the life of someone else. Many of her followers wore masks that resembled the ones worn in Africa by voodoo dancers. Beggars dressed like rich men and rich men like beggars. Virgins acted like ladies of the night and ladies of the night like saints. Everyone partook of spirits and got intoxicated.

When Jane was a little girl, she often wished that she had been someone else when Tom Lewis was pulling one of his stunts. Mama said that he couldn't help it, but Jane wondered because whenever they carried him to the doctor, for a few days, he could keep it together. One time the doctor in Kilmichael said that nothing was wrong with him. *If he only knew.* Jane thought. *I wonder if Tom Lewis has ever been to New Orleans and Mardi Gras.*

During Mardi gras, risks were taken by everyone at the celebration and most shed their inhibitions. The crowd was made up of freed slaves, slaves, the white people of New Orleans and people who wanted Marie's help with a problem. It didn't surprise Jane that Marie Laveau chose this night to increase her influence of voodoo on the people of New Orleans. Marie became more famous during Mardi Gras than she had been before.

James drove the buggy down a street close enough to the Square to see Marie standing naked on a platform stage and behind her Jane could see St. Louis Cathedral. Jane smelled the smoke from the large bonfire that lit up the night sky. Jane had the feeling that he'd done this many times before. She felt that he was very familiar with Marie. The hot, popping fire was hypnotic and the naked dancing women and men enticing. Mix in some alcohol and some of Marie Laveau's herbs, and she had control of throngs of people who worshiped her. As Jane watched, she saw people in the crowd that acted as bouncers or Marie Laveau's bodyguards.

In the background, Jane heard shouts, screams, and then the resonant voice of Marie Laveau loud above the others. There were drums beating a steady rhythm, but her voice sounded above everything else. There was an ancient looking man from Guinea who had played drums in Africa, who played for Marie Laveau at her performances. His music was hypnotic. Her sexuality was hypnotic. Then she saw Charlie bound to Marie's back with a white linen cloth. She wore nothing else and her large breasts swayed as she danced. This was the way women in Africa carried their babies with them while they worked. Shug had shown her how to wrap the long piece of fabric. Charlie looked to be asleep. Perhaps the rhythm of the drums or movement of Marie Laveau's dancing had lulled him to sleep. Marie swayed across the wooden platform to a large, bluish gray wooden box.

Gracefully, she reached inside the box and took out a huge snake. Jane knew that it was a python because she had heard Marie discuss it at home, but the crowd didn't. Marie danced and swayed as she let the python wrap around her and Charlie, too.

"Oh my," Jane said to James. "Now, you see why I have to get my baby away from this woman. That snake could kill him."

James nodded in agreement, mesmerized. "But I don't think she will harm Charlie."

The people in the crowd screamed and strutted like Banty roosters with their chests and tails stuck out as if they had tail feathers. "This is her trick," James said. "Nothing during Mardi Gras is quite what it seems. Marie Laveau included. Illusion is sometimes necessary. That is what voodoo is all about. Illusions of power. I've watched her perform before. She is very convincing, and then she takes a collection like they do at church. That is how she earns some of her money. She pretends she is overcome by a god she calls Damballah. The crowd really becomes obsessed with her charms and spells.

"But, I still have to remove Charlie from her influence before she turns him into a voodoo king or gets him killed. That is her intention," Jane whispered. "She wants my baby to be a voodoo king and replace her when she gets old, so she can still earn money with voodoo."

"Don't be scared, Jane," James said. "We must wait until she brings or sends the baby home tonight. Then we will take him and head toward Kilmichael before she knows what happened. He will be safe then."

"If the bandits don't get us," Jane answered.

He turned to Jane and pulled the dark blanket more tightly around her head. She didn't want Marie or any of the others to recognize her. While he was looking at her directly in the face, he quickly kissed her on the lips. "I know voodoo is an African religion, but I don't really know about some of the practices like worshipping snakes as gods and putting hexes on your enemies or making love potions. By the way, thank you for being so kind to my father. He misses my mother terribly, and you look so beautiful and innocent that I feel like a love potion has been used on me."

"Your father misses your mother so much. He was kind to me, too, and generous," Jane said. "He's a sweet man." She didn't say anything about a love potion.

"We need to get you back to your house before Marie sends Charlie home as most assuredly she will. She usually stops her performance around midnight. I will hide the horse and buggy away from the house and when they get home and the coast is clear, we will leave," James said. "Excuse the kiss. You are just so beautiful."

Chapter 35

Marie Laveau

"This snake is our surprise tonight. The people are eating this up." Marie said to herself. "They think he is a god. Damballah."

Marie handed Charlie to her woman servant, Gigi, motioning for her to take him home now, and then she moved toward the center of the wooden platform. She still had the python wrapped around her naked body. In the crowd, Marie saw the celebrant who had baptized Charles at St. Louis Cathedral. She slightly waved to him. He didn't wave back. He nodded his head to acknowledge that he recognized her.

"The Priest knows better than to believe in charlatans like me," Laveau whispered to herself. "I'm certain that he was just curious because I can draw such a large crowd and he wishes that he could. It couldn't be the naked women or men, could it?"

I guess that he's very threatened. Threatened by the thoughts of the people. The Catholic religion hasn't had a miracle since Christ Jesus arose from the dead. That miracle is the one depicted in the Cathedral stained glass window. Now, the people want and demand something more. Another miracle. Marie thought. *That's why they need, believe in, and pay me. He's not just curious. He's afraid.* She thought.

"Show us a miracle. Show us a miracle," the crowd chanted.

Marie moved to the beat of the drums and danced in the flicker of the firelight. The Mardi Gras crowd applauded. The drums beat louder and louder and faster and faster. Marie glanced at the priest standing defeated on the top steps of the Cathedral. Beside him on the steps of the Cathedral were choir boys swaying silver buckets of burning incense, warding off evil. She wondered if the priest now thought she was a devil. She was glad he had already baptized Charles, less the priest refused to baptize Charles now after viewing her dancing in front of the Cathedral. Or maybe he already knew. Maybe he had seen her before.

The only light on the Square were lighted torches and the firelight from the bonfire. It looked like this entire section of New Orleans was burning down.. Dusk had fallen hours ago. A full moon shone in the night sky. Marie attributed the large crowd to the full moon. She didn't think that she had attracted so many people tonight until she saw them in the moon light. She was the entertainment of tonight in New Orleans. She wondered if the priest had considered this.

She swayed, dancing to the beat of the drums. Then she wrapped her lined dress around her naked body. She stood to dance again. Her billowing, white linen dress flowed and swooshed around her body. Her head wrap came undone and flowed in the wind, making her look like an ethereal creature, ghostly, angelic, and yet sensual. She looked at the beautiful stained glass window of the Cathedral. A light shone behind it. It eerily shone for the drunken Mardi Gras crowd. Christ's arising from the dead was depicted on the lead and colors of the window while Marie's helpers sold voodoo dolls and gris gris right in front of the Cathedral, and she performed for the crowds. She made voodoo dolls and grips Gris for sale.

Marie kept dancing waiting for the spirit of Damballah, the voodoo god, to enter her. Tonight Damballah was taking his own sweet time. Until he showed up, she performed for the crowd as if he was already inside her. She had to have a better miracle than that depicted in the stained glass window, even if hers was fake. The crowd linked their arms and swayed to the rhythm of the drums. The drum's sound was hypnotic as was the glowing embers of the fire.

Marie surveyed the crowd. It was made up of poor black men, mulattoes, and slaves who had slipped away from their masters. There were a few whites and some freed slaves. What did they want from her? What did they expect? She couldn't send them back to Africa or Guinea from where they had come. She was scared. She did feel pride that these black people needed her, believed in her. She wanted to give them a miracle for Damballah.

Her helper chopped the head off a rooster with a sharp axe that he had brought with him and filled a cup with its thick blood. He handed the cup of blood to Marie. She turned it up and drank or pretended to, letting the excess run down her chin and onto her white linen dress. She was drunk with her own power.

Someone in the crowd yelled, "Marie Laveau is a fake." Marie surveyed the Mardi Gras crowd again.

Then Marie knew what to do. She again took the snake out of its box. The people near the front of the crowd tried to touch Marie, but not the snake. They backed up when she wrapped the snake around her shoulders. Its skin felt clammy and cold next to hers.

The crowd swayed and danced. They were still naked, although Marie had gotten dressed. Tensions ran high and several small groups fought-black and white, women and men, freed and slaves. In the distance, Marie saw the priest walking back and forth on the church steps. Still the crowd pressed closer to the platform as he paced. They paid no attention to him.

Marie made some loud, high pitched sounds and fell to her knees. She let her eyes roll back into her head. Her arms and legs shook and quivered. She stood and staggered under the weight of the snake. She coiled the python around her neck and cried, "Damballah, Damballah." The python stuck out its tongue.

"It will kill you," someone in the crowd shouted. Some of the crowd moved back from the snake. Some moved forward as if expecting a miracle and wanting to touch it. They thought that the snake was poisonous, but their desire for a miracle was stronger than their fear.

Marie moaned and swayed to the rhythm of the drum's beats. She danced with the snake and caressed the length of the snake. She kissed the snake. She threw dust over the crowd. She swayed to the beat of the drums. The crowd was mesmerized, waiting. Waiting for their miracle from Marie Laveau.

She walked to the very front of the platform and kissed the snake again squarely on the lips. Then, to the crowd, she offered the snake's face for them to kiss. They declined, but shouted "Marie Laveau, Damballah, Marie Laveau. Marie Laveau, the voodoo priestess."

Are they possessed or just pretending? She wondered.

"If you see a snake, you see Damballah. I make zombies. Walking dead. Zombies are the undead. Marie Laveau makes undead. Zombies," Marie chanted, hoping to gather the crowd. "If you see a snake, you see Damballah. I make zombies. Walking dead. Zombies are the undead. Marie Laveau makes undead. Zombies." Her voice got louder and more melodious with each phrase.

The crowd chanted and danced. Some just chanted, "Marie Laveau performs a miracle. Marie Laveau performs a miracle."

Some chanted, "Witch. Marie Laveau is a witch. Zombies. Zombies. Marie Laveau is a witch. Witch. Witch. Witch."

Marie knew how to make the living appear dead. Her grandmother had taught her to make the potion by mixing grave dust, dried cat's eyes, and a dead man's bone dust mixed with oil. Marie exited the platform and pulled a man from the audience. She had planted him there earlier. He was wrapped in strips of fabric like a mummy and until now no one had noticed that he looked like a zombie because they were dressed in costume. He looked dirty like he had been buried. She had rubbed him with her oily concoction before she wrapped him up like a mummy, and it slowed his breathing until it was barely noticeable. She made him look like a zombie, almost like a dead man, but he could walk.

"How did you do this?" one man in the crowd shouted. Marie had her helpers pass the collection plate. *I've caused so much fear in the crowd that they are afraid not to put money in it.* She thought. They are afraid that I'll put a zombie hex on them.

I'll never tell. Marie thought. She knocked the zombie to the floor of the platform and threw a cloth over him. Then she laid the python on top of him to protect him from prying hands. It lay stone still. Since the snake wasn't in a cage or wound around Marie now but free, the crowd began to disperse, but before they left, they put something in the collection plate. None of them acted like it wasn't poisonous and wouldn't come after them. They acted unsure. Just the way Marie Laveau had intended. They were mesmerized.

This was what Marie wanted. She was tired. She wanted to go home, kiss Charlie goodnight, and sleep. These rituals really took all her strength and left her listless and ready for sleep.

Chapter 36

Catherine Jane Lynch Tingle

Jane acted like she was in bed asleep when Marie Laveau's servant, Gigi, slipped into the house with Charlie. Now, he was fully awake and hungry, so the servant brought him to Jane to nurse. Jane acted like this woke her. Since having the yellow fever, Jane's breast milk had gotten less and less, but she hadn't let on to Gigi or Marie Laveau who was keeping her around to nurse Charlie. As soon as Gigi left the room, she got a bottle and added water to the goat's milk and fed him. She added some cereal and fed him more than she normally did, so he would go to sleep for a long while before needing to nurse again. Perhaps he would sleep eight hours, giving her and James time to get out of New Orleans. It would be easier for her to sneak him out of the house and into the buggy if he was asleep.

Jane knew Marie's servant often slipped out of the house to visit her boyfriend at night while she wasn't needed to take care of Charlie, and Marie Laveau wasn't home. "Please don't tell Missus," Gigi begged. Jane promised not to tell Laveau that Gigi was leaving the house. *How can I? I won't be here.* Jane thought. Jane felt excited to be leaving New Orleans and secretly, she vowed never to return if she got out alive.

She paced the floor and waited for James to come back after them. Her signal to James that the house was empty or the coast was clear was a lighted candle in her bedroom window, so as soon as Charlie went to sleep she lighted it, pulled the cloth curtains back, and waited for James to rescue her a second time in one night.

She remembered being hungry during her first trip down the trace to New Orleans. So she went into the kitchen to pack some food and more goats' milk for their trip. She packed left-over biscuits, corn bread, and some honey. She found some pork meat that had been fixed for supper and packed it, too. She found some Mason jars and filled them with goat's milk and sweet tea. Remembering her first trip down the Natchez Trace, she didn't want to be without food this time. Foraging for food had been alright then, but that was months ago. Some of the plants would be dead now although sometimes Mississippi winters were mild and sometimes not. As for her other possessions, she packed Charlie's clothes and some diapers. She definitely didn't want that whorish, red, frilly dress that Marie had made her wear to the brothel, so she put on a simple, black, cotton, handmade one that she'd had from school. She didn't take the time to pack any others. Charlie was too big for the basket she had used as a bassinet on the trip down here, so she got a large wooden, apple box with deep sides and put some feather pillows in the bottom of it to soften it. She would have to watch him more carefully now, since he could sit up and crawl.

James pecked softly on her bedroom window with some small pebbles like a lover wanting to be let inside or a teenage boy trying to get his girlfriend's attention without waking her father. She went to the back door in the kitchen to let him inside. If they hadn't been leaving, Jane would have been embarrassed at the disheveled appearance of the house, but tonight she didn't care. The kitchen cabinets had dirty dishes piled up and a large, gray granite dish pan sat on the wood stove waiting for heated water to wash the dishes.

"We are ready. We need to get out of here before Marie comes back. It won't be very long. I would say she's on her way now. She usually gets here a little after midnight. We also need to travel on a side street that she doesn't frequent." Jane said. Her heart raced, but she was thrilled to be getting away from Marie Laveau.

James picked up the wooden, apple box that held the now sleeping Charlie. Carefully, he carried the box outside to the buggy and placed the box on the floor of the buggy where Jane would sit on the front seat beside him. He had left the dark blanket in the buggy for her to wrap around herself until they were out of New Orleans in case they ran into Marie Laveau or some of her league of informants. She didn't need to be recognized.

Quickly, Jane placed her black leather bag of Charlie's clothes and the food pouch into the back of the buggy. She and James got on the front seat, and she wrapped the dark blanket around herself and over her head. She remembered when James had kissed her the last time she had worn it like a shawl. She remembered his lips against hers. The night air was cool and damp, so the blanket felt good against her skin, too, but not as nice as his lips had. She longed to feel his lips on hers again.

"Do you have somewhere that we can stay tonight? Tomorrow I want to go to the New Orleans Mint to get the gold coins that my husband had Matilda Mason melt for us," Jane asked.

"You have gold at the New Orleans Mint?" James asked. "My goodness, Jane, you never cease to amaze me. Of course, we can stay at my home here in New Orleans tonight. You can go to the mint in the morning."

James grabbed the reins, and they started down the street toward his home that happened to be only one block over from the brothel where he had rescued Jane. They drove past the brothel to get to his house.

Once they reached his home, James drove the horse and buggy through the magnolia trees and parked the buggy in the back of what Jane determined was a mansion with large columns on the front. A servant took the buggy reins from James. Then James helped Jane and Charlie walk across an enclosed, manicured courtyard and inside the house. *I wonder how Tom Lewis would have turned out if he had lived like this.* Jane thought.

His home was elaborately decorated in a way that Jane had never seen before and he had servants. She guessed that the décor was French. Jane wondered if he had ever owned slaves. James' house looked the opposite of the houses she had lived in Kilmichael with her mother and Tom Lewis or with Granny. Theirs was built for convenience; the Fares' home for an impression. Now, remembering the way her house and the disheveled kitchen beside Marie Laveau's had looked made her turn red with embarrassment.

Once inside his home, James had a servant show her and Charlie upstairs to their bedroom. In the bedroom, the servant had filled a ceramic basin with water. James' bedroom was across the marble floored hall.

"I'll wake you early in the morning," James said. "Let me take Charlie's milk to the ice box."

Jane handed him the Mason jar of goat milk. "We will need to get more milk tomorrow."

Good night, Jane. We will get more milk tomorrow." He said, taking the milk back downstairs.

***

Early in the morning, there was a tap on Jane and Charlie's bedroom door. Wanting to look lovely to James in the morning, Jane was already dressed and ready to go. She had already fed and bathed Charlie. Jane wasn't certain why she even cared what James thought of her, but she did. She guessed the *why* didn't matter.

"Jane, tell me about this gold that we are going to pick up. Where did you get it and why is it at the New Orleans Mint?" James asked, truly curious. "My servants have breakfast ready. You can tell me all about it during breakfast."

Jane placed Charlie in the wooden, apple box that she'd fashioned for a bassinet and tried to hide her embarrassment for using this box.

James carried the apple box with Charlie inside to the dining room and placed it in a couple of vacant chairs. He pulled another one out for Jane to sit in, and he took one across the table from her. As soon as they were seated, a large, yellow-skinned woman servant brought their breakfast plate of biscuits, bacon, and eggs. James drank coffee and Jane drank freshly squeezed orange juice. It was the first time she had ever had it, and it made her feel rich.

After James placed his napkin in his plate to signal that he had finished eating, James said, "Jane, I'm ready for the story about your gold now."

During the meal, Jane had wondered how much of the story about the gold she should tell James. After all, he was only her driver. Telling Johnny or giving him the gold had not worked out well, so she decided to tell James that she had found the gold brick in a creek near Kilmichael, and that it was Johnny's idea to have it melted into coins. Really, that wasn't a total lie. It really had been Johnny's idea to melt it into coins. She would omit the part of the story about the rest of the Confederate gold she had hidden in the grave box in the Berea cemetery in French Camp and about hiding with Tom Lewis in the Confederate tunnel that opened at the base of the angel statue.

James summoned one of his servants to watch Charlie for Jane until he and she went to the New Orleans Mint. Another servant brought the buggy to the front of the house, and he waited with it under the magnolias. *What is it like to live like this?* Jane thought. *I really do not like leaving Charlie here alone with these servants. Marie Laveau has followers everywhere. I'm certain some of these servants are her followers.*

Jane and James went outside to the front of the mansion and James helped Jane into the buggy. He drove to the Mint on the edge of New Orleans, and he and Jane went inside to summon Matilda Mason, and to get the gold coins or at least silver ones.

The receptionist asked them to kindly wait in the lobby while Matilda Mason was found. They waited for what seemed like an hour until finally a young woman came to the lobby to see them. She wore a printed, cotton dress, her hair wrapped in cloth, and sweat beaded on her forehead and wisps of blond hair slipped out from under the head cloth. Jane remembered Johnny's telling her about how hot it was inside the Mint. Matilda's face reflected the heat.

"Sorry for the delay," she said wiping sweat from her face. "What can I do for you?"

"I am Johnny Tingle's wife. He brought a gold brick to you to be melted into coins. I'm here to pick up the coins," Jane said.

"How do I know that you are Johnny Tingle's wife? I heard that he died of yellow fever," Matilda said.

"He did," Jane said. "He died six days after we got here to New Orleans which was June 2. I had the yellow fever too, so I had to have his body picked up by the funeral wagon. He's buried in the trench with the others in the New Orleans cemetery. There is a marker there with his name on it."

"Well," Matilda said, "I heard that, so I guess you really are his wife. I guess that I can give you his gold, but if I get in trouble with him, I'll find you and you will be sorry."

"I don't think a dead man can cause you any trouble," Jane replied.

"How many coins are there?"

"About 100. I think," Matilda said, still wiping sweat from her eyes with a handkerchief.

"Why don't you keep a few of them for your trouble?" Jane said. James looked at her in disbelief.

Matilda looked pleased and rose to go get Jane's gold.

"How do you know she hasn't already taken some of the gold coins?" James asked.

"It's simple. Johnny threatened her with a hex by Marie Laveau or a voodoo hex by him. I'm going to give her four coins. I believe that she's telling us the truth."

Matilda quickly returned with a bag of coins. She didn't hesitate as she had earlier. Jane opened the bag and without hesitating either, she gave Matilda four coins. The smile that crossed her face lit up the room. Jane didn't know the value of 4 gold coins, but it was evident from her smile that Matilda did.

James and Jane took the bag of coins and went back outside to the buggy. Jane remembered the last time that she'd been here with Johnny. She remembered the freed slaves huddling around the buggy, fascinated by Charlie, her "caul" baby.

They drove as fast as the horse would go back to James' mansion and collected a sleeping Charlie and their meager luggage. Then James drove out of New Orleans being careful to avoid the streets where they might run into Marie Laveau out and about New Orleans. They rode up Canal Street to Julia Street. Then they followed a street along the Mississippi River to Rampart. Glimpses of the Mississippi River with the steamboats intrigued Jane. Finally they were outside of New Orleans in the swamps, and the tiny trails that led to Natchez, Mississippi. The trail would run about 150 miles and take most of the day and on into the night if they drove as fast as possible.

"We will stay part of tomorrow in Natchez if we can make it there by tomorrow night and can find a place to sleep. My aunt owns The Burn on Union Street; well, on the north end. There is no rush, and we don't want you to get over tired, especially since both you and Charlie recently had yellow fever," James said.

"You are so kind," Jane replied. "Tell me a little about yourself. All your father said was that you were a baseball player. I played baseball when I was a kid in the pasture with the people who lived on our farm. That is about the extent of what I know about baseball except that once my brother slung the bat and it hit me in the stomach, knocking the breath out of me."

"Well," James said, "I am or was a baseball player for the Gulf League in Gulfport, Mississippi, but I messed up and twisted my knee and ankle. The coach thought that I only twisted my ankle and that I'd recover quickly. It was my knee, too. I don't think it is getting better. You probably noticed that I limp."

"Yes," Jane said. "It is hardly noticeable. I hope you get well soon. Thank you for being my knight in shining armor."

James grinned a wide grin but said nothing.

***

As they traveled north of New Orleans, they saw people in the streets dressed in costumes who had been celebrating Mardi Gras. "Some of them probably were at Marie Laveau's voodoo ritual last night," Jane said. I hope she isn't in this crowd, but she scanned the crowd for a white linen dress and a colorful head wrap.

"It's hard to say," James answered. During Mardi Gras all people look strange and in costume, but she usually looks the same.

Chapter 37

Marie Laveau
Saturday Night after the Voodoo Ritual

Marie felt so exhausted after her ritual at the Square in the front of the Cathedral with the python and the zombie, and the Mardi Gras crowds slowed her return to her house to a snail's pace. To tell the truth, using the python horrified her too, but it had worked on the crowds. As she entered the house, the clock on the mantle read one o'clock, and her house was deathly quiet. "Jane and Charles must be asleep," she said to herself. *I'm certain that Jane's day at the brothel was exhausting.* She thought, smiling to herself. *My night's ritual was extremely exhausting too-- with that snake being Damballah and the zombie but it should have been nothing to compare to hers.*

She slipped across the back yard and into Jane's house that was next door to hers as she often did at night. She cracked Jane's bedroom door about an inch and peeked inside.. She saw what looked like Jane sound asleep, covered with a sheet and blanket. Then she tiptoed over to Charlie's crib. Kissing him goodnight made her feel good. He wasn't in his crib. "Perhaps he's in the bed with Jane. I've told her not to let him sleep with her." She said to herself in a whisper. She was so exhausted that she couldn't talk much louder than a whisper anyway.

224

Marie slipped to Jane's bed. They weren't in it. Jane's head wasn't lying under those quilts? Marie jerked the covers back to find two pillows lying under the quilts, positioned vertically like a person sleeping under the covers. There was no sign of Charles.

"They're gone," she screamed. "Gigi? Gigi? Where are you? Where are Jane and Charles?"

No one answered her screams. No one was in either house. Both were empty. Marie Laveau's energy surged. She was no longer tired. She would have thought that they hadn't made it home if Jane hadn't made the bed to look as if she was in it asleep. "Where have y'all gone?" she yelled more as lights in houses along the street light up in the windows or her neighbors. Some came out into their yards to find out what had happened.

"Did y'all see anything unusual?" Marie asked her closest neighbors and customers. They were her followers or pretended to be for their own safety.

"I saw a horse and buggy leaving and a man driving," he answered.

Marie remembered that these were the people she made her money from, so she tried to calm her anger to act in control. She didn't want them to see her out of control. "Which way did they go?" She asked, trying to still her rage. *Marie Laveau is in control of all things.* She thought.

"North," his wife answered as she pulled her housecoat tighter across her bosom as if to keep Laveau's possible hex out. "She left with a man in a buggy, and they drove north toward Canal Street.

"She has gotten someone to take her and Charles back to Kilmichael." Marie said aloud. " It is no matter. I will follow her and get Charles Laveau back from her. He is mine. And I will have *him.*"

Marie went back inside Jane's house and looked around to see what was taken. Food, baby clothes, and goat's milk was missing. The apple box that Jane used for a cradle was gone too.

"As soon as it is too cold to dance in the Square, I'm heading to Kilmichael, Mississippi, to get that baby and kill Catherine Jane Lynch. She won't steal him away from me again. Charles doesn't really have to nurse her now, so he wouldn't even miss her. And I'll hide her body in that Confederate tunnel. No one else will miss her either. In the morning, I'm going to the brothel and find out who she got to help her. I'm surprised that she found a boyfriend so soon. No! That's it. She has more Confederate gold. She paid him or promised to pay him whenever she got back to Kilmichael. Well, no matter. I'll get all that gold too. Monday, I'm going to get that gold from the New Orleans Mint from that woman, Matilda Mason," Marie said to herself.

Chapter 38

Catherine Jane Lynch

After retrieving the gold coins, James and Jane rode the rutted buggy trail north toward Natchez, Mississippi, with full moon shone overhead lighting their way. Charlie woke up only once when the buggy wheel hit a large rock making it bump, but Jane took him out of the apple box and held him close, and the movement of the buggy lulled him back to sleep.

"You are a great mother, Jane," James said. "Tomorrow morning when we reach my aunt's house in Natchez, you can sleep and I'll watch Charlie for you."

"Thanks, but he's not a problem." *Jane remembered that Johnny Tingle's aim had been to steal Charlie for Marie Laveau, and James had admitted to watching Laveau dance prior to last night. It was possible that he and Laveau were friends, acquaintances, or more. He had driven to her house without asking directions when they had left her brothel.*

Riding up the trail toward Natchez gave Jane time to think about many things that had occurred in her life recently. She wondered how Victoria was doing in Memphis and if she would hear from her again, she wondered where Tom Lewis Lynch was- free or back in prison, and she wondered how Shug and Mr. Petey were doing. She even wondered about her brother Tommy and about Granny.

They had ridden for hours, and Jane was deep in her own thoughts when a tree fell across the trail in front of their horse, and a black bandit jumped out of the bushes. "Stop right there," he yelled. The horse reared up on his back legs.

James settled the horse, and he and Jane waited to see what the bandit wanted. Jane remembered her trip south to New Orleans and being stopped by a bandit when she came down with Johnny. Suddenly, it occurred to Jane that James didn't have a gun. She was so accustomed to men carrying guns where she was from that it hadn't been something she had asked him.. She had just taken for granted that he would have one.

"Give me all your money and jewelry," the bandit demanded. Jane noticed that he wore a red bandana scarf over the bottom half of his face, letting the whites of his eyes shine above it.

"We don't have either," James said. "Let us pass."

The bandit stood dumbfounded for a second. Then he said, "You, young lady, get off the buggy. You are coming with me," the bandit demanded. "I'll sell you or put you to work and make a killing."

"I have a baby," Jane replied. "I can't leave my son. He is still nursing."

"Leave him. I don't need no baby. I need a pretty young woman. I got no use for a crying baby."

Apparently, the bandit meant business, so Jane slowly climbed down from the wagon. *All she could think about was leaving Charlie with James. Although the bandit wasn't a little person, they thoughts of "little people slaves" filled her mind.*

James sat still. "Here, I have a few dollars." James said, throwing them at the bandit. "Take the money and leave her. She needs to take care of this baby. He's still nursing."

The bandit gathered the meager $20 that James had thrown on the ground. "Give 'em a bottle of milk. You can do it. I'm taking her with me. She will be very helpful to us under-the-hill. She'll be way more valuable than your $20." He grabbed Jane and pulled her into the bushes where he had been hiding. He tied her wrists with a leather strap and climbed on to his horse and pulled her up on his horse behind him. He made her put her arms over his head to hold her on the horse. Then he rode out into the trail beside the felled tree. "Take care of yo' son," he yelled to James. "I'm taking yo' woman."

Jane was horrified, but grateful that he hadn't harmed Charlie and James. She remembered him saying that she'd be helpful "Under the Hill." She hoped James heard what he'd said and would come on to Natchez Under-the-Hill to rescue her since he was supposed to stop at The Burn in Natchez anyway.

Once they were out of sight of James and Charlie, Jane tried to knock the rider and herself off the horse, but he'd looped the leather strap he'd used to tie her wrists over the horn of the saddle so she could do nothing except hang on. She and the rider rode on north toward Natchez.

***

Natchez, Mississippi, where the Natchez Trace really began, was nothing more than a wagon trail. The bandit told Jane that northern travelers floated their goods down the Mississippi River and lots of them stopped off at Natchez to sell instead of continuing on to New Orleans. He said that usually 15 flatboats arrived with goods to sell in Natchez daily. The flatboats with 20 men aboard were torn apart and scrapped in Natchez. He bragged that thousands of flatboats docked in Natchez, and they sold everything from furs to whiskey. Even those who floated on down the river to New Orleans came back through Natchez walking or on horseback, so drinking, gambling, and ladies of the night were readily available "Under-the-Hill", and thousands of men passed through Natchez and were anxious to indulge in whatever Natchez had to offer.

"I can sell you as one of those ladies," the bandit said. "You heard of Natchez Under-the-Hill? It is the rowdy part of Natchez, and the bluff area is orderly and respectable."

"Where is The Burn?" Jane asked. "I've heard of it."

"It is on North Union Street on the bluff."

I'm headed back to another brothel or a bordello. Jane thought. *I hope James caught the reference to under-the-hill, and I hope he takes good care of Charlie. Maybe he'll continue on to his aunt's house, The Burn. I'll count on that. I'm going to get away from this man.*

Chapter 39

Near daylight, lightening flashed and torrential rain had splashed on Jane and the bandit before they reached Natchez-Under-the-Hill. *She felt and looked like a drowned rat.* She thought. Still heavy clouds covered the sunrise and lightening flashed again. Jane had read about the Great Natchez Tornado in 1840 that had demolished Natchez-Under-the-Hill. Three hundred people had been killed in that tornado. She hoped that this thunderstorm wasn't involving another killer tornado.

Of course, Jane hadn't been able to get Charlie and James out of her mind. *I wonder where they rode out the storm during the night. I'm glad that they had that blanket to help keep the rain off them. I wonder if they spent the night on the trail or whether they had made it to The Burn.* She thought.

Totally, her trip from New Orleans had been about 170 miles. Finally after a few hours, he couldn't find a buyer for her under-the-hill, so he carried her down a muddy street to William Johnson's two-story, brick house near the riverfront on State Street. Jane had never seen a two story house with so many front doors. William Johnson had been a former slave, and now he was not quiet totally a free black man, accepted into the white man's world. His house was located in the commercial district of antebellum Natchez. Johnson, a handsome mullato, owned three barbershops and a bath house. *I'm going to be sold to work in a bath house.* She thought. *I hope that's better than a brothel.* She looked at a map of Natchez on the wall inside Johnson's library. *The Burn on Union Street was only three blocks to the east of here. I must escape tonight, so I can catch up with James and Charlie.* Jane thought.

As soon as she could get free from this bandit, she planned to make her way to The Burn on Union Street. Instead of going down under-the-hill, the bandit sold Jane to William Johnson at his two-story, red brick house for $50 dollars cash. Johnson took her to his library and looked her up and down and then locked her in by herself. He seemed to Jane to be in a hurry to go somewhere. She looked around to see that the floors in his library were pine and shone as if they were polished or waxed daily. On the south side of the library a floor-to-ceiling bookshelf held many books and interesting figurines and other kinds of knickknacks.

There was a roaring fire in the fireplace on the north wall with two large, over-stuffed, blue velvet chairs pulled up to the hearth, so she sat in one of them and dried her hair and clothes with the warmth of the fire. She felt like it had been built for her to dry her clothing. Once dry, she searched his book shelves and found works of Ralph Waldo Emerson, Edgar Allan Poe, and Melville. These books were very new, but others looked tattered and well-worn, well-read. She took down a book of short stories by Poe and read *The Black Cat* and then she read *The Raven.* She had read Poe in school, but she hadn't read these stories, yet. Then she stumbled on to William Johnson's desk chair and found diaries of the everyday writings and musings of the owner of the bath house. In his diaries were records of three barber shops that Johnson owned. For an hour while the rain fell, she read from his hand written diaries of the everyday life in Natchez, carefully putting the diaries back where she had found them on his large mahogany desk. She read that he often frequented the race track, and that's where she figured he was now, but in this rain, it didn't make sense. He had kept a diary every day for years. He had married Ann Battles in 1835. Apparently, Ann had given him one child per year, and he had written about all of them.

Maybe he will let me go back to get Charlie since he probably loves babies. Jane thought.

She checked the locks on the doors and windows to find them locked before she went over to the over-stuffed chair near the fireplace and sat down to figure out what to do next. She had to get out of here. She had to find Charlie. Her eyelids got so heavy and the warmth of the fire made her sleepy, so she was asleep in a few minutes from warmth and exhaustion. She was awakened by the turning of a key in the door that led to an interior hallway of the house. When Jane had been hauled inside by that bandit, she noticed that this hallway also had a staircase. Suddenly, the door that led to the hallway burst open and a very pregnant, black woman entered the room. "Come here young lady. Let me look at you."

Jane did as she was told. Somehow this woman, Ann, reminded her of Marie Laveau because she was beautiful and demanding. *She's carrying that baby low or it has dropped, as Shug had said about my pregnancy with Charlie.* Jane thought.

"You have been brought here to help me with my children," Ann said. "What do you know about children? Babies?"

"I have a baby. His name is Charles. He's going on nine months old," Jane replied. "We were separated when that bandit kidnapped me on the trail. Charles is with my driver. When is your baby due?"

"Your driver? Not your husband?" she asked, ignoring Jane's question about the baby's due date..

"No, Ma am. I don't have a husband. He died of yellow fever in New Orleans. His name was Johnny Tingle. There is an epidemic of yellow fever in New Orleans. We were on the way up the trace to my grandmother's house near French Camp when I was kidnapped and separated from my son."

"I don't know anyone named Tingle. Well, why didn't you bring your son with you? You left him with your driver?" Ann asked. "If you don't care for your son any more than that, I'm not sure you will be suitable to take care of my children. You may have to work in William's bath house instead. I need a girl who loves children," Ann said.

"I told you that the bandit separated us. He said that he had no need for another baby. Mis' Johnson, I need to go to where my son is. I need to find him. I'm certain he is terrified, being cared for by strangers," Jane cried. Huge tears rolled down her cheeks, and she wiped them off with the back of her hand.

"How do you know where he is? Do you think that driver will keep him?" Ann answered. "Men aren't fond of taking care of babies, especially babies that don't belong to them."

"I'm not sure, but I need to find them quickly before he leaves the country and takes my son with him. Mis' Johnson, please help me. I'm begging you. Don't keep me here. My son needs his mother." More large tears flowed down Jane's face.

Mrs. Johnson seemed to think about this for a long time. Then she said, "What about the $50 my husband paid for you? Mr. Johnson will not be happy that he's wasted $50. He's very frugal. He built all this. She waved her hands in the air indicating their house. Formally, he was a slave. But he is gone to the race track tonight. He doesn't know that I'm talking with you, and he will never know," Mrs. Johnson said.

"When I get home to Kilmichael, I will mail the money back to you. If you will please let me go. I'll repay the $50. I need to go find my son," Jane begged.

"Yes, you do. That much we are in agreement about. I'm going to unlock this outside door." She motioned to the door in the library that led to the street. "You may escape as soon as I've gone to bed. Sneak away in the shadows so Mr. Johnson doesn't see you if he's on the way back from the racetrack. Find your son. If you can't find him, come back and go to the back of the house then tell my servants that you must see me immediately. I must get out of here. This heat is making me nauseated."

Chapter 40

As soon as the house was quiet and all Jane heard was the pitter patter of rain and the sounds of night business on the street, Jane assumed that Mrs. Johnson and her children had retired for the night, Jane left the William's library through the door to the outside that Mrs. Williams left unlocked. She carefully closed the door behind her, trying not to make a sound. When she got outside the house, she heard a horse coming up the muddy street. She slipped into the shadows near the front of the house to wait for the rider to pass. The rider wore the same clothing the bandit who had kidnapped her had worn. He rode past the Johnson house and on down the street and headed to the west toward the bluff and the Mississippi River. Jane slipped around to the corner of the house, staying in the shadows, and peeked around to see where the rider had gone. Down on the river, Jane saw large bales of cotton waiting on the dock to be loaded onto a steamboat, and she heard the sounds of business taking place on the street and down on the river. She was amazed at the amount of business happening in the darkness of night and the intermittent rain, but Natchez Under-the-Hill came alive at night and a little rain didn't stop the festivities.

Jane heard thunder and saw lightening in the west over the Mississippi River. *The lightening looked very beautiful, dancing on the water.* She thought. When the lightening popped, she looked toward the east which was the way she was headed to The Burn. Lining the street Jane saw elaborate, two-story antebellum homes that had survived the Civil War or had been refurbished since. Some sat near the street and others had long driveways. She slipped east staying in the shadows toward The Burn on North Union Street. Hopefully, James would have Charlie at his aunt's house.

Jane hurried the three blocks from William Johnson's house toward The Burn where James and Charlie might still be. She couldn't get to Charlie fast enough. She missed him so much that her heart ached. When she made it to The Burn, she saw a large sign in the yard stating where she was. She ran around to the back of the house and knocked on the kitchen door where a lantern shone through the window. It was too late at night to knock on the front door to see Mis' Francis, James's aunt. A black servant came to the door. She wore a cotton calico dress and a white apron tied over her large belly. "Hello, I'm Jane Lynch and my son Charlie and James Fares' were coming here before I got kidnapped by a bandit. I hope they made it. Are they here? God, I hope so." Jane talked as fast as she could to keep the servant from closing the door in her face.

"Well, Mr. James came here and left the baby with my daughter, Tilly. My name is Gladys."

"Oh, thank God. Charlie is here," Jane said. "Thank you, Mis' Gladys." Jane wanted to hug her, but thought better of it. "Where is Charlie?"

"Then Mr. James went to Natchez Under-the-Hill to find you, but he couldn't. So then, he left the baby, Charlie, with us and went to gamble on the river boat, and, I guess, to look for you. Well. You know how men folks are. He left you a horse and buggy and a sealed box in case you showed up. He told me that you would show up, but God knows how he knew. I'll go get the box. Yo' baby is sleeping."

"I'm all wet," Jane said. "But, I want to see Charlie. I can't wait to see Charlie," Jane said. She slipped out of her muddy boots.

"What if I give you some dry clothes? My daughter is about the same size as you," the servant said. "Follow me. I'll take you to Charlie."

They walked up the circular staircase to a bedroom at the end of a hardwood floored hall with Oriental runners and opened the heavy, ornate door at the end of the hall. Jane peeked inside and saw an iron baby bed where Charlie lay sleeping. Jane tiptoed over to the baby bed. She leaned over the bed and gave Charlie a big kiss on the forehead, but didn't wake him. Gladys then took Jane back out into the hall, opened a large ornate cabinet, and gave her the box James had left for her and some dry clothes. Then Gladys slipped out the door, giving Jane time to get dressed.

Jane's curiosity got the best of her, and she opened the sealed box that James had left. It was a white cardboard box with a lid that had been sealed by twine. *I wonder if Gladys or her daughter had been curious or nosey and opened the box and retied the twine. I guess they could have just stolen the whole box.* Jane thought.

The box contained a letter to Jane and 94 gold coins wrapped tightly in fabric so they wouldn't rattle against themselves. She unfolded the letter that lay on top of the coins. The letter read: Dear Jane: I left you the horse and buggy and your gold and, of course, Charlie. I took two coins for my trouble and for the price of the horse and buggy. I hope you and Charlie make it safely back to Kilmichael. With your strength and determination, I'm certain that you will. If I am lucky, I will see you again someday.

Jane felt elated to have found Charlie, sad to have lost James, and hopeful that she and Charlie would make it back home to Kilmichael. She knew what she had to do. First, she would sell the buggy and buy a gun and ammunition. Never again would she travel the trace trail or anywhere else without a gun, and she thought she would make better time without the buggy. She had learned her lesson about traveling that trail without a loaded gun.

She slipped back down to the kitchen. "Charlie and I will be leaving early in the morning." Jane told Miss Gladys. "Thank you very much for caring for my son and for the dry clothes. Mine should be dry by morning, and I will leave these here." Jane took one gold coin from her pocket and pressed it into Gladys's hand.

"I want to pay you for all you've done for me and my son. I really appreciate it." Jane told Gladys, who looked at the gold in her palm and smiled a huge grin. "I'm going to sleep in the room with Charlie. I'm very tired, so I'm going to bed now." She left Gladys in the kitchen and slipped up the stairs to Charlie's room.

Jane slept in the room with Charlie that night, but she tossed and turned and slept fitfully. She felt grateful to have found Charlie and to be back on the way home to Kilmichael where there were friends and relatives she knew and that she could trust. *Something could be said for everyone knowing everyone else's business.* She thought.

Early the next morning, she loaded Charlie, who seemed happy to be back with her, and her meager belongings into a buggy. Gladys had packed them some food and some goat milk for Charlie. Jane drove to the nearest gun shop and traded the buggy for a .38 caliber pistol and ammunition. Tom Lewis had taught her to use a gun, and she was good enough to hit a squirrel at fifty feet. The pistol was large enough to kill a man and small enough to slip inside her shirt or coat.

Then she went to a Dry Goods store and bought a black, man's shirt, a black, leather coat, pants, and some black, leather boots. She also bought a hat to cover her long, brown hair that she had braided and pinned flat to her head this morning. Her plan was to dress like a man, to hide the pistol inside her coat, and bind Charlie to her back with a long strip of her cotton slip, much like Marie Laveau had used to hold Charlie whenever she danced with him in front of the cathedral. She also bought a saddle for the horse with straps to tie their bags of clothes and food to it during transportation. Paying with gold coins drew sideways looks by the owners of the stores, but they took it for payment. It seemed that she got a little more respect after she paid with gold.

Jane saddled the horse, and the gunsmith unhitched the buggy she'd traded for the pistol and rolled it to the back of the shop. Finally, Jane dressed in the male attire with the hat, loaded the pistol, and secured it inside her leather coat where she could get to it in a hurry. Then she tied their clothing and food bags to the saddle, bound Charlie to her back, and swung up onto their horse. She asked directions to the trace trail and set off on her journey to Kilmichael.

Chapter 41

Jane and Charlie rode north on the rough, trace trail still muddy from the rain. It was almost lunch time when they left the Dry Goods Store in Natchez, so Jane found a shaded part of the trail, dismounted, and tied her horse to a sweet gum limb. Mounting and dismounting with Charlie bound to her back took some effort, but Jane was determined to take Charlie home, and Jane was determined to make it safely back to French Camp and then on to Kilmichael.

So far, this morning, Jane hadn't seen anyone else on the trail which she found odd, but she was relieved. That way she wouldn't have to hide her identity. The rain and muddy trail may have hindered travelers because the trail was difficult enough without inclement weather.

Suddenly, around the bend in the trail, a wagon loaded with what seemed to be everything the family ever owned showed up. There were two men, a woman, and a child in the wagon too. Jane positioned her hat on her head and ducked her head low to avoid having them recognize that she was a woman dressed like a man. She ducked behind a tree to finish feeding Charlie. Then quickly, she bound him to her back and swung onto the horse again. He would go back to sleep quickly from the warmth of her body against his and from the steady galloping movement of the horse. As she passed the wagon load of people and household belongings, she tipped her hat and rode on. She had no time to waste. She had to get back to French Camp and Kilmichael to have complete protection from Marie Laveau if there was such a thing. She wasn't interested in meeting people or interacting with them in any way. She and Charlie needed to reach French Camp as soon as possible. *I hope Tom Lewis is back in town and not in jail.* She thought. If Marie Laveau shows up, I'm sure that he could be helpful.

A few more miles down the trail, she came upon a rough, hand painted sign that pointed toward Port Gibson Stand where she and Johnny had spent the night on the way to New Orleans. Jane didn't want to stop there because she didn't want to be recognized by the innkeeper and his wife, so when she got close to Port Gibson Stand, she moved out of the trail and made her way north through the forest 500 yards away from the trail. Others must have done the same because there seemed to be an animal path or something similar, but not really a clear, clean trail. Dodging limbs that had grown out into the trail and thick undergrowth, proved to be more difficult than Jane had imagined. Several limbs slapped her in the face, scratching her cheeks, and nearly knocked her and Charlie off the horse. She was glad that Charlie was bound to her back instead of her chest. *This horse needs to rest and eat.* Jane thought. *Really, we do too, but I'm going to ride farther north to be clear of this stand.* She heard a noise behind her and turned to look back. At first, she didn't see anything.

Then out of the corner of her eye, Jane saw someone else riding a horse behind her on the trail close to where she had just ridden to avoid the Port Gibson Stand. She reached inside her coat and took the .38 pistol in her hand. She put it under the folds of her coat where she could shoot it, but still it wasn't totally visible. As the rider neared her, Jane noticed that it was a man, but that was all that she could tell because she rode as fast as possible to stay ahead of him. He rode up on her from the back more quickly than she was getting away. He sat well upon his horse, and she had Charlie bound to her back making her movements labored. It seemed that this man was in a hurry, so Jane moved over to one side away from his path.

"Stop," he called to her. "Where did you get that horse?" the man asked.

Jane had passed the Port Gibson Stand by now, so she slipped effortlessly back into the main trail and broke into a full gallop.

The rider followed. "Stop, I say," the man yelled to her. He broke into a full gallop too.

Jane galloped on in the clearer path although it was muddy, but the rider's horse closed in on her.

"I asked you to stop," he yelled. "I just want to know where you got that horse. I'm looking for someone. I have no intention of hurting you. I don't even carry a gun," James said.

Jane stopped her horse and cocked her pistol, waiting for the man to catch up to her and Charlie. She pointed the pistol dead at him.

"What do you want?" she asked, trying to keep her head tilted downward so that he couldn't tell she was a woman. "I'm not a horse thief."

"That horse? I left that horse for a woman in Natchez. I'm trying to find her and her baby. Where did you get that horse?"

"James?" Jane asked. "Is that you?" She lowered her pistol and put it down beside the horse's back.

"Jane? I figured that I might catch up to you, but I didn't figure you would be on horseback. I'm so glad that I found you. You have a gun? You know how to use a gun?" James asked. "Why, of course, you do." He answered his own question. "Why would I think otherwise? I'm sorry I missed you at The Burn, but I searched but couldn't find you at Natchez Under-the-Hill. No one had seen you there. I figured that bandit had sold you to the men on the steamboat, so I boarded it to find you. You weren't there either, so when I got back to my aunt's house, you had already come to get Charlie and left. Mis' Gladys told me that you had come to get Charlie the very night that you were kidnapped. Well, it was over in the early morning when I got back there. How did you get away from that bandit? Now, I find you and

Charlie on a horse headed back to French Camp. What happened to the buggy? Oh, I see, I bet you traded it for that gun that you pointed at me. And you bought you some male clothing. What an ingenious idea. You are a very resourceful and brave young woman, Jane. Can I ride along to French Camp and on to Kilmichael with you?"

"Yes, you may," Jane answered, tears brimming in her eyes. "I thought that we wouldn't ever see you again. Mis' Gladys gave me the sealed box. Thank you. Also thank you for the horse and for taking care of Charlie while I was kidnapped. I can never repay you for that," Jane said.

"Well, from my calculations, we have a ways to go to get you home. I meet some folks back in a wagon carrying what looked like everything they owned. They told me that they had seen a lone rider who wasn't in the main trail. That's how I knew that you avoided the Port Gibson Stand. That's a great idea, by the way. I heard that staying at the stands is like taking your life in your hands. You are so shrewd and independent. Young lady, you amaze me. Did you have that pistol aimed at me? Would you have shot me?"

"I only avoided the Port Gibson Stand because my husband and I had stayed there before, and I figured the innkeeper would recognize me. Also dressing like a man seemed to be a good idea, but not where people knew me."

"It was, but I think you look better as a woman, but I'll take the pants, coat, and hat if that is all you have to wear until we get back to Kilmichael," James said.

"The next stand is the Raymond Stand. We should be safer with you along. Why don't you carry a gun?" Jane inquired.

"I was blamed with killing a man once," James replied. "You can't kill anyone if you don't have a gun. It is as simple as that. But I wished that I had one when that bandit took you."

"That's not exactly true," Jane said. "But let's not discuss that, now. When we get to Kilmichael, you may meet my stepfather, Tom Lewis Lynch. He killed a man, a deputy sheriff, and he was sentenced to life. But he escaped from prison and helped me get away from

Marie Laveau and her husband at a voodoo ritual she was holding in the Big Black River at Kilmichael. Tell me, James, how well do you know Miss Laveau?" Jane asked.

"She is partners with my dad in that brothel that she made you work in. Or should I say *she was* because as soon as she finds out that he and I helped you get away from her and out of New Orleans, I'm certain that she won't be very friendly to us anymore," James answered. "And I bet she will be even angrier when she finds that you and I picked up that gold from the New Orleans Mint," James said. He looked straight at Jane. "She sent Johnny Tingle to marry you. Didn't she?"

"Yes." Jane said. "Did she send you?"

"No," James stated simply.

Chapter 42

A Few Days Later
Marie Laveau

Marie Laveau hurried her horse and buggy by popping the leather whip sharply on the horse's back through the streets of New Orleans to the front on the New Orleans Mint. She was dressed in her typical long, billowing, white linen skirt and tunic although a cold wind blew out of the north hard today. She wore this same outfit year round as part of her trademark, letting the linen skirt blow in the wind. On cold days she wore more under clothing when the air was chilly. Today was one of those nippy days. She had wrapped her hair in an oblong, colorful, new, silk scarf. The scarf was yellow, green, blue, and red flowered. Today, she left the ends flowing. Wearing this outfit, she was easy to recognize by her followers in the city, and often people didn't have to ask who she was. Others whispered to them as she rode by saying, "That's Marie Laveau."

When she reached the front of the New Orleans Mint, she drove through the groups of loitering, freed slaves and tied her horse to the rail, many who hung around the front of the Mint building moved out of her way. She presented herself as someone to fear, and she was used to people recognizing her or respecting her enough to stay out of her way. She loved the fear she instilled in people. She loved the power.

She walked inside the front door as if all the gold and silver inside the New Orleans Mint belonged to her. Most people who knew Marie didn't know that she had deposited most of the money she earned in the Bank of New Orleans, and she lived as if she was poor. Actually, she was a very wealthy woman. Nobody was the wiser, especially the different men who were fortunate or unfortunate enough to be her boyfriends since her husband, Huerta died from snake bite and drowning during one of her rituals in Kilmichael.

The receptionist, Shelia Thompson, recognized her. "What can I do for you, Mis'. Laveau?"

"Awe, you know who I am. I came to pick up the gold that Johnny Tingle had melted into coins. I need to see Matilda Mason," Marie said.

"You can see Matilda Mason. But Mrs. Laveau, that gold was picked up by Mrs. Tingle a few days ago. Here is her signature on our log book. She came here with James Fares', the baseball player. I recognized him from the poster of the Gulf League," Shelia said.

Marie leaned over the counter and read the log book. "Catherine Jane L. Tingle" was signed in it.

The blood rose in Marie's face until she turned blood red. She felt angrier than she had felt when Charlie and Jane had not been in that bed after her dance in front of the Cathedral. Jane had gotten the best of her twice now.

"What do you mean? Y'all gave those gold coins to Jane. That was my gold. I sent Johnny Tingle to get it in French Camp. Someone here will pay for this," Marie said. "Maybe you, Shelia."

"Legally, the gold belonged to Mrs. Tingle. Mr. Johnny Tingle died with yellow fever. We read his obituary in the newspaper. She is the only heir," the receptionist Shelia said meekly.

"He died at my house. Who do you think owned, Mr. Tingle? I did. Go get that Mason woman. She's got some reckoning to do. That gold should be mine," Marie screamed. "I am the rightful owner of that gold. I sent Johnny Tingle to Kilmichael to get Jane, Charlie and that Confederate gold."

"Well, Mame, if that was Confederate gold, it didn't belong to any of you. It belonged to the government," the Shelia replied, summoning some courage.

"Well, Miss Shelia Thompson, I will show you who really is in control." With that Marie drew some kind of dust out of her pocket and threw it in Shelia's face.

Shelia immediately began to cough and sneeze. Then she fainted to the floor in a large pile of long, black hair and long, black dress.

At that time, Matilda Mason burst into the room. She ran to where Shelia Thompson lay on the floor. "Shelia, are you all right? What happened?" Matilda looked Marie Laveau up-and-down.

"Get away from her before you join her," Marie threatened. She wasn't intimidated at all by Miss Mason's gaze. "Johnny Tingle promised that gold to me. I want to see Matilda Mason."

"I'm Matilda Mason, and you are?" Miss Mason retained her composure.

"I'm the woman who is going to kill you or at least make you wish you were dead." With that Marie threw the same dried cat bone dust over Matilda Mason who immediately collapsed. "I will teach y'all to mess with Marie Laveau." She took out a black wax ball and some other gris gris and lay them near the two women. "Damballah, put a hex on these women. Make all their hair fall out and never grow on their heads again. Make the hair grow on their faces."

Marie jumped up and down in a rage near the two women, chanting and yelling until a security guard entered the room and pointed his gun at Marie. A few of the freed slaves also had slipped inside the front door. Marie wasn't fazed. She kept chanting and yelling until the rest of the freed slaves outside came into the room to see the frightened security guard huddled in a corner of the reception area. One of the freed slaves took the security guard's gun from him and ran out the door. He turned and smiled broadly at Marie.

"All three of you are cursed," Marie said to Shelia, Matilda, and the security guard. "Snakes will fill your homes, your beds, and your clothes and this mint. You will not be able to get away from the snakes until you are dead." She turned and strode to the door that led to her horse and buggy. As she left, snakes began to slither under the doors and through the open windows. The black cotton mouth snakes crawled toward the fainted women and over the security guard.

The freed slaves burst out the front door, stepping high so as not to step on a snake. Marie walked calmly to her horse, took the reins, and climbed into front seat of the buggy. She didn't drive back toward her house. She drove the horse and buggy north toward Natchez, Mississippi.

Driving north back toward French Camp without being prepared didn't seem to slow her down at all. At this moment, her confidence was soaring. She was determined to get Charlie, Jane, and the Confederate gold.

Chapter 43

Catherine Jane Lynch Tingle

Finally Jane, Charlie, and James reached French Camp on the old trace. Jane wanted to stop at the cemetery to check on her gold, but James didn't know that she even had more or where she had hidden the gold, so she didn't stop. They rode on into the night toward Kilmichael. As they rode through the wooded area near Bethsaida Church where the "little people" were supposed to live, Jane told James, "Have you heard of the little people who are said to live in gullies, gorges, and behind falls in different areas of the South. People say a group of them live near here, so keep your eyes peeled for movement low in the bushes and a few feet above the ground. They hide in the undergrowth and move quickly."

"Have you ever seen any of them?" James teased her.

"No, but I do believe they live here. They steal women and children and make them slaves. Several people have disappeared from this area, and folks said the "little people" got them.

As she was telling him, a large white owl swooshed across their path, scaring the horses and Jane. The horse reared on its hind legs. The rearing of the horse woke Charlie, and he cried and whimpered.

Jane tried to quiet him. She didn't want the "little people" stealing him or her, so she moved her pistol to the front of her coat so that she could reach it easily.

Nothing else happened after the owl lighted in a tall, loblolly pine tree, so the three of them kept riding toward Kilmichael. Finally at nearly 4 o'clock in the morning, they reached Granny's house. All the lanterns were burning. "Something is wrong. Something is wrong with Granny, Papa, or Tommy," Jane said.

"Who is Tommy?" James asked.

"Tommy is my baby brother," Jane replied. She dismounted her horse and tied him to the front rail. Charlie was still asleep, so with Charlie still on her back, she strode onto Granny's front porch. Mr. Petey was leaned back in a straight back chair on the front porch. Her foot falls woke him.

"Halt, who is that?" Mr. Petey asked, springing to a standing position.

"It's me, Jane," she said."What is going on? Why is the house lit up?"

"Awe, Miss Jane. It's yo' Granny and Papa. They got the yellow fever," Mr. Petey said.

"What about Tommy?" Jane asked frantically.

"He'd okay. He be at our house with Oma. He ain't got it." He stood and said, "Lawdy, Miss Jane, you lookin' good, except tired. Y'all been riding all night? Let me take that baby, Charlie, to Oma, so you can see to yo' Granny and Papa."

"Who's caring for them now? Shug?" Jane asked.

"She sho' is. She's doing the best she can, but I bet she won't mind yo' helping. You know yellow fever is catchy?"

"Yes, but I've already had it, and Charlie has had it too. You get it from mosquitoes." She turned to James. "James Fares', this is Mr. Petey, one of my very best friends in the world. Mr. Petey, this is James Fares'. He brought me home from New Orleans."

"Nice to meet you. Sho' is. If you be a friend of Jane's, you be a friend o' mine. Yes, Sir. That Jane is one fine lady. Sho' is," Mr. Petey said. "Give me that baby so he can get to sleep in a bed. I bet he's wore out, too."

Jane unwrapped Charlie from her back and handed the sleeping boy to Mr. Peter. He strode off the front porch and around the corner of the house toward his home, carrying Charlie in his arms.

"James, have you had yellow fever?" Jane asked.

"Not that I remember," James said. "We always slept under mosquito nets during mosquito season."

"Well, I learned how to care for folks who had it from Marie Laveau, but I bet my Granny and Papa are too far gone. It lasts only about 5 or 6 days. That is what killed Johnny Tingle, the man Marie Laveau sent to marry me. You stay out here until I get you a bed made up, I'm gonna see what I can do for Granny and Papa, too."

"You really are a nice woman," James said. "I'll wait here."

Jane went inside to find Shug mopping Granny's brow with a cool, damp cloth. Shug looked up at her with tired eyes, "Am I seeing a ghost? Or is that you Jane?"

"It's me, Shug. How are they?"

"I'm okay, but this is the fourth day that Granny's been sick. Papa got sick yesterday. Ain't you afraid you'll catch it?" Shug asked.

"I've already had it, Shug. Johnny Tingle and Charlie did too. Marie Laveau took care of us. Me and Charlie lived. Johnny died," Jane replied. "He's buried in the New Orleans Cemetery. I can't have it again. You go on home and let me take care of them. Mr. Petey took Charlie to your house. I'm sure you are tired. It's probably too late for Granny, but probably not for Papa. Have you ever had it?" Jane said.

"Yes, long time ago," Shug replied. She gathered her belongings and started for the door. Then she stopped. You said Johnny died, so who is that man on Granny's front porch?"

"He is James Faves'. He brought me here. He was a baseball player for the Gulf League."

"I figured that Marie Laveau had done got you and took yo' baby," Shug said. "She scares me to death."

"You never was scared enough for yo' own good, Jane Lynch," Shug said. "You is one-of-a-kind."

"I need some baking soda to bath them in. That is what Marie Laveau used on me and Charlie. I'm gonna fix a bath for them, but first, I need to make a bed for James."

"That bed in the back bedroom is already ready. I'll send him inside. Girl, you really are something. Bless yo' heart," Shug said, letting the front door close gently behind her.

James came to the door of the kitchen where Jane was mixing the baking soda bath. "Don't you think you should get some rest, Jane?"

"I'll bath them. Then I'll sleep in the rocking chair in their room. They will need this baking soda bath about every hour, but Shug did all that she knew how to do. I'm afraid that it is too late for Granny. She's had the fever for four days. That's a long time without treatments."

"Where did you learn to take care of yellow fever patients?" James asked.

"From Marie Laveau," Jane replied.

"Well, she was known all over New Orleans for being able to cure folks when the doctors couldn't. Which way to my bed?" James asked.

Jane pointed toward the back corner of the house. "Sweet dreams," she said.

With that, Jane carried the basin of baking powder water back into the bedroom where Granny and Papa lay sick and feverish. She took a dry bath cloth and dipped it into the baking powder solution, wrung it out, and began bathing first Papa and then Granny. Then she sat in the rocking chair and covered herself with one of Granny's crazy quilts. Just touching the quilt made her feel more secure and safe. She drifted off into a deep, dreamy sleep.

In Jane's dream, Marie Laveau was riding in a buggy toward Natchez, Mississippi. A heavy rain began to fall. Marie's buggy got stuck in the deep, muddy ruts, and the horse could not pull it. Marie, wearing her long, flowing white linen skirt and tunic, got out of the buggy, out into the mud and unhitched the horse from the buggy.

Mud soaked into the bottom of her skirt and ran over her boots. Marie shivered from the cold rain. She swung up onto the horse and rode him bareback on toward Natchez.

Jane woke from the frightful dream and looked out the front window. Sunshine beamed through the window onto her face when she moved the curtains back. She looked toward the bed to where the sun shone on Granny's face. She no longer looked drenched in perspiration. She looked peaceful, stoic, and still, except her eyes were still open. Jane walked to the bed and placed her hand on Granny's face. She was dead.

A single, large tear rolled down Jane's cheek.

Jane looked up and Shug was standing at the foot of the bed. A single, large tear also rolled down Shug's cheek, too.

"She's gone," Jane said, hugging Shug. "She won't be in pain any more, but maybe Papa can be saved."

"I'll go tell Mr. Petey. I'll lay out Granny's body on the dining room table this morning and get her ready for burial. Will she be buried in French Camp with yo' mama?" Shug asked.

"No, she has a plot in the Kilmichael City Cemetery. I'm sure Mr. Petey knows where her plot is because she's told him enough times. Can you wait until I wake up Mr. Faves'? He probably isn't used to folks getting laid out on the kitchen table." Jane said. "I'm sure they use a mortuary."

"You go wake him, and I'll bath yo' Papa with a fresh baking soda bath. Tommy is going to be upset at her death because Granny took care of him," Shug said.

"I can, now. I'll tell him," Jane replied. "I'll get something for Granny to wear. I'll hang it outside the amoire' in her bedroom. I'll help you prepare her body for the funeral."

Chapter 44

Jane carried some hot biscuits with pork sausage and hot coffee that Shug had brought to Granny's house to James on the front porch while Shug covered the dining table with an oil cloth and two sheets. Then Jane came back in, and they slipped the sheet from the bed by pushing the edges next to Granny's side and turning her over and then back. When they moved her body, the air expelled from her lungs, and it sounded like Granny groaned. The groan startled Jane. She jumped back and almost dropped Granny onto the dining table.

"That's just air, Jane. She ain't alive. That's just the air in her lungs. I forgot to warn you that this might happen." They lifted Granny's body using the sheet for a sling. Then they lay her body on the top sheet that covered the table.

Jane went back to the bed and slipped a fresh sheet under Papa, rolled him over, and pulled it to the side of the bed. Already, the baking powder baths were helping him. He seemed to be improving. "She died, Jane; didn't she?" Papa asked.

"Yes, Papa; Granny did," Jane said. "I'm sorry. You are getting better. I'll be helping Shug lay out her body. It's the least I can do for her."

"You are a good girl, Jane."

Jane went into the kitchen to help Shug. First, she and Shug stuffed Granny's throat, mouth, and nose with cotton and sealed her teeth and lips with glue. Then they tied a ribbon around her jaw to let the glue set up and keep her jaw from dropping. Then they rolled her to the side to empty the urine and feces into an old bowl. The smell made Jane's stomach lurch. Granny had been sick and feverish so long that this liquid was minimal, but the smell wasn't. Shug took the pan of liquid out the back door.

Carefully, Jane and Shug bathed Granny's body with a solution of lye soap and water to remove any excess bodily fluid that had escaped. Keeping smells down on a deceased body presented itself as a problem. The weather was cool, but the windows would have to be kept closed to keep flies from laying eggs on Granny's body, especially in her nose, mouth, and eyes.

"Jane, you will need to check her body this morning before you open the casket in the church. Cover her face with a cloth tonight. I'd do it for you, but you know me and Petey ain't welcome in a white folk's church," Shug said.

Jane couldn't tell if Shug had her feelings hurt or whether it was something that she accepted. "What do you mean? You are welcome as far as I'm concerned, Shug. You are one of my very best friends. Mr. Petey, too."

"Honey Child, yo' Granny would roll over in that casket if she thought that me and Petey was in her white folk's church. You know how she was. She was always worried about what folks thought about her, and she thought she was above darkies, as she called us," Shug said.

"Well, it is ironic that you can help nurse her while she's sick and lay her out after she dies and can't go to her funeral," Jane said.

"It's okay, Jane. Don't worry about it," Shug said. "Let's get this taken care of."

Jane raised Granny's bottom, and Shug placed a thick funeral diaper on her to catch any remaining liquid that might escape. They dressed her quickly in under clothes, a Sunday dress, and shoes. Then Jane applied a thin coat of fresh lard to Granny's face, lips, and hands to keep down the look of dehydration. They removed the top sheet and laid her on the second sheet, and then they put coins on her eyes to keep her lids closed. She would stay here laid out on the table until the casket arrived. They covered her body with a clean flour sack sheet. Then her wooden casket would be placed in the front of the church and her burial would be tomorrow.

"I'm gonna go get Petey to pick up a casket from Mr. Smith, the carpenter," Shug said. "You bathe Papa again with baking soda. It's helping him. He is getting better."

Jane bathed Papa again and cleaned up herself. Then she went to the front porch to talk to James.

"Jane, you are a very strong woman. You've got some grit. I admire you for being so good at taking care of those you love. I wish someone loved me like that," James said.

"Thanks. Speaking of those I love, I'm going to Shug's house to see Charlie. I bet he's missing me." Jane had not missed what James said or the way he had said it.

Chapter 45

Granny's funeral visitation or viewing of her body to pay respects was to be held that evening at 5 o'clock until the last person viewing the body had done so, and also one hour before the service. The service would be at 1:00 P.M.

Mr. Petey brought the wooden casket to the house in his wagon. They placed Granny's body inside, and he carried it to the Kilmichael Baptist Church. Mr. Petey and the Reverend would place it on some stands in the front of the congregational hall of the church.

"Mis' Jane said to leave the lid closed until she got there this evening and then after the viewing. She's gotta check the body before it's viewed again," Mr. Petey said.

"I understand," the Reverend said.

"Lots of folks around here think that yellow fever is contagious, but Mis' Jane said you get it from mosquitoes and can't have it but once. She done had it while she was in New Orleans. She said Johnny Tingle had it. You remember him. He and Mis' Jane got married.

"Is he with her?" Reverend Mayfaire asked.

"No, Sir. I think he died of the yellow fever," Mr. Petey said.

Chapter 46

Marie Laveau

Marie rode her weary, hungry, and tired horse into French Camp, Mississippi, at daylight the morning of Granny's funeral. Slowly, she dismounted and left her horse at the livery with Charlie.

"Well, I see you followed Jane Lynch back here from New Orleans. Lawdy, woman, you 'bout killed that poor horse. You been pushing it too hard. There ought to be a law against treating an animal like this. I heard that Mis' Jane's grandmother passed away yesterday from yellow fever. I also heard that Jane's cured her grandfather using a remedy she learned from you. Some kind of baths. You might have some good in you yet," Charlie the livery man said.

"Hmmm," Marie said, not replying to his compliments. "Where can I get a room? I'm exhausted." She didn't address any of his other concerns. *Anybody can find out anything from Charlie.* She thought. *He talks way too much.*

"Over at the boarding house. I think they are still renting rooms," Charlie said. "Of course, they might not rent to the likes of you." He frowned at her, scanning her filthy tunic and skirt.

"Since you love to talk, old man, don't tell anyone that I'm in town, or I'll put a hex on you. You'll have snakes in your bed," Marie said. "Would you like that? Snakes in your bed? Or would you like to bray like a mule instead of talk?"

"You better be careful who you be putting a hex on. You gonna need a horse to leave here on. You gonna need me," Charlie said. "I'm the only livery in French Camp."

"Lots of folks have got horses, Charlie. You mind your manners if you know what's good for you."

Charlie gawked at her with his mouth hanging open.

Marie left the livery and walked the short distance from it across and up the dirt street to the boarding house. Marie got a room and ordered a hot bath for 5 cents. She removed her muddy clothes and sent the white linen to the Chinese laundry. She put some rose petals in her bath, scrubbed her body with rose scented soap and washed her long, black hair. Bathing felt so good to her. By the time she had towel dried her hair, her white linen skirt and tunic were delivered from the laundry, smelling clean and fresh. She dressed in a robe that was hanging on the back of the boarding room door and lay down to sleep or just rest if sleep wouldn't come. She had traveled straight here from the New Orleans Mint without stopping to rest, and she was exhausted. She slept most of the day.

***

Upon waking, she walked to the livery to get a fresh horse.

"I need a horse to get to Kilmichael," Marie told Charlie.

"You going to Granny Lynch's funeral?"

"Maybe." This wasn't the first she'd heard about Granny Lynch dying. The girls in the bath house and the boarding house were talking about it and how crazy Tom Lewis Lynch was. "Remember what I told you last time about keeping your mouth shut," Marie said. "Too much talking will have you braying like a mule."

"You remember what I told you about "little people" living in the woods between here and Kilmichael? You would make a good slave for them," Charlie said, laughing at her.

"I ain't afraid of 'little people,'" Marie said. "I'm not afraid of anything. Especially you, old man."

Charlie saddled the fresh horse for her, and Marie swung her leg over the saddle and rode out the door of the livery. Her white linen skirt flowed in the wind behind her.

She rode the same trail between French Camp and Kilmichael that went past the area where the "little people" supposedly lived. She had been that way before with Huerta. By the time she made it to Kilmichael it was middle of the morning the funeral was in progress, and she hadn't seen any little people. Mostly, she believed them to be a kind of fairy story. She rode directly to Shug and Mr. Petey's house where Oma and Charlie were. She didn't knock on the door, but burst through it upon a frightened Oma.

"Show me that baby," Marie demanded. "Right now." Marie knew that she frightened Oma, and that was her intention.

Oma went into the next room to get him.

Marie took Charlie from Oma's arms. "Now, you go in that kitchen and make him a bag of food to take with us. You know what he likes to eat." Marie took a long piece of fabric like Jane and had used to bind Charlie to her back and bound him to hers. She took the bag of food and some cloth diapers. Then she flew out the screen door as rapidly as she had entered, but ran directly into Tom Lewis Lynch on the front porch.

"Where are you going in such a hurry, Marie Laveau? Oh, I see, you are kidnapping Jane's baby," Tom Lewis said, grabbing her by the arm. Oma had followed Marie Laveau to the porch, but she was frightened of both Tom Lewis and her. "Get his baby untied from her back, Oma. Take him back into the house and don't tell anyone that I was here," Tom Lewis said. "I'm gonna take care of this woman."

Oma did as Tom Lewis had instructed. She unwrapped the cloth that Marie used to hold Charlie, and she took a wide-eyed Charlie back inside.

Tom Lewis twisted Marie Laveau's arm behind her and then bound her arms and feet and threw her into the back of his wagon on the hard wooden bottom. He drove the wagon over the bumpy trail in the direction of Bethsaida Church and the hanging tree. Marie lay in the back and bounced on the floor with every rut. About an hour later, Tom Lewis stopped under a large, oak tree on a knoll with other smaller, scrubby pine trees around it and the old, white church named Bethsaida sitting in the background.

He threw Marie out on the ground and was in no hurry to hang her, but by now her white linen tunic and skirt was covered in dirt. She still had her arms and ankles bound, but he hadn't covered her mouth with anything, so she talked incessantly.

"I'm not afraid of you, old man," Marie Laveau said. "I'm going to put a spell on you. No one will want to be around you, and snakes will fill your bed."

"Lady, no, I take that back. You aren't a lady; you are a witch who steals babies and their mothers. You are really a witch who only frightens people into believing that you have special powers and can cast spells and harm people. You don't scare me. I watched you in the Square outside the St. Lewis Cathedral. That priest was so frightened of you, but all the time he paced back and forth on those steps, he called you a heathen not a priestess. Well, lady, it is my job to rid the world of heathens. God hates heathens and those who worship false gods like your Damballah. Yes, I heard you praying to Damballah and playing with that snake. Snakes don't frighten me. Usually snakes are afraid of me as you and your Damballah should be. That man you said was a zombie had been drugged and dressed up by you to look like he was out of a grave. You are not a priestess as you profess to be. I found out in New Orleans that you import liquor and run a brothel. You work in the brothel, dance naked, and have orgies. You have even had sex with me, but didn't know it. That makes you a heathen," Tom Lewis ranted excessively. "I rid the world of heathens."

"I made Catherine Jane Lynch work for me in my brothel, so she's not the pure, sweet mother of Charles Laveau like you think she is," Marie told him.

"Charles Laveau, his name is Charles Lynch. That is what Jane named him. I saw you dancing on that platform with him bound to your back. You witch," Tom Lewis said. "I followed you to the New Orleans Mint. I know you tried to steal Jane's gold, but Jane had already gotten it. I saw the hex you put on those poor people in that Mint. I saw the snakes, too. But as soon as I showed up, the snakes left."

Chapter 47

Catherine Jane Lynch

Reverend Mayfaire droned on and on a Granny Lynch's funeral. Apparently, he couldn't find much to say nice about Granny, so he took this opportunity to save the congregation. Jane had heard other preachers do this. She had even heard Granny talk about it. Jane was proud of the way she and Shug had "laid out" Granny. She looked very nice and respectable.

Jane had an uneasy feeling in the pit of her stomach that something else was wrong. Tom Lewis had paid his respects to Granny last night after the other mourners left the church, so he wasn't here. Oma had Charlie, and Papa's health was improving, so for the life of her, she couldn't figure it out. But, something was wrong, and Jane knew it.

Finally, Reverend Mayfaire said the prayer and "Amen." The congregation rose and filed out of the church behind the pallbearers carrying Granny's casket.

The Kilmichael City Cemetery was a few streets over for the Kilmichael Baptist Church, so her casket was loaded into a neighbor's nice wagon pulled by a mule. Jane, James, Tommy, and the rest of the mourners followed the wagon the short distance to Granny's final resting place. Reverend Mayfaire said a shorter prayer at the graveside, and her casket was lowered into the ground. Mr. Petey began filling the dirt in on top of her casket. Shug stood over to one side away from the white mourners.

"I've got to check on Charlie and Papa," Jane whispered to James. "And I must hurry. Something is wrong. I feel it in my bones. Could you stay here to help Mr. Petey and bring him home. I'm going to get his wagon and Shug and go home," She walked toward where Shug stood.

"How is the quickest way to get to Oma, Charlie, and Papa? I just know something is going wrong. I'm leaving James to help Mr. Petey. Can we go home in y'all's wagon?"

"Sure," Shug said. "Let me tell Petey. I believe in a woman's feelings. Sometimes we just know. Sho' do."

Jane climbed into Shug and Petey's wagon, and Shug drove as fast as she could back to her house.

As soon as they stopped the wagon in the yard, Jane ran inside to check on Charlie, who was sleeping on Oma's bed. Then she ran across the front yard to see about Papa. He also was asleep in his bed, and she touched his face; he had no fever.

Carefully, she eased the back screen door closed and went back to sit on Shug's front porch. Oma came out to join them.

"Shug, I'm sorry. I felt that something was terribly wrong; I guess I was wrong," Jane said. "Oma, did anything happen while we were gone?"

"No, Mame." Oma replied, but looked away in the distance instead of looking at Jane.

"Oma, tell the truth," Shug said. "You sound like you are hiding something."

"Yes'sum," Oma replied.

"What?" Shug asked.

"I's ain't supposed to tell. He told me not to tell anyone," Oma said.

"Who told you? Who's been here?"

"Mr. Tom," Oma said.

"Tom Lewis Lynch?" Jane asked, hoping he hadn't hurt Oma, but she didn't appear to be hurt.

"Yes'sum. He been here," Oma said. "If I tell y'all, y'all can't say I told."

"Girl, you better tell us," Shug warned her. "Or I'll beat the tar nation out of you."

"He took that witchy, voodoo woman."

"Marie Laveau?" Jane and Shug asked in unison.

"Yes'sum. She was trying to take Charlie, but he made her leave him with me, and he took her off in his wagon. He tied her up and took her."

"Where?" Jane asked.

"I don't know," Oma said. "He sent me back in the house."

"Which way did they go?" Jane asked.

"They went south," Oma said.

"Come on, Shug. We've got to follow him. I bet he's going to hide her in that Confederate tunnel."

"What Confederate tunnel?" Shug asked. "I don't know of no tunnel. And I ain't going nowhere close to Marie Laveau, tied up or not, and that crazy Tom Lewis Lynch. Jane, you can take the wagon if you want, but I'm gonna stay her with Charlie and Oma. I'll look in on Papa, too. But I ain't going where 'em crazy folks are."

"Okay, take care of Charlie. If she gets loose from Tom Lewis, she will come back to get Charlie," Jane assured Shug.

"I won't let him out of my sight," Shug assured her.

Jane climbed back into Mr. Petey's wagon and headed the mule south toward French Camp, the cemetery, and the Confederate tunnel.

The sun was setting in the west over the tree line as Jane reached the trail that led toward French Camp. She wished Shug had come with her to go through the section of woods near the hanging tree that Shug swore was haunted after dark and where the little people were supposed to live in a gully and come out at night. Because she had just come home from Granny's funeral, she didn't have her gun with her.

Chapter 48

As Jane neared the heavily wooded area near the haunted, hanging tree she heard a loud, shrill, piercing scream that made the hair stand up on the back of her neck. Then she heard a loud, gruff, coarse laugh that reminded her of Tom Lewis's laugh. She looked around to see if anyone was in sight because she felt as if people were watching her. She looked low in the underbrush, but saw nothing. She didn't know if what she heard was her imagination or if it was real. She did know that her nerves were on edge, and that she was frightened out here alone.

About the time she decided that it had been her imagination, she heard the loud, shrill, piercing scream again. It sounded like the scream of a frightened woman.

She drove the mule harder and faster to get to where the scream had come from.

In the clearing and under the large oak tree that Shug swore was the hanging tree, Jane saw the outline of Tom Lewis Lynch and Marie Laveau. She was standing in the back of the wagon. A noose hung around her neck, and the rope looped over the limb. It looked like Tom Lewis was going to drive the wagon out from under her feet and hang her.

Both he and Marie Laveau looked up at her as she rounded the corner of the trail within sight of the hanging tree. Jane jerked back on the reins, stopping her wagon next to his. She jumped into the back of the wagon where Marie Laveau stood. Jane had no idea what to do next. Part of her wanted Marie Laveau to be hung, but Jane knew in her heart that she couldn't take part in a murder no matter how badly she disliked Marie Laveau and all she stood for.

Suddenly, out of the bushes, a throng of little people appeared. Tom Lewis didn't seem to be disturbed at all. Marie Laveau looked more horrified than before.

"Do you little people know who I am? I'm the famous Voodoo Priestess Marie Laveau from New Orleans. One of you cut me down this instant, or I'll put a spell on all of you, and snakes will inhabit your houses and your beds."

One of the little men hopped into the wagon cut the noose around her neck, but he didn't unbind her hands and feet. He knocked her out of the wagon to the ground. Then about ten little men surrounded her, hoisted her into the air, and walked away into the forest with her upon their shoulders. Her screams pierced the night air like the sound of a screech owl.

Marie's scream would haunt Jane for a long time. Although Marie had worked in the brothel in New Orleans, nothing she had done there would compare to what the "little people" men would do to her.

Chapter 49

Tom Lewis Lynch's heart beat roughly against his big, hairy chest behind the blue plaid flannel shirt. In the cooler temperatures in Mississippi, a flannel shirt was what he wore with his overalls. The loud, hard thump of his heart tried to silence Marie Laveau's piercing screams that echoed across the damp swampy night air near Kilmichael, Mississippi. The sounds reverberated inside his head with the other voices that constantly persecuted him because of his schizophrenia. He hated those loud, shrill voices. Sometimes he squeezed his eyes shut as hard as he could until salty tears ran down his face to help silence them, and sometimes they were silenced briefly, but not today. There were no tears. *I almost hung Marie Laveau, the New Orleans voodoo priestess.* He thought and crunched his brow, failing to control his crazy, dizzying thoughts as he so badly wanted to do. But she ended up with a worse problem. Those "little men" will take care of her. You see, he had been diagnosed as paranoid schizophrenic and no medicine helped him. *But I can't get rid of Laveau that easy. She's everywhere I go, inside my head criticizing me, talking to me.*

After the little people took Marie Laveau to their camp in the Big Black swamp, from where he had almost hung her, Tom Lewis followed Jane in Petey's old wooden wagon back to the white house that was Granny's house. Granny's house looked the same with the wooden front and back porch and a porch rail with the running roses and the swept yard that was Granny's house. The "little people" had captured Laveau before Tom Lewis could hang her and carried her back to their camp. They carried her on her back held high over their heads. He knew exactly why he wanted to hang her. He could only imagine why the little people wanted her. He knew very little about this tribe of little people except that they lived like Indians, living off the land, but not as farmers as you would imagine the way others in this area did. They hunted and ate what they killed and tanned the hides for their clothing. They were clannish, but not really savage unless crossed. Then he had heard they were vicious. They didn't bother the people around them unless they were threatened. He had heard stories of the men capturing both white and black women, but he had no proof. Perhaps the women who lived to tell about it never actually wanted it told because he didn't know anyone who had ever been captured and lived to tell about it.

The rutted, dirt trail toward Granny's was eerily quiet today. The muddy ruts had dried to hard tracks. There were no screeching owls like there usually were. He had many memories from his childhood that happened along this trail. Today it was too quiet, making him feel strange and sad with grief that his mother had died from yellow fever, and he couldn't go to the funeral. He was a prison escapee. The sheriff and the other lawmen would have been looking for him there to take him back to prison. Now it was Papa's house, and Granny was buried in the Kilmichael Cemetery.

When he neared the house, Jane was standing on the front porch. "Laveau was trying to kidnap Charlie when I got to Shug and Mr. Petey's house. You were still at the Cemetery during Granny's funeral. She had dragged him out on the front porch in his nightshirt, and she was leaving with him," he told Jane, trying to justify his actions of hanging Marie Laveau. Oma was terrified of her." Although he wasn't even certain that Jane knew about his hanging Laveau, he explained anyway.

The whispering voices in his head started again. He hated the voices. As hard as he tried, he could not shut them up. And try he did. Sometimes the voices were in unison. Sometimes they were singular. Since he had met Marie Laveau, now some were communication from her. Some were individual and didn't really mimic people he had ever met. He couldn't get away from the voices for very long at a time. Laveau and the voices were like a reoccurring nightmare. He couldn't shut them up by himself, well, not for more than a few minutes at the time. *"You are no good. We are the heathens that you try to get rid of when you go preaching the gospel in the local country churches and on the street corners, and we will get you. You are most certainly a horrible preacher. And anybody can be a preacher."* The voices chanted. The voices loudly condemned. The voices tormented.

"I'm Marie Laveau." One of the voices said. *"Tom Lewis Lynch, you are a horrible person. You are ugly. You are stupid. You are bad to the core like a rotten apple. Shame on you for trying to kill me like you did that deputy sheriff,"* the voices whispered. Laveau's was loudest of all. *"You can't kill me. You should be back in prison for what you have done already. You can't win over me. I will get you."* Laveau droned on and on inside his head.

"I am trying to get rid of the voices," Tom Lewis said. "One day, I will." He was glad that Jane couldn't actually hear them, but he knew she was aware that they talked to him.

"Oh, I didn't know that she was trying to take Charlie, but it figures," Jane said. "I wonder what is happening to Laveau now out there with those little people. I hope they have her tied up. I thought she must have done something to you to make you that angry. James and I were still at Granny's funeral, and it lasted so long. During the funeral Reverend Mayfaire droned on and on and on." Jane looked at Tom Lewis's eyes. They looked glassy, cold, and distant, a look that she had often seen during her childhood, but she felt sorry for him and loved him anyway because he hadn't ever been anything but good to her despite his insanity. She knew the voices inside his head were attacking him now, persecuting him. She had seen this expression many times before when she was growing up. His expression looked crazed. His pupils still were small black specks. She wondered what that really meant because sometimes the expression left his face. There had been times during his episodes or periods of insanity that Jane felt slightly afraid of Tom Lewis. Her mother had helped him during some of these episodes, but her mother had been dead for almost a year now. "Since Reverend Mayfaire couldn't find much nice to say about Granny during the eulogy, he took the opportunity to try to save the congregation," Jane told him, thinking that he would get Tom Lewis' mind on saving people. "Sorry you missed it," she said aloud, but her face didn't seem to agree. Her expression looked like she was glad he hadn't come because she had been glad. "Granny looked very nice and respectable in her funeral clothes. I picked the pale, lavender dress that she had last worn to church before she got sick with the yellow fever. She loved that dress. It was her favorite I'm certain she sewed it. I helped Shug lay her out. Did you know that? You saw her at the viewing. Did you think she looked good? She was the first dead person that I've ever touched, and I hope the last. Laying out dead folks isn't for me. The sensation was odd. To me she felt like a cold stone. Well, I thought she looked as good as any dead person can look. We added a little rouge and powder to her face because she was so pale after being sick with yellow fever for the last few weeks. I hope we didn't add too much. Anyway, while they were burying her at the Kilmichael City Cemetery, I got an uneasy feeling in the pit of my stomach that something was terribly wrong. I thought it was because of grief, but now I guess it was because of Marie Laveau trying to kidnap Charlie. I know you couldn't be at the funeral because you are still hiding from Sheriff Marks. Are you still staying in that secret Confederate tunnel in the cemetery in French Camp? Does Mr. Petey still help you get food? I hope so. Have you seen Tommy?" Jane tried to reach him with her questions, but it didn't seem to be working. His pupils still were black and tiny. The voices in his head were more powerful than her love was.

"Whoa, girl, slow down. Yes, I'm staying in the Confederate tunnel in French Camp when I'm around here. Those Confederate ghosts are there too, now. They stay inside the tunnel with me. You shouldn't have taken their gold. They talk to me. They tell me things. They told me about the Confederate gold. And then sometimes I ride my bicycle to other parts of the country. I just got back from a trip to New York where I met an interesting man that was a lot like me, except he was a Yankee from Connecticut. We stayed at the Oneida Community up there. That's where I met him. It took me weeks to get there on that bicycle. I like to travel around, and Tommy is really growing up. What is he 12 going on 13 years old now? He wants to go down the Mississippi River to New Orleans on a raft like Huckleberry Finn. I told him that I'm his Huckleberry. I am going with him. I'm buying lumber, and we are going to build a raft to float down the Mississippi River.

Then Tom Lewis's abnormal thoughts took over again and his sanity was gone. Marie Laveau overwhelmed him again, persecuting him. He shook his head to and fro like a dog whose infected ears hurt, but he couldn't get her to be silent. "Too bad they didn't bury Granny in the cemetery near the Confederate tunnel beside your mother in French Camp. Granny's ghost could have roamed with the Confederate soldiers' ghosts. That way you could visit with her again. Well, you could visit with her spirit. I've seen those Confederate ghosts, felt their presence, and talked to them. They're amusing. Now they are angry about that Confederate gold y'all removed from their tunnel. They said 'stole.' They want it back. One soldier got it at the end of the war when they were moving the South's fortune from New Orleans to a bank in South Carolina to have when the South rose again and to keep it away from the Yankees. They want it back. The soldiers, I mean. They want their gold back. They plan to raise the South again. They told me so. Be careful. They are angry at Marie Laveau, too. But they can't find her because she's inside my head. She goes everywhere I go. She hates me. She comes out as those voodoo bugs like a monster inside me. She's so bad that she could scare those little people out there that took her, and they ain't scared of much. One of 'em will probably marry her or just breed her since they have her as their prisoner now. That scene of them hauling her off still tied up and held high over their heads was so funny looking to me. I enjoyed watching it even if I wanted to hang her. You couldn't really see them in the tall grass, and it looked like she was floating along over the tips of the grass, wearing the long white frock she wears, and screaming to the top of her lungs. Wonder what her baby fathered by a little person would look like? Short legs and arms and her skin color like local, wild honey. Might make pretty as a baby with her dark skin and all," he told Jane and laughed aloud. "It wouldn't be even a half-breed because she is mixed blood too. I'm not sure, but I heard that her father was a Frenchmen.

Marie Laveau, leave me alone. You can make a voodoo king of your own little person baby, and leave Charlie alone too," he said to no one in particular.

Jane knew that he was talking to the voices in his head. When she was growing up, he had done this often, and he was no better now. His talking alternately to her and to the voices made his conversations hard to follow. His hatred of Marie Laveau was as clear as hers.

"Laveau thought she was taking Charlie back to New Orleans to be her voodoo king, had him in her arms, and was leaving Oma by herself at Shug and Mr. Petey's. I guess Oma was scared of her, and I don't blame her. But I ain't. She may be inside my head, but I ain't afraid of her," he told Jane. Then he started twitching, wiggling, and acting like he was itching and was in church and couldn't scratch. "These voodoo bugs are all-over me, inside me, they come out in my pee, but I can't pee enough to get Laveau out of my body. I got to find that bag of sulfur Granny kept in her old, faded pie safe with the screen in the doors. I'm going to use the whole bag. You seen it, Jane?" He stood in the doorway, looking toward the kitchen with its red checkered, oil cloth-covered table, straight-back chairs and its wood, cook stove that hadn't been fired up since Granny got sick with the yellow fever. Granny's blue, gingham-checked, old, worn apron hung to one side of the wood burning stove on a wooden peg. Looking at it made Jane feel very sad.

Jane shook her head. "Shhhh. Papa is still asleep. He didn't go to the funeral because of the yellow fever; you know that's what killed Granny?"

"And get me some chewing tobacco. I'm gonna eat it, too, instead of just chewing it. That ought to get rid of these voodoo bugs. Kill 'em right off like tape worms. I actually like the taste and especially the smooth, mellow smell of chewing tobacco. Kill 'em off once and for all. I've got to get rid of these bugs." He scratched the itchy, voodoo bug bites through his overalls until a bright red spot stained the denim, making an island-like shape.

Jane came back with the bag of sulfur and some chewing tobacco. She handed it to him and looked down at the island-like, bloody shape on the denim.

These overalls will have to be boiled in the wash pot to remove that stain. Tom Lewis thought. He had watched Granny wash in an old, black, cast iron wash pot in the yard lots of times. To do laundry, Granny built a fire around the pot with oak wood and filled it with water. Once the water was boiling, she threw in Tom Lewis' and Papa's clothes. She boiled the dirtiest clothes in the water with strong smelling lye soap. Both men's clothes qualified as filthy. She used a long, wooden boat paddle to stir or agitate them. The end of that paddle had a bleached appearance from resting in the boiling pot with the strong lye solution.

"I'm going to the outhouse out back to shave myself. Tell me when your man friend gets here. I don't trust him. What's his name? I need to be gone when he gets here. He'd probably turn me in to Sheriff Marks."

"His name is James Fares', Tom Lewis. He helped Charlie and me get here from Orleans. He helped me get away from Marie Laveau down there. She had me working in her brothel. I climbed out the window, and he picked me up in his father's buggy. He drove us out of New Orleans in that buggy. We left it in Natchez, and he brought us here on horseback. Well, Charlie and I were coming on here on the Old Trace. He rode along with us. He's okay. I don't think he'd turn you in."

"You having another baby? His? If you ain't, you better stay away from the little people camp. I heard that they are kinda like those free-love folks up in New York in the Oneida Community as far as having babies is concerned." He laughed loudly. "Their camp's in the gully below Bethsaida church. They got another one out near Poplar Creek swamp. It's out near the hanging tree and the swamp. That's where they took Marie Laveau. You stay away, Jane."

Tom Lewis got the sulfur and chewing tobacco. He also got a straight-edge razor and a cup with lye shaving soap from Granny's medicine cabinet. He pumped the handle on the cast iron pump over the sink and wet the lye soap in the cup and lathered it up with the boar brush with the ivory handle. He walked out the back door to the back of Granny's house letting the old screen door slam, and opened the rough, wooden door with the peep hole shaped like a crescent moon cut in the top center of the old wooden door on the outhouse. He turned the wooden latch on the nail lining it up with the door frame to open the door. It squeaked open and he stepped inside.

Once inside, he hooked the door with a latch like the kind an old screen door has to keep others out. The barn wood outhouse walls had no finish on them. Inside the outhouse, he sat down on the wooden seat with the two holes in it for using the bathroom. He leaned on the seat more than sat on it. He set the shaving cup down on the rough, wooden board. The outhouse smelled of urine and other excrements that needed to be removed. He had cleaned it for Granny in the past when he was a young boy, but now it was Papa's job, and he had yellow fever so it needed emptying.

He stripped naked and sat on the rough, wooden seat. He lathered a small area of his skin with the wet boar hair brush and soap, rubbed the brush around and around in a circular motion on the round soap bar in the bottom of the cup to get a lather and then rubbed the boar hair brush on the area of his skin he wanted to shave.

The soapy smell of lye was stronger than that of urine, making being in the outhouse bearable. He scraped the hair off his body with the straight-edge razor like his grandpa had scraped the hair off a hog with a sharp knife at their last hog killing on a cold day in January. He sat there for a while looking at the carvings in the walls inside the outhouse. Names of people in Granny's family- Mavis, Conner, Jane, Victoria, Julia, Tommy, and John – had been carved in the walls. It was a type of rough-hewn family tree. A bucket of corn cobs hung by the bail on a nail by the side of a hole. Then Tom Lewis chewed a big wad of the chewing tobacco and swallowed the spit, an action that would have made anyone else sick enough to puke. It didn't even seem to make him nauseated. He would go through anything to get rid of the voices in his head-even eating chewing tobacco.

"You are no good," the voice in his head said again. "I'm going to haunt you for the rest of your miserable life. You can't kill me. I'm stronger than you. You are sorry. Why don't you cut your throat with that straight razor, instead of just shaving your skin? Those voodoo bugs are under the skin anyway not on top. You can't get them by shaving the hair off. Get rid of yourself. No one wants you around here anyway. My voodoo bugs are going to eat you alive. They'll take over your body. They'll make you itch. They'll hatch under your skin like on a squirrel with scabbies. Tom Lewis, you belong to me now. You look like a scraped hog. You're nothing," the voice of Marie Laveau in his head said. Then he took a large handful of sulfur and threw it into his mouth. He ate it, rubbing the rest of the sulfur on his freshly shaved skin that tuned red and now stung from razor burn and his scratching. After eating the sulfur and shaving, he put his blood-stained overalls back on. The roughness of the denim rubbed against the straight-edge razor burn and made the itchy rash bleed more, staining his over-alls more, but the blood dried quickly. He came out of the outhouse, sore and in pain, but his persecutors were still there inside his head.

"You all right?" Jane asked. She had gone to Shug's house behind Granny's to get Charlie from Oma and stood in Granny's backyard holding on to him, looking at Tom Lewis. She stared at the way Tom Lewis squinted his eyes and knew he wasn't okay.

"I'm going to look for Marie Laveau. I'm going back to the little people's camp to see what they've done with her," Tom Lewis said. "Don't worry. I'll slip in so they don't know I'm out there."

"Why?" Jane asked. "I'm glad to be rid of her."

"How you know?" Tom Lewis asked.

"What?" Jane asked. "How do I know what?"

"How do you know that you are rid of her? Ain't no one in this county ever gonna be rid of her. We ain't never going to truly be rid of her around here. She's the voodoo queen of New Orleans and the entire South. She's got followers in this area, too. We ain't that far from New Orleans. She's got kids. Her doings will be in this area a hundred years from now. Two hundred maybe. Why, Charlie is a caul baby. His daddy was Professor Huerta, Marie Laveau's husband. He's always going to be here. Marie Laveau will live on around here like those Confederate ghosts. She will float in an out, in and out, in and out. She's in my head now."

"Just don't bring her back here to Kilmichael. If you get her back from the little people, lock her in that Confederate tunnel in the cemetery in French Camp, and block the exit inside the church. Don't let her get out. Not now. I don't want her to kidnap Charlie or me again. She tried to make me work in a brothel in New Orleans. I got out by crawling out an upstairs window and then down a trellis. James waited below in his wagon and drove me and Charlie out of New Orleans. She thinks she is a voodoo priestess. She is evil. She wants to turn Charlie into a voodoo king." Jane said. "She even sent Johnny Tingle to marry me to get Charlie away from me." She had left out the part of going to the New Orlean's Mint because she didn't think he knew the truth about the Confederate gold."

"And that Confederate gold? Don't forget she wants that gold. I went there too and followed her to the New Orleans Mint to get those coins you and Johnny Tingle had melted, but you and James Fares' had already picked it up. She put a spell on those folks at the mint when they didn't give her the gold. A voodoo spell with snakes. You still got some of it? The gold, I mean. Don't you?" Tom Lewis asked.

"Why? Do you need some money to get away from Sheriff Marks? Or go to a hospital to get your mind better?" Jane asked.

"I ain't going back to any mental hospital, not now, not ever. I went to the Oneida Community in New York, and they made me worse, like they made Charles Guiteau. Do you know who he is? He's a politician who supports the Stalwart section of the Republican Party. He's like me. They made him worse too. They feed you glass in Oneida house and give you very cold, cold baths to shock you into coming to your senses they call it. They take pleasure in torturing crazy folks, their patients. They support free love. They are sicker than the patients. The folks that work there in those hospitals, they are mean. Nellie Bly."

"What in the world do you keep talking about Nellie Bly for?" Jane asked. "I heard you say 'Nellie Bly' that day as you rode away on your bicycle from Marie Laveau's voodoo ritual in the Big Black River," Jane said. "That was the same day she had the snakes attack Professor Huerta, causing him to drown. By the way, I never did thank you for saving me from Professor Huerta."

"Bly's trying to help patients in the mental hospitals," Tom Lewis said. "Folks like me and Charles Guiteau. She's on our side. I like Nellie Bly."

Chapter 50

Carefully and as silently as possible, Tom Lewis crawled on his hands and knees through the tall sage grass for the last 50 feet into the little people's camp where they had set up their homemade tents in a circle and had built a large fire pit in the middle. The tall Johnson grass made his shaved skin itch more or maybe it was the voodoo bugs still under his skin. There in the camp, tied with whitetail leather straps to a smooth well-used cedar tree post, he saw Marie Laveau, her long, black hair blowing in the wind. Her white, linen tunic and skirt had been ripped and part of her upper torso lay bare, showing the creamy, yellow honey-color of her bare skin that was streaked with bloody scratches. Her hair had fallen free of its wrap and touched her honey-colored shoulders. *She is beautiful.* He thought. *But I hate her and that alone makes her ugly* to me. While he watched, he laughed to himself at Laveau's plight. She screamed a piercing, blood curdling scream and held it loud and long, like the high-pitched, piercing screech of a screech owl as if she knew he was there hiding in the underbrush and could help her if he wanted to, but would not and did not. Perhaps she had smelled the lye soap on his skin. She screamed until she fell asleep or became unconscious. He didn't know which, but he didn't come here to help her. He didn't want to help her. What he did know was that she communicated with him through the voices in his head, but for the last few hours she had been silent. He felt her silence. He liked for her to be silent and not to torment him. Eating the tobacco and shaving the hair off his body had made her talk less inside his head. *Maybe it was because she was dead.* He hoped. He loathed the voices in his head. He loathed Marie Laveau.

Suddenly, she raised her head as if awake or at least not yet dead, her eyes rolled back in her head like she was having a seizure, and the voices in Tom Lewis's head began again. "Tom Lewis Lynch, you are no good. You are a sorry excuse for a human. I'm a heathen and I am better than you. I am a voodoo priestess. I have thousands of followers- freed slaves, and sinners. Even they are better than you. You are no good. I am evil, and I am better than you." She talked and his head ached.

One of the little men, who had been guarding her as Tom Lewis gazed on, noticed that she had raised her head. "She's awake," he yelled to the other little men in a rough voice. The others came running toward her.

All descriptions and sizes and shapes of rough-looking little people scrambled to where she was tied in a standing position to the cedar pole, and all of them surrounded her, chanting and screeching like screech owls. They were so loud that Tom Lewis put his hands over his ears. Some were men. Some were women. Some were children. But all were muddy, nasty, and dressed in rags or tattered leather. They had big heads for the size of their bodies, but folks said that they were normal people with short arms and legs and short torsos, like midgets, only they were an entire tribe of midgets. Of course, they were inbred. And according to all accounts in this area and the rest of the Southeast, they were mean, meaner than Indians on the warpath but not exactly savage. All looked as if they bathed and washed their raggedy clothes in the muddy, chocolate-colored Big Black River. One of them had dug a huge pit deep in the ground while Marie Laveau slept. They untied the deer leather straps holding her, tied up her stained, white linen tunic and skirt, and cast her feet first into the pit. Each one of them took turns throwing and kicking dirt in on her as she stood inside that hole until she was buried up to her neck in a hell pit similar to those used by Indians. It was a makeshift jail.

So as not to be the next one in a little people jail hell pit, Tom Lewis crawled backwards out of his hiding place in the tall, broom sage grass. Once out of their sight, he stood, and sneaked away from the little people's camp down the narrow but well-worn path through a thick undergrowth of sweet gum saplings and black berry briars back toward Kilmichael. He cringed at how close their camp was to town and at how unsafe the people who lived there really were and how they were so unaware of the danger lurking in the gully near them. "I wonder if they ever hear the screeching of the little people?" he said aloud.

While walking back to Granny's house, he had a feeling that he was being followed, so he took the long way across a log on Big Black River, meandering through the damp, swampy area near the muddy river. He had not seen anyone behind him, but he knew those little people were good hunters and especially very good trackers, so he cut through the swampy region, and waded through the shallow, muddy water in his path. Upon reaching the town, he ran as fast as he could though the city streets of Kilmichael. He wondered through the narrow streets back and forth, alternately running and walking, through the small town east and west until he felt like whoever had been following him had given up, or he had lost them. At first, he thought it was someone from the little people's camp, but then he remembered that he was an escaped prisoner, so he thought the person following him might be an informant or a deputy of Sheriff Marks. So after an hour of sneaking and backtracking, he thought he had lost them, or tired them out, so he walked to the back porch of Granny's house and sneaked across the bare boards of the old, wooden porch where the wooden door to the kitchen was open but the screen door was closed to let in fresh air and keep flies and mosquitoes out, and he heard James Fares' voice, so he peeked inside to see Jane sitting there and listened through the screen door.

James Fares' sat on a straight-backed wooden chair at the red-checkered, oil cloth-covered table cloth inside the kitchen. He said that he had received a letter from his father from New Orleans. It was brought by a post rider.

"Jane, I'm going to read my Daddy's letter aloud to you. I'm sure you will find it intriguing:

Dear James,

I hope you and that sweet girl Jane made it back to her home in Kilmichael. I truly would like to get to know her better, but it was obvious that she didn't belong in that New Orleans brothel or any other for that matter.

Apparently, Marie Laveau has followed you there. Well, I am certain that she did. I heard that Laveau went to the New Orleans Mint, but you and Jane had beat her there and gotten the gold coins from the melted brick of Confederate gold. Since then, Laveau has disappeared from here in New Orleans and word has it, she followed you and Jane to Mississippi that same day. I hope my letter beats her there, but I doubt it will. She moves very quickly.

This letter has two points. The first is to be careful where Laveau is concerned. She wants Huerta's baby Charlie and all that Confederate gold. You know what she is capable of. The second point is that I need Laveau back here in New Orleans to run the brothel and the liquor import business. I know she thinks that she is a voodoo priestess, and she may be, but she is a very shrewd business woman and was making us money with the brothel and the liquor imports. Now, we are losing money right and left. I need her back here.

I hired a man to run the liquor imports, but he was skimming money off the top, so I fired him. Madame Lucille is running the brothel, but she is not as good at getting the girls to do what they need to do as Marie Laveau was. I guess they were as afraid of Laveau as you and Jane should be. She's never cast a spell on me. As a matter of fact, she never has been anything but nice to me, but she knew where her bread was buttered, so to speak.

I heard that Jane and you took Jane's son Charlie with you back to Kilmichael. I heard, too, that Professor Huerta, Marie Laveau's husband, is that boy's father. The Lord only knows how that came about. I hate to venture a guess. I hope all is well with Charlie and, as far as Jane's concerned.

I also heard that Jane's step-father is insane, has killed a deputy sheriff, and then when convicted, escaped from prison. People saw him at the New Orleans Mint whenever Marie Laveau went to get that gold, so he knows that you and Jane have it. Son, be very careful. Both of those people are very dangerous.

Sincerely, your father,

Fares'

Tom Lewis listened as James read the letter to Jane. He wondered why James didn't let Jane read the letter herself. Tom Lewis figured that there was a part in it that he didn't want her to know about.

I knew that James Fares' couldn't be trusted. He thought. *He and his father are in cahoots with Laveau in business deals. She is money in the bank to them.*

"Do you know where Marie Laveau is? If she was here in Kilmichael, where would she be staying?" James asked. "I need to find Laveau to get her back to New Orleans to help my father," James said.

"I'm certain that I don't know," Jane lied, but having Marie Laveau away from here made Jane happy.

Well, it really isn't a lie. Tom Lewis thought. *She doesn't know that Laveau is buried up to her neck in a hell pit at the little people camp. Fares' doesn't know about the little people, and he doesn't know where they are living. I hope.*

****

Tom Lewis left Granny's back porch to travel back across the Big Black River to French Camp. He planned to drive his wagon across the Big Black River trail to the Confederate tunnel, so he could get some sleep. He would hide the wagon in the woods near the cemetery in French Camp where the Confederate tunnel lay.

***

Slipping down the rutted trail and across the bridge at the Big Black River was simple tonight because the moon was full and shone the way very well. Sparkles glistened on the leaves. When Tom Lewis neared the hanging tree, he heard very loud, piercing, screeching sounds like that of a half dozen screech owls. Then he heard a shrill, high-pitched laugh. He knew that Marie Laveau was still alive. He knew that these sounds were not inside his head.

He rode on south down the rutted trail, hoping that the little people were so busy with Laveau that they wouldn't know he was on the trail.

He was wrong.

Chapter 51

Suddenly screaming, screeching dirty, ragged little people that looked like magical fairies in the moonlight instead of humans surrounded the old, gray horse and wooden wagon with yellow wheels that belonged to Papa. His horse was bewildered and reared on its hind legs. "We've got you," one of them screamed in a form of English that Tom Lewis couldn't completely understand. It seemed to be a combination of rough, broken English and native Cherokee or Choctaw or other Native American language. "You can join that voodoo woman in the hell pit."

"Aarg, aarg," Tom Lewis replied to their screams. "Whoa, boy."

He tried to calm his horse, but it left pulling the wagon with her. "You may capture me. You may take me to your camp. But you don't have me. I will escape. You'll be sorry. I am not afraid of you fairy people. You should be afraid of me." Tom Lewis couldn't be certain that they understood his words.

"I'm sorry already," one of the more fairy-like, dwarfish women said as she walked next to Tom Lewis toward the little people camp. "We should have left you alone." He looked at her and saw a beautiful, miniature, almost child-sized woman with short arms and legs, but her clothing wasn't as shabby as theirs. Her clothes were made of leather and adorned with tiny sea shells and beads much like the ones the Indians wore. Her shiny, black hair mixed with silvery gray hung in loose curls half-the-way down her back. She seemed to be able to tell them what to do, and they listened to her as if she was the queen bee of the hive. "I'm Yunwi. Yunwi." She told Tom Lewis. He looked at her with admiration, gratitude, and now a feeling of love. Her name sounded like queen bee.

"Yunwi," he said aloud. "Yunwi. Queen Bee."

She is the kind of woman I heard my Choctaw great- grandmother telling stories about -little people helping people, but harshly punishing people who were disrespectful to them and their tribe. Grandmother said that these people were magical and like Indians, but not as savage. I'll be nice and kind to Yunwi. He thought. *Maybe she will be helpful to me.*

"Yunwi, you are a nice woman and beautiful," Tom Louis said. "Grandmother said you are magical. You smell nice, too."

"Not, magical. Nice. Respectful," Yunwi said. "But not magical." Her dark eyes sparkled when she talked.

"Yes, nice," Tom Lewis said, having made a friend in the little people camp. "I heard that you are able to disappear at will." She looked beautiful to him. He loved her dark, brown eyes that seemed to talk to him. He felt that he loved her too. He hoped that she wouldn't disappear.

"Yes, I can disappear," Yunwi said, laughing. "We all can. It is something that I teach my people to do as children. Disappearing is very helpful."

"My name is Tom Lewis, Yunwi," he said. "Teach me? Teach me to disappear."

"Yes, I know all about you Tom Lewis Lynch and about your situations," Yunwi said. "You be nice. I will help. I have an herb that will make you feel much better."

"What about Marie Laveau, Yunwi?"

"She's not nice. She is voodoo. You understand voodoo?"

"No, I don't. I don't like voodoo. Do you?"Tom Lewis said. "When I was a kid, my grandmother said not to step in puddles or you or some others like you would show up."

"You believe," Yunwi asked. "You believe your grandmother?'

"Yes, when I was a child. I did," Tom Lewis said, laughing at the absurdity of the idea. The voices in his head were silent when Yunwi talked to him, and whenever he looked into her eyes. This silence made him like her more and more. He liked the silent voices, and he liked Yunwi. Since his wife died, he had been looking for another woman to silence the voices. Yunwi did. Then, when his wife had been alive, the aliens or people from the sky started chasing him, starting the voices again. That was the day he dived into the pond and hid in the beaver hole where he could get air. He had come out of that pond looking as dirty as some of these little men did. Yunwi said that she knew about his situations. He wondered if she knew about the beaver hole. That was how he had disappeared.

They walked through the sage grass across the field, then across the Big Black swamp, and back up a hill covered in sand rocks for a short distance before they reached the little people camp where Marie Laveau was still buried up to her neck in the dirt pit. Tom Lewis looked around the outdoor camp where the little people lived. He felt sorry for them, but admired them at the same time. Their resourcefulness amazed him. They had their own civilization that in these times since the Civil War wasn't really civilized at all. They resembled Native Americans in their customs and ways, but they seemed to be less savage and more educated, if that was possible. His grandmother had told him that they were nice if you were nice to them. He looked at Yunwi as she interacted with the other little people in the camp. She controlled them; they did whatever she said to do. She was their leader.

Suddenly, a huge chaos or confusion overtook the camp. Tom Lewis understood what Yunwi said somewhat, but he couldn't understand what the others said, especially to each other and especially in their hurried excitement. He didn't know what was happening or what had caused the confusion, but he didn't think it had been him.

Tom Lewis looked around at their camp. The deer skin tents had been set up in a circle like a wagon train would have been to help ward off the attacks of savages. The center poles that held up the tents were made from peeled cedar poles. The smell of the cedar pole floated toward Tom Lewis. A flap hung in the front of each tent for an entrance. Tom Lewis wondered if the little people had been raised by the Indians or by those wagon train settlers traveling west to the territories. Maybe they migrated. They had to have come from somewhere. His grandmother had said they came from Georgia. *I don't think they are in this area all the time.*

"A storm is coming," Yunwi said. "I can smell it. We must move on toward the north. We must dig up Marie Laveau before the storm arrives. We have a weather man here in our tribe, but he didn't forecast this one. Although my bones felt like a storm was coming, this storm was a surprise to most of us. I guess it was also a surprise to him."

Suddenly with much thunder and lightning, the rain began, and the sky turned dark purple and red. The little people grabbed their belongings, homemade leather tents, food, pots, weapons, and children. With their backs and arms loaded, they rushed across the ridge with arms full of their belongings and tents flung across their backs. They swarmed down a trail toward the edge of Attala County where they had once inhabited an Indian cave to wait for the storm to pass before they moved to the North as the Indians had before them. Tom Lewis glanced at Marie Laveau's frightened face. The mud splashed on it when the rain hit the ground making her look as if she had small pox sores or bad pimples, but the cold rain woke her up. In their haste to leave, they had not taken time to dig Marie Laveau out of the hell pit that imprisoned her, and Tom Lewis didn't remind Yunwi. Laveau didn't matter to them now as much as their safety from the storm did, and Tom Lewis wanted to leave her where she was.

"I'll get her," Tom Lewis said in a gesture to help the little people more than saving Laveau. He wanted Yunwi to find him helpful. Suddenly, all the little people including Yunwi disappeared. While he was looking at Marie Laveau, they had quickly and, as soundlessly as possible, left the area. Tom Lewis looked around for the little people, but not one person was visible.

Then he heard a couple of horses coming up the trail toward the hell pit. The little people must have heard the horses too. Tom Lewis moved behind a large oak tree that was wide enough to hide his body. There was a male rider and one other empty horse. The rider stopped within inches of Marie Laveau in the hell pit. It was James Fares'.

***

Tom Lewis watched James Fares' dismount and stand over Laveau at the hell pit. He had a shovel in his hand and immediately began digging her out of the pit while the light rain fell and the thunder rolled. He threw dirt and sand every which way until she was free of the pit. Of course, her white, linen clothing was covered with dirt and mud stains, so James took some old clothes out of his saddle bag and threw them at her. Tom Lewis recognized them as patterns of clothing that had once belonged to his mother. Granny. He had slept under a crazy quilt Granny made from most of those patterns as random-sized scraps sewn together as a top and then quilted by a group of women from Kilmichael. He remembered his mother having quilting parties at their house and making some quilts with similar scraps. Often, he sat in the corner and listened to them talk.

Marie looked down at herself and her muddy, stained, white linen tunic and skirt and then took the clothes he had brought and moved behind the bushes to change. She came out looking like a dark -skinned Granny, but she carried herself in a more elegant posture that demanded respect and made her presence known; Tom Lewis still hated her.

How did Fares' know she would need clean clothes? Tom Lewis thought. *Why had he brought a shovel? Jane must have told him where Laveau might be, but how did Jane know where the camp was?*

Tom Lewis watched as Marie weakly walked out from behind the blackberry bushes, and Fares' helped her onto a spare horse that he had brought with him and told her, "My father is waiting for you in New Orleans. Don't make him wait too long. Do not stay here in Kilmichael. He won't be happy. He needs you to come back to work at the liquor import business and the brothel in New Orleans as soon as possible. You know New Orleans needs you. You are Marie Laveau, the voodoo priestess."

Marie Laveau and James Fares' mounted the horses left together. They traveled in the same direction that he had come which was back toward Kilmichael. Tom Lewis had a funny feeling in the pit of his stomach that he should warn Jane about Fares' and Laveau, but instead he wanted to follow Yunwi whose hold on him was stronger than his need to help Jane.

Tom Lewis followed the sparse tracks of Yunwi and the little people to the Indian cave in Attala county. They traveled across an upper ridge in the terrain that was littered with sand rocks and soon gave way to a different, harder, larger kind of white rocks and boulders. Some boulders were as big as half the size of a wagon, but some were small enough to build the walls of a house. On top of the ridge was the narrow opening of a cave in the side of a large hill, but once inside the opening, it opened up into a large, open room. A large fire had been started, and he in the flickering firelight he saw that the walls were covered with pictographs or hand-drawn pictures that seemed to tell a story of a hunt by the Indians hundreds of years ago. Tom Lewis wasn't certain which tribe had made the drawings. Perhaps it was Choctaw or Chickasaw. There was no way to know unless Yunwi knew. The cave was located in a rocky hill west of the trail. Large white clay rocks and scrub brush covered the front entrance, making it difficult to see its opening. The trail was littered with smaller, white clay rocks sticking out of the ground like parts of boulders. *I wonder if rattlesnakes live in this cave.* He thought, but decided the fire and smoke would run them out if they were there.

The other little people acted like he wasn't welcomed, but they respected Yunwi's wishes for him to remain. *He knew he might be in a pot of stew now if not for Yunwi.* She seemed to be a leader of the group. He and Yunwi were becoming good friends. He talked to her in her language and in his own, and she did the same. He told her about Fares' saving Marie Laveau. They learned from each other. That night, he made a pallet on the floor of the cave near her, and she moved close to him during the night. He squeezed his eyes tightly closed to silence the voices in his head. He tasted the salty tears that rolled down his cheeks.

Yunwi unbuckled Tom's overalls and moved her hands down to massage him until he was very erect.

He kissed her deeply and cupped her ample breasts in his hands. Yunwi responded to him until she was moaning with pleasure and all the other "little people" in the cave knew it. Of course, they didn't care and Tom Lewis loved it.

The next morning, he watched as the little people prepared a breakfast of roasted squirrel on a stick and a form of moonshine like mead that tasted sweet like honey but was made from corn like moonshine. Tom Lewis loved the moonshine made from corn. This had less fire than the moonshine the men who lived around French Camp made. Even the little people children drank it. This was the only beverage besides milk and water that was drunk with meals. Lunch was more of the same. From the warm flicker of the fire, he examined the cave walls and the visible little people. The walls were rough as if carved, but some of the drawings had colors. Yunwi seemed to be the most intelligent and beautiful woman there. No wonder she was the queen bee. The little people women had gathered wild rice, berries, and fruit for them to eat. These they cooked into some of the most wonderful meals. They made some of the fruit mixture into flat, pressed patties and cooked them until brown and dry. These patties resembled pancakes. They wrapped them in clean skins and put them into their pouches for eating later. He noticed that the women were equal to the men in strength and endurance, but they had other duties that the men didn't share like shelling corn for moonshine and taking care of the children.

They all stayed together for several days and nights inside the cave until the rain storms cleared the area. Tom and Yunwi spent all their spare time having sex. It was a time that he wouldn't ever forget.

Yunwi enjoyed everything Tom did to her. He loved the oral sex that he did to Yunwi until a fluid that squirted all over his face. She was uninhibited, and he loved every minute of it.

One of the younger little people's babies was born while they were inside the cave. Tom Lewis noticed her sneak away deeper into the back of the cave, but not a sound could be heard from her until the cry of the newborn baby awakened the others. Tom Lewis was amazed and no man seemed to claim being the child's father.

One morning, Tom Lewis made his way out of the mouth of the cave to relieve himself. He noticed that the rain had stopped. It was difficult to tell in the rocky terrain how much it had rained or how muddy the trails would be farther up the trail. Tom Lewis was amazed at how afraid they were of storms. Generally, nothing else seemed to frighten them, but the storms really had.

The next day, one of the little people men came into the mouth of the cave and announced, "Whacko, whacko ball time!" in a mixed language that Tom Lewis was beginning to understand. Apparently, the storms had ended. When he announced this, the rest of the men and a few of the women got excited and jumped up and down, dancing in a circle around the fire pit in the largest part of the cave. Their dancing reminded him of children playing games in the church yard or the school playground. Then they pulled open some large, leather, hand-sewn bags and took out sticks with webbed deer leather strips at the top and handles at the bottom, and an oblong leather ball that appeared to be stuffed with more leather and sewn by hand at the seams. It reminded him of a crude baseball.

Yunwi told Tom Lewis the rules of whacko ball. The rules of the game were similar to what Tom Lewis understood Native American stickball to be which meant that there actually were no rules and could involve hundreds of players and uneven fields which often left injured players. Yunwi said, "The object of the game is to drive the leather ball between two trees that had been previously designated as the goal posts. She pointed in the direction of the two trees. They drop kicked the ball and often they competed to see who could kick it the farthest." Although the Indians played a similar game called stick ball, the little people handmade their own rackets and balls for this game, and they looked different from those the Indians used. A racket was a throwing stick or arm extender, which the little people needed to play because of their short arms and legs and to add force and distance to the reach that the ball could travel. The curved rackets had netted ends of woven bark or rawhide from deer skin. Some of these rackets measured 5 feet long. They were longer that the people were tall.

"We feel like giants using these," Yunwi told him. He chuckled at her making light of the fact that they were short. He liked her more and more each day, especially since the voices in his head were silent whenever she was around. She gave him some kind of herb, and it helped his problems tremendously. But she kept the herbs in a pouch around her waist. It was a plant that he didn't recognize. She called it lamb's ear.

Finally, the whacko game began, and Tom Lewis watched as the fastest runners in the group ran at full speed ahead toward the opposite end of the field area, and the larger men and boys stood their ground in the center of the field. He looked around to see where the women had gone, but none were visible. Once the ball was tossed into the air, a violent scuffle began to recover the ball. Some players got whacked so hard on the head that they were rendered unconscious. Tom Lewis noticed that the injured were left to wake where they had fallen, and he didn't offer to go help them because Yunwi laid her hand on his arm when he indicated that he was going. This is where the name of whacko ball originated. Yunwi said. "A period of practice has been added into each day for the young boys until they learned how to play, so these players are experienced."

Finally, Tom Lewis asked Yunwi where the women were.

"They hide naked in the bushes to entice the opposition players away from the game. It is not unusual to find girls and the opposition team's players having sex. All the players have to do is slide the flap covering their erections to the side and enter the naked girls from the back. Often more than player entered more than one naked girl. Or to at least the naked girls distract them," she giggled. "Lots of them get pregnant during these games and don't know who the father of their baby is."

"Hmmm," he said. He was intrigued. "Perhaps that is why no man claimed to be the father of that girl's baby who gave birth in the cave, and it could also explain the men's excitement about playing."

"Exactly," Yunwi answered.

After two days and one night, the whacko games ended and life for the little people returned to normal. While the women set up the skin tents again outside the cave but near the mouth of it, Yunwi taught the children writing with pictures. It wasn't unlike those drawings Tom Lewis saw on the cave walls. The children wrote on large pieces of slate with pieces of dried clay that Yunwi told him had been gathered out of the creek beds and put in the sun to dry. She taught classes of magic spells and potions, but none of the spells used snakes like Marie Laveau's did. And Tom Lewis was glad of that. Some of the men taught the children to hunt and to dress the game animals. But Yunwi was the one who taught them to tan the hides for leather to make clothes or bags or tents.

Tom Lewis watched and learned, too. He had learned much from Yunwi and enjoyed every minute of it.

Yunwi instructed, "To tan the hides, you scrape every particle of fat and fleshy meat from the hide with a sharp knife." She gave Tom Lewis a rabbit hide and a sharp knife. He scraped until no fat or rabbit meat was left on the hide. He wanted to please her.

Yunwi explained that this scraping kept the hide from rotting and that Tom Lewis had to be careful not to cut a hole in the hide with the knife. To begin the tanning process and preserve the hide, she covered the scraped side of the hide with a generous layer of plain salt. Tom Lewis helped her rub the salt into the rabbit skin. Some of the salt got into cuts on his hands and stung.

Others of the little people tribe soaked their hides in a large vat of salt solution. Their hides were stretched to a frame and left to dry. Tom Lewis found that this hide tanning was a time-consuming procedure and that the salt or the solution was removed, and if the soaking solution was used, the hide was wrung dry. Then a pound of alum was dissolved in hot water. The skins were soaked in this liquid for about three days. Yunwi helped him wring this solution out of the hide and hang it on low branches.

After it was dry, they rubbed a stinking mixture of animal brains and boiled vegetable broth into the hide to soften it. It took days, but Tom Lewis enjoyed being with Yunwi. He enjoyed watching her. He enjoyed the silence inside his head while she was around. He thought that he was going to marry her if she would. Although nothing about marriage seemed a practice of these little people.

A couple of the little people males made moonshine outside the entrance to the cave. At Yunwi's insistence, they let Tom Lewis watch. They had fashioned a whiskey still and worm out of a pipe and began by boiling a mixture of corn mash made from crushed corn that the women had grown and crushed with rocks and water to a high temperature. Yeast that they had stolen from a local moonshiner near the hanging tree was added. The smell alone could knock you out. They laughed when they talked about stealing the yeast and the pipe, sure that Tom Lewis couldn't understand what they were saying. The skinniest little person that looked as if he had drunk his share of their moonshine stirred the mash mixture every once in a while and then let it set to ferment.

After 7 days, this mixture was put into their homemade whiskey still, and the sediment was left in the clay vat. This solution was cooked and then water and sugar were added. They aerated the mixture by dumping it back and forth into two buckets. Then it was cooked again and run into clay whiskey jugs and corked with a corn cob to be drunk later. Corn whiskey was their favorite everyday beverage, but mead or whiskey made from honey was their special drink.

Yunwi offered Tom Lewis some of the moonshine, and just as he was about to drink it, Sheriff Marks rode into the little people camp. Finally accepting Tom Lewis as a friend not an enemy, the little people surrounded the Sheriff to protect Tom Lewis and tied him with leather deer straps to a similar cedar pole like Marie Laveau had been tied to.

"Yunwi, I need to take him back to French Camp," Tom Lewis said. "I'm gonna put him where he can't get away." He drank his moonshine from the gourd that was handed to him. Tom Lewis liked it, too. The more he drank; the bolder he became.

"I'll help you," Yunwi replied. She had a puzzled look on her face.

"Ok, we will tie him up and take him to a place where I can lock him in," Tom Lewis said.

"You mean tunnel?" Yunwi asked.

"Yes, the Confederate tunnel," Tom Lewis said. "At the cemetery."

"Ghosts. Ghosts are in that tunnel. I'll not go inside there. You take him inside by yourself," Yunwi said. "I'll help you get him there, but I'm not going inside that tunnel."

"Okay, Yunwi. Thank you," he replied. *I wonder how she knows about the Confederate tunnel.* He thought.

Chapter 52

Tom Lewis and Yunwi rode on a horse into the Cemetery at French Camp, pulling a makeshift sled behind the horse with Sheriff Marks tied to it. As they rounded a corner near the old, white church, Tom Lewis saw Marie Laveau sliding a stone back on top of a grave box near the angel gravestone statue in the cemetery where he entered the tunnel. He and Yunwi stopped their horses, and they both watched as Laveau swung two, cotton, cloth bags or heavy looking pouches over the horn of her saddle.

I'm leaving now. Yunwi motioned to him, not saying a word. "I'll wait over there. Laveau is stealing Satan's gold."

Tom Lewis blew Yunwi a kiss, but stayed still until Laveau rode away. Laveau hadn't noticed either of them because she seemed to be very excited about the two canvas bags she had taken out of the grave box and loaded onto her horse. As she rode away toward the south, Tom Lewis noticed that she still had on some of Granny's clothes. After Marie Laveau left, he rode his horse to the angel gravestone and knocked on the special place to open the Confederate tunnel. The tunnel had been used during the Civil War by the Confederates to hide from the Yankees. He dragged Sheriff Marks from the makeshift sled and into the mouth of the Confederate tunnel. He unhooked the sled from the horse, and Yunwi took the horse back to the little people camp with her. He closed the angel statue from the inside, so Sheriff Marks couldn't get out and so no one would know that they were there, just as the Yankees hadn't known that the Confederates were inside the tunnel. Then he left the sheriff tied up on the cool stone floor of the entrance and made his way toward the other end and out the door inside the church. He locked the tunnel door inside the church, so the Sheriff was locked inside.

Chapter 53

Sheriff Marks

Sheriff Marks wiggled and squirmed on the cold, stone floor of the tunnel until he was free from the tight deer leather straps that held his hands and then he untied his ankles. Finally free from the restraints, he stood up in the tunnel by inching his way up the stone walls. Luckily, Tom Lewis and that little people woman, Yunwi, hadn't searched his pockets, so he still had a few strike-anywhere matches. Those little people amazed him and terrified him at the same time. *I will be glad whenever they leave this area.* He thought. Carefully, he struck a match on the stone wall to light the pitch-black, stone prison he had been left in to die. He looked around, getting his bearings until his match went out, and then he struck another match. He slipped one hand in the pocket with the matches and counted about ten matches. He watched the flame. It followed the draft. He walked south toward the direction Tom Lewis had gone while he had some faint light from the match. Of course, the match went out quickly, too. So he felt his way along the stone walls of the tunnel. He felt the smoothness as if the stones had been polished, but surprisingly, they were not damp as he had expected, and he knew the creek that ran beside the library wasn't too far away. When he had gone about 25 yards, he noticed that the texture of the walls changed. He struck another match and saw what looked like iron hinges or some other iron apparatus, so he carefully watched the red glow of the match's flame and the smoke. The smoke followed a draft that came from around the iron appendages. He knocked on the iron like Tom Lewis had knocked on the angel gravestone. First to the left, then the top, and to the right he knocked. Tap, tap, tap. He knocked. A stone-like door opened into the same cave where Jane had found and removed the Confederate gold. He knew that she had carried some of it to the New Orleans Mint because he had heard Charlie, the livery stable owner talking about it. No gold remained inside, but Sheriff Marks thought that this cave led to the creek that ran by the library. He saw bats hanging from the ceiling. He smelled the musky smell of them. *The bats didn't enter the tunnel like I did through the angel gravestone, so there must be another way in and out, and I will find it. If they can get in, I can get out.* He thought. He waved his arms around, and the bats fled out into the Confederate tunnel where he had been previously. He was glad that they were gone. Bats horrified him, and they carried rabies. Although there was a vaccine, he didn't like shots or doctors or hospitals, and he was locked in this tunnel with them.

Sheriff Marks had only one main problem now. He needed a light source, so he stuck his hand in his pockets to find another match. He struck it and looked around inside this cavern for something else to burn as a light. He found an old, cotton, canvas sack on the floor of the cave. He stuck the match to it, but it didn't ignite. He reached into his pocket for another match. He felt and counted the matches he had left. He had only five. He felt thankful for the coolness of the cave; otherwise, he would be sweating and the matches could be ruined from the sweat.

He struck another one of the limited number of matches. He picked up the cotton sack and held the match under it. At first, there was a small ember. Then the cotton sack ignited, glowing brightly. He held it to one side and watched the smoke. He surveyed the cave. In the dim light, he saw two old, army muskets leaning on one side of the cave, several tattered, woolen, gray, Confederate uniform coats, some old cotton shirts, a tiny shovel, and more old cotton sacks like the one he had set fire, enough to keep a flame burning for a few minutes. He followed the smoke deeper into the cavern, taking 5 of the dirty cotton sacks with him. They had straps, so he hung them over his shoulder. Later, he might have to come back for the old, cotton shirts to burn, but now, he took the shovel deeper into the opening. The entire cave smelled putrid of bat droppings and urine. The smell reminded him of cleaning an outhouse.

As he went deeper into the cavern, the cave opening got narrower and narrower until he was crawling on his belly like a snake, but he still followed the smoke. The smoke had to escape somewhere. As one sack burned out, he lit another and followed the smoke, still crawling on his belly. Gradually, the opening got so narrow that his shoulders wouldn't fit, so he backed out to where he had seen the tiny shovel about the size of one used to remove the ashes from a fireplace or wood burning stove. He saw a Confederate soldier sitting on a rock on one side of the cave. Sheriff Marks thought he was dreaming. He dragged the shovel along until he reached the narrow area again, and then he began to dig. This part of the cave was only dirt, not stone walls like the tunnel. *I bet the Confederate soldiers built that part of the tunnel themselves.* He thought. The dirt tunnel could fall in on him. So digging was possible even easy, but extremely dangerous, and the narrowness and his broad shoulders made it very difficult to do. He loaded the loose dirt onto an old, cotton sack and dragged it back into the cave. He heard the soldier laugh at the absurdity of his digging. Again he thought he was dreaming, but his survival demanded that he dig. He made his way back into the opening and started digging again. Once he began filling the cotton sack with dirt, he felt someone or something touch his ankle. Thinking it was a bat, he turned to look, but saw nothing or no one.

For hours, he dug the opening larger and larger and deeper and deeper, carrying each cotton sack full of dirt back to the larger opening in the cave where he had found the cotton sacks. He dug until he thought he could smell fresh air and hear the tinkling of water flowing like a small waterfall. He felt thirsty and his mouth felt dry from all the digging, but perhaps not so thirsty as to imagine the smell of water. *He had imagined the Confederate soldiers or were they really ghosts? Had one of them actually touched his ankle? One way or the other, he had to get out of this tunnel.* He dug for a few more hours until he fell face and shoulders into a pool of water and had to drag his feet out of the hole. The cool water felt refreshing, but he was afraid to drink it because of the bats. He knew that they carried diseases.

He stood in the shallow underground stream. The eerie sound of laughing inside the cave became louder. *Were the ghosts laughing at him?* Getting his directional bearings, he walked quickly through the creek being certain to step carefully along the creek bed and toward what he thought would lead outside beside the French Camp library. He knew the creek flowed past the library. Of course, his matches were now wet, so he inched his way along in the darkness of the creek until he saw intermittent light streams through the thick overgrowth of bamboo leaves.

I hope there are no snakes. He thought.

***

Tom Lewis Lynch

Tom Lewis wanted to travel on a raft with Tommy south down the Mississippi River to New Orleans from Natchez, but he didn't want to be trailed by the lawmen, so he was going to fake his own death like Huckleberry Finn.

Yunwi gave him a large, black wild hog. Some of the little people had snared him in a trap and then killed him with a spear. She thought Tom Lewis wanted it to eat. It was an old boar hog and much too tough to eat without boiling it for days in a large black pot. It was too tough to cook it wrapped in wet sheets or large, lily pad leaves in the ground in a pit of coals, the way he usually did a domesticated hog. The huge wild hog's tusks curved up around its nose and its coarse black hair was matted with mud that mixed with the musty wild smell of the boar. The boar weighed about 200 pounds. Tom Lewis didn't plan to eat it as Yunwi thought. Slaughtering it and letting the blood drip everywhere was a diversion he would use to throw the lawmen off his trail, so he stuck a sharp knife in the pig's neck cutting a jugular vein, making blood gush out in big, bright red spurts. Then he let the pig's blood drip onto some bloody old clothes that he had worn. He left them lying in the Church cemetery near the angel gravestone. He wanted to make everyone think that he had been murdered in that cemetery, especially the sheriff's office and Marie Laveau and James Fares'. This was his way of making Sheriff Marks think that he was no longer available for capture, but, in fact, was dead. He loaded the hog carcass into his wagon and rode into town He gave the hog carcass to Mr. Charles at the livery in exchange for a fresh horse to pull his wagon load of lumber for the raft to Natchez.

"I'm like Huckleberry Finn, you know, Mr. Charlie. I'm going on a raft trip with Tommy," Tom Lewis said.

"So you are building a raft to float down the Mississippi River? Are you? How 're you going to keep them steamboats from running you over?"Charlie asked. "Y'all be careful. Take care of yourself and Tommy. He is a fine boy. As a matter of fact, that Jane is a fine young woman, too."

"Ah, but she married that Fares' man from New Orleans. She's gonna have another baby."

Mr. Charlie helped Tom Lewis load the wagon with some rough lumber that he had bought at the saw mill earlier. Tom Lewis had bought some rope and long nails at the hardware. Carefully, he laid the wood on top of the hog's blood to cover it up, but Charlie said nothing about the stain.

He drove toward Natchez as soon as the last piece of wood was loaded into the wagon. He didn't even bother to load any food or other supplies, but he did take a rifle with him.

Chapter 54

Jane needed to go to the outhouse. Her baby's head resting on her bladder made the need to urinate happen more often now. She slipped out of the bed that she shared with James Fares', trying not to wake him. She was still too shy to use the enamel pot with the red rims that Granny had left under the edge of the bed where Jane and James slept. Opening and closing the lid made a tinkling noise, not to mention the actual noise made by urinating. She opened the squeaking back screen door and slipped across the yard toward the outhouse. A full moon illuminated her way, and having lived in this area for most of her life, Jane wasn't frightened of the dark, and she knew the way by heart. Jane turned the latch on the outside of the outhouse and peered inside. Even in the daytime, she hated going inside and closing the door to a dark closet room that could contain spiders or snakes, so she twisted the globe on the lantern, making a squeaking sound, and struck a match, smelling the sulfur smell. She didn't see any snakes –chicken snakes or rattlers - or spiders as she peered inside. She hung the lantern on a large nail inside the outhouse. Then someone tapped her on the shoulder, and she jumped almost wetting herself.

"Give us our gold. Give us or gold." Jane wondered if she was getting insane like Tom Lewis and hearing voices, but these voices weren't just in her head. Someone or something was talking to her. As she turned to face the attackers, one of the ghosts grabbed her shoulders and shook her hard enough to make her wet herself. "Give us our gold. We need it. It isn't yours to take. We plan to build up the Confederacy again with it. And that will be to your advantage."

"I will give it back to you. But first, I have to find it," Jane lied. She knew full well that it was still hidden in that grave box in the same cemetery where she had stolen it from their tunnel. That was unless someone else had found it. "I don't know where it is. My husband hid it from me. You will have to ask him. Maybe he put it in the bank."

"Liar," one of the ghosts said. "If you don't give it to us now, you will be very, very sorry. We know your husband doesn't have it. We already asked him and scared him half out of his wits, if he had any. This is the deal we will make with you. You give us our gold back, or we will take away all that is precious to you. You think about that, Missy."

With that, the ghosts disappeared.

Chapter 55

"James, is Charlie out there with you? He was playing here in the front yard inside the fence while I was hanging out clothes, but he is not there now," Jane yelled from the front porch. Her voice sounded frantic.

"No, he isn't. Have you looked at Shug's house?"

"Yes, he is not there either. Shug, Mr. Petey, and Oma are helping me look for him. He must have wandered off somewhere," Jane said. The terror in her voice reflected the terror she felt. She remembered what the ghosts had promised.

"Charlie," Jane screamed. "Charlie, where are you?" Jane's second pregnancy showed under her dress as a small mound. She was in her last month. She had not tried to hide this pregnancy since she was married to James now, but she couldn't say that she had enjoyed being pregnant since Marie Laveau was visiting in French Camp, but had disappeared which was her way.

"I was going to town; I've got to get some supplies at the hardware; I'll look on the way there and around town. Someone may have seen him," James said. He didn't sound very concerned. "He's probably playing around here somewhere, Jane. Don't worry. We will find him. Did you look under the house? He may be playing under there. I've seen him hide under there when the kids play hide and seek. I'm going into town, and if you like, I'll ask the sheriff's office to come help us."

"The sheriff's office? Do you think Charlie has been kidnapped again?" Jane demanded. "Do you know something that you aren't telling me? Has Marie Laveau been back near here? Have you seen her? I know you like her because she worked for your father, but I'm telling you from personal experience that she's a demonic creature, and she's really all about herself." Jane hadn't told anyone about the visit from the ghosts except Shug.

"No. Well, I haven't seen her and she's not demonic; she just practices voodoo. Jane, you don't understand voodoo. The folks in New Orleans worship it much like a religion like being Baptist is around here, and they are entertained by it. I'll ask Mr. Charlie at the livery stable. He would know if she is here. Y'all keep looking around here. And look under the house. Have you looked everywhere inside Granny's house? Charlie is very small. He could hide most anywhere like under furniture or in closets. I'll be back as soon as possible. If I find him, I'll bring him back with me and give him a good whipping for running off."

"You will not," Jane replied. "Charlie, where are you?" Jane screamed until her throat hurt. "Charlie?" As James rode away, she opened the screen door to look inside the house again. Not finding him there, she ran out the back door and across the yard to Shug's house.

"Shug, I can't find Charlie. Can you?"

"No, Mis' Jane. I cain't," Shug replied. "Petey is looking under the house."

"Charlie," Jane screamed. "Charlie, where are you?"

∗∗∗

After digging his way out of the Confederate tunnel, Sheriff Marks eased open the door of his office and dripped creek water and mud on his floor. His deputies slept off their drink from the night before sitting in the straight back chairs, leaned back on the back legs with their feet propped on his desk. He slammed the door hard, waking them. One fell back on the floor and the other jumped to his feet. "Sheriff, where have you been? We looked everywhere for you," one of the hung-over deputies said.

"Not everywhere," he said with a touch of anger in his voice.

"While we were looking for you, we found some old, denim overhauls like Tom Lewis Lynch wears. They were drenched in blood. They were in the cemetery near that statue of the angel. I think someone murdered Tom Lewis Lynch. We thought you did, but we didn't find his body. We didn't find a body at all," the deputy said. "And we couldn't find you."

"I guess not," he said, indicating their drunken states and the bottles on his desk. "We wouldn't be that lucky," Sheriff Marks replied, "for Tom Lewis to have died. He should be wearing prison clothes, but instead, he's traveling all over the South like he owns the place. I guess he does. Well, as you can see, I'm alive, but wet and muddy. I'm going home to get cleaned up and get some dry clothes. Then we will question everyone we can find in town." He didn't tell them where he had been. He didn't tell them about the Confederate tunnel. He didn't tell them that Tom Lewis and that strange little woman he called Yunwi had captured him and locked him inside that haunted tunnel. "Get these bottles of booze out of here before you lose your jobs."

As he was leaving, James Fares' burst through the door, "Jane's baby Charlie is missing," he said. "I think Marie Laveau took him."

"Maybe Tom Lewis took him. These deputies say that he's disappeared too. Let's go talk to Mr. Charlie at the Livery. He'll know either way," Sheriff Marks said.

James and the Sheriff walked down the street to the Livery Stable.

James didn't ask him about the mud and his wet clothes. James detected his bad mood.

Once they reached the livery, Sheriff Marks questioned Mr. Charlie. "Tom Lewis's gone to float down the Mississippi River to

New Orleans with Tommy. He thinks he is Huckleberry Finn," Mr. Charlie said. "But he didn't have that baby Charlie with him."

"Does he know that Jane Lynch's baby Charlie is missing? I wonder if Marie Laveau took him," Sheriff Marks asked. "You talked to Tom Lewis?"

"Yes, but I don't think he knows. He was probably kidnapped by Marie Laveau. She wants Charlie so she can train him to be the next voodoo priest like his father was. And although she didn't say so, I know she has left going back to New Orleans. I sold her a horse and buggy," Mr. Charlie told them.

"Lordy, man, you are aiding and abetting criminals. I ought to lock you up."

***

Within an hour, James returned to Granny's house. By that time, all three, Jane, Shug, and Mr. Petey, were waiting on the front porch.

"I've reported the baby missing at the Sheriff's office. I talked to Mr. Charlie at the livery. I hate to tell you, but he said that Marie Laveau was here in town," James said.

Jane stared at him in dismay. "How did she sneak in here and take him right out from under our noses? Why didn't any of us see her? Why didn't he scream? I 've told him to scream if anybody tries to harm him." Jane collapsed into a rocking chair on the front porch, her large belly making her feel crowded. She was so pregnant that she filled the entire seat of the chair. "We have to go to New Orleans immediately. I'm certain that is where she took Charlie. When we were there before, when she had him baptized at the Catholic church, she said she wanted to train him to take over her voodoo business one day, to be a voodoo priest because his father was Professor Huerta, and Charlie was a caul baby. She said he was royalty because of Huerta's bloodline. She said people would pay good money to watch him perform rituals and cast spells. She said he would be more popular than she was."

"She's right," James replied. "I'll go get him. Jane, you are in no condition to make that long, rough trip to New Orleans on horseback, in a buggy, or on a riverboat. Don't you remember how hard it was to get back here? And you weren't pregnant then. If she has Charlie, and she thinks he is royalty, she will take good care of him, and we will get him back. Remember she told Shug that he was royalty and that she must treat him well. If she has him, I will bring him back."

Chapter 56

"James, I want to go with you to New Orleans. We can take the buggy," Jane said. "Shug, can you go with us too in case I go into labor?" Jane sobbed. "Oh, Charlie. My baby."

"Awe, Mis'Jane, I can't do that. I'm scared to death of that woman. That Marie Laveau. She will put a spell on me. She warned me. You needs to stay here with me," Shug said. "You wouldn't make it very far in a bumpy wagon as pregnant as you is. And remember those bandits that you told us about? Then how much good will you do Charlie if you have a tiny baby too? How you gonna take care of both babies and yourself?" Shug asked. "Lawdy me. That woman is evil." She mopped Jane's brow with the damp cloth.

"Jane, I'm not going to take you or Shug with me. I can make better time on horseback by myself. I can ride straight to Natchez without stopping to spend the night at the stands. I want you to stay here and take care of yourself and my baby. I'll get Charlie from Laveau, and I'll bring him back," James said. He held his hat in his hands. Then he returned it to his head. "I've decided."

Jane knew from experience that arguing with James was useless. She knew he was right. Laveau would treat Charlie like royalty, but Jane worried about the voodoo she would teach him, and she worried about his impressionable age. He would soak it up like a sponge.

"Let me pack you some food, Mr. Fares'" Shug said. "I got some ham and bread."

"Thanks," James said. He and Jane went inside to pack him some clothes. She packed a bag for Charlie too. James sat beside Jane on the bed and rubbed her hand and kissed her goodbye. "I'll leave as soon as possible. I'm certain that Laveau won't harm Charlie. She will take good care of him."

Then he called to the kitchen, "Mr. Petey, I'm going to go saddle my best horse and return that exhausted one to the barn lot for water and food? Do you care to go with me?"

While no one was in the room with James and Jane she whispered, "James, stop by the Cemetery beside the Old Trace at French Camp and get some of that Confederate gold out of the grave box beside the angel statue gravestone. The gold is there inside several old, canvas bags. I'm certain you will need it. I've kept it for emergencies. This is one. An emergency." She burst into tears.

He looked at her in amazement, not saying anything about her tears. "You have more of that gold than what was at the New Orleans Mint?"

"Yes," Jane replied. "It is Confederate gold and hidden in that grave box plus what we brought back with us from New Orleans is in there too, except for what I spent in Natchez for that horse."

"Woman, you amaze me," James said. "And all this time, I thought we were dirt poor."

"We are," Jane replied. "My most prized possession, Charlie, is missing. Oh, James, you've got to bring him home, and I've had nothing but bad luck since I took that Confederate gold. I think it's cursed. I plan to put most of it back in the Confederate tunnel, so they will leave me alone."

James didn't reply, and Jane was glad. He headed to the back of the house.

***

Within fifteen minutes, Mr. Petey and James brought the fresh horse to the front of the house.

"Good bye, Jane," James kissed Jane good-bye again. Taking his bag and the one Jane packed for Charlie, he went to the front porch to mount his horse. He waved as he rode down the street on his way. He rode swiftly back across the Big Black River toward French Camp. *He thought about the silence. Usually, when he rode this way, he heard the horrible screeching of owls. He wondered what the silence meant.* By the time he reached the rutted trail of the Old Trace near the old sorghum mill, he decided that he would take all the gold from the grave box in the cemetery. He didn't believe in ghosts anyway although he had seen some.

Quickly, he rode to the cemetery near the Old Trace. He dismounted and quickly strode across the cemetery to the grave box. He slid the heavy, four inch stone lid to the side and peered inside. There were no bags of gold inside. The grave box was empty. He reached inside in the corners with his hands and felt for the bags. Daylight had dimmed. No bags were there, so he carefully replaced the thick, heavy lid. Not once had he ever considered the poor soul who was buried there.

Marie Laveau or Tom Lewis Lynch. He wondered which had taken the gold. Then he remembered the Confederate ghosts and winced. They would not be happy.

"My bet is on Marie Laveau," he said aloud to himself. "She knew Jane had the gold, but how did she know where Jane had hidden it?" He wondered aloud.

James remounted his horse without any gold and rode hard down the Old Trace in the direction of Natchez toward Raymond Inn. *I'll overtake Marie Laveau and Charlie before they reach Raymond Inn.* He thought.

Chapter 57

Finally, after riding hard in the moonlight south on the Old Trace, around 2 o'clock in the morning, James reached Raymond Inn. The Inn was quiet and the kerosene lanterns were turned low. He tied his horse to a sweet gum sapling near the front of the barn where the horses and buggies were kept. The tracks of his horse mixed with others in the mud outside, so they wouldn't be noticed. Silently, he slipped inside the barn to check for Marie Laveau's buggy. There is was. He saw the same buggy that Mr. Charlie had had in the livery. He tiptoed across the barn lot to examine it. He forgot about Charlie. Only the Confederate gold concerned him now. Since he had met Jane, he had wanted that gold, but didn't know where she had hidden it or how to ask for it. Now, he had a chance to get most of it. Greed overtook him. As silently as possible, he searched the buggy. From past experience, he knew that most buggies had secret compartments in the bottom. He found the compartment on the right precisely where he thought it would be under the front seat. He turned and slid the latch to the side and silently, raised the lid. Inside the black silk lined compartment lay two Confederate canvas bags, similar to those he had seen carried by Confederate soldiers in Marie Laveau and his father's brothel. He tried to lift one of them. It felt very heavy. He strained to lift it. Being rearranged, the coins clinked together.

He looked around to see if anyone had heard. Nothing stirred in the barn--not even the other horses. Quickly, he took both of the heavy canvas bags and tiptoed back across the muddy barn lot and out the old wooden door to his horse that he had tied to a sapling. He tied the two bags together and swung both bags across the horn of his saddle one on each side of the horn. The clink of the gold coins made him smile. He went back into the barn to get some hay for his horse. After the horse ate about half of it, he swung himself into the saddle and walked his horse toward a small pond behind the barn. Once the horse stopped drinking, he made his way farther down the Old Trace trail toward Port Gibson Inn with the gold.

A few miles down the trail, he stopped to wait for Marie Laveau and Jane's baby Charlie to come by. He hoped that Laveau wouldn't notice that the gold was missing before she left the Inn.

He was wrong.

Chapter 58

Early the next morning, the sunlight streaming in the window through the tattered, lace curtains of their private room in the Raymond Inn awakened Marie. One of the gold coins had insured the private room.

Carefully easing out of the bed, Marie Laveau dressed in a long, flowing, white, linen tunic and skirt and left Charlie asleep in the deep, feather bed she and he had shared. She had long ago ditched Granny's old clothes that Fares' had brought her. She slipped outside to check on the gold hidden in her buggy. She tiptoed into the muddy barn lot and opened the door of the old wooden barn.

Marie Laveau sensed that someone had been there. She often just knew things. It was like women's intuition. It was more intuition than anything else. She climbed over into her buggy and turned the latch on the hidden compartment. The lid squeaked and opened. The compartment was empty except for a chicken snake, a 24 inch long rat catcher let live in the barn to help rid it of rodents. The heavy canvas bags of gold were gone. Her intuition had been correct. Someone had definitely been there. Someone had taken the gold.

Incensed, she reached inside and caught the chicken snake behind its head. Although it wasn't poisonous, she knew it would be useful to trick whoever had taken the gold. The long snake wrapped its body around her arm. She had practiced playing with snakes for her voodoo performances often in New Orleans. It was something that she would teach Charlie how to do. In the back of her buggy was a wooden box with a lid that contained some gris gris dolls she had made to sell when she returned to New Orleans. Selling gris gris made her extra money during her voodoo rituals, and people believed in them so they were important. With her other hand, she unwound the snake from her forearm and slipped the snake into the wooden box and closed the lid, and then she slammed the compartment shut. The noise aroused the horse's attention. She strode back into the kitchen where the sleepy lodgers and owners of the Inn sat around the large, farm table eating a quiet breakfast. "Which of you took my belongings out of my buggy in the barn? Tell me now. I am Marie Laveau," she demanded. "Tell me or I will cast a voodoo hex on you and all your future children or grandchildren will be deformed."

The lodgers ceased talking immediately at the mention of Marie Laveau. Each looked at the others. The women looked terrified. No one said anything. No one knew anything. "She's Marie Laveau. I suspected so last night," one of the elderly women at the table whispered. "She is my aunt's hair dresser in New Orleans. She is also a voodoo priestess. Oh, my God, she is carrying a wooden box. They keep voodoo gris gris in wooden boxes and snakes too."

"I am Marie Laveau. I can do what I say. I am the voodoo priestess from New Orleans. If you don't answer me, you will be sorry. Answer me." Laveau stood there with her hands on her hips, but she held the wooden box under her left arm. She wore the white linen outfit that was her trademark.

One woman at the table began to choke as she tried to swallow her scrambled eggs. Her husband tried to help her, but couldn't.

"Leave her," Marie Laveau demanded. "I will make all of you choke it someone doesn't return to me what you took," she said. Her brown eyes glared at the people.

"What is missing?" A man across the table from the choking woman asked.

"Never you mind what is missing," Laveau screamed and raised her hands high in the air, letting the wooden box fall to the floor with a loud thud.

Rubbing his eyes, Charlie opened the wooden door of the hallway and wandered into the kitchen. He stood watching Laveau as if in a trance.

She glanced in his direction. She knew that she must make an impression on him to win him over to voodoo and this was her first chance, so she introduced him, "This is my son Voodoo Charlie. He can cast voodoo spells on all of you. Like me, he can command snakes."

They all turned to look at Charlie. While they were looking, she opened the box that held the chicken snake. She held it by the certain spot on the back of its neck, and it hung straight like a stick.

"Come here, Voodoo Charlie," she demanded. "I want you to walk around this table behind these folks and stop whenever you reach the one who took my belongings. I will put this snake on that person." Marie Laveau thought that this would bring out the confession from them.

Reluctantly, Charlie walked over to where she stood.

"Go on," she said. "Walk around behind their chairs. Stop behind the person who stole our belongings from our buggy. "

Two of the women at the table immediately fainted, and the one who had been choking began turning green from lack of oxygen. Charlie slowly walked behind them. He stopped near the corner of the table nearest the choking woman. He pointed to her plate.

"So she is the one who stole from us?" Laveau screamed. She strode to the choking woman and threw the snake into her lap. The woman fell backward in her straight back chair, and the snake slithered away under the table. Instantly, the others cleared the room.

The choking woman lay unconscious, so Marie grabbed her around the rib cage and knotting her fist under the woman's sternum, Marie jerked hard. The large piece of scrambled egg flew out of the woman's mouth, and she began to breathe again.

"I have the power to grant or take away life," Marie screamed. Somehow she realized that none of them had taken the gold. The person who took the gold had not stayed for breakfast.

Marie grabbed Charlie and went back inside the room where they had slept. She set him in the middle of the soft feather mattress. I'll take us some breakfast to eat in the buggy, and we will be on our way. She stuffed their things back into the carpet bag and led Charlie back into the dining room.

Take a napkin and fill it with biscuits and ham. Then wrap the ends together. She demonstrated what to do for him. They took the remaining food from the table and walking outside to the barn, climbed into the buggy. Then Marie harnessed the buggy to the horse. She set Charlie in the front seat beside her. Then she ran back into the kitchen and took two large fruit jars of milk and some blackberry jelly and a fork and spoon.

She and Charlie left Raymond Inn on the Old Trace trail as quickly as they could. Somehow, Marie knew that her intuition was correct and no one inside the Inn had taken the Confederate gold.

Chapter 59

James Fares' sat in a cool, shady oak tree thicket near the Old Trace trail waiting for Marie Laveau and Charlie to appear. He took off his black suit coat and replaced it with a leather buckskin that made him look more like a rogue, riverboat gambler than a respectable husband and soon to be new father, both he hadn't chosen to be. His conscience was nagging at him. *Finally, I have what I've always wanted—gold.* He thought, arguing with his conscience. *With this Confederate gold, I am a rich man, even richer than my father ever was or most anyone else that I know in New Orleans. With this gold I can go anywhere and do anything; I can build anything and run anything; I can have much power with this much wealth.* His conscience told him to travel on to New Orleans and forget about being tied down to a wife and two children—one of whom he was supposed to be rescuing. If the truth was told, he had always resented Charlie because that caul baby got special attention everywhere they went. *People sensed that Charlie was a caul baby, especially older, black women. He had he heard them state that Charlie was special and all-knowing.*

"I guess if she teaches him to do voodoo, he really will be special," Fares' said aloud to himself.

He looked up as two buggies approached his hiding place. The occupants of the first were elderly and well-dressed. The man wore a black suit and lacy white collar and a black top hat, and the woman wore a deep pinkish purple or magenta dress that he had seen women wearing on gambling river boats. He liked to see women dressed up like that. He liked fancy women like some of those he had dated in New Orleans. He hated the drab, flour sack dresses that Jane often wore. She dressed no better than Shug, her mid-wife friend who had been a former slave. He hated feeling dirt poor; he hated being dirt poor. He felt that Jane was beneath him. He was reared by aristocratic parents in New Orleans. No matter how they earned their wealth, at least they were not dirt poor. According to a fortune teller in New Orleans, he was destined to be a wealthy man and finding Laveau's Confederate gold had made him one.

After the first two buggies passed by James's hiding place and Marie Laveau and Charlie weren't in them, James Fares' climbed back onto his horse and rode south down the Old Trace trail on toward Natchez. "I can wait for them more comfortably in Natchez. I can stay at The Burn with my relatives. I need to hide this gold somewhere that Laveau can't find it, and somewhere in Natchez will be perfect," he said aloud to no one as if he was trying to convince himself. "If I wait here for her with the gold swung on my horse, she or someone else will probably steal it from me. I really need to hide it in a safer place."

He rode straight for two more days without stopping to rest. He ate the ham and bread that Shug had packed for him. He only stopped for the horse to eat and drink. Finally, he reached Natchez and The Burn. The Burn was a white, antebellum house a few blocks up the bluff from the Mississippi River and Natchez Under the Hill. He left his horse to be cared for at the stable in the back, but he removed the bags of gold and carried them with him into the kitchen. "Please tell my aunt that James Fares' is here to visit," he told the kitchen help.

"Yes, Sir, would you like something to eat?" the butler asked. "We have biscuits and ham and sweet tea."

"Yes, thank you," James said and sat down at the red gingham-covered table to eat a repeat of biscuits and ham like Shug had packed for him. He drank his glass of sweet tea in one continuous gulp, and the cook poured him another. He hadn't realized just how thirsty he was.

Finally, his aunt walked into the kitchen. She was dressed in the latest Paris fashion, a dark green brocade with fashionable long sleeves and white lace cuffs and lace around the collar. The bodice had pearl buttons down the front, and his aunt wore a matching strand of real pearls around her neck. Although she was old, she looked lovely. "James Fares', what brings you back to Natchez?" she exclaimed.

"I'm here for a brief visit. I'm going back to New Orleans. My father needs me." He rose to kiss her hand.

"Can we take your bags to your room?" she asked, noticing the two Confederate canvas bags lying with a leather duffle bag under the table near his chair. "My, my, aren't those Confederate bags?" she asked. "Where in the world did you get them?"

"Yes, Ma'am, they are. If you don't mind, I'll take them to my room myself." He replied without explaining about the Confederate bags. "Thank you for allowing me to stay here at The Burn. I really appreciate it, and I'm excited to get to visit with you."

"Show him to the second room on the back at the top of the stairs when he finishes eating," she told the butler. The church bells rang, telling the town that it was 5 o'clock. "James, I was just going out to a gala on the riverboat Natchez by invitation from the riverboat Captain. Would you care to accompany me? I would love it if you did. Get some rest and freshen up and then come on down to the riverboat. I'll tell the Captain that you are coming later this evening, so you can board. I remember how much you liked the cards and the ladies. Especially the ladies. Is that how you were going? back to New Orleans? I think the boat departs in a couple of days."

"Thanks, Aunt Burns. That would make me very happy. Living in Kilmichael, I've missed socializing so much," James replied. "Well, social functions there are church related. His mind drifted to where he could hide his gold while he was on the boat.

"I see that you are wearing a wedding ring. Who is your lovely bride?" Aunt Burns asked.

"Her name is Catherine. She couldn't travel with me because she is with child," James replied, wishing that he had removed his wedding ring sooner.

"What was her maiden name?" she asked. "You know we Southerners still like to know the bloodlines of everyone. Our kin is very important to us."

"Lynch," James replied, but gave no other information.

"Hmmm," she said. "I don't believe I know that name."

"Please excuse me, Aunt. I'm going upstairs to freshen up now." James rose and took the two canvas bags with him. He picked them up carefully to keep the gold from moving around and making noise. "I'll see you later this evening on the riverboat. Thanks for the invitation. I'm so looking forward to being there. It has been too long since I really had fun."

James followed the butler to the top of the stairs and then the second room on the back. The butler turned the large key in the key hole and opened the door. Then he handed the key to James. Knowing that he could lock the door, didn't make James feel more secure; in fact, he felt less secure from the way the butler handed it to him. James remembered seeing women at the brothel unlock doors with their hairpins. These looked like the same kind of locks, and he felt certain that a hairpin would unlock them.

This bedroom had polished hardwood floors, but a lack of Oriental rugs. James had planned to hide the gold under the floor boards under a rug. It a bed with tall, ornate posts and hooded wood framed canopies. The most obvious place to hide the gold and the first place the butler would look was under the mattress, so James flipped over the chaise lounge and ripped the lining loose from the bottom. He took a pillowcase off one of the pillows and stuffed the gold inside the pillowcase. He kept three gold coins out to use for gambling on the riverboat. These he stuck deep into his pants pocket. Then he tied the top of the pillowcase securely and pushed the gold inside the bottom of the chaise lounge behind the springs but not far enough to make the seat look too lumpy. Then he tied the wire springs horizontally to secure the pillowcase holding the gold. He set the chaise back upright and surveyed his plan. Carefully, he positioned the chaise in exactly the same spot it had been previously so if the butler came into his room, he wouldn't notice. Then he removed the other pillowcase and stuffed it into one of the Confederate canvas bags. This one he would take with him when he went back down stairs, so that it would appear to the butler that he had carried the bags with him, leaving the butler nothing to search the room for. He removed his dirty, white shirt that smelled of dust and perspiration and placed it in the other canvas bag and left it lying on the bed.

He walked to the dresser and poured fresh water into the basin. Carefully, he groomed himself. James was so excited to go to the riverboat. Traveling and gambling on the Mississippi River could be his new occupation since he was both rich and, in his mind, now a free man. He had totally forgotten why he had come to Natchez in the first place.

Chapter 60

Jane sat in the rocking chair on Shug's porch until sundown. Shug sat out there too. Jane rocked back and forth, back and forth. Her grief consumed her.

"Shug, I need to tell you something," Jane said. "It is very bad."

"What is it?" Shug asked. "Is it time? It ain't gonna be long. That baby's coming soon. Maybe tonight."

"No, that's not it. Do you remember when Tom Lewis was staying in that Confederate tunnel, and Mr. Petey carried him food? Well, I hid from Huerata in there with them. You know that. When I was leaving the tunnel, I noticed another room attached to the west side of the tunnel. There was Confederate gold inside that room. Victoria and I took it. I hid most of it in one of those grave boxes beside that angel statue. When I married Johnny Tingle, I took some to New Orleans Mint to be melted into coins. Well, I took one gold brick. The other night when I was going to the bathroom at the outhouse, some of those Confederate ghosts found me and said that they wanted their gold back. Tom Lewis already told me that they wanted it back and that they were angry that we took it. The ghosts threatened me. They said if I didn't give it back, I would lose all that was precious to me. Do you think that is why Charlie was kidnapped?"

"Could be," Shug replied without missing one forward or backward movement in the rocking motion of her chair. "Could be. I don't want nothing to do with no ghosts, Mis' Jane. Lordy be. You's mean to tell me that 'em ghosts was here? You better give them what they want. If you's got their gold, you give it back to them. They's some mean folks, those Rebel soldiers. And as ghosts. You better be careful girl. "

Chapter 61

Within three days, Marie Laveau and Charlie reached Natchez in her buggy. Although she had lost the gold, she had not been in a hurry because she began the journey exhausted from being in the little people hell pit. In Natchez, she sold the buggy and bought them tickets to New Orleans on a riverboat named the Natchez. Their tickets were cheap ones for the lower deck with the cows and pigs. No one who might recognize them would be downstairs with the animals in this lower area designated for transportation of livestock. All the aristocrats and those who wanted to be aristocrats rode above. They wouldn't lower themselves to ride below deck. She made Charlie comfortable on a pile of hay and feed sacks and waited for him to fall asleep. The trip down the Old Trace had exhausted both of them, but exhausted or not, she had things to do. Then she dressed in her finest, white linen, tunic and a black head wrap and went upstairs to see if she recognized anyone who might have stolen her Confederate gold out of her buggy at Raymond Inn or anyone who might be spending her gold coins. The riverboat Natchez would venture south within 72 hours, but it would take several days to travel down the Mississippi River. She planned to deal with whoever was onboard the riverboat using the power of voodoo.

At first, she removed her black head wrap and eased around the edges of the gambling hall in the shadows. Wearing the head wrap had become a habit when she fixed hair for her clients in New Orleans. Some of them had sparse, thin hair, and hers was thick and luxurious; so she wore the wrap over her own hair so that her clients wouldn't feel jealous or expect their hair to mimic hers. As she surveyed the hall, she kept her chin tucked and didn't make eye contact with anyone who might recognize her. She stood behind a large support beam and watched and waited. She recognized some of the people from the Stand. These were some of the same people who were at the Raymond Inn at the breakfast table. Patiently she watched them for any sign of their having stolen the gold. She saw none.

For once, she didn't want to be the center of attention. She needed to be a wallflower. Not being the center of attention was totally foreign to her because of her voodoo presence, a presence that she had worked hard to achieve. This voodoo presence frightened people and her trademark costume made people recognize her everywhere she went in New Orleans. Being recognizable was to her advantage. It was a way of advertising her wares and business. Since the fiasco at the Raymond Inn, she wanted to blend in, not stand out. She wanted to blend in just long enough to find her gold.

Hiding behind a column, Marie looked at the elaborate décor of the gambling hall. It resembled the inside of the grand hall of an antebellum house, very Victorian and very over-decorated with rich velvet sofas and heavy drapes. Victorian furniture sat everywhere.

Suddenly, a familiar figure strode into the gambling hall from toward the dock or wharf. James Fares'. *Why hadn't she thought of James Fares'? Of course, he had followed her to rescue Charlie, and realized that she had taken the gold. Jane probably hadn't trusted a bank to deposit the sudden inheritance and had hidden it in that grave box, so Fares' had gone there to remove some gold for his trip. During Marie's stay in French Camp, no one had mentioned Jane Lynch's newfound riches. It made perfect sense.* Marie Laveau thought.

Laveau stepped back behind a large, white upper deck support to watch as James joined an older woman at the gambling table with the riverboat captain. He kissed her on the cheek. Clearly, she was too old to be a girlfriend of his, so Marie moved closer to them so she could hear what was said.

"Hello, Aunt," he said, smiling that toothy, white grin that Laveau recognized. His father, who owned the brothel, had that same grin. "Thank you so much for the invitation."

"I'd like to join this game." He laid a gold coin on the green felt of the poker table.

"Oh, my," his aunt exclaimed. "You must have robbed a bank. Gold? I didn't know the Lynch's of Kilmichael or French Camp or Mississippi or wherever you said you'd been were that wealthy. Surely I would have heard of them before. Not even the Fares' of New Orleans deal in gold coins." She seemed to be enjoying the asset of having a wealthy relative like James Fares' sitting near her.

"They're not," he laughed amused and reached to kiss her on the other cheek. "Let's keep it to ourselves," he whispered and winked at her.

Marie Laveau watched the game from the fringes of the gambling hall and listened to their conversation long enough to know that James was staying at The Burns. She figured he had left the rest of the Confederate gold there, so she went back below deck to check on Charlie.

She roused a farmer who slept near them on some hay-covered, burlap bags.

"I've got to check on something on shore. Could you watch my boy while he sleeps? I won't be gone more than an hour, two at the most. When I get back, I'll pay you handsomely," she told the man who was carrying a load of hogs to New Orleans.

He grinned at her at the mention of payment for watching a sleeping boy, a job that required no effort.

"I'm Marie Laveau, the voodoo priestess. If any harm comes to this boy, I'll put a spell on you and all these hogs. They will die." She reached into her carpet bag and tossed him a gris gris voodoo doll.

It was her calling card of sorts. She stuffed another one in her pocket and carried the empty bag with her. When she found the gold, it would come home with her in the empty carpet bag.

With that she didn't wait for the man to reply, but ascended the stairs as quickly as possible. She felt certain that he would carry out her wishes. Most people did what she asked out of fright.

The dirty, hog farmer grinned his toothless grin at the swish of the white, linen robes and pretended to go back to sleep. He looked at the sleeping boy out of the corner of his good eye. This was a story that he could tell his friends.

Marie strode across the upper deck and toward the lowered draw gate that allowed her to transfer to the shore. The sound of the paddle wheel muffled her steps. She hurried back to the level of the brick streets above Natchez Under the Hill where the riverboat was docked. She hurried past the cemetery on the bluffs and east toward The Burns, the antebellum home belonging to James Fares' aunt's family. A light mist had begun to fall. The coolness of the rain was refreshing to Laveau as she walked in the shadows toward The Burns, letting the mist bathe her face. She replaced the black wrap on her hair. She truly didn't want her hair to get wet from the misting rain and turn frizzy as it sometimes did from lack of care.

When she reached The Burns, she hurried breathlessly to the back of the house. This was the servants' entrance, and although she considered herself to be better than the servants, this was where she felt that she had an advantage. She knocked lightly on the kitchen door entrance. It was near a brick courtyard that was edged with thick hedge bushes. A short, heavy, black woman cracked open the door. She wore a ragged apron over her blue, flour sack dress.

Eyeing Marie Laveau, the woman was awestruck. "Hello. I'm Marie Laveau." Quickly, she took the gris gris out of her pocket. "I'll give this gris gris to you, and it will bring you good luck if you allow me to go to the room of James Fares'; but if you don't, I'll put a hex on you and everything you touch will turn to mush, gore, and muck. I met him tonight, and he asked me to wait for him here in his room;

if you know what I mean. He said you would let me in. I want to wait for his return, and I don't want Mis' Burns to know I'm in there."

The cook was so stunned by the boldness of Marie Laveau that she could do nothing except grin. "'mon in," she said, stepping backward to allow for Laveau's entrance into the kitchen. Marie saw that the woman was tongue-tied with fear and awe.

Master Fares' room is upstairs second on the back. Here's a key." The cook eyed Marie with a look of distrust and fright.

"Thank you, kindly. I don't need a key," Marie retorted, quickly hurrying up the carpet-covered stairs. "Mr. Fares' gave me his key," she lied.

Upon reaching the landing and making her way down the hallway, Marie slipped a hair pin from the pile of dark brown hair on top of her head, inserted two loose ends into the lock, twisted it a few times, and unlocked the door. She looked behind her to make certain that the maid hadn't followed her and that no one else was looking. The hallway was empty.

Once inside the room, Laveau closed and locked the door. She surveyed the Victorian, although sparsely decorated room. One wall had a large four poster bed made of dark walnut. The top had a hand-crocheted canopy that hung down a foot around the top. Laveau looked around the room. Something puzzled her. Something was missing. Something was wrong. Laveau tiptoed across the floor and sat on the chaise lounge to think.

Then it occurred to her that there were no Oriental rugs. She observed the room to see where James Fares' could have hidden the Confederate gold. The most obvious place was under the mattress, but that didn't seem logical since he had left one of the Confederate canvas bags lying on the top of the feather mattress. Leaving the bag there was an obvious move. She felt certain. Someone must have seen the bags in his possession whenever he got here. Perhaps his aunt that he had asked to keep quiet about it. The Confederate bag proved that he had taken the gold. So she looked more intensely at the room. There was a fireplace on one wall. She walked over to it to see if any of the bricks were loose.

None were.

There was a bookcase on another wall, but oddly, it didn't contain many books. She picked up each of the cloisonné ginger jar vases and shook them gently, but all were empty. She knocked on different areas of the bookcase to see if a secret compartment opened up.

None did.

Thinking that James might have stuffed the gold under the mattress, she walked over to the bed. Besides the Confederate canvas bag that had been left on the bed, something was wrong with the bed. She looked at it intently. The pillowcases were missing. That was it. He must have transferred the gold from the canvas bags to pillowcases. This suited Marie.

Marie Laveau walked back to the Victorian chaise to sit again. This chaise had lumps that needed to be smoothed. She smoothed one and in the silence of the upstairs room, she thought she heard the clinking sound of gold coins hitting together.

Quickly, she flipped the sofa over and found that someone had pulled the fabric back from the bottom of the chaise. She stripped the loose backing quickly and there were the pillowcases being used as bags for the gold. They were stuffed inside the Victorian chaise like a turkey stuffed for Christmas. Relief and greed rushed through her. She removed the gold from the chaise and stuffed it in the pillowcases that housed it into the carpet bag that she had brought and tiptoed back down the stairs, but instead of exiting through the kitchen where the cook was, she went out the front door of The Burns, carrying the heavy bags of gold. Laveau smiled to herself.

Carefully so as not to be caught with a carpet bag full of gold , Marie Laveau walked down the street to Natchez Under the Hill and the riverboat where Charlie slept. She slipped along with the heavy bags across her shoulders staying in the shadows. The docks were lined with men who called to her, but she strode onto the deck of the riverboat as if she owned it and slipped down the stairs to the below deck where Charlie still lay sleeping. Lugging the heavy carpet bag had tired her, so she handed the man who watched Charlie sleep a coin and a gris gris and waved him on.

Charlie, tired from the trip down to Natchez down the Old Trace, slept and didn't know anything had happened or that Marie had left.

Using the carpet bag as her pillow, Marie fell into a nightmarish, fretful sleep. As long as the Confederate gold was in her possession, sound sleep would not come to her again.

Chapter 62

James Fares' and Aunt Burns stayed on the riverboat gambling, dancing, and partying until around 4 o'clock that next morning. When they reached The Burns mansion together in Mis' Burns fancy black carriage with James' horse tied behind, all the kitchen staff had retired for the night.

Soon after the party ended, the riverboat left the dock. It was before dawn and before James Fares' found out that Marie Laveau had entered his room at The Burns and stolen the Confederate gold. Early the next morning, he rode his horse hard and fast toward Natchez Under the Hill, but the boat was long gone. He was too embarrassed to return home to Jane without the gold or Charlie, so he entered a bar in Natchez Under the Hill to inquire about the next riverboat to New Orleans. Another riverboat wouldn't dock at Natchez for four or five days.

Within two days, Charlie and Marie Laveau reached New Orleans on the riverboat Natchez. Charlie looked exhausted and both of them smelled of farm animals and manure. "Don't you worry," Maire Laveau told Charlie, "when we reach my house, I'll prepare us a huge feast and we'll take a long, hot bath. And you can sleep for two days." As they stood on the dock, Laveau summoned the driver of a horse and buggy parked near the wharf to take Charlie, the gold, and herself to her house. Otherwise, she could not have made the trip with the heavy gold and the heavy child. She still felt very exhausted.

***

Having reached New Orleans on the raft that he and Tommy built a half day before the riverboat, Tom Lewis Lynch watched Marie Laveau ride away from the wharf with Charlie, but he did not follow. Tom Lewis knew to watch and wait until the time was right. He stayed in the shadows making certain that she hadn't seen him. He knew that Laveau had scouts all-over New Orleans that reported back to her.

Chapter 63

One Week Later

"Everyone make way for the Voodoo Queen."

Marie takes the rooster's heart and touches it to Charlie's mouth. She puts her bloody fingers to Charlie's lips. "The grand Zombi is coming." The python comes out of the box. It winds around her. "The snake gives sight."

The crowd gathered around her. They acted mesmerized with the creepy scene and with Marie Laveau. The python kissed and teased her with its forked tongue, and her followers knew that she was the Voodoo Queen. She didn't act frightened by the snake. "Believers, receive your vision," she shouted to the throng of people who surrounded her. There were freed slaves, blacks, sailors, aristocrats, and even people she'd seen in church in the crowd earlier that same night.

The crowd was afraid of the snake. Only Marie wasn't afraid of the snake. Then Charlie reached out to touch it as if it was his toy or pet. He didn't act afraid of it either. Each man and woman in the crowd held its breath, waiting for the snake to strangle the small boy or bite him.

"Charlie, this is my advice to you: With the weak, you demand. With the strong-willed, you pull one way. They pull the other. With the proud, you dare. Are you afraid? Is a dare."

Charlie looked at her wild-eyed, but interested. He wanted to play with the snake. He was a typical boy. "Spirits make gris gris. Spirits make spells," Marie said. "Snakes enchant people. Snakes make people do strange things."

Charlie watched her wind the snake around her shoulders. He watched as the python's tongue kissed her. He reached toward the snake again to stroke it.

"When we begin, demand that the crowd receives the vision. Risk your life for their belief. Superstition claims that this python is poisonous. But he isn't," she said teaching Charlie to be a voodoo priest. "Another thing, Charlie, don't deny Damballah."

Charlie watched the snake and listened to the rhythm of the drums. He felt the drum beat deep in his chest. He fell into a trance and accepted the serpent's kiss. Some of the followers shook violently and fell listlessly to the ground. To calm the crowd, Charlie touched them and then touched, rubbed, and petted the snake. The snake seemed to like Charlie's touch. Then those who had fainted rose again saying, "I was blessed. I was blessed by Marie Laveau. Saint Marie."

"And Voodoo Charlie," Marie shouted. "Voodoo Charlie is your new voudon."

Now, all want the snake's kiss and move toward them. All press toward the stage, Marie, and the boy. Both Marie and Charlie panic. Marie shouts, "Stop!" But the crowd of followers pressed nearer to both of them. Charlie felt their bodies.

Finally, they stopped, but it was the snake the made them hesitate. They were pleased. In reality, they didn't want to touch the snake. The snake frightened them.

Marie was pleased with their response. She kissed Charlie. "How does it feel to be a saint?" She asked him. "Saint Charlie Laveau."

Marie knew that voodoo was a religion of lies and horror. It was a way to have power and to make money. She still believed in God, but she wanted Charlie to feel the power of voodoo. Marie called a man from her audience. She had previously spoken with him, and he knew exactly what to do. Marie Laveau had previously coached him. The man said that someone had put a hex on him. He said, "I can't eat. I can't sleep. I don't know who did it or why they did it." He turned his hollow eyes toward the crowd so they could get the full effects of the problem. One that Marie Laveau had created for Charlie to cure before the crowd.

"Charlie will help you. Come to our house tomorrow. We will help you," Marie said loudly so that the followers would hear that for a price, they could get help with their problems from Marie Laveau and Charlie.

Marie held Charlie high above her head before the crowd. "Praise the serpent. Eve came into the world blind. The serpent gave her sight. The serpent helped her. I am Marie Laveau. This is Charlie Laveau. He is our next voodoo priest. Praise Charlie Laveau."

The man screamed and bowed to Marie and Charlie. "Charlie Laveau. Charlie Laveau. Charlie Laveau." The crowd began chanting. The drums began again in rhythm with the chanting. "Charlie, Charlie the Voudon. Charlie," he cried. Their chants turned into, "Voodoo Charlie. Voodoo Charlie. Voodoo Charlie."

Charlie began to smile and cry at the same time. Finally, Marie slowly stopped the drums, and the crowd eventually dispersed two or three at the time in different directions.

Tomorrow people would be talking about Voodoo Charlie and his power. They would add to it and make it bigger. People would say that Voodoo Charlie had raised a man from the dead only by touching him, kissed a poisonous snake, and eaten a rooster's heart.

Charlie went inside the house and went to bed, but he couldn't sleep. He heard drums. He tossed in his bed, but the rhythm crept into his heart. He jerked fully awake. Then he heard nothing. The world outside was silent, and he pulled the covers over his head. He wanted his mother, but instead, he only had Marie. Then he heard the drums again.

"Voodoo Charlie. Voodoo Charlie. Voodoo Charlie."

Charlie slipped from his bed. He tiptoed to the window. The moonlight shone on the beach of the Gulf of Mexico, making the sand shine like silver coins in the moonlight. The waves rushed to the shore as if summoning him to come closer. Marie was calling him, calling him toward the shore.

He opened the bedroom door and crossed the room to the adjacent door that led to the outside. He felt like he was floating across the sand, but slowly he walked toward the shore. He stopped. He heard the voice of his mother inside his head. "Charlie, where are you? Come home, Charlie. I love you." He felt the tears on her pink cheeks with his fingers.

Again Charlie heard the drums. He saw a group of people standing near the water of the Gulf of Mexico singing and chanting, "Charlie, Charlie, the voodoo priest." The sound was lovely, soothing, and peaceful. He felt like he was floating. Then he saw her. It wasn't Marie. It was Jane, his mother. He wanted his mother more than he wanted Marie.

Charlie was enchanted. The spirits drifted into the top of his head. His head tingled as if he had fever. He felt lost. The crowd parted and then closed in around him, sucking him in. One man picked him up and let him ride on his shoulders.

Marie had a knife in her hand. She thrust it into the goat. The knife rose and fell again and again. The crowd cheered with a rhythm that matched the spurting blood from the goat's heart beat.

"Charlie," his mother hit him with a switch. "Stop it. Get back to the house." Charlie felt nothing except excitement. He didn't want to walk back to the house. He wanted to see what excited the crowd.

His mother pushed him back through the crowd toward the house. She still whacked him with the switch, but he felt nothing.

Jane pushed him forward. He looked back at the crowd and Marie. She seemed demonic. Charlie screamed. He looked back. He saw curls of something swirl out of Marie's mouth.

The next morning Charlie felt feverish. The stripes on his back stung. He asked Marie, "What happened last night at the shore, and where is my mother this morning?"

She said, "I was asleep last night. As a matter of fact, I slept very well. I haven't seen your mother since she gave you to me. She didn't want you."

But Charlie knew what was real and what had happened last night. He knew that his mother loved him. His skin stung from the blow of his mother's switch. He remembered her pushing him through the crowd. He remembered her kissing him and reading him stories at night. Large tears rolled down his face.

Marie and Charlie sat on the front porch all the next day, but when she stood to come back inside she stumbled, but she caught herself on the porch railing. People often left Marie gifts on the porch. Charlie liked looking at these gifts. He liked playing with them. They left things like a crooked twig, a bird or turkey feather, a curl of hair, a scrap of a love letter, or a broken piece of jewelry.

Charlie looked at these gifts and asked Marie, "Why? Why do they worship you? People I knew at home didn't do these things."

Marie didn't answer. She stared at him. "I heal people," she said finally.

"Your mother or Granny didn't?" she smirked. "Who there where you lived heals people?"

"Shug. I guess. She brought me into the world. My mama said I was a caul baby. Special."

"Yes, Charlie. You are very special. I'm gonna make you a voodoo priest. I want you to have what I have. I will call you Voodoo Charlie Laveau from now on. You will be famous."

Charlie wanted what Marie had. Marie was famous in New Orleans. He liked voodoo. He liked the power, but he wanted his mother too. He never quit wanting his mother.

***

Marie hung quilts over the doors and windows. Candles burned about the room. A crowd gathered outside, leaving more gifts for Marie and Charlie. Marie taught Charlie his voodoo lessons.

"When the right time comes, I will call you," Marie told him. "Damballah will tell us—both of us."

Charlie had learned of Damballah from Marie. She said that Damballah was a serpent who hissed life into the earth's creatures. He ruled the lakes, rivers, and streams and the land.

Marie taught him that every living creature and non living thing had life. Spirits to be contacted, with its own personality, but the spirit's gate was guarded. She started the chant, "Spirits let me pass through. Remove your barriers." She motioned for the drums to start. The rhythm became more intense. She broke out the rum and passed it around. Charlie took a sip, and Marie smiled.

Suddenly Charlie saw spirits everywhere. They entered him. He drank another small sip of rum. The spirits surrounded him. Charlie was hooked.

Charlie stopped drinking. He tried to speak. Gurgling sounds came out of his mouth. He didn't remember how long he had been there. He wanted his mother. He wanted to go home. He felt heavy. He felt attached to the floor. He didn't want to be Voodoo Charlie. He wanted his mother. He wanted to go back to Kilmichael.

"We will call the snake, but the snake does not speak."

Charlie felt that he was the snake. He slithered across the yard. He felt the earth shake under his belly. He dreamed that he saw people being born and watched them die. Millions of years flowed through his mind. He planted seeds. He felt the spirits filling him deep into his soul. He heard Marie singing. Marie cried. Charlie felt the rum had unhinged him. Damballah filled him.

Charlie cried. The peacefulness he felt was so great. He felt feelings he had not felt before. He shivered; his arms stung. The crowds watched.

"You were the serpent? Damballah had you?" Charlie felt light, but his clothes were covered with mud from crawling around like a snake on his belly.

The crowds closed in on him. "Touch me; Voodoo Charlie, bless me. Bless me."

"Marie, tell them to leave me alone," Charlie clung to Marie.

"Get used to it, Charlie. You are the voodoo priest now. You are Voodoo Charlie. They worship you now. It is what I wanted."

"I don't want to be worshiped. I want my mother. We worship God and Jesus—not snakes and Damballah."

Marie slapped Charlie hard across his face. "Stand up, Charlie. You are theirs. Accept this."

Charlie did as he was told.

Hands touched him. Fingers tugged at his hair. These hands had rings, calluses, bracelets, long nails, short nails, and bitten nails. The hands pulled at his clothes and his hair. Charlie stayed very still, waiting for it to be over, hating them and loving them at the same time. Each person wanted a souvenir to take home, a personal charm from Charlie the new voodoo priest to protect them from harm. He was replacing Marie. She had become old and ineffective for them. Some of them touched his cheeks and his nose. *How did Marie stand it? He thought he would die.*

Marie sang: If you see Charlie,
He is your savior.
If you see a serpent,
You see a voodoo priest.
Charlie Laveau is the voodoo priest.
Voodoo Charlie.

Voodoo followers threatened Charlie. He tried to get away; Marie called him back. "Call Damballah, he will help you." Marie shook him hard. "Go through this. My business will be ruined if you don't."

Charlie gasped. He cried. He tried to wiggle free.

"Charlie, summon him," Marie demanded.

"Damballah," Charlie whispered.

"Good, Charlie. Good."

Charlie felt very sad. "Damballah," Charlie choked through the tears He prayed, "Bring my mother to get me. I need Jane Lynch please."

Marie whispered to Charlie, "Shut up."

Chapter 64

Labor pains racked through Jane's body as Shug held the burning mugwort cigar near her swollen extended belly. Jane lay on the crazy quilt on her bed. Grasping the quilt when the pains came made Jane think about Granny. It made her think of Charlie. She wanted Charlie back. She wanted this baby. She wanted Granny back. She wanted her mother back. She wanted Tom Lewis to be okay. Jane screamed in pain. She wanted to be free of Confederate ghosts and Marie Laveau.

"Oh, my, Shug, the pain is worse than last time," Jane told Shug.

"No, Mis' Jane, you just forgot. Women tend to forget the pain of childbirth very quickly. If they didn't, they wouldn't have no more young 'uns."

"Oooooh," Jane screamed again.

"It ain't turned right. We need to stop it from coming."

"I can't. It is coming. I feel her head," Jane said.

"It's too late, Jane. She's coming," Shug said.

The baby would be born today, but it was twisted and not head down in birthing position. Charlie hadn't been in birthing position either, but Shug had been able to bring him into the world with no harm to him. This baby wouldn't be so lucky. It was coming too fast.

Jane screamed in pain. She felt like her insides were being ripped out. The baby was coming no matter which way it was turned. The pains had started the same evening that Charlie had been kidnapped, and James Fares' left her to rescue him.

James hadn't come back. Charlie was still with Marie Laveau. Apparently, James and the Confederate gold were too. Jane wished she hadn't told James about the gold. She hadn't known he would take all of it. It was his ticket to freedom--freedom from poverty, freedom from her and this new baby, and freedom from Charlie, the caul baby. His freedom had cost her plenty. She hated the thought of Charlie learning voodoo from Marie Laveau. It made Jane's pain worse. Jane wanted to give the gold back to the Confederate ghosts, so they would leave her alone. She wanted life to be plain, dull, and boring again.

It was her secret. The Confederate ghosts haunted her almost every night. They showed up everywhere. They were in the cemetery. They were in the yard when she walked to the outhouse. They were even at Granny's kitchen. They frightened her more than Marie Laveau had. Each time she saw them; they asked for their gold. They said, "Until we get our gold back, you will never have a healthy baby. You will never have peace. Nothing will ever go right for you, Jane Lynch Fares'."

Jane's baby was born with the umbical cord around her neck. She died from strangulation.

Jane, Shug, and Mr. Petey buried her in the cemetery in French Camp next to Jane's mother. The ghosts didn't come out in the bright sunshine, but Jane felt their presence.

Chapter 65

As soon as Jane was able after losing her baby daughter, she mounted a horse and rode down the Old Trace toward Natchez. The Confederate ghosts had taken her baby girl, but they would not take Charlie from her. She rode straight for two days. Since she had no money, she camped out on the Old Trace. After 4 nights, she reached Natchez Under the Hill, but there was no riverboat in sight.

Instead of riding to New Orleans down the Mississippi River on the riverboat as she had planned, she hitched a ride on a flat raft with a group of men from up North. She didn't want to wait however long it took for another riverboat. Northern farmers built flatboats for about $75 and carried $3000 worth of corn, wheat, potatoes, flour, tobacco, wheat, hay, cotton and/or whiskey to New Orleans. Sometimes they carried chickens, iron ore, pigs, or lumber. Often people hitched rides on the flatboats.

This flatboat was made of logs put together to be about the size of 50 feet by 60 feet. It was rectangular. In the center of the boat was a small cabin. On one side of the raft were two sails to help the boat move southward in shallow water as was often found in the Mississippi River. Two long oars stuck out on the other side.

Jane hired on to be their cook and wash their clothes. She explained to one of the men from Memphis that her son had been kidnapped, and that she was desperate to get to New Orleans. After she finished her story, Jane cried so hard that Rolo took her into his arms to console her. "When we get to New Orleans, I'll find your boy. I promise," Rolo assured her. New Orleans was the destination of the flatboat. There the goods could be shipped to other countries.

"But it will take us weeks," the man from Memphis told her. Jane found out that his name was Rolo. Rolo was a professional flatboat hauler from Missouri to New Orleans who hitched a ride back up the Mississippi River on a riverboat.

"I can make it," Jane replied. "I have to find Charlie."

"So how old is your son, Charlie?" Rolo asked.

"He will soon be 5 years old," Jane replied.

To get her mind off her troubles, Rolo asked, "Did you know that Abraham Lincoln was once a flat boat man like me?"

***

Already in New Orleans, Tom Lewis slipped through the darkness and the shadows around Laveau's voodoo rituals keeping an eye on Charlie and waiting for the time to steal him and take him back to his mother. He learned from one of Marie's servants that the Confederate gold was now in the Bank of New Orleans, having been put there in a safe deposit box by Laveau.

So early the next morning, Tom Lewis walked slowly into the Bank of New Orleans with a black scarf around his neck. He pulled the scarf across the bottom of his face and demanded, "Raise your hands. This is a hold up," Tom Lewis told the Bank of New Orleans teller. "Open that safe deposit box that belongs to Marie Laveau and give me all its contents. I want the gold that belongs to Marie Laveau. Well, it actually belongs to the Confederate army."

"We don't have any Confederate gold here, old man. Marie Laveau took all her money out of the bank yesterday," the teller said. "She took out everything that she had in her box."

Tom Lewis stood in disbelief while the voices in his head screamed at him. "Shut up," he screamed. A loud shot rang out. Then he fell to the cold marble floor. He had been shot in the back by a Bank of New Orleans guard.

Later that afternoon, Jane and the flat bottom boatmen Rolo reached New Orleans. She heard the horrible story of Tom Lewis's murder on the streets.

Chapter 66

Jane and her new friend Rolo made arrangements for Tom Lewis's body to be transported back to Natchez. She wired Papa to pick it up in Natchez and take it back to French Camp to be buried beside Jane's mother. Tommy traveled along with him.

"At least now the voices in his head are silent," Jane told Rolo.

"May he rest in peace," Rolo replied.

"You have no idea," Jane said. "He can roam with the Confederate ghosts."

Jane and Rolo got a house on St. Rue Ann near Charlie and Marie Laveau II. Jane took to wearing men's clothing whenever she was out and about New Orleans. She changed her name. Rolo understood and didn't mind. Often she went to watch Marie Laveau and Charlie's rituals. She watched Marie. She watched Charlie. Charlie's power over the people astounded her. They worshiped him. Marie already had him inducted into voodoo by the time she made it to New Orleans on that flat bottom boat.

So she watched and waited for the perfect time to win Charlie back.

Often when Marie went to work at the Liquor Import Business, Jane visited with Charlie. He still loved her so much, but he knew the hold that Marie Laveau had on him. Jane was frightened for Charlie, Charlie was frightened for Jane.

One day Charlie told her, "Marie says that James Fares' is now her boss. His father passed away."

"Good to know," Jane replied. She had no desire to ever see James Fares' again, but she didn't understand how he could work for Marie.

Chapter 67

Ten Years Later

Charlie slept late from exhaustion of the previous night's rituals with Marie and the sips of rum she allowed him to consume. The story around St. Ann was that Charlie liked rum, but he disliked wine, so rum was often left on the porch for him.

He sneaked from his bed and went to find Marie. She sat in the rocking chair on the front porch of their St. Ann cottage. She wasn't moving; she was dead. Sitting beside her on the old wooden porch, Charlie found the black carpet bag full of Confederate gold that now belonged to him.

News traveled through the neighborhood of St. Rue Ann very quickly. Jane heard about Marie's death and smiled to herself. One of the presents left for Marie had been from her. It was wine laced with arsenic. For once, Jane had won and no one else was the wiser.

Charlie summoned the funeral wagon and instructed Marie's servants to bury her in a crypt in the Saint Louis Cemetery with her ancestors, but in reality, she was buried elsewhere. He knew that her grave would be famous for years to come, so he purchased two plots. She wasn't buried in the one that was posted in the newspaper, but in another secret tomb in St. Louis Cemetery No. 2. Others claim

Marie Laveau is buried in St Louis Cemetery No. 1 with her family. Only Charlie knows for sure.

Later one of Marie's friends claimed that she died of a heart attack in 1897 at a ball and was buried in the Basin Street Cemetery St, Louis Cemetery No. 1. She claimed that Marie Laveau II was put in the same tomb with her mother and the rest of the family. That is the tomb that Charlie told all the stories about. He used Marie's friend's claims to his advantage.

The death of Marie Laveau II brought out several secrets that Marie Laveau had kept for many years. Her mother Marie Laveau had lived in the same house at St. Rue Ann. The first Marie Laveau had lost her memory and her looks, but both Maries lived in the same house and both practiced voodoo, so whenever the first died, the second took over causing people to believe that Marie Laveau was perpetually young. People believed that the first Marie Laveau still walked the streets of New Orleans. Charlie knew the truth, but would not clear up the mystery. It was to his advantage not to.

True to what Marie Laveau taught him, Charlie planned to make some money from her death. He invented stories of seeing naked men and women dancing near the proposed grave of the Laveaus. These naked people were lead by a tall woman wrapped in a huge snake. He told his followers that Marie wasn't dead. She would live forever. He told them to leave offerings of money on the tomb, and she would grant their wishes. He collected these offerings.

A few weeks after the private funeral ceremony, Charlie hitched the horse to Marie's black buggy; he put the gold in the secret compartment and closed the lid. Early the next morning, he headed over to Jane's house in the St. Rue Ann neighborhood. Jane packed her bags and made them some sandwiches and drinks. He didn't tell her about the Confederate gold hidden in the buggy nor did he tell her about it as he boarded the riverboat.

He and Jane traveled back toward Natchez on a riverboat. Charlie was now almost 16 years old, but wise beyond his years from living with Marie. Like her, he wasn't afraid of anyone or anything. He had their belief in voodoo on his side, but Jane didn't believe in voodoo.

She explained to Charlie about the ghosts and how they had caused her to lose her baby girl. She explained how they wanted their gold back.

"I think Marie Laveau spent it," was all that Charlie said. He wanted to return it to the Confederate ghosts without his mother knowing about it. After a few months, if the ghosts stopped visiting her, he planned to tell her what he had done with it.

Later that night while Jane lay sound asleep, Charlie saddled his horse, eased it out of the barn, and rode south across the Big Black swamp where his father had drowned and to French Camp to the cemetery where the angel gravestone stood at the entrance to the Confederate tunnel. Charlie instinctively knew where to knock on the angel gravestone to open the base. Whenever it opened, he entered, but he carried a lantern that illuminated inside the tunnel. Charlie opened another secret room inside the tunnel and replaced the Confederate gold. He hoped the Confederate ghosts would appreciate his generosity. He hoped they would leave his mother alone.

Then he exited the tunnel through the opening in the church. As he walked out the front door of the church, he whistled, and the horse came to him. He mounted his horse and headed back toward Kilmichael to spread voodoo throughout the area because after all he was The Voodoo King.

The End

Story's Origin

This story has been pinned by me as it was told to me by an elderly man, long deceased. It was handed down through the grapevine by the older people of Kilmichael and French Camp, Mississippi, and their relatives and friends. Many locals have searched for the Confederate gold and the secret Confederate tunnel. There have been several newspaper articles written about the Confederate tunnels. So far, no one has found them, taken the Confederate gold, and lived to tell about it. Historically, the gold brought nothing but bad luck to whomever had it in his possession.

To make the story of the Confederate gold more interesting, no local people have been brave enough to tell the story of Marie Laveau's voodoo connection to this area. Most people think she stayed in the New Orleans area. That isn't true.

No one tells the history of the "little people" either because their relatives still live in the area. No locals will give anyone assistance in locating the Confederate gold. Who wants to rile the Confederate ghosts? Who wants to inherit the curse?

No one tells any stories about the hanging tree. While researching this story, its actual location was debatable. All the locals I asked placed it in a different area.